SLEY HOUSE PUBLISHING

Tales of Sley House 2022

First published by Sley House Publishing 2022

Copyright © 2022 by Sley House Publishing

First edition

ISBN: 978-1-957941-90-5

Editing by Trevor Williamson
Editing by Lillian Erhart
Cover art by Kristina Osborn Truborn Design

This book was professionally typeset on Reedsy.
Find out more at reedsy.com

Contents

The TALES of GENEVIEVE SLEY — 1

The Tasting Notes of John McKinney—Ryan F. Love — 4

Invasion of the Bong Snatchers — Justin Moritz — 10

Here in the Stacks — Hannah Gilchrist — 23

Hauntings — Katerini Koraki — 34

Final Score, in B Minor — Karl Lykken — 50

Gardens for the Dead — Benjamin Thomas — 65

Forest Cactus — Sharon Cabana — 85

The TALES of CHARLES SLEY — 95

The Lady Who Dances in the Ashes — Judith Crow — 97

The Winsome Boy — Shelagh Smith — 114

The Collectors—Jen Mierisch — 127

Relationships Cultivated on the Bike Trail — Edna Cartwright — 146

Black Mariah's Final Form—Michael Gray Baughan — 160

Hunger — Curtis Harrell — 173

Waif(u) — J. D. Keown — 186

The TALES of RG SLEY — 203

Three Days of Darkness — Tiffany Stewart — 206

Telethon — TM Morgan — 220

Lord Carrington's Guest — Erik McHatton — 237

Hear the Ghosts After — J. Rohr — 247

The U Train—K. C. Grifant — 272

The Hunger—Frank Coffman — 288

In Search Of—Catherine Fields — 310

The TALES of GENEVIEVE SLEY

These stories bring to my mind my father's library, and Father himself. I can still see him in there, wandering the stacks, a glass in his hand—whether of wine or whisky—or a pipe in his palm.

Running his fingers over the leather-bound spines. Taking a taste from his glass, swirling it over his tongue—none of that vulgar swishing you see today. The satisfaction of a first sip, or a first inhale, the smoke encircling his head, sharp, acrid, welcome. An old, dusty Victrola sits silent in the corner now, but it used to play, ghostly strains that echoed down the hallway, even with the door closed.

These stories each have elements of the familiar, the surprising, the disturbing. They leave a memorable taste or a hint of smoke, or a note of music that lingers in the air long after you turn the page.

Charles has taken over Father's library now, adopted it as his own, as his birthright though he isn't the eldest. He doesn't look like he belongs there, yet, not like these stories. I rather think Father would have liked them.

The Tasting Notes of John McKinney—Ryan F. Love

Ryan F. Love teaches high school English in the Finger Lakes region of upstate New York, where he earned a degree from Alfred University. He and his wife live in a Victorian with pairs of daughters and beagles. His short fiction has appeared in The Blue Mountain Review, Sleet Magazine, The Copperfield Review, Blue Lake Review, *and* L'Esprit Literary Review. *He is currently writing his second novel and seeking publication for his first.*

* * *

McKinney could taste the ladybug in your wine. Any wine drinker worth a damn can tell you that a handful of them would give an undrinkable funk to a swimming pool of wine, let alone a barrel. You buy a bottle, you don't have to worry about it; anything ladybugged enough to get the taint never makes it to the shelves, and if half a little one gets ground up in the press, no one's the wiser.

But if you opened a bottle with John McKinney and a ladybug so much as looked at the grapes, McKinney would know. Then he'd tell you how many spots it had.

I know that's not why you're here with your notebook. It's not the brilliance you're researching. But the man was more than his end.

Thirty years ago, he sold his liquor store for a tidy sum and founded McKinney Vineyards. He searched for months until he found the right location, the right *terroir*: "the soul of the place in the wine," he defined it. To this day, there's no other winery on that stretch of road. State Route 90, east side of Cayuga Lake, just doesn't get the same traffic as 89 on the west, but McKinney didn't care: he had his *terroir* and limestone soil.

There never was such a man for limestone. He spent months sampling soil to find his spot, the only limestone within a hundred miles. McKinney was a particular man. He never did build a showroom for tastings, just set up a card table in the barrel room. "Limestone, Dan," he told me there, "is the foundation for everything you taste."

It was his first vintage. He must have talked to me about *terroir* and limestone and pinot noir for thirty minutes. His son Mark was there, too. They lived in a cabin to one side of the sloped driveway; Mrs. McKinney had been out of the picture for a while, she was a good friend of my sister, and no you can't have that story. It was no secret that McKinney was grooming Mark for succession: he conceived his vineyard as a New York answer to those French chateaus. Mark wasn't quite 21 then. His dad handed him a glass and he looked at me a little embarrassed, since I was a policeman. I told him as far as I'm concerned, the law doesn't have much to say about family business. He said, "Thank you, Officer Dan," and took a pour. He held his father's wine up to the light and looked at it like it was rubies.

Word got around. Locals found that wine right away. Then industry people. There was camaraderie in those days, when all winemakers scrabbled for a bit of good press for the region. They told any customer with a palate for the good stuff to head down the state route less traveled. Eventually, the critic came.

Nobody knows who sent the critic that bottle. I'd swear on my sister's grave it wasn't McKinney. He never advertised. Some fool well-wisher must have done it, and once the critic tasted that pinot, he set out directly for Cayuga Lake.

That's not the way these publications work, you know. You're supposed to send them complimentary bottles, letters requesting they please deem you worthy of review. If anything, you get back a number, and if it's lower than 88 you just hope to God no one notices. But this critic, whose name I will not repeat, tasted that wine and drove here before three days passed. McKinney Vineyards Pinot Noir, 1999. It was that good. McKinney produced 1,440 bottles, and I bought 24 of them. I wish I'd bought more.

You know the story. Things start well, but at some point, McKinney runs the critic out of the barrel room, throws empty bottles after him. The guy's furious, calls the police—me, as it happens. The critic shouted about pressing charges until I talked him out of it. Maybe I shouldn't have, I don't know. There was broken glass everywhere, but you have to understand, McKinney was a particular man, a brilliant man. The critic wasn't hurt. He was angry, though. Back in the city he wrote a blog post, and John McKinney was forever "Mad McKinney." That's who you came here to research, isn't it? "Mad McKinney?"

McKinney didn't go around much after. I needed wine a few weeks later and saw him in his barrel room with his son. He pulled some 2001 pinot out of a barrel with a wine thief – that's what they call the pipette they draw samples with – and he said he was going to harvest all his grapes beneath a waxing gibbous moon.

It's called biodynamics; I looked it up. Hundreds of vineyards around the world practice it, so as much as I'm sure you'd like to write about Mad McKinney and the moon, he's not alone, and you don't know how brilliant he was. If you saw him at work, you can never forget it. McKinney swirled, lifted the glass to his lips, closed his eyes for a minute, maybe two, and said, "I can taste it, Dan. The moon. *Terroir* is more than just soil, limestone or climate. It's the soul of the grapes. Their light. No matter what they say, I taste the moonlight."

I did not ask if "they" was the critic because it did not matter. You understand? It was the wine and his love for it, for the depth of it. God knows I'm not a poet and I'm not a genius. But when you tasted wine with John McKinney and listened, you could taste it, too. *Terroir.* "The land is alive in your glass," he'd say. And it was.

He made 60 cases of the 2001 vintage, half of before. I didn't know how he'd make a go of it, financially. At the start he made riesling beside his pinot; it's the big grape in the region, so you can sell it easy. He stopped making it. Maybe he viewed the riesling as selling out, or a distraction. He was always a particular man. He tended those pinot noir vines like they were children. He was less tender with Mark.

I was on patrol that evening, driving north maybe six miles up Route 90. Someone was walking through the rain. He had a bundle covered with a trash bag on his back, and his coat didn't look near weatherproof enough, so I pulled my car over. It was Mark.

I joshed him. "Not enough sense to keep out of the rain, Mark McKinney?"

"Will you take me to the bus station, Officer Dan?" he asked. "I have to leave."

There were bruises on his face, ugly ones. On the drive I was quiet to give him space. The rain was loud enough.

"He said there's spirits," Mark said.

"What's that?"

"In the vineyard. He says the spirits are part of the *terroir*."

"What?"

Mark said no more until the bus station. He paused with the door open. "Check in on him, Dan. He's… I don't know. I don't know what's happening to him." We were beneath an awning, and the wipers kept switching over the dry windshield.

"He's a particular man."

"Yeah," he said.

I didn't see Mark for ten years. He sent me a postcard with his address. Maybe he meant for me to write him. Maybe he saw what was coming.

I stopped by to taste wine with McKinney once in a long while. He talked less. "*Terroir* runs deep," he said, "deeper than even I imagined." He wouldn't explain, and I wouldn't ask. But the wine was beautiful. He cut production to 25 cases. "Only the most expressive grapes," he said.

He kept the doors open, somehow, until he didn't. He barred the drive with the gate and hung a sign: "McKinney Vineyards CLOSED to all visitors." I didn't want to disturb the man. I thought of checking in, but then I got a package in the mail: two bottles of McKinney Vineyards Pinot Noir, 2010. No note. I figured it was his way of saying he was alright. Two bottles came yearly after that, every glass a work of art. I missed him. I could only imagine how his wine would taste with McKinney offering notes like the old days, but I kept away. Some people question that. But if you have the privilege to know a genius, a real genius, you give what he needs. You give him space; that's the bargain. Say what you like, but I kept my end.

The bottles stopped after four years. I waited weeks, making sure they weren't just late: nothing. It was time to see McKinney.

I went one night after my patrol. I parked my car on the roadside and walked past the locked gate. The sign hung in the same spot, though some punk kid had spray-painted "Mad" above "McKinney Vineyards." I ascended the slope, vines on both sides. The night was clear, and the fruit glowed softly: a waxing gibbous moon.

The cabin to my left was dark with broken windows, and for a moment I wondered why McKinney hadn't replaced the glass. Then I saw the one light burning beside the door of the barrel room. Where else would McKinney live?

I knocked, I called, I nudged the door—open. It felt wrong and I drew my .38. "Police - I'm looking for John McKinney," I called. "If you're there, John, it's Dan. Dan Bledsoe."

I heard something behind me then, or felt it; I could not tell you which. It was nothing I could see. The wind, maybe.

Sharpie covered the barrel room walls. Red, black, crossouts. It seemed haphazard until I recognized a rough map of the property. Red words were scrawled over vineyard rows, sometimes over top of one another. "Thick limestone." "Chestnut taproot." "Hail storm 84." "Wolf haunt." "Lovers' sweat." "Solar flare." "Fallen warrior." "Smoke." "Unknown spirit - old." "Lake mist." "Cayuga spirit." "Pioneer child." "Sadness." "Unknown spirit - young."

I knocked on the barrels. Only one was full, and an envelope addressed to Mark lay on it. I heard nothing but the wind.

I called it in. We searched the vineyard by flashlight: nothing. I tried to match vines to the notes covering McKinney's walls like wrinkles on a brain. In the next day's sun, we saw fresh earth, which we dug up: nothing. Just vines all around.

Two days later I took Mark through the yellow tape. He saw the walls and shook his head. "You should have written me."

"I didn't know."

"You should have."

He read every note, twice, then stood silently. I handed him the envelope. He pocketed it.

"That's evidence," I said.

"Of what?"

"I just thought you should read it first."

"You can have it tomorrow," Mark said, exiting into the vineyard.

"We'll find him," I called. My words echoed off the walls, and Mark kept walking.

He told me the letter got stolen; I couldn't prove otherwise. I have no idea what it said. He never talked to me again, but he stayed in town while the wine finished aging in that one barrel. One weekend I was driving by and saw him carrying bottled cases—McKinney's last vintage. Since then the grapes have rotted in the vineyard. Mark won't sell it.

I check the internet sometimes. You can't find McKinney Vineyards Pinot Noir any more than you can find the man himself. I suppose Mark still has what he carried out that October weekend, and that's what's left of John McKinney. You'll call him what you like and I can't stop you, but he had brilliance like you can't imagine. He bottled it.

Since you ask, yeah, I've got three bottles downstairs. Two 2012. One 1999—what that critic drank.

You'd probably like to see what you taste. Limestone, moonlight, *terroir*. Spirits. Genius.

And you can go to hell.

Invasion of the Bong Snatchers — Justin Moritz

Justin Moritz (They/He) is a non-binary writer of queer horror, exploring the grotesquely campy and the filthy underside of society. Raised on true crime and horror movies from way too young of an age, their work tends to explore the terror of living as a queer person in modern times, while adding a speculative and often disgusting and comedic twist. They spent four years studying chemistry at the University of Colorado-Boulder, only to abandon a doctoral program to pursue an MFA in Screenwriting at the University of Texas at Austin. Their short fiction and poetry have been featured in Leviathan Libraries' Twisted Anatomy: A Body Horror Anthology, Death Knell Press' Nightmare Sky: Stories of Astronomical Horror, and several upcoming Scare Street anthologies. You can follow them on Twitter at @jeepers_justin.

* * *

It's starting to feel like I'm out of the loop, unable to pinpoint whose latest offspring is McKinleigh or who bought a boat or whose stock portfolio is up 115% this quarter. I guess I should be thankful that my college friends still get together, graduation a decade behind us. When we meet up in the Rockies for our annual camping trip, a sort of homage to the disastrous one we attempted junior year that in the moment felt like the end of our friendship but somehow solidified it in mutual trauma, I feel like I'm the odd one out. Thirty-three years old and my Saturday mornings look the same as those of my friends' children. Cartoons and a bowl, but I substitute a bowl of Fruit Loops for a bowl of the strongest pot I can afford on minimum wage.

"Anything new with you, Heather?" Connor asks, white-knuckling the handle above his head as if Margo's husband Tim is about to drive the SUV over the mountainside.

"Same old, same old. Cashiering during the day, painting during the night," I say with a sigh. "More importantly, are you okay, bud? You look like you're ready to rip that handle off."

Connor doesn't loosen his grip as he replies, "Having kids changes you, Heather. I'm scared of everything, can't even go five over the speed limit without imagining what it would be like if I passed and left them and their mom all on their own..."

Connor nonchalantly wipes a tear away as if that isn't the weirdest shit to be crying about on your way to a weekend of binge-drinking. Margo sits in the front seat, cute as she was in college, but now rubbing at the swelling baby bump she hadn't bothered to mention. My guess is her and her fucking badminton-coach-turned-husband Tim are hoping to make it a big deal. The sort of surprise announcement that everyone already knew was coming since they've been popping them out every year or so since they got married three years ago, but still must pretend to be caught off guard by. *You're pregnant? I couldn't even tell*, I imagined myself exclaiming in fake joy.

"You're a regular Van Gogh, aren't you, Heather?" Tim smiles back at me with the sort of preppy grin that I wish I could smack off his face.

"Oh, leave her alone, Tim." Margo swats at his shoulder. "She isn't an Impressionist or anything. Her art isn't fine art..."

"Ouch, Margo," I say, grinding my teeth.

"What I mean to say is your art is cool, Heather. It isn't the sort of thing you see in a museum. If you walk into someone's house and see it on the wall and say, 'Wow, that's interesting'. And that's what I love about you," Margo course-corrects, reaching behind her to give my hand a pity squeeze.

Here I was, still being called the cool and interesting one a decade while my friends were getting promotions or knocked up or planning their next trip to the Bahamas. College-me would have worn this like a badge of honor, the unique one in a group of kids who would grow up to become investment banker girlbosses and stay-at-home dads, but it stung now. It meant that all these years later, I was still just Heather, the stoner, the artist, the one who people expected great things from but never lived up to those expectations. As I wallowed in it, I thought about badly I wanted a joint.

While years before we had simply hiked off-trail, staking our claim to some unclaimed section of woods, this campground sported the amenities of a hotel without four walls and a roof. Kids ran past the car to climb on the jungle gym or jump into the chlorinated pool. Their folks sip beers and barbeque at their campsites just a few dozen feet away. No peace, no quiet, only screaming children.

"There's so many fucking kids here," I whisper, clearly not quietly enough.

"Don't worry, we asked for the furthest site, so we can participate in all of our tomfoolery," Margo says.

I feel my anger cool the longer we drive, leaving behind the domestic drama as the car turns around the bend. Half a tent is already assembled when we pull into our spot, and even before I open the car door, I can hear Nico and Wayde arguing over a set of tent poles. Whoever said gay men have happier marriages than straight folks have never listened in on the couple's squabbles, which get hot and loud to the point that it's a nuisance. I practically jump out of the car to get away from the middle-age air stinking up Tim's car.

"Heather!" Nico lets go of the tent pole, causing the entire structure to collapse as he runs over to hug me.

"How are things?" I say, latching onto him as Tim tries to shepherd us to unload the SUV.

"Just lovely. We just moved into a new place with a doorman and a sauna!"

"A doorman and a sauna!" I feign excitement.

"Oh, and Wayde just made junior partner."

Wayde stands above the ruins of the tent, red-faced, shouting, "I'm going to take your ass to court if you don't help me pitch this tent, Nico."

"You know how good I am at helping you pitch tents, babe. I haven't seen Heather in ages!" Nico yells back.

Thwack! Thwack! Thwack! My attention is drawn away from Nico to the sight of an unknown woman mid axe-swing, her biceps glimmering with sweat as she cuts a log down the middle with ease. She's butch in the way I like. Purple hair chopped short, a flannel tied around her waist, tattoos snaking their way around her legs and arms.

"This is our roommate, Bernadette. She's a playwright," Nico says, pushing me towards her.

Bernadette flips her hair out of her eyes, wiping sweat from her forehead as she says, "Hi all, hope it's okay I'm crashing your camping trip."

Margo rushes to hug Bernadette, which seems to make her wildly uncomfortable. Tim approaches in tow, offering out his hand, saying, "Name's Tim. That fine filly is my wife, Margo. What kind of plays do you write, Bernadette? Or should I say Lin Manuel Miranda."

"I don't write musicals, but I appreciate the compliment. I wouldn't want to bother you all with the details though."

"Oh, come on, Bernadette, they'll love to hear all your genius," Nico insists.

"Well, the current one is about a race of aliens who wage war on each other by playing a tournament of competitive water polo."

"Oh, that's cool," Tim replies, unsure what to say.

"Yeah, yeah, that's interesting," Margo adds.

It's then that I realize Bernadette and I are kindred souls. In our 30s and the only ones who are still cool and interesting in the group, instead of junior partners or mothers-to-be or crying about their own mortality.

"Bernadette, this is Heather. I think you two are going to get along," Nico says, pretending to smoke an imaginary joint.

As the others begin to unload the campsite, Bernadette gives me a look. I nod at her, grabbing my bag from the car. We meet on the edge of the campsite as I announce, "We're going to take a walk and find the bathroom."

We're not going to find the bathroom. Everyone knows it too.

Bernadette and I trek up a wooded hillside, both of us in agreeance that if we're going to be high all weekend, we might as well start smoking somewhere pretty. We struggle up the incline, regularly stopping to catch our breath. Smoker lungs after all aren't designed for such rigorous activities. But eventually, we come across a rocky bluff that offers quite a view of the surrounding woods and the campground below.

"Shall we?" Bernadette says as she scales a nearby boulder to sit upon.

I hand the backpack up to her, then climb up to join her. I unpack the contents of my backpack, revealing a considerable number of provisions concealed within several gallon bags.

"Shit, you've got the works." Bernadette laughs as I begin to prepare a bowl in my trusty pipe, the very pipe I've been bringing on these trips since college. A sacred pipe for this journey and this journey alone.

"I always bring extra. You know, in case one of the others wants to smoke. But if they don't, the worse that can happen is I have enough to keep myself blissfully unaware of how their lives are passing me by," I explain, holding out the pipe so she can see, "This pipe here has come on every one of these stupid camping trips.

I fill the pipe with bud, offering Bernadette greens. But she struggles with the lighter, causing me to instinctually shield her from the wind with my body as I light the pipe for her. She smokes like a pro, filling her lungs to their capacity, holding for a few seconds, then exhaling without so much as a cough directly into my face. I breathe in her air, savoring that she doesn't move away even after exhaling.

"You're living with Wayde and Nico?"

"You want to know the answer to the question behind the question, don't you? No, they don't need a roommate, but Nico and I got friendly at my bartending job, then when my girlfriend kicked me out, they offered me a room and wouldn't take no for an answer." Bernadette looks out stoically at the horizon, but I'm unsure if it's because she's embarrassed or cause she's high. "I think they think just because I have artistic ambitions, it means I can't keep my money straight."

I fill my lungs with smoke, but like an amateur, I cough in a way that is neither interesting nor cool. She pats me on the back, pantomiming deep breathes till I get my composure. It's then that I feel myself blush, suddenly aware that I didn't look cute either, and that it matters if I look cute or not.

"I get you…I get you…One time, Margo and Tim offered to buy me groceries, as if I can't afford my own ninety-nine cent ramen."

"I guess we can't blame them. When you have your whole life put together, it must look like everyone who isn't on the same life track as you have their shit absolutely rocked." Bernadette laughs before she takes another hit.

The weed has hit my brain at this point. Puff, puff, pass and I'm swaying along with the trees, wondering if Nico and Wayde had ulterior motives for bringing Bernadette along. She's pretty in the sort of way that doesn't feel forced, her confidence the sexiest thing about her. I might just be high, but she seems to be everything I'm not. Well-spoken, individualized, the sort of person who doesn't latch onto the identity of being in a friend group that has long since grown apart.

"You okay?" Bernadette taps me on the shoulder, holding out the pipe once more, "Whatcha thinking about?"

"I just wonder what my friends think of me. Like if they still think of me as Heather, their trailblazing, crazy artist friend, or if I'm just some woman they feel bad for. I wonder if they would call me for help, like they expect me to do when things get tough."

"You seem like the sort to do what has to be done, even if people don't expect it of you," Bernadette says.

It really is a beautiful day, a gently breeze creating a visible sway of the trees down the mountainside below us. The sun blazes down on us unrelenting, and it is when the sky somehow gets even brighter that my attention is drawn upwards. I shield my eyes, but still something blinds me. A ball of blue light that slices across the horizon. Before I can point it out to Bernadette, but it makes its presence known, booming as it is dragged downwards by the earth's gravity.

Bernadette jumps, the pipe falling out of her hands, shattering against the boulder. I don't have time to grieve for this heirloom from my youth, because the meteor hits the ground so hard that the two of us are nearly knocked down the backside of the rock. I try to gain my composure, but a surge of energy explodes against my frontal lobe, overwhelming my thoughts with a burrowing, razor-sharp blue light. There is a whispering in my ears, a throbbing in my temples that is at first all-encompassing, but it suppressed by a familiar sensation: the head high of the marijuana in my system. Whatever struck us is quelled by the psychedelics already in my system, dissipating until it is once again just Bernadette and I sitting on the boulder.

"What the fuck was that?" Bernadette says, tilting her head as if trying to dislodge water from her ears.

"A meteor, but I felt like I was getting skull-fucked by a goddamn lightsaber, Bernadette. That isn't normal."

"Neither is that," she says, pointing down the mountainside to where glowing teal light rises from the ground in the middle of the campground.

"Shit, everyone is still down there."

We were as urgent as humanly possible for two people high of their asses trying to run straight down a mountainous hill. There was definitely something wrong. While the birds sang softly in the boughs above us, the day was eerily quiet. I couldn't hear any people. No families playing catch, no children yelling as they splashed in the pool, not even a commotion surrounding whatever had crashed directly into the center of the campground.

"Do you feel like someone is attempting to crack your skull open with the world's tiniest chisel?" Bernadette says as we approach our campsite.

I didn't need to ask what she meant. I had hoped it was just a bad reaction to whatever strain I'd been talked into buying at the dispensary. But there was a subtle aching in my forehead as if someone was trying to crack through the skull to slither into the folds of my brain and take root.

"Something is wrong," I say as I begin to run faster. Bernadette stops in her tracks.

"Cease your movement," She shouts in a flat voice unlike how she's been speaking all afternoon.

I turn to look at her, expecting something odd, but Bernadette just stands there, her gaze unmoving but unfocused. I shake her by the shoulder, then she's back with me again.

"Why did you want me to stop? I demand as I pull her along.

"I didn't say anything."

"Yes, you did. Just now. Cease and desist or some shit," I explain, as she caught up, holding her head as if in paid.

There's a rhythmic thud. A sort of metal-on-metal sound just on the other side of the trees. As soon as we step into the camp, I see Tim with an axe in hand, swinging it vigorously at the door of his precious SUV, the one he had sent me pictures of like it was a newborn child chopped to pieces. I suppose a psychotic break wasn't out of the question for a dude who had three kids with Margo and a fourth on the way, but then I see Margo scrambling inside the vehicle, desperately trying to get away as Tim's blows start to break through the glass.

"Heather, they've all gone crazy," She screams as Tim busts through the back window.

"Tim, put down the axe." As soon as I say it, his attention snaps to me, his chocolatey brown eyes now a glowing icy blue. The chiseling against my skull intensifies with every step he takes towards me, but I'm frozen, unsure what my plan was in the first place.

"Hey! Over here you preppy fuck!" Bernadette runs around the perimeter of the campsite, chucking stones in Tim's direction. He hardly flinches as she cracks one against his temple, but it draws him away from me. Even when he swings at her, Bernadette keeps drawing his attention, saving me from being split in two.

"Surrender your individuality, find comfort in uniformity or die, human." He drones in the same monotone voice Bernadette had used in the woods.

The further away from me, the more my composure returns to me. He almost hits her, causing me to rush to the barbeque grill, grabbing hold of a hefty metal extinguisher. Before Tim has a chance to realize it's two-against-one, I crack him over the head. He crumbles to the ground, which causes Margo to scream.

"You killed him, Heather. You know I can't raise four kids on my own, but you killed my husband anyway," Margo sobs as Bernadette helps her out of the car.

I can see the slight rise and fall of Tim's belly. He's knocked out cold. "He's alive."

"What happened?" Bernadette asks as she dusts off Margo.

"We got the camp set up and Tim was going to make some burgers, but I was so hungry so I thought I would have one of those brownies you made, Heather," As the still-crying Margo says it, I see the tray of pot brownies on the nearby picnic table, one large square cut out. "Nico, Wayde, and Connor went swimming. But I was feeling dizzy, so Tim and I stayed behind, but there was a bang and a flash of light. Suddenly, my Timmy was chasing me with an axe."

"Sit down, Margo. Now, I don't want you to freak out, but those were pot brownie."

This makes Margo cry harder as she cradles her stomach. "But what about the baby?"

As much as I wanted to comfort my friend, my attention lay elsewhere. On the discarded axe near Tim's body. One swing of its sharp blade against my skull, and the force pressing against my temples would be gone. But then Bernadette was shaking me by the shoulder, the tray of pot brownies in her hand.

"Heather, I think that the marijuana is the reason we're not effected by whatever is happening since that meteor hit the ground. Margo isn't effected cause she had one. As we ran down the hill and the weed started to wear off, I started to feel like less of myself," Bernadette says, grabbing a fistful of brownie.

"So, we have to get extremely high to stop us from turning into one of those things?"

"Exactly," Bernadette shoves the fistful of brownie into her face.

I do the same, then take another handful. The two of us are practically smashing chocolate down our own throats by the time we finish the tray. A belly full of pot brownies gives me an awful stomachache, but for the first time since we returned to the campground, I feel like I can think for myself.

"Margo, I want you to go into Wayde and Nico's car and lock the door," I say as I grab hold of the axe, "Bernadette and I have some alien ass to kick."

The rest of the campers are partaking in a procession of sorts, dragging their feet in an eerily synced manner. Some have even lost shoes, but they continue their trudging towards the glowing crater at the center of the campground. Bernadette gives me a sort of *What The Actual Fuck Is Going On* look. This isn't something you want to see when you're high off your ass, but Bernadette and I fall into their rhythm, two interlopers on our way to make this right.

"So, what's the actually plan?" Bernadette whispers into my ear as the unearthly light becomes stronger, my skull vibrating more with each step.

"The fuck if I know."

"What do you mean the fuck if you know? You were the one with the one-liner. You were supposed to have the plan." Bernadette is sweating now, white knuckling the fire extinguisher. "We could have left in Wayde and Nico's car."

"We're too stoned to drive," I say, noticing the way the campers ease their pace.

"But we're sober enough to fight aliens?" Bernadette hisses.

I shush her, grabbing her by the arm to keep her from falling into the crater. Everyone else, Wayde, Connor, Nico, and a half-dozen of creepy as shit possessed children and their parents, stop on the rim of the impact site.

"We are the One Consciousness, the one made of many," They drone, moving their arms in a sort of rhythmic dance. An extraterrestrial macarena if you will. "The Earthlings won't perish. Instead, they shall join our rank. This here crate is our origin, our holy site, our most precious source."

Bernadette and I struggle to remain inconspicuous, lacking the hive mind's knowledge of the complex choreography. The ground trembles beneath us in a series of pulses. The glow growing stronger as the dancing becomes more rigorous.

"It's going to happen again, Heather. Another pulse and that be the end of us and the rest of humanity," Bernadette says, readying her fire extinguisher.

"Let's show these fuckers that a couple of stoner fuck-ups can save the world." I raise my axe.

Bernadette and I's badassery lasts exactly two seconds as we both tumble down the side of the much-deeper-than-expected crater. The glow seems to be corporeal within it, striking at our temples as we push ourselves onto our feet. But whatever emanates from within the strange object is no match for pot brownies, causing the glowing tendrils to reel back as they try to infiltrate our stoned minds. We collect our weapons, ready to go in for the kill.

"We are the One Consciousness. We are inevitable," The crowd chants as Bernadette and I strike at the glowing meteorite.

Cracking through its hard exterior, there is a cylindrical-shaped glass object concealed within the meteor. But no matter how much we strike it, the substance proves undamageable. Bernadette moves to try from a different angle, then lets out a large gasp.

"It's a bong."

I move to where she's looking. From her point-of-view, I can see what she's talking about. The cylindrical object emanates its glowing force through an opening at the top, some sort of bowl-shaped breathing apparatus at its base. What Bernadette fails to point out before I look is that within the capsule, submerged in some sort of jelly, is a goddamn baby alien fuck, all bulbous and misshapen like if you inflated a fetus with a bicycle pump. Its oversized eyes release a glowing pulse, cueing its underlings to enter the crater to protect it.

Bernadette tries to smash the alien bong, but her weapon bounces off.

"Fuck, it's not working."

"If it looks like a bong, we have to treat it like a bong," I say, pulling my backpack off my shoulders.

Bernadette swings at the approaching campers as I grab my supplies, filling the concave piece at the base of the capsule with weed.

"Hurry, Heather!" Bernadette screams as she's yanked off her feet by the campers.

I take the alien capsule and press my lips against the end. Lighter in hand, I scorch the shit out of the weed. The smoke fills the capsule, causing the alien within to squirm, releasing one last pulse that goes straight into my system. I am suddenly no longer myself. I see the primordial ooze of planets long dead, oceans forming and life brewing only to be destroyed by bursts of fire. I see the beginning of the universe and the end of it too. I see the face of God and the faces of those who tear him apart limb-by-limb. I see it all, but eventually my lungs fill with smoke.

I exhale and I'm stoned out of my mind, sitting on my ass surrounded by a bunch of people who have no idea how they ended up in the bottom of this crater. Bernadette runs to my side, grabbing hold of my arm, shouting, "You did it, Heather!"

"Dude, I'm so goddamn high."

Bernadette laughs, looking close at the alien bong in my hand. Whatever is inside still slightly squirms, but now, its eyes are bloodshot, its powers nulled by the THC in its system. She touches my face, concern registering on her face as she says, "I'm sorry I broke your pipe on the mountain. I know it was special."

"It's okay, we have a new one."

Bernadette smiles, wiping tears from her face. Then she's wrapping her arms around my neck, pressing her lips against my own. I kiss her back for too long, the sort of stoned-out-of-your-mind make-out session that no one else wants to see. But we just saved humanity, so I don't let her go until she starts to laugh, separating her face from my own.

"Look, Wayde, you owe me ten bucks cause they got together," Nico says as he watches Bernadette and I embrace. "You two are a match made in heaven."

Bernadette laughs, clarifying, "More like a match made in outer space."

I kiss her like it's still the end of the world.

Here in the Stacks — Hannah Gilchrist

hatever you think about her, you are probably wrong. Hannah likes to subvert conventions. Her only other publication, aside from a small blog no one reads, is the story "Souling" published in Tales of Sley House 2021.

* * *

The old man stepped down off the bus and winced at the pain ripping through his knee. The pain was as familiar to him as the quirks and foibles of the old two-story limestone with iron latticework on the windows in front of him. The interior mostly dark now in anticipation of closing, successively dimming lights not a subtle hint for those straggling patrons lost in the pages of some tome who had forgotten such trivialities as the passing of time. The old man cinched his coat tight about his thin frame and noticed a young woman in a white dress staring out of one of the semi-dark third story windows. He regarded her only a moment before ascending the wide stone steps and pulling open one of the two heavy oak doors. In the small foyer, he shed his outer coat, shook off the cold, and hung his navy blazer on the coatrack in the corner before turning to the second set of doors that led into the interior. A young boy no more than six held his father's hand as they came for the exit.

The old man said: "How are you boys tonight, Eric, Mr. Missini?"

"Great, Mr. Eubanks," the boy said as the father said, "Hey Layne," and wished him a good night. Layne held the door open for them with a wide, denture-filled smile before shuffling to the front desk. The evening desk girl, barely old enough to drink, her dark hair streaked pink and a sterling silver loop through her upper lip, greeted him with a smile as he walked up. She was a nice girl but hadn't worked there long, yet still the customers responded well to her despite the overall conservativeness of the community given her daily appearance. Tonight, her black leggings stemmed out from under a wide pink tutu, and she wore black lipstick, her short hair spiked.

"Are all the patrons gone?" he asked. The wide desk she manned in the front hall held everything: the computer she used for check-ins and checkouts, a phone connected to a PA system where she made the time known every few minutes for the last stragglers, a locked drawer directly underneath the computer's keyboard holding a till with enough cash and coin to accommodate the meager fines that came with overdue or damaged books. To the right of the monitor a double row of smaller screens, their views focused around the upper two floors, showing the stacks and empty reading areas, tables and microfiche machines. The only cameras downstairs showed the lobby where they stood and the two meeting rooms, one in the east wing and one in the west. The rest of the first floor was filled with private offices where cameras had not been placed. The front desk girl took a cursory glance at the row of screens and nodded.

"I still have to go upstairs and check, though," she said, her eyes wide.

Layne offered her a warm smile. "This is a place for seekers of knowledge, a warm and comforting place."

"They just…they wait, always. Why do they wait till after dark?"

"This place gives them somewhere to belong. They are a family." That wasn't much of an answer, he knew, and thought of the girl he glimpsed in the third-floor window. "I'll go upstairs for you," he said. "Have a good night."

Because of her scare last week, and that he'd only worked with her a few times – her name was Rebecca, but she went by Becca or something like that – she seemed no different from the other girls who'd come and gone, and so he figured she'd turn out the same way. She was a sweet girl, but if she couldn't get a handle on what happened upstairs, she wouldn't last long here in the stacks.

She didn't leap up, however. He tried to meet her eyes, but she focused on the desktop. Usually most were anxious to leave when he offered to check the upper floors for them, and in fact he'd anticipated such a response from her. But not this acquiescent silence; her dress suggested a character that rebelled against submissiveness.

"Are you okay, dear?" Layne asked.

"I'm fine," Becca said after a deep sigh, and rose and kissed his cheek. She forced a smile with no real power behind the lips. "Thank you, Mr. Eubanks."

Layne locked the door after Becca left and dropped the keys into the breast pocket of his shirt. He adjusted his tie, then walked to the far end of the hall, taking the elevator up to the third floor to begin his rounds.

He hadn't always followed the advice he had offered Becca. Back when he started at the library, just after college, when he was a single young man starting out in the world, there were plenty of times the bumps and shadows and glimpses in the dark had made him question his position as the new night librarian. Back then, his life still before him, his master's in library sciences diploma fresh in frame, he questioned often the position he had been relegated to. Never with bitterness did Layne feel he deserved more; his momma did not permit an entitled outlook from her children. At that point in his career, it was not the hours or the small-town library with little chance for advancement that gave him pause, nor the realization that of all the applications he had sent out and all the interviews he went on, the only job offer he received came from this library. No, what gave him pause, when he was twenty-four, were the after-hour's patrons that frequented the stacks between ten p.m. and seven a.m.

On the third floor in the fiction shelves, Layne found the night's set of stacked books. The first night Layne found the titles, oh so many years ago, he had to restack *The Count of Monte Cristo, The Tell-Tale Heart and Other Stories by Edgar Allen Poe, A Tale of Two Cities, Pride and Prejudice,* and *Robinson Crusoe.* Over the years the stacks of books had different themes, and he'd managed to only memorize the most unique collection of titles. Tonight's stack contained more modern authors: *Hard-boiled Wonderland and the End of the World, Libra, Red Dragon, The Road,* and a thin, little-known work by a regional author, a journalist by trade—John Cross' *Renegade Mustang.*

Layne paused, held the spine of Cross' book up to his lips so that he could breathe in the yellowing, fading paper, that acrid smell common only to old bookstores and the libraries and attics of literature professors. A moldy smell, the fiction stacks of the library were segregated between serious literature and hard Sci-Fi/Fantasy/Horror, Romance, Young-Adult, Westerns, Short Story Collections, and Mysteries. He might have found five Mysteries or five Westerns, but never had the genres been mixed. Even those first books, who the layman might argue came from different genres, were all of the same time-period and all classified by author in General Fiction. While he was not an expert on the paranormal by any means, he had spent enough time with the inhabitants here to know they were all creatures of habit.

He finished his rounds upstairs and found Mr. Lorenson, the head librarian, readying the deposit at the front desk. Mr. Lorenson was balding with some white hair tufts over his ears and sprouting from the back of his scalp, and he had a gut, but he was probably twenty or thirty years younger than Layne. Layne liked him well enough. By the time the position had come available, and Mr. Lorenson joined the team, Layne had become settled into

his nightly routine. He had been offered the job first, of course, by the county, which would have allowed him better hours, a raise, and more responsibility, but Layne politely absconded and said he'd like to stay right where he was. By then the after-hour's patrons here in the stacks were old friends. When Layne had finally learned to accept them, he also learned not to fear getting older.

"You wear the same suit every night, Mr. Eubanks," Mr. Lorenson said.

Layne nodded. "It don't get dirty here in the stacks. I don't sweat much, and I have it dry-cleaned once a week."

"Layne, I been thinking. You, you have a minute?"

"All the time in the world, Mr. Lorenson. What's on your mind?" Concern wrinkled his brow, made thin his pale lips. Layne was no stranger to the conversation that was about to begin. He and Mr. Lorenson had been having one form or another of it on and off over the past few years. At least Lorenson wasn't petulant and at least he wasn't tenacious.

"This work, these hours, they don't bother you? I mean, these aren't the hours of the day mostly frequented by men our age."

Layne smiled. "The work ain't hard, Mr. Lorenson. And if I might admit something to you, I don't think the county would begrudge me a nap for a time after my nightly work is done."

"No, Mr. Eubanks, I'm sure they wouldn't."

The two men shared a chuckle followed by a moment of silence, punctuated with a few quick steps from the floor above. They cast their eyes up as if they could see through the eight-foot ceiling to the second story stacks, then Mr. Lorenson hurried to gather up his paperwork and the rest of the day's deposit. Bustling toward the front doors, he offered Layne several well-wishes and goodbyes and, fumbling with his keys, finally made his way outside. Not many day-employees cared to discuss what happened in the stacks after the library closed.

* * *

Around three in the morning, a knock came at the outer double doors, rousing Layne from his short nap behind the front desk. He'd been dreaming of the pretty little girl he'd dated for a time when he first took the job. Once she'd accepted a proposal he'd offered. Then she vanished. He'd been dabbling in poetry at the time and had a few poems published and had tried his hand at a one-act play that he was sure would get published. He'd based their wedding and their futures on such hopes. This wasn't enough, he realized, when she'd sent him a telegram announcing her marriage to a literary critic in St. Louis.

27

His arms were folded across his chest, crinkling his tie. He smoothed it out as he hobbled to the front doors as on a floor above, he heard the heavy legs of a reading table scoot across the tile.

Persistent rain on a flat roof was always a concern with the library, that the rainwater would collect and soak the plaster and drip into the attic, but weekly diligence on Layne's part had so far dammed nature's efforts. He'd spent many a weekend with a strapping young man tarring the roof, years after he was able to physically patch and tar the flat roof of the library himself. Tonight, with the storm overhead, Layne took some notice of the ceiling tiles as he hobbled toward the front door, where he found a young girl, soaked to the bone and staring up at him, her eyes the color of the jade dragon statue that perched on a pedestal as patrons entered the Asian studies section of the library on the third floor.

"Library's closed, miss," he said, and then recognized her rain-soaked form as the front-desk girl. She'd changed since leaving earlier.

"Please, Mr. Eubanks." Fear swirled in the undercurrent of her green irises, swam and danced as her pupils constricted. She forced a smile but her lips quivered, and the smile looked as though its wearer was without confidence in the smile's authenticity.

"Becca?" the old librarian said and unlocked the deadbolt and let her in before securing the lock once more.

He brought her a few towels hoping she had stayed on the entryway carpet, a bit disappointed when he found her by his desk, staring anxiously at the front door. He'd have to get out the mop bucket later. Wouldn't do to let the water stand overnight till the janitor came in at five. She thanked him and dried off, never taking her eyes off the door, never losing that worried, furrowed brow. She had removed the wet slicker and draped it over the desk, which he hurried to remove for fear that rainwater would ruin the monitors.

"Doors are locked," he said, following her gaze.

"He won't care."

Layne asked who but Becca said she didn't want to talk about it. He said he had some books to reshelf on the second floor and she asked desperately if she could come with him, and he wondered what had changed since earlier, or if she had just not wanted to go up alone before.

A second-floor patron delivered a mournful cry and sniffling sobs that gave Becca pause as Layne went about his nightly duties. She crept right behind him through the low-lit stacks, illuminated by the dimmest of county-approved nightlights just bright enough for him to see objects and furniture (he operated the book return with a small flashlight he kept in his right front pocket), and at the sound of the wail he felt her fingers on his elbow and heard her breath catch and suck at the flesh on his neck.

"I wish we were alone in here," she said.

For his part, Layne continued humming a tune he hoped was soothing as he worked. A couple of notes mimicked a yes sound, and the girl's grip relaxed a little. Only when a silhouette passed in front of a lightning brightened window did she squeal and grip his arm so tight he nearly dropped the three books he desired to re-shelve.

"This building is over a hundred years old," he said. "A lot of people have come here over the years, and this building was not always a library. It started out as a hospital, then was converted to a tuberculosis ward, then an orphanage. But even as a library it has had its history; I've worked here for fifty-six years and have known five people that have passed away on the premises during my employment."

"How can you stand it?"

Ignoring her, Layne continued as though he were giving an historical tour. This he did as he examined the spines of the books he held and delivered them to their proper space on the shelf. "They say the wail you just heard is from a woman who died during childbirth back when this was a hospital. The story goes that she was murdered by her physician because he, a married man, was actually the father of the baby and didn't want to be found out by his wife."

"How many are here?"

He'd always fancied giving a guided tour, but the times he'd had this opportunity were few and far between and didn't seem to warrant his memorization of the history of the place and its patrons. Didn't warrant, but still he'd memorized. "A man suspected of multiple killings around the turn of last century was brought here when, before his trial, he was diagnosed with tuberculosis. In a controversial move, the CEO of the ward opted to stick the man in solitary in a fashioned cell down in the basement. He was neglected, denied visitors, denied treatment, and died screaming in pain."

"Does he ever leave, the…um…?"

He met her eyes in the dim light. Her features were soft, and he felt at that moment what it must be like to be a grandfather, staring at the expected hopeful youthful child wanting to be told everything was going to be okay. When his wife passed ten years ago, he knew it was too late to marry again, to have children, but he had seen so many of his friends look at their grandkids the way he now looked at this young girl.

"No, sweetheart," Layne said. "He doesn't come out of the basement, but we don't go down there, not by ourselves and not after dark." Off in the darkness, another sniffle, another sob. "They were people once, like you and me. Mostly they can't hurt you now. I've gotten to know each of them, in my way, they're like family."

"What about the killer in the basement?"

The library had only been open a year prior to Layne's hiring when his predecessor suffered a mysterious and violent death. During his nightly duties, he found he had business down the in the basement. He had of course been told the history of the library, but he went downstairs alone after dark anyway. Layne was hired before the funeral was even scheduled.

Before he could answer her there came such a pounding on the front door; her eyes grew wide with more fear than any mention of ghosts could conjure. Layne started for the stairs, but she pulled him back.

"He's big," she said. "He could bust down the door. Especially if he sees you."

"Who is he?"

"He won't leave me alone. He doesn't care. He won't obey the restraining order."

"I'll be okay. They'll make sure of it." Layne smiled then walked down to the lobby, leaving her on the first floor.

Between the thin panes of front door glass came the heated conversation.

"Bitch in there?"

"I truly don't know what you are talking about, sir, and I don't appreciate the language."

"She ran this way man and I ain't stupid. You let me in right now and let me take what's mine."

Layne unlocked the door and stepped aside. "You may go upstairs or down each wing, but I must say you should stay out of the basement."

"Basement, huh," said the hulking man. "Which way is the goddamn basement?"

"Sir, the basement is off limits."

He pulled Layne up by the collar till the tips of the old man's loafers barely scraped the tile. His breath smelled like alcohol. His face was pockmarked and ruddy, his nose fat, his eyes black and soulless.

"Where the fuck is she, you old codger?"

Layne merely lifted a hand, pointing a finger aiming down the ground floor wing to the left, where the stairs to the basement stood behind a closed door.

"Take me!" the bull snapped.

"Okay," Layne nodded. "Just let me fetch my keys." He backed away from the behemoth slowly. The man had such hate in his eyes, Layne dare not anger him. Still, what if he opened the basement door and the man descended and nothing happened? Then this night, Layne realized, glancing up the stairs to make sure the coast was clear, might be the night he joined the family he'd acquired here in the stacks.

He walked with the man, removing his large ring of keys and unlocked the basement door. Only the first few steps could be seen from the hall, and then only darkness. But a shuffling from below helped convince the brute that his destination was downstairs, so with a triumphant *Hmph!* he stormed down to the basement and after fumbling for a light switch, he called Becca's name in a tone with as many flourishes of filth as he could muster.

Calmly Layne shut the door and looked back down the hall. Becca had ventured nearly to the bottom of the steps and peeked over the railing down the hall to watch Layne, who only smiled at her and gave her a nod. The residents would not disappoint. They hadn't yet, tonight, and he was sure the basement's visitant would deliver the same.

Sure enough, a scream, followed by the thud of steps, and Becca hurried up the stairs. The door flew open and out ran the hulking man, his rain-soaked shirt and jacket slashed across the torso, blood around the edges. Layne judged the wound superficial, but the man didn't stop to give him a better look. He sprinted down the hall and out the front door. Layne locked the basement door first then raced to lock the front doors again, smiling to himself. When he turned, he jumped a little; Becca stood at the base of the stairs, a smile unpunctuated by her sad eyes.

"Thank you," she said and when he approached, she hugged him.

"He won't come back here, and he shouldn't bother you again."

"No," she said, and hung her head. "He'll find me once I leave. He always does."

"Don't you have any family? Anywhere to go?"

She shook her head then looked around. "I could come here."

"You have no one to care for you?"

She laughed—a snort or a chuckle, something selfish. "I work at the shirt factory part time when I'm not here. I sew pockets on men's shirts. I'm one of twenty women in my department who sew hundreds of pockets on hundreds of men's shirts each day. I barely scrape by with the two jobs."

"I guess I could watch you here," he said. "There is no going back. Once your mind is made up…"

"I understand," she said, and hung her head like she was being scolded. Then she bit her lip and regarded a thought briefly. "But the others have interesting stories. They sound so memorable."

"I think this night would be memorable," he said.

Layne took her by the hand and led her up the stairs. They sat at the top of the wide spiral case, and he spent the rest of the night telling her about all the ghosts in building—how they died, how they revealed themselves from time to time. At a quarter of five she yawned and stood and leaned against the rail.

He stood. "Are you ready?"

"Yes," she said. Her voice was a singsong. Her eyelids drooped as if she'd already slipped into a dream. He hugged her, kissed her cheek and felt her kiss his cheek in turn. Layne smiled at her as warmly as possible, staring into her eyes. He did care for Becca, but he'd known this, that she'd turn out like the others.

"I'll care for you, like I care for the others."

She nodded, seemed to consider something. When she looked back up into his eyes, there was an assuredness. "Thank you for tonight."

"You're welcome," he said. And then he pushed.

There is a story at the Region Hills Public Library, about a girl on the main staircase, her neck broke. She appears most frequently of all the spirits at the century old building. Some people say that she is the newest spirit, so that's why more people claim to see her. Others suggest she is searching for her murderer, or regrets committing suicide (depending on whether you believe she was murdered or killed herself). The official report listed suicide—Layne told the police most of what happened that night, told them about her boyfriend coming, about how sad and afraid she was, and this meshed with what others who knew Becca told the police.

If you go to the library and meet old Layne Eubanks, still the night librarian, he'll tell you about the ghosts of the building. But of Becca, the former night clerk, he will only say this: When she came to him that night she was in search of a home, a family. And now she has one.

Hauntings — Katerini Koraki

Kat Koraki is a speculative fiction writer and student based in Boston. You can find her work published in Quill and Crow's Carnival Macabre *anthology,* Jayhenge Publishing's Grandpa's Deep Space Diner *anthology, and in* Luna Station Quarterly, *among other places.*

***

Sensation was the first thing that came back to me: hard concrete cooling my skin, the scratchy wool of my skirt clinging to my hips, the feeling of the back of my head against the floor. Slowly, my sight refocused. Rows of wooden catalog cabinets appeared on either side of me like the walls of a labyrinth. On the ceiling, a single light bulb hung from a frayed wire, giving out its pathetic orange light. In front of me, a plywood staircase seemed to stretch out forever. My hearing was the last to return, maybe because it was all so quiet. When it did, I could barely make out the chug of the boiler in the next room. On the level above, chairs scraped and footsteps beat against the floorboards. Pain throbbing from behind my eyes, I pushed myself up to sitting.

I was in the basement of the library.

I wasn't supposed to be there.

Bile pushed its way up my throat but I choked it down as I dragged myself upright and up the stairs. When I reached the top, my stomach dropped. On the ground floor, the walls were lined with floor-to-ceiling windows, a modern response to the dark, claustrophobic design of the older buildings. Paired with the white linoleum lining the floors and columns, it created an almost glow in the afternoon sun. Daylight pouring through the windows, reflecting off of the linoleum, these were the last images I remembered before the black of the basement. Now, though, the day was replaced with the electric blue of the sky after sunset. I looked over to the clock on the wall next to the reference desk. Quarter after five, the minimalist numerals read. Fifteen minutes after the end of my shift.

My head spun. Five hours, unaccounted for. How?

Slamming my hand against the top of the bookshelf to steady myself, I ran through the facts I knew to be true. Back then, I still remembered my name, my hometown, the month and day that I was born. Small details like that have long since disappeared, but they calmed me in those initial moments. Now, all I can recall are the broad strokes. 1959, my third year of undergrad. I was a full-time English major and part-time page at the largest library on campus. Newest one, too, at the time. Most of my workday was made up of rearranging catalog cards and restocking the shelves in the stacks. On special occasions, when we were short-staffed, I would get to fill in and field a question or two at the reference desk.

Not on that day. From where I stood, I could see my supervisor, the Head Librarian, sitting behind the desk. She was an old owl of a woman, a fixture of the library as much as the mahogany shelves or plaques on the wall. She must have been eighty, at least, and had been working on campus since she was a student back in the last century. This fact she'd drilled into all of us doe-eyed new pages on the first day of the job, and she reminded us of it every time we put a book out of place, missed a spot of dust on the shelf, or did some other task in a way that didn't meet her standards. Miss Callaghan. That's one name I'll never forget. In the three years I worked at the library, I never saw her smile, laugh, or show any expression on her face besides her neutral mask, mouth drawn firmly into a line of vague disapproval.

That's why the wide-eyed look of concern on her face that night as she stared at the clock took me by surprise. After reaching into her pocket to double-check the time on her tarnished brass watch, she cleared her throat and picked up the intercom.

"All library staff remaining on the premises please report to the central reference desk. I repeat, all library staff please report to the central reference desk. Thank you." Miss Callaghan hung up the receiver with a satisfying click.

Ready to pour out apologies, I made my way over to the desk. Countless times I'd watched Miss Callaghan ream the other pages for being late to work or late to leave. *You aren't getting paid a cent more than you're supposed to,* she'd nag, tapping the page schedule with a long, manicured nail. But she didn't yell or lecture when I reached the desk. She just sat, hands folded, eyes scanning the room. If she was silent now, I guessed, that probably meant she would unleash a tidal wave of fury later. I choked down my apologies and stared at the floor.

Within a few minutes, the night-shift page, the two full-time librarians, and the janitor stood at attention in front of the desk. At the end of the line, I braced myself for a humiliating dress-down in front of my colleagues. Instead, the frown on Miss Callaghan's face grew deeper. She asked the assembled staff if any of us had seen…me.

I looked up to meet her eyes. "I'm right here, ma'am."

Total silence, like I hadn't even spoken. I looked at the rest of the lineup. All of them shook their heads. Speechless, I walked forward, trying for the first time in my employment at the library to draw attention to myself. It didn't work.

"Alright, well, let's see here," Miss Callaghan placed a small notepad on top of the desk. "It seems that today, she was assigned to reorganize the catalog archives down in the basement. Perhaps she did not hear my announcement and lost track of the time. Two of you, go down there and fetch her."

One of the full-timers and the page volunteered and headed over to the staircase. I followed, desperate to find out what was happening to me. Around me, the library seemed to spin and dissolve. As we wound through the stacks to the corner where the basement door stood tucked in between two unused carts, I felt like I was walking in a dream. I struggled to keep up with the pair's pace.

"It's still open. I bet she's down there." The librarian gestured at the door, which was slightly ajar.

After my struggle up the stairs, I must have forgotten to shut it behind me. The page nodded in agreement. With a shrug, the librarian opened the door fully and looked down the stairs.

The librarian was a tall and broad-shouldered woman, almost comically large compared to the short and stocky page. So, it was obvious, even from behind, when her shoulders and back tensed. One hand she clamped over her mouth and the other, she used to point down the stairs. Worried now, the page pushed past her to see for herself. As soon as the page's eyes hit the staircase, she started to shriek. Still screaming, the duo sprinted back to the reference desk, drawing the panicked stares of every patron along the way.

A black snake of dread coiled around my throat. Step by shaking step, I walked to the precipice of the stairs. When I reached it, I screwed my eyes shut, not wanting to see whatever terrible thing lay before me. I think I knew, in that moment, what I would find. After a few moments, I forced my eyes open.

My body lay at the bottom of the stairs. A pool of thick, coagulated blood poured from the back of my head. My jaw hung limp and open. Catalog cards lay scattered across the stairs and the floor of the basement, their box upturned and empty by my feet. Under the light of the single bulb, my eyes shone as they sat locked in their unblinking stare. I was looking at myself.

Gripping the railing with white knuckles, I descended the stairs. Up close, I could see the viscera. A ring of blue-gray bruising ringed my neck, punctuated with the angry red slashes of thumbnail marks just below my lymph nodes. Coral lipstick, the one my mother had given me for Christmas last year, was smeared from my bottom lip down to my chin. *Your mother,* an absurd voice in my head crowed, *she'll be ashamed of how you look right now.* It was true. My skirt was in disarray, my collar was messy, my once-blonde hair was matted the deep red-brown of dried-up blood. Far from presentable, far from a good reputation for our family. Seeing this scene, seeing myself, dead, in some dark basement of the school she didn't want me to go to, would kill her. Of that I was certain.

And yet, I felt nothing, just a void like the blank haziness right before you wake up from a dream. I crouched down until I could see the red veins of my bloodshot eyes. Carefully, I reached out and grazed my fingers over the ridge of my cheekbone.

Instantly, a soft, charcoal darkness took over my field of vision. I was back at the top of the stairs, holding a cardboard box of soon-to-be-organized catalog cards. Alive. The incessant beating of my heart, a sensation I didn't know I'd missed, told me that much. Midday sunlight warmed the back of my neck. Skimming my fingers over the tops of the cards, I counted the names of at least four textbooks that had been removed from the collection. I was just about to slide them out of their row when I heard a set of footsteps stop just behind me. From their heavy, plodding sound, I could tell it was a man.

"I'm sorry, but the basement is restricted to the use of library staff only. You can request to see our catalog archives at the reference desk in the front. You probably passed it on your way in." I didn't turn around to look at him, not wanting to lose the offending cards I'd found.

No response from the man, but he didn't leave. In the quiet corner where we stood, the library's patrons were hidden from sight and sound by stacks of shelves. Which meant that we were hidden to them, as well. All I could hear in that moment was the man's heavy breathing and the sound of my quickening heart.

The rest of it happened in a flash. With the grip of a vice, the man grabbed me by the forearms and whirled me around to face him, sending the box of cards tumbling down the stairs. Before I could make a noise, he clamped one massive hand over my mouth and another around my neck. I tried to scream, but all that could make it out of my windpipe was garbled chokes. By then, he had moved both hands to my neck. When I clawed at him with my fading strength, he just chuckled and dug his nails deeper into my skin. Reliving it was like watching a film: I could see what was happening, but thanked god that I didn't feel the pain of it all again.

His face, amused and smiling like a child ripping the heads off of paper dolls, will be etched into my memory forever. A thick, knotty scar ran from just below his left eye down to the curve of his jaw. Bright blue eyes, laughing at me, were the last thing I saw before it all faded away. As my vision tunneled, I felt the sensation of falling.

I was back in the basement, looking at my lifeless body.

Most certainly, I wasn't supposed to be there.

Hyperventilating, I paced the basement until Miss Callaghan tiptoed down the stairs. Averting her eyes from the nastiness, she walked up as close to my corpse as she could and made the sign of the cross.

"The police will arrive in ten minutes or so. Oh, Christ, how could this happen? She was such a lovely girl. Who could possibly…" Miss Callaghan's voice evaporated into a wet trail.

I walked right up to her and waved my arms around, desperate for any kind of acknowledgement. "I'm here! I'm right here in this goddamn basement with you!"

My boss's shoulders tensed and shook with a chill. Aside from that, no one moved a muscle.

For as long as I could muster, I ran around the basement like a crazed animal. Bellowing, crying, rocketing from wall to wall, I tried whatever I could think of to get anyone's attention. Slamming my fists against the walls made no sound. Kicking my corpse just showed me how my legs would pass right through physical objects as though they were bathwater. Shrieking my voice ragged up against the page's ear resulted in nothing but another chill. By the time the police bounded down the library stairs, caps in hand, I sat in the farthest corner from my body, curled up and weeping.

Three cops arrived at the scene. One I recognized as the lanky, miserable old man assigned to the campus beat. Prowling the school, he wrote up dozens of noise complaints. As he looked around the basement, his permanent scowl somehow grew graver. The second cop, at first glance, could pass for thirteen years old. Wide-eyed, he flashed photos with a handheld camera and murmured about how it was such a shame, such a tragedy. The last police officer's badge glinted in the sparse light. Sheriff. I'd seen him a few times before, patrolling the perimeter of town, buying a coffee at the delicatessen across from the village green. Now, instead of the courteous nod I was used to, he frowned in concentration as he surveyed the room. Once he was satisfied, the sheriff turned to Miss Callaghan, who stood, back against the wall, twisting her pearl necklace around her fingers.

The police spent hours questioning every member of the library staff, scratching down notes, and placing evidence markers around the room. I didn't get up from my seat until more visitors arrived: the town coroners. Reverent as a pallbearer, I followed them through the cleared-out library until they lifted the stretcher down the front steps of the building. Much as I wanted to hear how the police planned to proceed with the investigation, the clawing need to stay with my body pulled me forward. With a deep breath, I stepped through the door of the building and into the darkening night.

As soon as my foot left the threshold of the library, I appeared back where I'd started: in the catalog archive room of the basement, standing in the exact spot where the outline of my body was drawn in chalk on the floor.

"I must have done something wrong," I assured myself, bounding back up the stairs and sprinting towards the front door.

Back in the basement again. Same spot.

Embarrassingly, that didn't stop me from trying each and every entrance and exit. In a fugue state of fear and desperation, I hurled myself through every inch of every wall. By the time I had tested every spot I possibly could, desperation turned to rage. Standing in the middle of the reading room, my brick wall of resolve collapsed and anger took its place. Rage at the supreme unfairness of the circumstances I found myself in boiled in my chest until it was too unbearable to ignore. My heart raced and my chest felt as though it would burst as I pictured the image of my body discarded like trash on the concrete floor of the basement. As the feeling came to a crescendo, my arms shot out to either side.

As soon as my arms moved, the upholstered reading chair to my left and shelf of magazines to my right ricocheted back as if in the impact zone of a bomb. The clatter of their falls rang throughout the building, silencing the sheriff as he instructed the library staff to go home. Every head in the room swiveled to look at where I was standing. For a fleeting moment, I thought that maybe they could finally see me. But they weren't looking at me. They were looking at the beaten-up old chair turned over on its side and the issues of *Popular Mechanics* and *Vogue* littering the floor. No one said a word. I could almost hear the rationalizations playing through their minds.

The young cop broke the silence. "Probably a freak boiler issue. Basement door's not supposed to be open, right?"

Everyone nodded and carried on with the prior conversation. The two full-time librarians picked up the chair and tidied up the magazines. The group, it seemed, was ready to move on. They'd reached their limit for the day on the unexplained and wouldn't waste a moment thinking about my outburst.

Still, the drumbeat of hope pounded in my ears. If I could move objects, it meant that, albeit in an awkward way, I could communicate with the living. If I could communicate with the living, I could give the police a description of my murderer. And if I could somehow guide the police to solve my murder, then maybe my loose ends would be tied and I could move on. Or, at the very least, leave the library.

Bone-deep exhaustion washed over me. As much as my mind urged me to do whatever it is I did to move the chair and the magazines again, I didn't have the strength. As the police walked the three librarians to the parking lot and the page back to her dorm, I searched around for a soft spot to sleep. The linoleum of the main floor wouldn't do, and the hard, crusty carpet of the reading areas and study rooms wasn't an improvement. Out of the question, obviously, was the basement. Soft desk chairs in the office seemed promising, but it somehow felt invasive to take over another person's private space like that. After floating around for what felt like half the night, I finally decided to curl up on the carpeted floor of the Children's Corner, with its few plush chairs and rack of picture books. Created the previous summer to enhance the college's elementary teaching program, the space was now used mostly by bored children of professors while their parents researched in the reference section. I fell asleep staring at the worn-out copies of *Goodnight Moon* and *Little Bear*, trying not to think about how I'd never read them to children of my own. That night, I did not dream.

Loud footsteps and white noise from two-way radios startled me awake in the morning. More police. In addition to the three from the day before, half a dozen cops from surrounding towns had joined the investigation. Walking shoulder-to-shoulder, their uniforms created a muted rainbow. As they passed by the children's corner, I stood up and straightened my clothes before remembering that I was invisible. Old habits die hard, I suppose. The sheriff brought the new guys down to the basement to see the crime scene while the other town officers sat at the reference desk and took over the phones.

Not wanting to see my death scene for the hundredth time or bear the humiliation of listening to the officers call my family and friends, I decided that now was as good a time as any to form my plan for getting the officers' attention. While I perused the nonfiction shelves, hysterical laughter wracked through my body and poured out of my throat. Nothing was funny but all my body could manage to do was double over, abdomen burning with laughter. The stern, rational voice in my head begged to focus on the task at hand, but it was drowned out by the id voice crowing about the absurdity of the situation. I fought my parents to go to college and become an English teacher or a librarian, whatever job I could find that allowed me to surround myself with books. Now here I was, in the darkness of the stacks, stuck with a thousand books that I could never read. Maybe this wasn't really happening. Maybe I was in Hell.

Banishing that sobering thought, I spent the rest of the morning searching for books that could describe my killer. I left the nonfiction section and its musty, dark, nondescript covers and moved over to the shelves of novels and poetry. It turned out that learning how to haunt was only half the battle. Unfortunately, there wasn't a book titled *I am the Girl Who Died and My Killer is a Man with Bright Blue Eyes and a Facial Scar.* I considered removing all the blue books, but realized what a leap of logic that would require from the police. None of the novels or magazines had covers with pictures of men that even vaguely resembled the murderer. For a brief moment, I thought about stacking up books so that the first letter of their titles would form a sentence, but once again decided that it would be too hard to decipher. After my third turn about the fiction section, I flopped down on a chair in the reading room and gave up on cleverness.

What I needed to do was scare the hell out of them.

Camping out in the ladies' room, I summoned my strongest emotions and tested out different kinds of haunts just to see what I was capable of. Once I exhausted my body and mind with this training and left the bathroom, I found myself, once again, alone. All around me, the too-familiar sights of the library stood, silent except for the faint rumbling of the radiators. I spent the whole night pacing the floor, trying to recall the facts of my life again to calm down. Already, the edges had started to blur. Already, I was starting to forget. The name of my second-grade teacher, the color of the pillow cases in my dorm room, what dress I wore to my senior prom, the details of my life had already begun to pour out like a sieve. I wouldn't have even noticed if it wasn't all I had to think about. Now, the thought of losing memory struck the deepest chord of fear within my soul. Unable to entertain the thought of what it would mean to forget myself without being paralyzed with dread, I forced myself to think of a truly desperate feat to get the police's attention. Surely, I reasoned, the investigation in the library had to end soon. This could be my last attempt. I thought of the pulp horror digests I would to buy at the grocery store back home, of the stories whispered by the older children in the darkness when I used to trick-or-treat. By the time that pre-dawn bathed the library in weak, grey light, my next move was planned.

Shortly after sunrise, the gaggle of police barged through the front entrance, just as they had the day before, sheriff speaking as he led the way. "Today, I need you to crack down on this case. I want you to follow any lead, even if it's based on the weakest and smallest shred of evidence. Half of us will stay here and keep calling the girl's close contacts and the rest of you will canvass the town. State troopers will be arriving shortly to aid with the investigation, and you should defer to them when they arrive. Clear?"

Everyone nodded, then divided themselves into the phone callers and the search party. To build up my strength for the haunting, I decided to rest in the chair until the state troopers arrived. More people to bear witness to my message. I shut my eyes and tried to stoke the ashes of emotion until the time came. I heard the pair of state troopers before I saw them. Their boots made a different, louder sound on the hard floor than the local police's shoes did. I waited until I heard their small-talk greetings with the current investigators. Then, careful not to disturb my emotional state, I opened my eyes.

When I did, I saw my killer.

The crisp, clean lines of his black, militaristic uniform contrasted with the sloppy plaid button-down that he wore in my memory. A round, wide-brimmed hat cast a shadow over his face. But he was unmistakable to me. Those blue, blue eyes pierced through the shadow, as did the thick, straight, keloid scar.

At the sight of him, the wind was knocked out of me. I could still feel the grip of his hands on my neck, the pain points where his thumbnails dug into my skin. Terror from my memories paralyzed me, rendered me mute as I watched him nod at the briefing from the sheriff. Voices and noises around me sounded like they were coming from a swimming pool.

Slowly, I regained my sense of reality. As soon as I was able to move my limbs again, I ran to the administrative offices. Getting my killer as far out of eyesight as possible was the only thought in my mind. Forcing myself to take deep breaths, I repressed my memories of the murder. Now was not the time for pain. Now was not the time for cowering. Now was the time to plan my attack, the only opportunity I'd have to face my killer directly. Mentally, I twisted the plan I'd made the night before to serve the circumstances at hand. I laughed then, bitter and dry. *Good,* I thought. *This will make it easier to do what I have to do.* Once I steeled myself for the sight of the blue-eyed man again, I walked back to the reference desk, the home base of the cops. All I had to was wait, eyes following the killer like a cat tracking its prey.

My opportunity presented itself at midday. *Full circle,* I mused, seeing the afternoon light in my memory. A giant map of the town lay open on the table, each police officer tracing out their theory for the perpetrator's path. As the young, local officer and the other state trooper argued about motive, the blue-eyed man peeled away from the table and towards the bathroom. The sheriff was the only one to notice his absence, and he headed to the bathroom in lock step behind. I brought up the rear, passing through them on my way to the only room of the library I had never seen. The men's bathroom was dark, even at noon, with a single porthole window too high on the wall to see through. As the two men used the urinals, I faced the mirrors over the sink and prayed to whatever God had abandoned me here that my plan would work.

I reached a shaking arm out to the dingy mirror. At first, my palm met the resistance of the cool, hard glass. Pushing harder, I allowed myself to remember death, that cold ocean I fell into, right before my vision went black as I tumbled down the stairs. Little by little, the glass turned into viscous water, clear but thick as marmalade. Floating on my feet, I pushed myself through the mirror and came out the other side. Everything was flipped, of course, and I stumbled with the disorientation of it all. As I heard the urinals flush, I snapped back to the task at hand and turned myself around.

From here, the mirror was a window to the sheriff and the state trooper. The sheriff made a joke about state bureaucracy as he flipped on his sink, and the state trooper gave a pitying laugh in return. Urgency turned my veins to fire. *Now or never, only shot.*

All at once, I let myself feel every emotion I'd buried in my mind. Grief, at the images of my mother, father, brother, friends, dog, classes I'd never get to take, life I'd never get to have. Stomach-roiling horror at the thought of this library as the afterlife, as eternity. Rage, my old friend, when I looked into my killer's cold blue eyes and remembered everything he'd stolen from me for no reason other than his own sick entertainment. I sensed every feeling on an almost molecular level even as I let them crash over me like waves. Power flowed through me and the pressure built as the emotions grew stronger. Hot, angry tears poured down my face as I let out a wet, guttural yell. It only took a few more seconds for the dams to burst, in real life and in my mind. I watched as the bathroom mirrors filled with blood. Like a severed artery, the blood gushed from the mirrors, coating the sheriff and the murderer from head to toe, stopping only when I willed it to. Spitting red and streaming profanity, the sheriff scrambled until his back hit the wall behind him. My murderer had no reaction. He stood, still as a tin soldier, staring straight ahead.

Needing to up the ante, I cleared the blood from the center of the mirror, leaving a red crust on the rim. I walked right in front of the murderer and willed the reflection to reveal my face. If he saw it, he didn't react, just continued with his thousand-yard stare. I only knew it worked from the sheriff's bewildered yelp as I materialized in the reflection. Inch by inch, my skin turned to the grey, bruised, and bloated mess that he'd left me as at the bottom of the basement stairs. I wanted the man to see what he had done.

"You." My voice came out gritty and visceral, the words like knives in my throat. "You did this. I know what you did."

"Holy shit!" The sheriff cowered in his corner.

I locked my glare onto the murderer, hoping to make it clear to the sheriff that the state trooper had killed me. In my heart of hearts, I hoped that the sight of me would break my killer, too. That, confronted with my face, he would collapse into guilty sobs, confessing exactly what he'd done to whom. Aside from the hard clench of his jaw, though, it was like I wasn't even there.

Maintaining the stone wall of his face, the killer finished washing his hands and shook them out to dry, glancing at his companion in the mirror. "You all right, Sheriff?"

The other man sputtered. "The mirror! Look at the mirror!"

"What on earth are you talking about?" Knitting his brows, the state trooper turned towards the sheriff.

"You don't see that? The girl, right there, in the mirror, saying we killed her!" As the sheriff pointed emphatically to where I stood, I felt my power fading fast. The haunting wouldn't last much longer.

My killer looked back in the mirror, back to me, and feigned ignorance. "I don't see anything. Nothing but my own face. You been hitting the bottle, Sherriff?"

Using the last of my strength, the last crest of despair, I spoke again. "Murderer!"

As the shaken sheriff continued to insist on what he saw, the state trooper pushed back against him every time. Power spent, I fell through the cold glass of the mirror, back to the side I came from. A slow river of anger continued to course through me, and I used it to keep the edges of the mirror painted with blood. Exhausted and sick to my stomach, I lay back against the bathroom wall, begging the sheriff to trust his own eyes.

The plea was of no use. My killer walked over to the sheriff and clamped his hands over the other man's shoulders. "Listen, Sheriff. I've been in law enforcement for over twenty years. Such a nasty business. All the things you see, the horrors, like what happened to that poor girl… Well, it can play tricks on your mind. Make you feel guilty, feel responsible. Now, I know you've been working night and day on this case. Losing sleep. We all do, especially with a case like this. How about you go home for the rest of the day and rest, alright?"

The sheriff shook the state trooper's hands off his shoulders and stared at the mirror for a long while before letting out a deep sigh. "You're right. I guess I'm just shaken up. Much more shaken up than I thought. I'll let the boys know I'm leaving for the day and head out. I'm sorry."

"Don't be sorry. Rest up and come back tomorrow." The state trooper smiled his too-wide grin.

With a slam of the door, my killer and I were alone again. At last. Arms and legs heavy as lead weights, I knew I was too tired to move from my spot on the floor. All I could do was sit and watch as the blue-eyed man stepped up to the mirror. For a few moments, he looked at his reflection, crowned in crusted blood. Then, like a shark moving through water, he brought his face up to the mirror and licked a stripe of blood away. Wiping his mouth with the back of his hand, he walked out of the bathroom, the echo of his boots ricocheting off the wall.

I never saw him again. As far as I know, he was never caught.

A sense of emptiness filled me then, one that has never left in the decades since. Until I heard the sounds of the policemen leaving, I lay in the same spot on the bathroom floor. Sleep was fleeting, inconsequential, doing nothing to restore my will. At some point during the night, I forced myself up. I sat in front of the tall windows until the sun came up, staring out at the winter air that I would never feel again.

They kept the library closed for another week after that. Crime scene investigation over, however, the police never returned. I suppose they closed the library out of respect for me. Somehow, that week felt like both a year and an instant. Time never felt the same after I gave up hope of moving on.

Years passed like steady spinning wheels as I paced the floors of my home, my prison. Miss Callaghan died a few months after I did, honored by a plaque on the wall that fewer and fewer people stopped to look at each year. Wherever she is, I hope it's not like this. Students came, students went. New pages and librarians and janitors joined and left the staff. I wondered if they could feel me reading over their shoulders, following their paths. Bored and numb and resigned to my fate, I could never muster up the energy to haunt them. Eventually, once all of the liberal arts schools in the state went co-ed, most women's colleges couldn't survive. Ours was one of the first to go under, the pitiful enrollment not even enough to pay to keep the lights on. Sitting on the reference desk, I watched as movers hauled away cart after cart of books. I imagined the hailstorm of words Miss Callaghan would rain upon them if she was still alive. My only companion now are my thoughts and my imagination. Maybe someday they'll knock the walls around me down while I am still inside.

Until then, I tell what parts of my story remain in my mind so that I will remember it. I mutter the facts to myself as I tread the long-abandoned floorboards of the library, passing rows and rows of empty shelves. I've forgotten my name. I've forgotten where I come from. The faces of my parents have blurred, erased from my memory like the faded names etched into the stone of an eroded tomb. It would be so easy to let go of it all, to give into the bedrock of wrath that has been my only constant all these years. Each day, I lose more of myself.

When I forget the story of my death, I fear what I'll become.

Final Score, in B Minor — Karl Lykken

arl Lykken writes stories and software in Texas. His work can be found in Daily Science Fiction, Theme of Absence, *and* Love Letters to Poe.

* * *

Monica often forgot a face, but never a violin. Certainly not a violin like that. A trained ear would struggle to differentiate it from a Stradivarius, and a trained eye from a teenager's final project for shop class. Though she had never seen it in person before, Monica had no doubt it was the violin Boris Boureanu used for his album, *My Insides Out*.

After all, how many times had she stared at its picture on the cover of her most prized vinyl record? Not quite so many as she'd heard it play on the same. She knew that violin. She signed up for Boris' class on "Translating Memories into Music" because of what he had done with it. Well, that and the mystery of why he had done so little else.

The mystery preoccupying Monica at present, though, was why this violin, this piece of music history, was in the hands of Morty, whose skill level she considered far more in line with the violin's look than its sound. But as she listened to Morty play, Monica wondered if she underestimated his abilities.

She didn't like his song, exactly. It exuded smugness and arrogance, which in Monica's ears made it perfect as Morty's theme music but far from her taste. Nevertheless, she could not deny the mastery required to produce a sound so emotive. She always freely admitted Morty had natural technical talent (though not quite as freely as Morty admitted it) but making music at this level required more. It took a devotion to the craft, a love for it, an obsession with it. In short, having the kind of feelings about music that Monica doubted Morty could have towards anything besides himself. The Morty she knew in school, at any rate.

Those first few months after graduation, filled with failed auditions for progressively fewer elite orchestras, surely gnawed away at Monica's confidence, and she supposed they might have shocked Morty out of his lazy, self-congratulatory ways. She frowned, reflecting that his apparent choice of audition piece suggested otherwise.

The song concluded with a coda that seemed to simultaneously scoff at the notion that the applause of an audience full of inferior talents could possibly matter while assuming it must be coming. This assumption, however, proved false. What came was total silence, which, in a practice room full of a dozen musicians all vying for the same spot on the Silver String Screen Orchestra, constituted far higher praise. But not high enough to prevent Morty from rushing out of the room, red-cheeked and teary-eyed.

"Morty!" Monica called, pursuing him into the hallway. "Stop!"

He obeyed, using his sleeve to mop his eyes before turning to face her. "What do you want?" he mumbled.

Boris' violin, she thought, but she said, "To know how you could play like that."

Morty bit his lip to keep it from shaking. "I would say you don't have to rub in how much I suck, but I guess maybe I deserve it after subjecting you guys to my so-called music."

Unsure of how Morty—previously so full of unearned cockiness—could now be so full of unearned self-dissatisfaction, Monica decided to forgo any niceties and take a more direct approach. "I want to buy Boris' violin. How much did it cost you?"

Morty smiled, though no one would mistake his expression for mirth. "Nothing. He just gave it to me."

"To you?" Monica's indignation crowded out any concern for tact. "Why?"

"As a mean joke, maybe? I don't really know. I ran into him a couple days ago, when I was going to see Dr. Goldmeyer to ask him about how he liked working on film scores. As if I might actually get this gig. Man, I'm such a jackass." He ran his hand through his hair and looked down at his feet. "Anyway, Boureanu asked me what I was doing, and I told him I was wondering if film work was too far beneath me—as if! —and then he just took me back to his office and gave it to me. He said he thought playing it would make me a better man. As if anything could make me better than useless. Do you know I didn't even practice on it before today? Man, I'm deluded."

"You're right. You don't deserve a violin like that." Monica meant what she said, but she told herself that she didn't mean for her words to make him feel the way he looked. Since when was he so fragile? Morty extended the violin towards her, and she was thankful for the excuse to avert her gaze from his face.

"Take it." His voice held no anger, no resentment, and Monica felt all the worse for this.

"Morty, I didn't mean—"

"You didn't say anything that wasn't true. I don't deserve this, and I don't need it, because unless the conductor is a child murderer, he doesn't deserve to hear me scratching away at strings I should only use to hang myself." He pushed the violin into Monica's stomach, and she reflexively grabbed it as he let go and turned around.

"Morty, you're not really thinking about..." Monica trailed off as he strode decisively away down the hall. She lowered her head, and her eyes followed the worn strings from the neck to the tailpiece of the violin she wished she hadn't recognized. She heard the distant click of the door at the end of the hallway closing, then plodded back into the practice room.

"Monica Vinceres?" inquired a man standing in the doorway on the opposite side of the room.

"That's me." Monica stepped inside without looking up from her new violin.

"Well, now that you've deigned to make an appearance in the waiting area, perhaps you'd be so kind as to audition for us? You're up." The man turned abruptly and left, letting the door fall shut behind him.

Monica stared at the violin and saw the expression Morty wore when he handed it over. Forgoing her audition seemed like an appropriate act of penance, but she knew her atonement would have to take a different form. Her music came first. If it didn't, it might not come at all.

She crossed the room and passed through the door into a small antechamber, and then on into the rehearsal room, where the auditions were held. Three men sat side-by-side near the far wall, partially hidden by shadows due to lighting that Monica assumed was purposefully dim. Nevertheless, she recognized among them both the designated fetcher and Serg Warstein, the SSSO's conductor whom she painstakingly stalked online the night before.

Monica came to a halt in the center of the room, working on the theory that her evaluators aspired to an aura of mystique. "I'm Monica Vinceres," she said, listening intently to verify that the room, though cavernous, allowed no echoes or reverberations.

"While it is no doubt a novel experience for you to have anybody actually know your name, we do in fact have it written down," Warstein replied, holding up his clipboard. "We'd introduce ourselves, too, but odds are we won't meet again. So, let's proceed, shall we?"

Prepared for such a greeting by her research and newly convinced that such abuse was her karma, Monica readied her violin. Boris' violin. The violin that she had never played before, never gotten a feel for. The violin that her preoccupations prevented her from remembering to switch out for her more familiar (and properly tuned) instrument.

Going back for her other violin was not an option, she knew, so she tried to put it out of her mind. She took a deep breath, let it out, and accepted that her traditionally solo Paganini caprices would now be accompanied by a mix of guilt and terror. She put the bow to the strings and began to play.

Not Paganini, though. She played something else, something new. Something dreadful, not in the sense of being poorly played, but in the feelings it inspired. She transformed remorse and anxiety into sound, without any trace of the beautiful, sentimental coatings so often applied to music dealing with such emotions. In short, she played exactly what she felt.

Or, at least, exactly what she felt was played. Her arm moved the bow, but she put no thought into moving her arm. Her mind remained clear of any contemplations about what notes to play, or musings about what might have induced this bizarre extemporaneous musical episode in someone who as a rule never improvised. She focused solely on her guilt and worries, from her first note until her last. Then, as the final troubled reverberations of the strings subsided, she smiled.

As did Warstein. "You get it. You actually get it. I can't tell you how many prima donnas come in here and make some beautiful music, not realizing that for us, it's not about making the music beautiful. It's about making music that makes us feel, that adds the emotion to the film. And you—if you can play like that, you can play for me. Well done, Miss…" He paused to consult his clipboard. "Vinceres."

"Thanks. I guess I'll see you at rehearsal then," Monica replied. Warstein chuckled, while his unidentified companions frowned at her presumptuousness. She turned to leave, unperturbed by the mystery men's reactions. She knew Warstein would override them. She knew she was going to be a star. And she knew, without the slightest doubt, that she deserved it.

* * *

The next several days served only to reinforce her convictions. From the call formally offering her the job to the subsequent flood of messages from friends, family, and networking-focused acquaintances affirming her talent, dedication, and all-around perfection, she received enough external validation to drown out the voice telling her to stay focused and keep practicing. After all, she reasoned, she deserved a break.

Consequently, she showed up to rehearsal on Monday prepared to put an end to her longest vacation from the violin since she fractured her wrist in the sixth grade. As she removed Boris' violin from its new case, though, the remnants of her prior anxiety began to multiply. Where exactly did that audition piece come from? Was it just some freak occurrence? The product of a mental breakdown that happened to rub Warstein the right way? Could she do anything like that again? Or would they realize that was just an aberration and regret hiring her? Why in the world did she take the weekend off?

Her neck prickled under the eyes of her fellow musicians, though judging from the cellist who declined to stop staring when Monica returned his gaze, their interest—disgust? —centered less on Monica than her instrument. She imagined playing a few notes could clear up their misconceptions about the quality of her violin, but for fear it might bring other misconceptions to light as well, she sat in silence.

Within a few hours (or possibly minutes), Warstein entered, followed by the third man from Monica's audition and a petite, young woman whom Monica found vaguely familiar. Warstein stepped up onto his podium, which now was bathed in overly yellow light, and the sounds of strings and chatter fell away.

"There are a few new faces here today," Warstein said, "but still none as beautiful as mine, so you can keep your focus up here." He paused for a laugh, and the orchestra obliged.

"You all should have received sheet music when you came in for a new score by Rich Sterhol," Warstein continued, gesturing towards the third man. "Before we dive into that, though, we should see the actual film. It's called *The Bitter Start,* and the director, Miss Heidi Ingle, would like to say a few words about it."

Ingle approached the podium, then stopped to wait for Warstein to finish aimlessly shuffling through his papers before stepping aside. Ingle pulled in the center of her mouth, forcing the corners into a small smile, which Monica and a few others reciprocated.

"Thank you for the introduction," Ingle began, speaking in a contralto voice Monica was sure she had heard before. "This movie is very near and dear to me because the themes and plot draw heavily from my life experiences. I think a lot of you will be able to relate to it, too. It's about a young musician, a girl in the suburbs of Philly trying to cope with the reality that she will never realize her parents' dream of her becoming a successful, professional violinist. Well, I guess none of you will quite relate to that part."

This drew some self-satisfied laughs, but not from Monica, who began studying her knees in hopes of hiding her face from Ingle. Monica remembered where she had met Ingle before. She remembered that audition back in high school, back in Philly, for the Rising Suns Youth Orchestra. Monica earned a seat, though she never knew whether to attribute her success to her performance or to her words, the words that drove teenage Heidi Ingle out of the practice room in tears.

"Anyway," Ingle went on, "I suppose movies are better watched than talked about, so we should probably get to it. I hope you get something out of it. And if you notice any continuity errors or anything, let me know. It's too late for me to actually fix them, of course, but it will let me get a head start on beating myself up about them."

Ingle nodded her appreciation for the applause she received before taking a seat near the podium. A large screen descended from the ceiling in front of the orchestra while the lights dimmed, and the scoreless cut of *The Bitter Start* began.

On the rare occasions Monica watched a movie, she typically devoted her full attention to the score. This time, though, she barely noticed its absence. This was a film she understood, a film that understood her. The mix of love, ambition, fear, and doubt that drove the protagonist fueled Monica as well, and the scenes from this fictional childhood felt all too real. When the screen finally rescinded back into the ceiling, Monica re-watched scenes from it inside her head, with her younger self recast as the lead.

A sprinkling of subdued clapping alerted her that Sterhol's turn on the podium was ending, from which she inferred that it had previously begun. Warstein left her no time to fret about missing Sterhol's speech, though, as he prepared to lead the orchestra through a trial run of the score.

Monica looked at the sheet music, though she still saw the film. She raised her bow as Warstein did his baton, but they promptly ceased to work in unison. The emotions that drove Monica to play—that had driven her to play since the second grade—vibrated out from the strings of Boris' violin, in a different key and at a different tempo than the notes played by everyone else.

Monica paid no mind. She ignored the scoffs and glares, and she played on after the others cut out. She poured out her insides, and she didn't stop until she sat empty in her chair.

"I told you taking her was a mistake," Sterhol said. The staring-prone cellist grunted his agreement. Monica didn't care. The prospect of getting booted from the SSSO didn't faze her, and she mused that, for the first time in her life, it made no particular difference to her whether or not she ever played the violin again.

It made a difference to Ingle, though. "That was it. That was the soundtrack to my movie."

"No," Sterhol said. "That wasn't it at all. This alleged violinist was just making it abundantly clear that she can't actually read music. My score is nothing like that."

"Then I guess your score will have to find a new movie to accompany," Ingle replied, "because I'm using hers."

"An excellent choice," Warstein chimed in. "Miss…" he paused to consult his chart, "Vinceres, would you kindly talk to us in my office?"

"But Serg—" Sterhol objected.

"Don't worry, Rich. I won't make you squeeze in there with us."

Monica beamed as she followed Warstein and Ingle into the spacious office adjoining the rehearsal room. Muted though her ambitions had become, she still appreciated a good complement, as well as the overt envy and outrage on the faces of Sterhol and the other musicians.

Warstein closed the door behind Monica, who noted that the only chair in the room sat behind Warstein's desk. He soon occupied it, while the two women stood. "Just to confirm, that was your original composition, yes?" he asked, lounging back in his seat.

"Yes," Monica replied. "Well, sort of. I mean, I didn't really compose it, per se, I just played it."

"Can you play it again?" Ingle inquired.

Monica looked down at her violin, in part to avoid making eye contact with Ingle. "I don't know."

"What do you mean you don't know?" Warstein reverted to the tone of voice from when Monica first met him, and the old feeling of discomfort began creeping up inside her.

"Well, I don't know that I can play that exact piece again, since I was kind of playing on the fly." Monica glanced up at Warstein, but his expression chased her eyes back to her violin. "But I'm sure I can play something similar."

"Wonderful," Ingle said. "So, what's the process? Do you need to write it out, or just play?"

Monica paused, now studying her violin out of a genuine fascination with it. "I think I need to watch the movie again first. Or maybe I should do it a scene at a time. I'll watch a scene, and then I'll play the score for it. Would that work?"

Her gaze found its way back to Warstein's face, which wore a grin. "Perfectly. We can record tomorrow." He turned to Ingle. "You know, a lot of conductors don't put any emphasis on actually watching the films. But me? I do. And the results speak for themselves."

"So I see."

"Now, if you'll excuse me, I'm afraid the rest of the orchestra will be rather lost without me, but I'll be back to work out the details in a few minutes." Warstein made Ingle step aside to let him by on his way out, rather than passing around her.

After he left, Monica found avoiding looking at Ingle increasingly difficult, especially since she could feel Ingle looking at her. "Do you know why I ended the movie before Lily finds out if she makes the orchestra?" Ingle asked after an uncomfortably long pause.

Monica finally made eye contact, and immediately felt the tension in her shoulders ease. "No. Why?"

"Because it doesn't matter what the judges—or any of the other kids—say to her. That's not what drags her down, and I don't want the audience to scapegoat anyone. After all, they probably don't deserve to be villainized." She smiled, then looked at her feet.

"It really is a great movie," Monica said, quite certain she could play the perfect theme for the ending of an antacid commercial.

* * *

Monica couldn't say how she felt about the actual recording process, filled as it was with dramatic swings in her emotional state, but she certainly enjoyed the aftermath. When Ingle hugged her and thanked her for making a better score than she could have hoped for; when her old college roommate congratulated her stiffly over coffee and fell into a discernibly foul mood; when her parents said they were proud of her—these moments made Monica never want to play Boris' violin again, lest the feelings that arose in her fade away.

Monica reversed her position on this, though, when Warstein called to ask her to score another film. Boris' violin in hand, she arrived in the rehearsal room the next day to meet with Warstein and the new film's director, Eddy von Treves.

"There's my girl." Warstein gestured toward Monica as she approached the men. "Just wait until you hear the work she does for me. The Academy won't bother nominating any other scores."

"It's a pleasure to meet you," Monica said, extending her hand to von Treves, who kissed it rather than shaking it.

"The pleasure's all mine, I'm sure."

Monica resisted the urge to agree, forcing a small laugh instead. "So, I hear you have a movie in need of some music?" she said, inching backwards.

"Right to business, she is," von Treves said, exchanging a glance with Warstein.

"When making music like we do, business is pleasure," Warstein replied.

Monica only managed a smile this time. "So, what is this movie about?"

"This picture," von Treves began, "is about life itself. Though if you need a summary to fit on the back of your DVD case, you could say it is a poignant character study of a boy in the grips of remorse after his involvement in a tragic accident that claims the life of his friend."

"Sounds beautiful," Monica said.

"Or it will after our score is added." Warstein clapped von Treves on the back.

"Can we watch it, then?" Monica asked.

"But of course." Warstein took a remote off his music stand and, with the click of a button, turned down the lights and called down the screen. "For a lot of conductors, the film itself isn't a focus, you know, but then those conductors don't understand the intricacies of our craft."

"It's always embarrassing, having people watch my pictures," von Treves said, giving no indication he heard Warstein. "I just feel so exposed."

Monica took a seat on the far edge of the first row of chairs, while von Treves sat beside her. She crossed her arms so as to put her bow between them, while Warstein sat down on von Treves' other side. The movie began, and from the moment Monica saw the title, *Invisible Tears*, superimposed over a discarded kite, she doubted the film would prove absorbing enough to distract her from the less-than-subtle peeks at her expression von Treves took every few seconds. The next three hours proved her right.

"Did you hate it?" von Treves asked, as the lights came back on.

Monica forced the image of a Schnauzer begging for a treat out of her mind. "I hate that it had to end."

"Don't we all?" Warstein piped in.

"You're too kind," von Treves said to Monica, reaching his hand toward her shoulder. She reflexively jumped to her feet and stepped out of his reach, then froze, her left hand strangling the neck of her violin.

"What's wrong?" Warstein inquired, his tone suggesting he left off an implied "with you."

"I'm just so excited to play the theme music I thought up for you," Monica lied, watching the affronted scowl disappear from von Treves' face. "The movie really inspired me."

"Wonderful," the director said, clapping his hands together. "Let's hear it."

Monica took a breath, trying to summon to mind some semblance of *Invisible Tears'* sparse yet confusing plot. Closing her eyes to block out von Treves, she began to play. Her strokes switched back and forth from frenetic and off paced to slow and tentative. What they evoked, however, never changed: discomfort. An almost palpable uneasiness that hung in the air and constricted the chest. A feeling that only increased in Monica when Warstein grabbed her wrist, preventing her from finishing the tune.

"You'll have to forgive Miss Vinceres, Eddy," Warstein said, looking hard into Monica's now-open eyes. "Sometimes she likes to joke around. But obviously she knows that what she is playing is all wrong."

"I should hope so. That noise didn't match the essence of my picture at all."

"Why don't you play the real piece, Miss Vinceres?" Warstein squeezed Monica's wrist until she winced. "You don't want to make me look bad in front of my good friend, now, do you?"

"I don't feel well," she replied, her voice shrill. "I'm on this new diet, and I don't think it's agreeing with me. Would it be alright if I played it for you tomorrow?"

Warstein gave her wrist another squeeze. "What do you say, Eddy?" he asked, his face still inches from Monica's. "Shall we reconvene tomorrow?"

The director sighed. "I suppose."

"Well then, I hope you feel better tomorrow, Miss Vinceres." Warstein released her, and she hurriedly made her leave. Upon arriving at her apartment, she discovered a voicemail from Warstein, expressing less civil sentiments.

* * *

Monica awoke the next morning to a pounding both in her head and on her door. Her night of drinking failed to deliver the creative breakthrough she needed, but it did leave her an empty bottle with which she armed herself in case Warstein had come to kill her. She took a stance against the wall beside the door and put her bottle-free hand on the lock. "Who's there?"

"Morty. Open up."

Monica hesitated, then set the bottle down on the table and opened the door. "What do you want?"

Morty squeezed past her into her apartment. "I want my violin back."

"Well, we can't always get want we want. Believe me."

"Funny how listening to you always results in me losing out. Seriously, did you really think I wouldn't figure out what it does once the effects wore off? Do you think I'm stupid?"

"I think you're crazy, and I have no idea what you're talking about."

Morty snorted. He scanned over her living room and kitchen before heading into her bedroom, with Monica in pursuit.

"Get out of my room!" She side-stepped in front of her closet while Morty rifled through the dirty clothes on her floor, but he noticed her movements.

"It's in the closet, isn't it?" he asked, straightening up and closing in on her. "I do want to hurt you, but I won't if you get out of my way."

"I'll call the police if you don't get out."

"Good. Bring them here. Then we can tell them all about how you stole my violin."

"It's Boris' violin!"

"Which he gave to me!"

"Only so you'd be less of an arrogant prick!"

Morty opened his mouth, then closed it. They glared at each other in silence for a few moments before he opened it again. "Fine. I don't need it anyway because I actually have talent. But anytime someone complements you on your little score, know that the real musician isn't you. It's that stupid piece of wood. That inanimate object that you had to steal from me, because Boureanu knew you didn't deserve it."

With that, he turned and walked out of her bedroom. Monica glared at the space he previously occupied before following him into the living room. "If I don't deserve it, then how come I'm the only one in this room who made it play something beautiful?"

Morty turned to face her. He took a couple steps toward her, then broke into a run. Monica dodged out of his way, realizing too late where he was headed. She chased him into her bedroom only to find him already emerging from the closet, violin in hand.

"Give me that back!" She tried to grab it from him, but the extra eight inches he had on her allowed him to hold it out of her reach.

"I'll tell you what I'll do," he said, heading back into the living room. "After you've been kicked out of the SSSO in disgrace and I've become a platinum-selling rock violinist, I'll let you have it for an hour every month—so you can polish it for me."

Morty flashed her a grin before reaching for the door. Monica watched him crumple to the floor before it sunk in that she'd grabbed the empty vodka bottle back off her table. Her eyes flicked from the cracked glass to the red puddle forming around Morty's motionless head. She dropped the bottle.

"Oh, God." She fell to her knees and rolled him over, then frantically slapped his cheeks. He didn't respond. "This can't be happening. It just can't."

She felt in vain for his pulse, then got to her feet and paced back and forth. At length, she paused, staring at the body. "I'm so sorry, Morty. I didn't mean to. I swear I didn't mean to."

She put her hands over her eyes and pressed. When she pulled them away, the body was still there. This time, though, it reminded her of something. A boy accidentally killed by his best friend. *Invisible Tears.*

Monica knew she had to hurry. She bent down and grabbed Morty's feet. "I really am sorry," she said, struggling to pull him out of the doorway. "I'm going to dedicate this score to you. Maybe not formally, we'll have to see how things play out. But definitely in spirit. I promise."

* * *

"Feeling better?" Warstein asked.

"Yes, much." Monica nodded to von Treves as she made her way into the recording booth.

"Good, because I would hate to think someone I took under my wing would request going straight to the studio if she didn't have something truly worthy of recording."

Monica ignored him. The body growing cold in her apartment wouldn't wait for her to make small talk. Besides, she knew her song would say it all.

The red light went on, and she played. She poured out her feelings, and by the time she finished, all she could do was curl up and cry hysterically. "I guess that one wasn't for you after all, Morty," she whispered between bitter sobs. "Or for *Invisible Tears*."

Monica couldn't recall the plots of most of the movies she'd seen, but she remembered the scores. And as she played back through her song in her head, it struck her that she had never watched a film with such triumphant music.

Gardens for the Dead — Benjamin Thomas

Benjamin Thomas writes from New England where he unequally balances time between hiking, writing, and quoting seemingly random movies. His short fiction has appeared in a variety of publications, while his medical thriller, Jack Be Quick, *is available from Owl Hollow Press. He is the guest editor on the* Tourmaline and Quartz *fantasy anthology,* Kingdoms of Wrath and Ice, *and hopes you'll get in touch at benjiswandering.com or on social media @benjiswandering*

* * *

I get a call just before midnight and, like anyone, expect the worse. A siren blares by my New York City apartment, so I wait before muttering hello.

"Marybeth Hannigan?" The voice sounds tired. His words are punctuated by a faint, rhythmic beeping. I put my e-reader on the nightstand and sit up. The motion causes Ellie to roll over.

"Speaking."

"This is Dr. Carlos Gunderson with Bowers Regional Hospital. I'm sorry to wake you."

Suddenly, I can't swallow. You can expect the worst all you want but there's such a violent contrast between *expecting* and *receiving*. In my head, I run through all the names he could potentially say, but even before he utters another word, I know who it is.

"Your mother was brought to our facility tonight. We have you listed as her next of kin?"

I put my head in my hand. "Is she okay?"

"She was found confused and walking down the side of the road. An ambulance: a bystander called 9-1-1. When we examined her, we found she had sustained a significant head injury. It's hard to say when it occurred, but after running a CT scan, we found a large amount of intercranial bleeding. I'm sorry to tell you this, Ms. Hannigan, but your mother has passed away."

After the call disconnects, I sit in silence and listen to Ellie's breathing while tears pool in the corners of my eyes. I pad into the kitchen and pull out a chair. Sitting with my elbows on my knees, phone in hand, I dial a number that is not in my contacts, but one of only three that I actually know.

"Catherine?" I say when she picks up. "Mom died."

* * *

It's not quite dawn when Ellie comes home balancing two coffees and breakfast from the diner down the block. The plastic bag rustles when she puts it on the counter. She brings over a coffee and kneels in front of me. I don't think I've moved since I called my sister, not even when Ellie found me and immediately wrapped her arms around my shoulders.

"Should eat something," she says.

She pops the plastic lid from a foil container and scoops seasoned home fries and pale-yellow eggs onto a plate. Tops it with switchback trails of ketchup and just a bit of mustard on the side. Despite the crushing weight on my shoulders, I smile. Ellie has been a constant light since the day she t-boned me at a four-way intersection.

Sometimes damage is okay.

While I take toddler bites, Ellie uses her thumb to spin her engagement ring around her finger. I stare at her hand, her long nimble fingers. Think of my hair curled between them. "I never got a chance to tell her you said yes."

"I mean," she shrugs. "It's only been a week and we've been, you know, celebrating."

"I still should have said something."

She takes a mug from the cabinet and reaches toward the coffee pot only to realize it's empty, and that her takeaway cup from the diner is next to the sink. She takes it from the counter and thumbs the popped-up plastic tab on the lid.

"I'll chalk it up to you were too excited to have finally asked me and was lost in a haze of happiness."

I stop chewing, leave the unbitten bits between my cheeks, and stare at her until she meets my gaze, then abruptly we both start laughing. When we finally stop, my side hurts and I have to wipe tears from the bottom of my cheeks.

For what it's worth, we crawl back into bed and lie there. Neither one of us touches the other, just finds comfort in their presence. Catherine told me she couldn't accept my choice with Ellie not because she disapproved of it per se—Catherine jokes that she knew I was into women before I did—but because she found Ellie overbearing.

I'd argue with her if she could see us then: lying there under a blanket of mourning, Ellie's arm not around me, but the idea of it being there, being present if I needed it, more than enough.

* * *

Our house breathed when we were children; at least that's what our mother told us. When the flames would waver in the great room's fireplace, she would say the old Victorian was whispering secrets in our ears. My sister and I would sit on the massive stone hearth and hold our little hands to the fire, trying to feel it exhale. At night, the floors and walls would groan.

Creaks that echoed in the darkness, punctuated by brittle branches scraping against the windows.

"It's singing you a lullaby." Mom would say. "Helping me take care of my two little ones."

She'd hush us. Tuck our comforters close to our chins, and hum along to the sounds until Catherine would groan and tell her houses don't talk, *mom*.

"Of course, they do, hunnie." She'd smile. "And you better listen when they do."

"Or what?" I'd ask quietly. Our mother hummed softly and ran her hands along the front of our pants, as if she didn't hear me. "Mom? What happens if you don't listen?"

"Listen to a house, or you won't have a home; listen to a house, or you'll be all alone."

* * *

Our house sat at the end of a gated gravel drive that formed a horseshoe in front of the Victorian. The front porch wrapped around the right side, and a swing hung just next to the front door. Our bedroom was on the second floor along with our mother's room, and a playroom in the turret. Catherine and I weren't allowed on the third floor. Adjacent to the house was a greenhouse and behind it there was an expansive garden and then two acres of woods that separated our home from Lake Kurnugia. There was never anyone on the water aside from the rare townie who happened to drag his canoe from the dirt road to the tree-lined shore. It was one of the few small lakes in upstate New York that remained truly hidden. Our property lined almost two thirds of the shore, and the opposite side was primarily undevelopable wetlands. We were children with a kingdom.

Our favorite game was hide and seek. Between the dusty crawlspaces, dirt-bottomed basement, and the garden out back, the pickings were ripe and always fresh. On sunny days, the garden was pristine. Its hedges were overgrown, and deep green vines wrapped their way around stone figures like earthbound tethers. I imagined if they weren't there, the cherub statues and carved animals would float away, lost in the sky like balloons.

"Close your eyes, Marybeth!" Catherine would shout.

"They are closed."

"You're peeking through your fingers. I can see you."

I wasn't; I never did. I just always knew where she was hiding. When I walked through the garden, it was like the flowers would whisper to me, guide me to my sister in near silence. I'd see which way the leaves would turn, notice snakes slithering in the same direction, and there she'd be, tucked behind a gargoyle, her knees against her chest.

"Mom!" Catherine found her in the greenhouse, tending to a row of thin plants with white blossoms. She was wearing gloves and clipping dead leaves. "Mom, Marybeth is cheating again."

"Is that so?" She looked at me and grinned. "Are you playing fair?"

"I am. It's not my fault I'm better than her."

"You're only better because you're a cheater." Her face was flushed, and her eyes were filled with rage. "That's why you don't have any friends, because you cheat at everything so you can win. You're a bitch."

The door clapped shut, causing us both to jump. "Catherine Alice Hannigan." My sister stepped back, her eyes on the ground as our mother pointed. "Go to your room."

"But it's not fair."

The greenhouse glass creaked as if the panes were expanding. Our mother slammed her pruning shears onto a table. "Go. To. Your. Room."

"I hate it here!" Catherine screamed. "I wish this whole house would burn down with both of you inside!" She stomped her foot then stormed off.

Mom's chin waivered slightly. I was young at the time, maybe ten, but I knew the words had hurt. You don't say things like that to your mother unless, somewhere deep inside, you mean them just a little bit. When Catherine was gone, our mother leaned against the table, her shoulder brushing the plants she had been tending. It could have been her breathing; it could have been a tremble in her tired muscles, but to this day, I swear the plants were moving behind her. Little white blossoms and green-leafed stems caressing her arms.

* * *

Ellie offers to make the five-hour trip upstate with me. "I'll even drive. You can rest, get your mind right."

I love her for her generosity. And for her intelligence. The way she smells, and the way she lies in bed with me for hours simply listening to the rain against our windows.

"It's okay. I—I think it would be good if it were only me and her at first. Just let me get things squared away, and then I promise I'll call you to come up."

"Do you really think she'll show?"

"I hope so. I think she'll regret it if she doesn't."

The road winds upstate like a familiar river. It's cold for September. Leaves that have met a pre-mature death skitter across the pavement, their colorful kin still hanging in the trees. Stopping just outside of town, I grab a deli sandwich and a soda from Mark's Gas & Go, and use the hood of my car as a table.

I'm plagued by dreadful familiarity. Everything from the stones on the ground and the way the trees sway in the autumn breeze. It all reminds me of my childhood. A car pulls in and parks next to a gas pump, obscuring my view of its occupant. Is that Catherine's car? Does she even have a car? It mortifies me that I can't remember, and this could be her.

When it isn't my sister, but some man that exits the vehicle, I exhale a breath I failed to realize I was holding. He walks toward the convenience store and pauses, looking at me. "Do you need something, sweetie?"

I instantly snap to. Start chewing the wad of bread and bologna in my mouth. I shake my head, too embarrassed to be angry at *sweetie*.

* * *

The gate at the end of the drive is rusted; it creaks when I push it open. Mars-colored chips rub off and flake away. Welcome home.

The old Victorian is a queen, and at her feet are trees, shrubs, and derelict grounds. Bushes are overgrown. Weeds and vines overshadow the season's last remaining flowers, drowning their fading fall colors in a sea of poison green. I hate myself for not visiting more, for leaving my mother with all of this. Ellie would tell me it wasn't my choice to make—her having stayed. She'd say people do what they want.

Overhead, the sun plays hide-and-seek with a band of clouds. The wind blows and a shutter claps. I follow the sound to the side of the Victorian and see the half-dome roof of the greenhouse. One of the glass panels is missing. The metal frame lined with jagged shards that glitter like gemstones.

I leave the greenhouse, climb the front steps, and go inside. The door clacks shut behind me and I hear the faint creak of the porch swing hinges like someone is sitting there, feet barely gracing the ground as they swing and swing and swing.

Unlike other Victorians, ours has the kitchen closest to the front of the house. There's a great room through the door to the right, while straight ahead is a small hallway that leads to a bathroom, formal dining room, and the stairs. I pass by the great room and dining room, deciding to rip the band-aid off even though it will undoubtedly result in some residual bleeding.

The stairs creak. Directly across from the top step is a faded wooden door with chips missing near the handle. Mine and Catherine's old bedroom.

Inside, our beds are made. They both look so small. I wonder how I ever slept in a twin past eleven years old. A waist-high bookcase, filled with more of my stuff than Catherine's, is under one of the windows. A toy chest our mother refused to part with sits between two radiators.

The turret room our mother recommissioned as a play space while we were growing up is on the other side of a folding door. I don't go in; if I did, I doubt I'd make it much farther before needing to sit down and stop.

I'm surprised to find the bathroom is as clean as the kitchen. Our mother was always a bit. . .messy? She refused to wear gloves while working with plants. I can hear her voice in my head: *you need to feel the dirt beneath your nails, May. It'll connect you to the Earth.*

The second-floor hallway is lined with green carpeting while the walls are adorned with paintings on either side. They are all portraits with the exception of two: one of the house, and one of Lake Kurnugia. The others are a range of people whose story would change over the years. When I was a teenager, I started to think our mother found them at various yard sales and thought they needed a home.

I shudder. My mother would chuckle at me if she saw. She never grew tired of me being unsettled by this place. Though as an adult I tell myself it was more nerves than fear. I had been nervous because our house seemed real in a sense beyond the physical. Like it and the world in its bubble was alive in ways neither should be. The oddities bred my fear which led to Mom's babying that in turn caused Catherine's teasing which, in the end, just seemed to make the house feel more alive. Like it was protecting me.

Mom's bed is a four-poster king. There's a dresser on one side of the room and a vanity in the corner. The latter was a gift—Catherine's idea—that our mother never used. She dressed up occasionally when she would take us out to dinner, but despite having enough family money to only work part-time her entire life, the woman defined 'down to earth'. There's a jewelry box on the vanity, along with a box of tissues and a couple orange pill bottles. I pick one up: zolpidem.

I pull my phone from my back pocket and type the name into Google. They're a sleeping pill more commonly known as Ambien. I know that name. Remember reading news stories of people who would do crazy things while taking them then wake up and remember nothing.

The dent in her truck's front bumper... Now that I think about it, she never told me about that. Nor did she tell me about starting medication. I try to replay phone conversations with her. Ones where I was only half paying attention because I was focused on something else—dishes or an email from work—things that could have waited.

"Fantastic daughter you were," I say to no one.

I take a picture of the label and tell myself I'll contact the doctor who prescribed them in the morning. When I put the plastic bottle back down, I notice an oversized bracelet with large teal stones. It's cheap, almost tacky, and something our mother would *never* wear.

"Why would you have this?" I look at her bed as if she's there, lying in it, sick or maybe dying. I put the bracelet down. "Sorry."

A soft sound of weight on stones crawls through the window. With it comes what must be my sister's car. I stare through the window as she parks, readying myself.

I make my way from the second floor, heart fluttering like I've drank nothing but coffee and haven't eaten for days.

Catherine's door *clunks* shut. She sports an athletic tank top and jeans. Takes a second to tie her hair back. Her tattoo, an orchid wrapped in vines, is visible on her left arm. I breathe like I'm approaching a podium, speech notes clutched in shaking hands.

She takes a deep breath and puts her hands on her hips. "Well, shit. This sucks." These are the first words Catherine has said to me in person in over three years.

I've been telling myself it's because we've both been busy, that once things settled down with Ellie, or Catherine's seemingly overbooked schedule would allow it, things would revert back. Resemble normal. But, standing in the driveway of our childhood home, the monolith looming behind us, I know our concocted excuses were just a ruse.

Without a word, I throw my arms around her shoulders and cry.

* * *

We didn't move into the Victorian after a tragedy. Nor was it some family estate passed down when our grandparents passed. The house was my mother's—was ours—since the day we were born.

Our father died when we were babies. Well, Catherine was just born; I was the oldest an Irish twin could be. According to our mother it was from a car crash. Catherine assumed the role of armchair detective but could never find any records of the accident… or his existence. I would wake up at night and see the glow of her laptop under the blanket. Search as she might, there was never anything of sustenance on the screen's other side. No news reports or records. Just the web's endless abyss.

"I don't understand." Catherine would fume. "You don't have any photographs of him! Not even in the boxes in the attic or your room. How is that normal?"

"Catherine, there are rules about going through other peoples' belongings."

"*Ugh*, stop talking to me like I'm a child! I just want to know."

When I went to our mother's room later that evening, to ask a question about a plant in the greenhouse, one that blossomed this oddly-colored amber flower, well, it was the first time I found her door locked.

* * *

I bring a bottle of wine and two glasses out to the porch. Catherine is sitting on the swing, has been since she arrived an hour ago. The sun has started to set, and the sky burns an autumn orange.

"Ah," she eagerly takes a glass. "Thank you much."

I pour. We say cheers. The swing sways front to back like it did when we were children and would sit on it with our mother. The wind blows and I smell pine in the air.

"So, how's that girl of yours?" Catherine asks. "Still with her?"

My lips part; the words are ready. And the thought is jarred from existence by the sudden bang of a window slamming shut. Catherine and I both look up and over our shoulders. We stare at the house, at the roof of the porch as if we can see through it. But neither of us needs the ability to peer through solid surfaces to know that a window closed on its own accord. It's the same kind of odd thing that happened our entire childhood.

"So, Ellie?" Catherine says.

But something in the way the window closed. The glass panes sealing off what was inside? "Yeah—yeah, she's good. We're still together. Talking about getting a puppy."

"That's good," she says quietly. "Mom really liked her, May. She was happy for you."

"I know," I say quietly.

The conversation descends into silence, our words falling away with the last rays of sun as it disappears behind a tree-lined horizon. Massive pines tower toward the sky. I wonder how many have fallen over the years, their weight subjected to thunderstorms and blizzards. High winds and heavy snow. My sister finishes her glass of wine. The bottle is almost half gone.

"So, what do we have to do?"

And like that I'm reminded of the daunting tasks ahead. Before I left, Ellie helped me make a list. Things like *meet with the mortician; pick out a casket; get a headstone.* I want to do none of them.

"I um, I wrote some stuff down," I say. "I guess go into town tomorrow and talk with Mom's lawyer or the funeral director, make sure everything is all set and then figure out a date?"

Catherine nods. A yawn creeps up and she succumbs. "Alright, well I think I'm going to shower and turn in. Think our beds are still upstairs?"

* * *

There's a hallway. The walls are adorned with portraits of men and women. They all hold the same pose; hands folded atop one another; legs elegantly crossed at the knee. There's no door at the end of the corridor, just a dim orange glow. My skin crawls. Cold air settles on my shoulders like a layer of dust.

Painted eyes stare down at me. I can't help it: I hunch as I walk. I want nothing more than to reach the end of the hallway. Push open whatever door or window I can find and jump outside, but the light stays out of reach.

Liar.

I freeze. I'm scared to look behind me, but when I finally do, I find nothing there.

A liar.

My heart pounds against my chest. There's movement in the corner of my eye. The lips of the closest painting—a grey-haired man in a collared shirt. He sits with distinction. His eyes bore into me as his lips move in jittery motions like a cheap holographic trick on a child's toy.

She's a liar.

* * *

The next morning, Catherine finds me in the greenhouse, mug of coffee in my hands, walking down rows of dead and dying plants. They need water. And so much more. Fertilizer. Fresh soil. Trimming of leaves that are no longer green. Empty pots and aluminum containers the size of bathtubs line the wall.

"Weird, huh?" she says and yawns.

I nod, though I don't know what she's referring to. Either being back in this house or walking through a greenhouse with holes in its roof. Her footsteps push little stones into the ground. She picks a wilted flower—*snap*. I shiver.

"Said you made a list?" Catherine says.

"I did."

"Might as well start running down it. Hell, if we're lucky maybe get a for sale sign at the gate before the end of the month."

The sound of glass shattering causes us both to jump. I drop my mug and cover my head as glass glitters down like deadly snow.

"Ugh, seriously?" Catherine winces and points to an old claw foot tub filled with dirt.

A crow lies there, a carcass amidst weeds. The jagged hole in the roof drips red while black feathers float down like autumn leaves.

My sister shakes her head and walks back toward the door. She holds the collar of her shirt to her lips. "Good on the dead birds, thanks."

"It's just one bird," I say. "Though it is sad."

"Shouldn't have hit a window then."

I look up. "I don't think it was on purpose."

"Well, what do you think happened then?"

"I don't know. Maybe it had a heart attack and died mid-flight."

She scoffs. "Birds don't have heart attacks... Do they?"

"It's actually a common way for hummingbirds to die."

"Huh. Alright, maybe it had a heart attack."

She lets the fabric drop from her chin and the bulky teal end of her necklace bounces against her chest. My fingers twitch. I recognize it instantly: it's the same design as the bracelet on our mother's vanity. Catherine's been here.

"Right," she brushes her hands dismissively against her thighs and I get the feeling the gesture is not directed toward the bird. "The list."

We form a plan. A column of checkboxes, the first of which is to meet with Mom's

attorney—a man with greying hair who still wears suspenders even though... they're

suspenders. "Catherine, good to see you again. You look well."

"When did—"

"Thank you," Catherine cuts me off. "This is all just a little much, you know? We don't even know where to start. You know you see all these movies and tv shows with death in it and things happen so smoothly you forget that's not really what it's like."

What? I stare at my sister as she rambles.

Our mother's attorney clears his throat and adjusts the waist band of his pants even though... he's wearing suspenders. "Yes, well, the movies are an oddity."

He does the human thing and offers condolences. Tells us our mother had her affairs in

good order. Was a *responsible woman.*

"Least that's good," I say.

He walks us through everything. What Mom wanted. What she planned for. And then we get to the bottom of the list, and he carefully reads off what our mother left behind. Nothing of particular value; just odds and ends and a few small accounts.

He flips the page. "And as for the property."

As he reads the document, my fingers tighten around the arms of the chair, color syphoned via my grip, leaving nothing but numb tips and white knuckles.

* * *

Catherine slams the passenger door shut. "Just stop, May. Seriously."

I hurry after her, dropping my keys as I try to put them in my purse. "Then just tell me why you did it."

"I didn't do anything!"

"Really? You didn't do anything? Mom just changes her will right around the same time you called us looking for money? And you were obviously at the attorney's with her! *Good to see you again. You look well*? What was that?" Her lip curls, but I don't stop. "How'd you convince her to do it? Huh?"

"May, she practically left everything else to you! Everything inside, all the money in her accounts except for one. Mom left me the house. She probably realized I need the help and you don't. So, stop being selfish and get over it."

"It's not about the money," I scream. "You hate this house! Why do you want it? So, you can slap on a for sale sign on it and be done with it? This is our home."

She turns at the top of the porch steps. "No—*your* home is in the city. Mine, is in Michigan. This house… is being sold. You are right about one thing, May, I do hate this house. I hate everything about it. You know what? Maybe I'll start a fire and just let it burn. How's that work for you?"

Wood cracks. In a flash her foot and lower leg are gone, fallen straight through the board she's standing on. Catherine screams and slumps back, her other leg weirdly contorted on the porch.

I lurch forward but stop. Hesitate and stare as she tries to extricate herself from the splintered wood. She cries out, tries to push herself to her feet but her pants—or her skin? —are caught on something. Slowly, the porch swing begins to sway. The rusty chains make a sound like… like someone laughing.

* * *

Catherine needs stitches. And a tetanus shot. A rusty nail embedded itself in the soft side of her thigh and carved a jagged valley from her knee to the top of her leg. On the way to the hospital, we don't talk about what happened. Just have a back and forth of *put pressure on it,* followed by, *I am, Jesus.*

While the physician assistant cleans and begins stitching the gash in her leg, I wince at the lip-like edges of flesh and leave the room. I hear her laughing when the curtain's closed. Hospital staff brush by me, only a few look up from their phones or wheeled computer stations. I'm a fixture to them. A piece of furniture they have to navigate around.

I look from room to room and wonder which one my mother was brought to. How many people have laid on the same bed she died in? I clench my jaw and push through the double wooden doors leading to the lobby.

The emergency room waiting area is a square with chairs along the far walls. Several people are waiting to be seen. I can only handle the sounds of someone retching for so long before I stand and head through one of the other doors. I follow the corridor until it changes from linoleum to carpet. I assume I've made it to an old wing of the hospital. It was a manor before it was a place for care, and according to the sign on the wall the upper floor is still used as office space for a select group of administrative staff.

I turn left and walk into a large foyer at the front of the building. There's a floor-to-ceiling bookcase on one wall and a row of paintings on the opposite side. Portraits of the original homesteaders.

I try to think of how long I've been at our mother's house—*Catherine's* house. Has it only been a day? It feels like weeks. My blood churns at the thought of Catherine inheriting the house on her own. She hated it. *Hated* it, and here she is, the sole inheritor.

Maybe Catherine was right, and our mother thought it best given where she is in life. I can't be mad that I'm doing better and don't need the help, can I? But I wouldn't sell our home. I look at one of the portraits, an older man with thin grey hair and wrinkles on his forehead, and think of the building around me. Was it his choice to create a hospital? Or would he have rather kept it in the family? Maybe I can convince Catherine not to sell it.

I lean forward to try and read his name when a voice is in my ears. *"Liar."*

My mind flashes to the hallway and the door behind the light. All the eyes boring down on me, and I try to back away, suddenly falling backwards.

"Whoa." Hands are helping me from the floor. "Are you okay? I'm sorry, I didn't mean to scare you."

I look up and find myself staring at a middle-aged man in a janitor's uniform. His beard is patchy, and his fingers smell like cigarettes. There's a cart of cleaning supplies behind him, angled in the middle of the room. I quickly get to my feet and take a step back.

"I'm really sorry, miss," the janitor says. "I didn't mean to scare you."

My mouth is dry, and it feels like my lips are cracking. "Why did you—why did you say that? Why did you call me a liar?"

This time, the surprise is on his face. He recoils ever so slightly and then rubs the back of his neck with a chuckle. "I didn't call you a liar. I said *Lionel.*" He points to the painting. "That's Lionel Bowers you were looking at."

My lips refuse to close. I look at the name plate and there it is: *Lionel M. Bowers.* I slowly realize that this makes sense: I'm standing in the foyer of Bowers Memorial Hospital. I close my eyes and try to fight away the embarrassment.

* * *

Walking into the house, the sun now down and the moon risen, I full-heartedly know what I heard in the hospital foyer. It was not a janitor saying the name of a healthcare founder; it was the word *liar* because that's who I'm with… A liar. Her jewelry on our mother's vanity, the attorney's recognition…

"I need you to tell me the truth, Catherine." I put my bag on the table and scrub my hands under the tap until my skin is red. I still smell the hospital. The janitor's nicotine nailbeds. "Did you trick her? Were you here last year?"

She slams the fridge door shut, wedges the top of a beer bottle against the edge of the counter and slams her palm down. The cap snaps off and with it comes a chunk of the red laminate. The floorboard creeks beneath my feet and I feel something tighten in my calves.

"Catherine!"

She looks to where the piece is missing and rolls her eyes. "This is why mom left this place to me. She knew you'd never be able to sell it. To wrap up her business and move on."

"It's our house!"

"It's *my* house. You weren't even supposed to be here."

Catherine gulps away half the beer and slams the bottle down on the kitchen table before stalking to the bathroom. The sudden jolt has caused her drink to fizz and rise above the top of the bottle, spilling over the sides and onto the floor. I grab a stained dish rag from the counter, pausing to rub my thumb along the curved chunk missing from the counter and realize what she said, the word that slipped out of her mouth: *weren't*

Liar.

I drop the towel.

She's a liar.

"She is a liar," I say softly.

I ignore the spilled beer and walk toward the hall. The house has gone silent. The sour smell of fermented yeast fills my nose. A few feet down the hall is the bathroom door. The toilet flushes. The sink turns on. When the water cuts out, I hear another sound: the soft click of a lock being turned. Then the rattle comes. Followed by Catherine banging—softly at first and then pounding against the inside of the bathroom door.

"May? May, seriously? This is how you deal with a bad situation?"

I'm confused at first, because I didn't lock the door. I try the outside handle, but it won't move. Just rocks against itself in cut-off turns. I tell Catherine to stop twisting the other side and just let me try it. The knob still doesn't move.

"Catherine!" I've had enough. "Let go of the door"

"I'm not touching the damn thing."

Liar.

She's lying!

My lips start to shake, and I let go of the door. "Okay—okay. Hold on."

I remember there being keys in one of the drawers in the kitchen. One of them an old-fashioned skeleton key for the old-fashioned locks. The junk drawer in the Victorian isn't like my junk drawer at home. There are no cables. No random cell chargers or take-out menus. Just a phone book, coins, and—I yank my hand away and curse. My fingertip is bleeding from a clean slice right down the center. Blood drips to the floor and splatters like rain drops on dry concrete.

My sister calls from the bathroom. Starts pounding on the wood again. I peer down and reach inside the drawer more carefully. Inside are my mother's pruning shears. There's a smear of blood on the side where my finger ran along the edge.

There are tears in my eyes, and it surprises me. I remember her using these. Feel her hand wrapped over mine as she guided me to dying leaves and overgrown stems. I hear her voice in my ears telling me where to cut and how it will help the plant grow.

The memories are severed by the serrated blade of Catherine cursing from the bathroom. She curses me then curses this place. In the pause of her taking another breath to start again, I suddenly remember that day in the greenhouse: *I wish this whole place would burn down with you inside.* And then again out on the porch: *Maybe I'll start a fire and just let it burn.*

I lower the shears and stare through the kitchen and down the hall to where she's volleying a string of swears and fists. The bathroom door violently shakes against its frame. "May!" I hear the vitriol dripping from her voice like sap from a poison tree. There isn't a place for the amount of hatred festering inside her. Not in this house, this home, this life.

And like that it snaps together. I wasn't supposed to be here. Catherine's bracelet in our mother's room… The doctor on the phone—I can't remember his name… what was his name? He said our mother suffered a head wound and I so easily assumed she had fallen down the stairs or tripped in the bathroom.

Catherine was here.

Catherine was here and she had it all planned out: it would have looked like our mother had an accident, one like I initially thought, and it could have been blamed on grogginess from the sleeping pills. But whatever happened hadn't been enough and somehow our mother was able to get out of the house. After Catherine did whatever horrible thing she did and then left, thinking our mother was dead. Except she wasn't, and Catherine didn't think to change the paperwork with the hospital. Why would she?

The curtain over the kitchen window suddenly wavers and falls from the hook fixed to the side of the cabinet like an invisible hand gently pulled it shut.

I wipe away tears and take a deep, heavy breath. I walk to the front door, shut it, and turn the lock. As I softly pad to the bathroom, I grip the shears tighter. White-knuckle them. Surprisingly, my hand isn't shaking. It's barely moving as I hover my palm above the door. Catherine shouts for me to let her out, and with a split-second of doubt, I look to the front door, my last chance to turn away.

No. This is my home. The shears gleam and when I touch the knob, the bathroom door unlocks on its own.

* * *

A few days later Ellie makes the drive from our place in the city and finds me in the greenhouse, a pair of overalls on and a bandana holding my hair back. She knocks softly on the open door, but I already knew she was there. I felt her hands against the front gate when she pushed it open like her palm was pressing against my own chest. The Victorian whispered her arrival in my ears. Sang me the song of someone coming.

She simultaneously looks relieved to see me and yet so sad at the circumstance. Near the door is a thin cardboard box and inside are two replacement panels for the broken ones in the roof. I still need to find a ladder. Along the wall, the empty pots and large containers have been filled with dirt. Empty bags of fertilizer are weighed down by broken pieces of beige ceramic. New seeds have been planted, and the plants left to wilt when my mother died are rebounding.

"Catherine didn't show, did she?" Ellie asks.

I exhale, look at the table and the pair of pruning shears lying next to the plant I'm working on. The blades shine like new. Hours of washing and bottles of dish soap. I put one finger on the handle and spin them like wayward clock hands. "No, she did. But she left. Like always."

Ellie comes over and hugs me. I'm bathed in her smell and would be wrong to say I didn't miss it. I breathe her in until our arms tire and we separate, each of us realizing we're both crying. Her hands trail down my arms until they take my fingers within her own. She holds them up with a laugh and shakes her head. "Look at these! You should wear gloves when you're doing this stuff. It's going to take you forever to clean up."

I shrug and pull my hands away. "I know, but this way… I don't know, makes me feel closer to the Earth, you know?" I gesture at the tables. "Closer to my mother."

I rest my palm on a pot with a lively plant growing inside. Thick leaves of deep green are punctuated by fresh violet flowers. Ellie puts her arm around me and rests her head on my shoulder. When she closes her eyes, the flowers sway and the leaves touch my skin. It's such a comforting feeling to be home.

Forest Cactus — Sharon Cabana

Sharon is an autistic, queer author from just outside Portland, Oregon. As a current student of creative writing, she is interested in crafting stories that inhabit grey spaces and create engagement with the deep humanness that defines emotional experience.

* * *

I was nine years old the day we planted my mother in the Old Grove. Great sheets of driving rain folded over our skins as we made the slow walk to her rooting place. Her Rooting was a beautiful one. Bright green life unfurled from her branching arms, stretching out for all of her six feet in height. She grew and expanded until we knew we would need the wagon and four of our strongest Clydesdales to roll her into the grove. As a blessed oak, she would stand beside her father and her father's mother and their grandmothers before them. Beside the most venerated of our ancestors, she, an honored one, would take her place among the most precious of our people.

Barely a child, I didn't understand the honor bestowed upon my mother. I could not understand the aching emptiness in my chest that told me my mother's Rooting was a permanent change in my life. And while I knew I could still speak with my mother and learn to climb in her branches, bark was no substitute for skin. Even as a sacred oak, she would not smell like cinnamon and chocolate, the smells I liked best in all the world.

My brother's fingers nipped my chin.

"Cheer up, small one," he said in his slow drawl. "You do not know how lucky we are that Mother's Rooting came so late. You had nine whole years with her and I almost twice as much."

Together we followed the wagon, our steps long and slow behind the horses who heaved the great weight of my mother deep into the forest. Though tractors and trucks worked faster, we Tree People leaned into the old ways. Horses' hooves were softer, and the trees would more readily yield to them than the grind of an engine and tires. Mother's place, already prepared for her, had been lovingly dug with shovels in the days before the planting. The rain poured down, droplets escaping the hood of my raincoat to tease the hairs on the back of my neck. I shuddered at the cold.

"Yes," I agreed because he was my older brother and that was what he expected me to say.

I didn't tell him that I had nine years with my mother, but I wanted ten. I wanted ten, eleven, fifty, a hundred thousand million years with her. I wanted to feel her laughter in my cheeks and smell the rosebud soap in her hair. I wanted to snuggle under the blanket she quilted for me and eat popcorn with too much butter.

I did not want a tree for a mother.

I did not tell him that no matter what happened, no matter how much the gods of a forgotten species called forth the ancient magic inside of us, no matter the glory to the stalwart wooden guardians of the forest, no matter how much that ancient wisdom burbled in my bones, the path would be different for me.

I did not tell him the truth I knew inside myself from the moment my mother told us about our fates as the Tree People, guardians of the old forests of the world.

I would never accept the Rooting.

Instead, I just looked up at my big brother and forced a smile.

"I know," I said. "I just hate the rain."

* * *

I was seventeen years old the day I turned my back on the grove and the countless centuries of tradition. I turned my back on the farmhouse that began as a cabin over three hundred years ago when the grove was new. I turned my back on the old dirt road that led to a civilization I knew only from attending school in the small town thirty miles away. I left the herd of twenty horses, the Clydesdales that hauled our loved ones to their planting place and the Mustangs and Arabs that carried us deep into the heart of the grove to sprinkle ashes of lost family, to clear away the undergrowth, and to tend to the sick among the Tree People. For eight years, the dandelion bitterness of my mother's death soured in my chest. For that reason alone, I accepted a scholarship to a school two hundred miles away from my homeland. I pretended I did not hear the call of the forest, closing my ears to the song imprinted on my soul since birth. When I told my brother, he raged.

"You have an obligation," he said.

"I have a prison sentence for the crime of being born," I snapped. "*You* have an obligation."

Six months and my brother grew more and more stubborn and withdrawn. Although he was seven years my senior, Ashton was bound to the land on which we were born. Ever dutiful, he tended the grove, fixed the house, and lived his life in the ways of old. He knew how to repair a wagon and take care of a Clydesdale's feet. While I sought to silence the song of the forest, that ever-grinding hum of the grove come to life, my brother sang with them, a sing-song chorus of family I did not understand. My brother would keep his life firmly planted in the past, in the old ways and traditions of a hundred thousand years. I, on the other hand, could only chase a sunrise I had never seen. I tasted the lemon pepper sour of regret on my tongue for all the hurt I was causing.

I loaded the last of my things in the beat-up Volkswagen I bought for $500 from an old woman on the internet. As my brother's heavy footsteps followed behind me, he stopped at the threshold of the garden and the road.

My brother, loyal and strong to the depths of the roots he had yet to grow, would never stray beyond the grove. My feet, however lighter, glided over the rocks and stones until the asphalt reached up to welcome the soles of my shoes.

I took one last look at my brother through the side window of the car.

"Ash can handle things while I'm gone," I said, unsure to whom I actually spoke. "It's just a couple of years."

As if they sensed my lie, the trees of the grove straightened, the turgor pressure of their cells hardening their bark into living rock. I heard the hum grow louder, a kind of wail from the old forest keening, keening, keening. Tears poured down my face as I tried to tell them what was in my heart, what had been in my heart since the day we planted my mother in the grove. But I could not open myself to their song knowing my path was to suffer the same fate.

I did not look back to see my mother, high on the hill in the center of the forest. She, whose mighty limbs drooped for the first time from her great height and wept acorns long into the night.

* * *

I was twenty years old when summer began with June. I was a scrawny sapling, dressed in faded, torn up dark jeans, hiking boots and sensible flannel. I sat at a table in biology class waiting, as I did every day, for my life to begin, when she flew into the room on the scent of pine needles and sage. Long hair trailed to her knees. She wrapped herself around me like ivy. I felt her presence squeeze my chest, robbing me of breath. She wore green boho pants and an ivory crocheted top that was two sizes too large over an orange tank top. Baubles dangled from her ears and wrists and the rings on her fingers glinted against the light. I wanted to drink her up, invite her to coffee and then coffee forever.

I don't remember much more about that day or the weeks that followed. I grew accustomed to her next to me every Tuesday and Thursday. Her scents changed by her moods. Jasmine and vanilla when she was happy. Lavender when she was stressed or tired. Peppermint when she had a headache. My favorite was the pine and sage; that was when her wildness came to the surface, and I would spend the hours helping her catch up while trying to hold on to the flights of thought whirling around her. When we were assigned a lab project, she asked me to be her partner. When the semester ended, I asked her to be mine.

"You were so prickly," June says now. "You reminded me of a cactus. Y'know, like the prickly pears."

Our first anniversary, June bought me a cactus in a terra cotta pot with a small card that said "Elowen." I placed it in the window.

* * *

There were five cacti sitting in the window the day my summer ended.

"How was your day?" She asked me.

I flung my keys in the ceramic bowl by the door, slid my aching feet from my flats and dropped my purse to the floor with a thud.

She turned to me and smiled, "That good, huh?"

"I'm for the sauna," I said, and dragged my weary body to the bedroom we shared in the 1980's Cape Cod we rented in a suburb just north of the city. With her income as a therapist and mine as a science teacher, we just about made enough money to pretend we were adults. We had a cat named Palm, and a garden with a sauna in the back of the house. The only thing we didn't have was permanence. After five years, June wanted to make things official, to settle us into marriage and begin to build another kind of life. But permanence held no meaning in the context of my inevitability.

I sat for what felt like hours in the sauna, the heat penetrating the existential cold in my bones. I slipped the towel from my body and began to make the cursory inspection. Along the way, I paused to rub the soreness from my muscles. As my fingers trailed over my neck and shoulders, I groaned at the tension living there. I noticed the smoothness of my skin. I unaccountably thought of my mother. I felt the callouses on my hands and the wrinkled patches of my knees and elbows. I rubbed the left foot

89

gingerly, noting the tension in the fascia from a lifetime of walking.

I put my right foot on my left knee and began to rub.

I froze.

There, just inside the arch, a small dime-sized bump had appeared. My heartbeat quickened and the cold in my bones became an eternal shiver. I breathed a ragged breath and gazed down at my foot. In the bump, a fragile green tendril grew, spiraling downwards towards the light.

I thought of June and my family and the children I would never have. My fingers touched the fragile growth and a sob burst through my chest.

The Rooting had begun.

* * *

That night I laid in bed, remembering all the lore of our people.

I turned and looked at June on the bed, sleeping quietly and smelling of jasmine and vanilla.

She shuffled a little in the bed.

"When were you going to tell me?"

"Tell you what?" I asked.

"Do you know," she said softly. "When you talk about home you smell like petrichor? And when you have nightmares, you vow never to tell me that you're a Tree Person." She paused. "Elowen?"

"Yes?"

"What the fuck is a Tree Person?"

I blinked, wrestled with the question of whether or not it would be better to lie about it. Tell her that it was just a nightmare I had as a child after I lost my mother. Tell her that I had a weird phobia of forests and trees and that's why I moved away from the farm. Maybe, I thought, if I didn't tell her the truth, I could save us both from the Rooting.

Instead, I told her everything.

"Tree People are like humans, but not. We're sort of in-between beings. Our stories say we came with the fae people across the stars. We are families, kin, spread out in groves throughout the world. The farm back home?

That's my family's grove. We have groves all over the world. Most of us stay in the groves and never leave." I rubbed my fingers on the bed quilt. "I chose to leave, to try to find a life." I smiled softly.

June sat up in bed and turned on the light. Her expression was cold and flat, clouded over like the new moon. Her scent changed to sea brine, and I knew she was angry. She blinked slowly and took a deep breath.

"All this time," she said softly. "All this time I thought it was something about me. That maybe you thought I was too flighty or stuck in my work or you didn't love me like I love you."

I sat up, too.

"It's not that…"

"And really, it was just because you knew you were leaving before we even began." She snorted bitterly. She shook her head. "No wonder you didn't want to marry me."

I swallowed over and over again until my eyes filled with tears and my sinuses filled up with regret.

"I wasn't supposed to meet you," I whispered.

"But you did."

"Yes," I replied simply. "I met you and asked you to be my partner knowing that I was going to have to leave."

I told her about the Rooting and how it had already begun. I told her how my people became part of the grove, our roots tangling up with each other, sharing sentience. I explained how our bodies changed and disappeared with each transmutation, our tree forms chosen by the same force that brought us to the groves. I showed her the bump on my foot. She touched it gently then pulled back, reality burning her fingertips.

Silence.

Then.

"So, what do we do now?" She asked, her tone hard. Her eyes focused on the far wall where five years of photos documented our story.

"I want to marry you. I want to spend a thousand sunrises watching you. I couldn't promise you forever when I didn't know when it would come for me."

"I wish you had trusted me enough to tell me," she said softly.

Before I could respond, her scent changed, and she cocked her head to the side with a funny snort. She laughed, a little wildly. "Although what would you have said?"

"I'm sorry I can't date you. I'm actually a tree? I have a distant uncle that married a ginkgo?"

June laughed again, really laughed and then her scent turned again to wild rain. There was anger and relieved joy and sadness in her now. She rubbed her face and sighed deeply.

"Why did you run away?" She asked. "If you knew you were going to disappear anyway?"

My voice broke when I told her about my mother. I sobbed at the emptiness inside my chest. I told her that I would sell the sun and moon for another day with her and that I had been scared for five years every day that I would lose her because of what I was.

June took a deep breath, shook her head. She looked at me, her soft lips pressed together. I saw the love and hurt fighting for dominance on her face. She laid back on the bed and turned off the light.

"We need to get you home," she said simply. "Everything else we'll take a minute at a time."

I got up and opened the window as if the fresh air would cleanse away the pain in the room. A piece of forest song crept into my heart. I hummed it to her while breathing in the smell of lilies and moonlight. That night, she fell asleep inside my arms, both of us listening to the song of my people.

* * *

I was twenty-five years old, when I returned to the grove. Heart full of June, I pulled up the old house at the base of the forest. My breath caught in the center of my chest.

"Elowen," June cried. "What's wrong?"

I leapt from the car to the base of the grove. My right foot pounded an instant slower than my left due to the pressure of the roots against the sole of my foot. June ran behind me until we skidded to a stop together.

"Ash," I said softly.

There at the base of the grove, next to a wagon, my brother stood, his feet already beginning to grow and stretch with The Rooting. My brother's head leaned awkwardly down to gaze upon me. His branching fingertips nipped my chin. His eyes fell to June.

"This is June," I said.

He smiled, the leathered skin of his face carving crinkles in his cheeks.

"I always knew," he said softly. "I always knew you would be the one."

"What 'one'?" I asked.

"The one to go. The one to stay. The one that would bring forth the next generation. Mother never told you. She never got the chance. She was too worried it would feed a wildness in you and if her guess was wrong you would never forgive her. I am sorry, Elowen."

It was then that I understood the truth about my people. Of course, I realized. Some of us had to stay as mostly human. I looked at the ones who loaded the wagons and cared for the horses with my family. Of course, of course.

The Rooting came upon me so suddenly, even my brother shuddered at the power. There would be no ritual for me. No, this was wilder, raw...like me.

June stepped back, overcome by the force of song swirling all around me. My heart cracked open, and I heard the shouted cry of joy from my brethren. My mother's voice, who last wept when I spoke to her, sang out, cheering her pride and asking my forgiveness. Roots swirled inside my bones strengthening them, giving them life. My once shorn hair hung heavy like vines swinging against my hips. I rose up for a moment and saw all the grove before me, the past, present, and future of our kind and of the world we were sworn to protect and nurture from the beginning of time.

I looked at June and all the future laid out before me.

I was twenty-five years old when The Rooting came for me.

* * *

Standing in my mother's house, I listened to my ancestors in the grove. I hear the songs of elm, pine, elder, maple and oak. I hear my mother's voice ringing loudest, her long bark-covered limbs reaching towards the stars. I watch my extended kin and those trusted to bear our secrets as they prepare to load my brother into the wagon. He will complete his transformation tonight. We will dance in the grove, our bodies rocking, our feet stomping with the song of my people. I will lay the blessed water at his roots to encourage him to grow and be strong for generations. I will carry our lore and our song in my heart to share it with the Tree People like me, the guardians of our kind.

June comes up behind me and wraps her arms around my waist. She props her chin on my shoulder and together we watch the ritual as old as the earth begin to take hold.

It's a full minute before I realize the hand resting on my belly is holding something. I smile when I see it and the joy causes a burst of life from my brother's head. He sprouts another layer of canopy.

"Ready?" She asks.

I nod and take her offered gift.

"This belongs here," I say.

"You both do," she replies.

I smile again and with a deep breath, I place the cactus in the window.

The TALES of CHARLES SLEY

Figure Charles Sley, portrait in Sley home library

Younger siblings are so precocious, aren't they? Sorry, sis, but once you hit a certain age, precociousness becomes a fallible trait. I think I will get that old Victrola up and running again. Our young editors, as well as schooling us on social media – phenomenal idea, truly – tell me that vinyl has come back into fashion. So too have the classic horrors.

Gothic tales, tales of things from beyond the stars, things that shouldn't be but are, that are created and set upon the world in the most familiar of settings. An estate. A Civil War battleground. An old European city. A metropolitan trail usually traveled by pedestrians and lovers and those looking for physical activity. Things that shouldn't be lurk in these familiar places, much like the strangely ancient and vascularly hungry plants you grow in Mother's conservatory. Sometimes the classics can still terrify and awe, much like the stories assembled here.

The Lady Who Dances in the Ashes — Judith Crow

J udith *was born in Orkney, grew up in Lincolnshire and now lives in the far north of Scotland. Her work draws inspiration from folklore, experience and the natural world.*

The Backwater, *Judith's debut book, was a finalist in the Wishing Shelf Book Awards 2019, and her most recent novel,* Honour's Rest, *was a finalist in the Eyelands Book Award.*

When she isn't writing, Judith is a teacher at a primary school in Caithness. She sometimes finds that writing gets usurped by crafting, music, and being a generally doting spaniel owner.

* * *

It has often been suggested to me that, having worked with the insane for the best part of five decades, I should have no shortage of chilling stories to share. Indeed, my patients have communicated stories which have devastated my spirits and forced me to question my vocation, and there are countless faces which haunt my waking and sleeping thoughts: tormented for my mortal duration by those I could not save and those who would not allow me to try. Yet, I have also experienced more moments of success than I had anticipated as a young man, and wisdom leads one to view the world through a lens of lives preserved, rather than those which were lost.

But there is one particular story which is inclined to raise its head whenever I am called upon to share a dark tale on an autumn evening, or a ghost story on Christmas Eve. It is no use. My tongue ties and my speech chokes me as I attempt to form the words which would reveal the story, but perhaps I will finally be able to share the truth in writing.

To comprehend the setting, I would first direct the tale to the summer of 1862, when I undertook a trip north with my friend, Felix DeCourcy. He had been my good companion at Harrow and then Cambridge and, while I would inherit my father's comfortable estate in Suffolk, DeCourcy was the fifth son and would inherit little in the way of property. His father suggested he purchase his own estate and, to that end, we travelled to Yorkshire together that summer to view one which had been recommended.

Hedgwick Grange reminded me of Emily Bronte's *Wuthering Heights*. Its remote location evoked a sense of foreboding which filled me as I accompanied my friend up the long drive. The rattling cries of unseen crows and the trees which, twisted by the wind, leant over on either side of us, gave a claustrophobic ambience to the estate. DeCourcy, however, seemed not to notice it in the slightest, and only commented on its acreage and his plans to join the local hunt which took a route through the grounds.

The estate was being sold after the death of Rupert Hedgwick, whose solicitor acted as our guide. With no known surviving relatives or friends, the old man's estate was in danger of falling into disrepair unless an owner was found quickly, and DeCourcy was determined to be its saviour. Having accepted my friend's substantial offer for the property, which I thought was rather too generous, Hedgwick's solicitor assured us that the previous owner's final effects would be removed by Michaelmas. We spent the remainder of the day strolling through the grounds and rather lost track of time. Consequently, we were forced to spend the evening in The Drop and Cage, a shabby tavern in the neighbouring village of Rukby-on-Stane.

Whilst there, some of the local men seemed to get wind of our purpose for visiting and took it upon themselves to share their knowledge of the estate with its new owner. DeCourcy was unperturbed and, I suppose, I was too. It is easy with the curse of hindsight to believe I felt some deeper sense of dread after the words which were spoken, but I cannot claim it with any conviction. The old men told us 'the Grange', as they called it, had been built by Ezra Hedgwick, a notorious executioner some two hundred years earlier. It had never had any occupant save the Hedgwick family, and each generation lost their eldest son in punishment for their ancestor's crimes. It transpired that Ezra Hedgwick did not so much take a pride in his work as a pleasure, and was known to allow witches to burn alive, rather than garotte them at the stake as was the standard sentence in the area.

DeCourcy would not be swayed, and he stayed up into the small hours that night expressing his dislike for superstition and his excitement at the prospect of developing Hedgwick Grange into a family home. I had no greater interest in superstition than he had himself, but had no taste for the house or the local people. Although I never voiced my feelings aloud, I must have expressed them in my attitude and actions, for DeCourcy and I drifted apart over the years which followed, not through any disagreement, but simply through the unforgiving passage of time. I discovered a calling to my work and, eventually, DeCourcy married Louisa Elphinstone who was, like him, the youngest child of an earl. I read the announcement of their marriage in The Times and was pleased he had found happiness with a wife, but it brought a certain pang of disappointment to consider how our friendship had faded over the years until I did not even merit an invitation to his wedding.

When my father died, I took up permanent residence in London and, as I had always intended, put all my energy into the treatment of the sick, specifically those suffering from mental infirmity. During visits to my patients, I noted how fortified they were when in the company of some or other family member, and I began to theorise there may be scope to treat such patients at home, providing they posed no threat to themselves or those around them. I believed it with such fervour that I presented it as a paper to the *British Medical Journal* and was overjoyed when it was printed.

However, I had not reckoned with meeting ridicule and stifling traditionalism from my colleagues, who believed nothing could be gained from such a gentle method of treatment for the insane. I unwittingly made myself the laughingstock of London and, with a sense of deep personal despair, I resigned my post as a Junior Physician at the Bethlem Royal Hospital and returned to Suffolk. No doubt my family feared for my own mental state, as my sister quit her house to come and live with me to ensure I did nothing which might endanger myself.

It was during these dark days in Suffolk that I received a letter from DeCourcy inviting me to stay with him at Hedgwick Grange. I admit I railed against the idea at first, believing he had discovered something of my downfall, but a conversation with my sister led me to realise it was unlikely he would have known of it without any connections within the medical circle. I therefore wrote back to him and expressed my intention to travel up to Yorkshire immediately, privately hoping I would find the Grange to have become a less dismal place. I arrived to discover that someone had rejuvenated the avenue with new trees, which had not yet been crippled by the inclement weather, but the house itself was quite how I remembered it.

DeCourcy seemed pleased enough to see me, as I was pleased to see him, and he introduced me to his family: Louisa, his wife; Matthew, his eldest son; Henry, his second son; and the baby, who was named for her mother. I found it rather overwhelming to see how easily my friend had embraced the role of husband and father, while I still viewed myself as a young man with the world at my feet. It was both humbling and astonishing to retire to my room and stand staring at my reflection in the glass, seeing myself as DeCourcy must have seen me. I had not noticed until that point the grey hairs in the temples, and those in my beard too. I shook my head and rebuked my reflection for so unsettling me, telling myself I still had years to achieve the high ambitions I harboured.

Dinner that evening was a quiet affair, and I got the impression that Hedgwick Grange was not as lively at it had seemed in the daylight hours when the children had been presented by their governesses and nursery maids. DeCourcy and his wife barely spoke a word to one another, and it was not until Lady DeCourcy had excused herself at the end of the meal and we gentlemen had withdrawn for a glass of brandy that my friend began to speak anything more than pleasantries.

"I see little point in maintaining the play-acting," he said with a sigh, before taking a sip of brandy and gazing out of the window for a moment. "I will admit, Lockman: I had an ulterior motive for inviting you to Hedgwick."

I said nothing, uncertain what could be the mannerly response to such a frank admission. Instead, I followed his gaze. Although he seemed to be staring into the darkening estate beyond, my own eyes watched a large moth beating its wings frantically against the glass panes. DeCourcy turned back to me after a second and smiled.

"You always had a masterful way of making people talk," he said, and I nodded my head in appreciation of what I hoped was a compliment. "You would have done well to have entered Her Majesty's service, rather than dedicate your life to those who will not miss you when you are gone."

I frowned at his damning definition of my work but, to maintain politeness, I did not comment on his dismissive view of my career.

"Then tell me your ulterior motive, DeCourcy," I said quietly, and he gestured that we should both take a seat. Once sitting down, he took another drink from the glass and then proceeded to explain the reason for my being at Hedgwick.

"Since my daughter was born, my son, Matthew, has not been himself. He talks all day about speaking with insects and animals, or else some soul which no one but him appears to see. I have attempted without success to engage him in the usual pursuits I would recommend for a boy of seven years, and I am nearly at my wits' end. I have wondered whether school will be the making of him or the breaking, but I am afraid to risk the latter." DeCourcy paused to take a breath and, when he spoke again, he looked down at his hands instead of making eye contact with me. "In truth, Lockman, there is madness in my wife's family, and I fear Matthew may have inherited some tendency towards the same. Will you speak with him and establish an opinion? As a medical man?"

He looked up and stared at me with such desperate pleading that I could not refuse his request even if it had been my intention to do so. I agreed to speak with his son and attempt to form an understanding of the boy's claims, reassuring DeCourcy it was quite usual for children to claim to have befriended animals or people who were nothing more than an imaginative fancy. It seemed to calm my friend knowing I would address it with his son though, and our conversation gradually developed into a discussion about the many things which had happened since we had first set eyes on Hedgwick Manor fifteen years earlier.

To conduct the examination DeCourcy had requested of me, I invited Matthew to go hacking with me the following day, and we set out immediately after breakfast. The estate was somewhat larger than my own in size, although the house itself was smaller, and we kept within its boundaries. Matthew told me he disliked the local people and I had similar feelings towards them. The ride took us through woodland, heath, and then finally to the farmland at the edge of the estate. Here, I suggested we stopped a while to have a drink and something to eat. I had carried a flask of water and some cake myself, not wishing to betray DeCourcy's confidence by allowing any other soul to join us.

As we sat down and began to eat, Matthew looked out onto the open landscape of the fields and then turned to me with a smile. It was strange to think I had met his father when he had been only a couple of years older than the boy who looked at me now, and yet more of my false sense of youthfulness slipped away. I said nothing to my young companion as, no sooner had I opened my mouth to speak, than he placed a small finger over his lips.

"Look," he whispered, plucking a blade of grass from the earth and putting it carefully between his thumbs.

As he blew, the whistle sounded, and I caught a glimpse of movement in the field in front of us. He had seen the hare already, and now seemed to be using the whistle to lure it towards us. It ran in our direction and then stopped suddenly as it caught sight of us both, tilting its head as though questioning our existence. Then, with the air of someone taking umbrage for a reason known only to themselves, it turned on the spot and began to dart back into the field.

Matthew sighed. "Usually, she comes. It's the same sound her leveret makes, so she comes to make sure that everything's alright. She must not like you."

"Did you learn that from the gamekeeper?"

"I don't like the gamekeeper," Matthew replied. "He kills hares. He sets his dogs on them."

"So, who taught you about it?"

"The lady." Matthew put the grass whistle down and picked up a piece of fruitcake. "She taught me how to catch moths too, without damaging their little wings." He took a bite of the cake and chewed thoughtfully for a while, before going on. "I talk to them all, you know. Papa thinks I am mad, but the lady says it's not madness to speak to the earth's creatures."

"And do they speak back?"

Matthew laughed. "They are dumb animals, Mr Lockman. I speak to them, but I don't expect any response. The lady says they talk to her though."

"Who is the lady, Matthew?"

The boy stared at me again and then shrugged. "Just the lady," he said at last. "I call her the Lady Who Dances in the Ashes, but I don't know her real name."

"Ashes?"

His words sparked memories of my own boyhood growing up as the eldest son of an estate. It was easy to feel lonely or burdened by a responsibility which you had been born to rather than sought. My father had been furious when he discovered my friendship with the gardener's daughter. Innocent as it was, he had thought it unthinkable that a child of the House should form any connection with one of the servants. I supposed from Matthew's words that he had been speaking with the scullery maid and I decided to protect his secret while it was causing no real concern.

Matthew seemed to relax into my company after sharing his secret with me, and we rode back together in time for lunch at the Grange. Later that day, I assured his father that the boy was simply a child with a vivid imagination and a deep love of nature. Now, I am able to regret my words, and blame myself for everything that followed, but then I was just relieved to reassure him that his fears about his son were not justified: while sensitive, the boy lacked nothing in the way of sense. I made no mention of the scullery maid at the time and hoped DeCourcy would come to thank me for respecting his son's confidence.

Despite having invited me to examine the mental competency of his son and heir, my friend made it clear I was welcome to stay for as long as I wished. To that end, I wrote to my sister in Suffolk and advised her to return home, saying I was feeling more myself and would stay in the north until I was required to present our youngest sister at the Queen Charlotte's Ball in July. I then put all my efforts into an attempt to distract myself from the situation which had arisen since I had submitted my paper to the *British Medical Journal*. I achieved this solace by undertaking long, solitary rides beyond the estate, sometimes visiting Sir Randolph Devon, with whom I had lost touch since Harrow, and other times just riding until I was confident no soul would see me.

On one occasion, about a week after I had spoken with Matthew, I returned to Hedgwick Grange to find it in something of an uproar. It became apparent through a conversation I finally managed to secure with the butler that Master DeCourcy had disappeared for nearly the entire day. After his father had led a search of the estate to find him, Matthew had wandered alone back into the Grange and had been surprised to find he was in disgrace. I nodded my head as the man explained the situation and then, handing him my hat and coat, walked into the drawing room, where DeCourcy was in the process of reprimanding his son.

"Well, Lockman," he said, drawing me into the conversation before I could back out of the room and close the door behind me. "Perhaps you can speak some sense to the boy. Tell him how he has ruined his mother's nerves. And how half the county has been out looking for him today."

DeCourcy got to his feet and marched out of the room, leaving Matthew staring at me with a deeply unhappy look on his face. I was not a father at the time and had little intention of becoming one, so I felt no small discomfort at being put in the position where I had to adopt a role for which I was woefully inexperienced. However, I sat down at the seat recently vacated by the boy's father and asked him for the truth of what had happened.

"I swear to you, Mr Lockman," Matthew pleaded, "I didn't realise how time had passed. The Lady Who Dances in the Ashes, she took me into the woods for the morning. I must have fallen asleep, but I lost track of the time." He held out the fob watch in his small hand. "It's broken," he whispered. "But I didn't dare tell Papa so, for he bought me it as a gift."

Whilst I could assure him I would not tell his father about the watch being broken, I realised I could no longer keep his secret about the scullery maid. As my friend had mentioned, Lady DeCourcy had been deeply shaken by her son's disappearance and I instructed Matthew to go and reassure her while I spoke to his father. I found DeCourcy in his study, and his brow furrowed as I entered the room.

"He will not talk to me, Lockman," he said, before I could utter a syllable. "But I hope he has shared the details with you?"

I nodded slowly, cursing myself for betraying Matthew's secret. But it was in the boy's best interests for his father to know as, while the maid may have been well-intentioned, her actions proved she was rash and unthinking at best. I began to explain how Matthew had told me about the scullery maid taking him out onto the estate and teaching him about the natural world, and how they had become close enough for him to trust her when she guided him into the woods and let him fall asleep there. My friend's face grew scarlet as I spoke but, when he replied, his tone betrayed none of the anger I assumed he was feeling.

DeCourcy insisted I stay to witness his dismissal of the scullery maid, who was brought forcibly to her master's study and made to stand in front of us both. Memory plays tricks with the mind, and I don't know now whether I felt as sorry for her then as I remember, but she certainly cut a pitiful figure. I recall her dress was too tight and rather short, but her apron was spotless and too large for her, so I imagine she had quickly been provided with someone else's to make her presentable for her master. She wept as DeCourcy levelled the charges against her: accusing her of insolence and attempting to lead his son and heir astray. When he had finished, he invited her to speak with no intention of hearing the words she attempted to say. Once she tried to protest her innocence, he just shook his head and gestured for the waiting footman to remove her from the room. I listened to her cries as she was removed from the house and, finally, saw her being cast out of the back door. From the sanctuary of my room, I kept my eyes fixed on her as she stumbled down the path which led from the house into the village.

To ease my remorse, I attempted to remind myself that DeCourcy and his family were my social equals, and chastised the radical in me for believing friendships could exist across class boundaries. Still, I could not help but feel that my old schoolfriend had mishandled the situation. That evening, I excused myself after dinner and returned to my room, pondering whether to quit the house immediately and spend the night at The Drop and Cage before returning to Suffolk the next day.

Perhaps it was the memory of the village tavern which infected my dreams so my sleeping mind recalled the story of Ezra Hedgwick, who had burned witches alive for the pleasure of it. When I awoke in the middle of the night, I remembered what the local people had told us when we had first visited the Grange so many years earlier. I thought of their claim that every Hedgwick generation had lost their firstborn son and wondered whether it was the fear of losing Matthew which made DeCourcy so incensed at his son's behaviour.

When sleep returned, I dreamt not of Ezra Hedgwick, but of the witches he had burned. I stumbled, as Macbeth and Banquo on that blasted heath, through the moorland near Hedgwick Grange to find myself faced with a young woman who danced ahead of me, a cloud of dust swirling in her wake. As a storm gathered in my sleeping mind, she cavorted and screeched as though possessed, before finally scuttling up to me and looking me in the eye.

"Children should be seen but not heard," she sang. "For he who hears them shall hear me."

Upon forcing myself awake, I could scarcely remember her appearance, but something about the manner of the gaze and her manipulation of the words from the Gospel would not leave me. I went downstairs early and requested breakfast, intending to leave the house before my host and his family were even awake. I did not contemplate the ill manners of my decision, but only wished to get as far from Hedgwick Grange as possible. However, the fates had an alternative direction for me, and I was distracted from my breakfast by DeCourcy hurrying into the room.

"Please, Lockman," he said, rushing up and taking my arm as I got to my feet. "Please. Lady Louisa – my wife – I fear…"

He had no need to say anything further. I could see the panic on his face and could not leave another human being, let alone a friend, to suffer whatever was so terrifying. I established that Lady DeCourcy, with her genetic predisposition to mental fragility, had attempted to pacify her nerves with the inadvisable consumption of laudanum. Her maidservant had alerted DeCourcy after she had been unable to rouse her mistress from sleep.

Lady DeCourcy was dangerously fragile for a time, but I worked alongside the local physician, a man called Jensen, to first treat her and then to fortify her mental and physical health. My intentions to leave Hedgwick Grange had to be put aside, as I was bound by the Hippocratic Oath to do all within my power to preserve life. But, while I served Lady DeCourcy faithfully and attempted to keep an eye always on Matthew as well, I found my own mind began to creak under the pressure, not only of caring for my hostess but from the dreams which haunted me each night.

A week after I had first meant to leave Hedgwick, I voiced my renewed intention to DeCourcy, who only nodded. If my visit to Hedgwick Grange had proved anything to myself, it was that its master and I no longer had enough in common to sustain a friendship. In my dedication to his wife and son, I had not stopped to question his deception in drawing me back to Yorkshire. However, once it occurred to me that evening, I could not shake free from the sense of having been used for his own purpose.

That night, I once again found myself on the Shakespearean heath by Hedgwick, watching the woman who danced and leapt in front of me, and unable to persuade my feet from following. She swung from laughing to screaming, and I wondered if my imaginings of her final moments were about to play out before me. I hardly dared to look for fear of what I might see, but my vision was as fixed on the woman as my feet were in following her footsteps. Eventually, she turned around and hurried up to me, and I prepared myself to come face-to-face with her again.

"Earth to earth," she chanted, and I recognised the words I had last heard at my father's funeral. "Ashes to ashes. Dust to dust." The witch uncurled her clenched fist to reveal a handful of ash, which she threw up into the air. In the confusion which followed, she disappeared into the cloud and transformed into a moth. The creature, which had only moments earlier been a woman, fluttered into my face, causing me to splutter in panic as I attempted to wave it away.

I awoke to find a real moth had landed on my cheek and, although it was harmless, my heart pounded as I enclosed it in my hand and felt the furious beating of its fragile wings. The memory of how the woman had effortlessly turned into the insect chilled me so, for a moment, I considered crushing it beneath my grip. But Matthew's words about speaking to creatures came back to me, and I decided to grant it freedom by releasing it through the window. The moth beat its wings more furiously as I pulled up the sash and, at first, seemed reluctant to leave my hand. I shook it away and watched as it fluttered down into the courtyard below, catching the moonlight on its translucent wings. My still sleepy imagination pondered where it would go now I had put it out of my room, but my attention was diverted as a much larger animal darted out from near the house.

As it was running, its lanky gait almost equine in the faded light, the hare looked back at the house for a second. I felt its gaze strike me and I backed away from the window under its disapproving stare to return to my bed, sitting for a while in the darkness and trying to ignore the palpitations which almost prevented me from falling asleep. Perhaps because the final character in my mind was Ezra Hedgwick, my sleep was plagued by a recurring image of him burning the witch from my earlier dream, her screams sounding like a bloodcurdling mockery of the grass whistle Matthew had used to lure the hare.

The following morning, I took my breakfast and prepared to leave, but was surprised when one of the footmen offered me a telegram which had just arrived. Its contents had been diverted by my sister, who it appears was still in Suffolk, so I was receiving it a day later than intended. It contained an invitation from a Doctor Bartholomew Hill, who was the Principal Physician at a new hospital for the insane, in Wakefield. He professed to have been deeply impressed by the paper I had written and wished me to begin a new post immediately.

I could hardly believe my good fortune, not only in securing a position when the medical world believed I was mad myself, but in having an opportunity and excuse to leave Hedgwick without causing any offence. I shared the news with my host, who politely congratulated me, and then made my final preparations to leave.

In apparent gratitude for what I had done during my time at Hedgwick Grange, the entire family congregated to bid me farewell. I went first to Lady DeCourcy to thank her for her hospitality, and to remind her there were more effective ways to calm her nerves than to medicate herself with laudanum. I then thanked DeCourcy for inviting me, choosing not to reference the fact he had his own intentions for having done so, then turned to the boys. Each of them shook my hand, before Matthew looked up at me, with a stare which seemed darkly reminiscent of how the hare had glared at me last night.

"The Lady Who Dances in the Ashes isn't pleased with you," he said, his voice low so his parents would not hear. "She is cross with you for putting her out of the house."

I thought of the scullery maid stumbling down the path from the house and into the village, and could only smile down at Matthew. I did feel remorse for the fact she had been dismissed, but she had overstepped her boundaries in a way which had nearly brought tragedy into the house. Although her intentions may have been good, I was now convinced I had done right by the boy.

"I'm sure she will find another place," I said quietly, although in truth I knew my words were a lie.

It was a relief to be travelling away from Hedgwick Grange, and I felt the pressure which had enveloped me there beginning to ease with each jolt of the carriage. By the time we had reached the nearest railway station, I felt nearly myself again, and could not help the boyish sense of excitement which bubbled up within me at the prospect of my new position. Not only a new role, in a new place, but one which had been created for me on the merits of the paper everyone else had discredited.

The train was busy and, with only one space remaining in First Class, I found myself sharing a compartment with a group of young gentlemen who had been at a hunt. They shared their stories with boundless excitement and, whilst at other times I may have found their enthusiasm jarring, I could not help but feel it was emblematic of the adventure I was embarking upon myself. However, I did not want to intrude on their conversation, so did everything I could to distract myself, including gazing at the landscape as it hurtled past us.

To this day, I do not know whether I was dreaming or lucid but, as I stared out of the window with little intention of seeing anything, I caught sight of something which seemed to make no sense. Galloping beside the train, and almost matching it for speed, was a brown hare. I felt myself jolt as I noticed that clenched between its teeth was the prone body of a small bird. Despite my initial horror at the sight, I had hardly a moment to consider it, as the conductor marched through the train announcing that we would soon be arriving in Wakefield. I told myself I had imagined or misinterpreted the strange sight and, as I disembarked the train and walked along the thronging platform, it slipped away from my mind.

I took a carriage immediately to the hospital and met with Doctor Hill. He was as excited to meet me and discuss my radical theories on the treatment of the insane as I was to meet him and thank him for providing the opportunity to prove myself. We sat in his office and discussed our plans for the asylum and for the treatment of the sick within the community, until he was called away some two hours later to oversee the arrival of a new patient. As he was about to leave, he handed me an envelope and apologised.

"I had meant to pass it on to you straight away, Doctor Lockman," he said, and I felt a thrill of proud excitement to hear myself being addressed in that way again. "But I was too excited to discuss everything with you. It slipped my mind."

I assured him there was no harm done, and he invited me to stay in his office for as long as I needed, so I remained on my seat as I opened the envelope to read the telegram.

PLEASE RETURN TO HEDGWICK ON RECEIPT. MATTHEW MISS-ING. I WOULD NOT ASK YOU TO RETURN UNLESS IMPERATIVE. DECOURCY.

I took a deep breath and shook my head, feeling a strange sensation of hysteria course through my body at the memory of how relieved I had been to have escaped from Hedgwick Grange, only now to be summoned back immediately. And surely, I told myself as I attempted to decide whether to return or stay, Matthew could not have been missing for too long. I had seen him safe and well that morning.

However, the sense of duty I felt towards the boy and his father led me to approach Doctor Hill and request I be spared for a few days while I returned to Hedgwick on pressing personal business. He acquiesced and even loaned me the use of his carriage, as the last train north had already departed. It took me the best part of the night to reach Hedgwick and, when I did, I once again felt the despairing claustrophobia of the house and estate bearing down on me as I approached.

Matthew had not yet been found and, although I was utterly exhausted from a full day's travelling, I joined DeCourcy in his search. As before, he had enlisted every servant in the house and almost every local man for twenty miles. It was dawn when someone raised the alarm and we hurried across the heath in the grey light to see what had been found.

The boy's little body was lying on the ground, seeming a good deal smaller than he had been in life, and encircled by a thick ribbon of ashes. Matthew's hand was clenched, but the rest of his body looked utterly calm, almost angelic. I crouched down beside him and carefully opened his fist. A handful of ashes scattered across him, leaving only the crushed body of a moth in his hand. I jumped back, suddenly unnerved.

His father stood as silent as the son, and I was about to direct one of the men to cover the child's corpse when I noticed something in the ashes which surrounded it. There were prints preserved in the dust. Some were from a human being who, from the lack of any heel prints, had cavorted and twirled on their bare toes. But intermingled with those were other prints: a hare had bounded and danced along with its human companion, and sometimes one seemed to naturally dissipate into the other, as though they were one and the same.

The local people, many of whom had gathered to observe the child's dead body, were quick to reference the curse which had claimed the eldest sons of Hedgwick Grange since Ezra had built it two hundred years ago. They did not seem to notice the strangeness in the circumstances of Matthew's death, but just assumed it was acceptable that the heir to the estate had met an untimely end, taking a macabre satisfaction that their local curse had stretched beyond the Hedgwick name.

Matthew's father, by contrast, immediately placed the blame on the scullery maid. He would not listen to the reason which stated she could not have possibly been on the heath that night when she had been seen in the village by plenty of others, all of whom offered themselves as witnesses in her defence. After the coroner reported that Matthew had died from asphyxiation, DeCourcy pursued the prosecution of his former maid, and demanded punishment to the full extent of the law.

As much as I wished to see some justice served for the death of such a sweet boy, I could not endorse DeCourcy's crusade to see the scullery maid hang. Throughout and beyond her trial, the girl protested her innocence, and I attempted to reason with the magistrate to make him realise she had been blameless. However, the witnesses were not called and my own responsibilities to my patients precluded me from making a claim as wild as my belief that Matthew had been charmed, entranced, and murdered by the shape-shifting spectre of a woman who had been executed on the heath hundreds of years earlier. I had to accept it was I who had misunderstood Matthew's words about the Lady Who Dances in the Ashes, assuming it was something as everyday as a scullery maid.

DeCourcy broke all ties with me after I sent a plea to the judge to grant the scullery maid a stay of execution. I could see how deeply he needed to find someone who would answer for the crime, but it broke my heart to know a young girl had gone to the gallows, still desperately professing her innocence. It led me to marry my expertise in the fragility of the human mind with a developing fascination for folklore, and I wondered whether the malevolent spirit which had killed Matthew had been a witch when she was burned alive, or whether it was the brutal sadism of Ezra Hedgwick which had turned her into one.

'Earth to earth. Ashes to ashes. Dust to dust,' she had said in my dream. Perhaps, too, 'hate to hate' had an equal truth to it.

At Wakefield Hospital for the Insane, I realised my vocation. I worked for many successful years under Doctor Hill, finally marrying his daughter, Harriet. We named our first son 'Matthew' in remembrance of the boy whose death continued to haunt me. When Hill finally retired, I was appointed as the Principal Physician at the hospital, where I worked until my own retirement forced my return to the fresh country air of Suffolk.

Murderers… rapists… victims… All the things I saw and the stories I heard, each one of them personal to someone, I faced with a calm demeanour and a reassuring approach. Yet the one thing I can never bear to see, without panic, is ash. For the duration of my life since those dark days at Hedgwick, I have employed someone whose sole responsibility is to ensure my family and I never have to look upon the dust of a dead fire. For, in each particle, there is the possibility of finding the footprint of a vengeful woman, denied a name and a grave, and burned alive by Ezra Hedgwick.

I must not fail to protect those around me. I must never allow her to dance from the ashes and realise her insatiable revenge.

The Winsome Boy — Shelagh Smith

Shelagh's previous publishing credits include New England's Best Crime Stories 2017 and 2018, Tempest Literary Journal, and Embracing Writing. In addition, she is also the recipient of the PEN New England Susan P. Bloom Discovery Award. She teaches writing for Massachusetts Maritime Academy and Bridgewater State University, and lives in a creepy little New England village.

* * *

The locals called it Crazy Sister Island, but that wasn't its real name. It was officially named Winsome Island, after the family who'd set down stakes a century ago, after it had been stolen from the Muskogee. Its real name was lost to history, but the people who lived on the coast just called it Crazy Sister Island.

As the boat sliced through the water, Elliott looked at his dog-eared notebook, a relic he couldn't bear to part with. His colleagues had switched to apps to track notes, but he was old-school, learning journalism from an old professor who'd put his faith in handwritten notes over technology, and Elliott knew that he was the kind of writer Elliott wanted to be. Part of that was keeping it old school.

He steadied himself as the launch bucked through waves to smoother water. The ocean had never been his thing, much to the delight of his ex who got the Miami Beach condo in the divorce. Good riddance, thought Elliott on the day the papers were signed, to both condo and ex. He skimmed his notes.

"Is that a four?" he mumbled, and Roger, the launch captain, looked over a tanned shoulder.

"Huh?"

In the distance, Winsome Island grew larger.

"How long?"

Roger grinned, his teeth the color of his sweat rings. "Ten minutes. You're nuts to go," he said, and hawked something sticky over the side. Elliott braced for another round of questions – or cautions.

"So I've heard."

"No good comes off that island."

"Heard that too."

It was true, Elliott mused. No good had come off the island, especially no good records. He'd started the assignment with hopes of tracking down hidden gems along coastal waterways, a puff piece about the abundance of natural beauty. Quickly it turned into a serious piece about the abundance of the ultra-rich. Private islands were big business. He'd started with realtors who showed off their million-dollar wares, and then moved into stories of islands stolen by white men, then the one percent. It had been shaping up into a nice series when he came across Winsome Island.

"You're nuts to go," echoed Stan, a local who occupied his own spot at the Grub Hub's bar. Elliott settled beside him one night, hoping to add color to his piece.

"Why?" asked Elliott, feigning ignorance. He knew the island belonged to Petra and Castor Winsome. He also knew the island had its skeletons, including a series of questionable probate and tax assessments. And then there was the story of the missing tourists who'd set out for the island, but hadn't come back. Vagaries of time and tide, Elliott figured. Just one more reason to hate the ocean. "What do you know about Mr. and Mrs. Winsome?"

"Mr. and Mrs.?" laughed Stanley, pulling from his beer. Droplets of condensation pooled on the teakwood bar.

"Should be, eh?" joked another local, sliding into the empty spot opposite Elliott, drawn by conversation or Elliott's bankroll. Elliott signaled another round, pretending not to notice the looks exchanged between his new friends.

"What's that mean?" asked Elliott, feeling unease in the pit of his stomach. He'd felt it before, usually when he was on the cusp of a good story – no, a great story.

"Brother and sister," said the friend.

Elliott paused, thinking of a way to frame a follow up, but didn't need to. They were suddenly eager to talk, like someone who'd held a secret too long.

"Family's not right," said Stan, and his partner nodded. "They stick to themselves."

"No one comes or goes from that island. Except the preacher."

"Preacher?"

"When the old man died, they called the preacher. Buried him there next to his old lady."

"And that was the last time anyone saw them? Why?"

Stan shook his head, but not in denial; more like resignation. "They ain't right in the head."

"Castor left for a while, didn't he?" mused the other, scratching his hairline with a stubby pencil pulled from behind his ear. Elliott looked at the gray streak left behind, thought about mentioning it, but didn't.

"Where'd he go?" asked Elliott.

"College maybe? Long time ago. When he left, his sister went nuts. Walked the beaches, screaming and hollering. Tried to drown herself, they say."

"*They* say," snorted Stan. "Who's *they*? I never saw it."

"Doesn't mean it didn't happen," said his friend, looking hurt. "Ain't called Crazy Sister for nothing."

"What happened?" asked Elliott.

Stan answered. "All we know is they ain't left since. Must be nice to have that kind of money."

Elliott saw resentment there, and asked, "Where's their money come from?" He thought back to outstanding tax bills but no motions to seize the land.

"Who knows?" said Stan. "They pay, that's all I know. Roger Jardiniere drops off food every couple weeks. Ask him."

"Why you want to know?" asked his friend, and Elliott saw their resentment turn toward him, quick as a squall on the water.

"I'm writing a story about the island," said Elliott.

"Leave them alone," said Stan, but there was no malice there, more like worry, thought Elliott. Maybe fear. "Last guy who went never came back."

Elliott looked at him for a long time, trying to judge if he was serious, but he gave no indication he was joking. Finally, he said, "You're pulling my leg, right?"

Stan leaned close, pulled down the skin under one eye with a gnarled finger. "Maybe. But do yourself a favor, friend," he whispered, and Elliott recoiled at the smell of bad breath and stale beer. "Stay away from that island."

* * *

But of course, Elliott couldn't. The island history had been interesting, tax records intriguing, and the warnings damn near irresistible. He'd tracked down Roger Jardiniere the next day, pressed a fifty into his palm, and persuaded him to bring him along on his next supply run. As the boat glided over water that turned from turquoise to steel, Elliott asked, "When was the last time they came off the island?"

Roger squinted at the sun. "Probably not since their folks died. Long time."

"Isn't that peculiar?"

"Yep," said Roger, and nothing more.

Elliott remained quiet, watching the water change color, from gray to green to aqua, until Roger pulled up to a dock so rickety Elliott feared it might buckle under the weight of the throw rope. It swayed underfoot as he clambered out. To his surprise, Roger didn't join him. He simply leaned over and snatched a plastic bag tied with a red ribbon to a post.

"Tell Miss Petra I'll be back." The sputtering of the outboard motor drowned out Elliott's protest, and then he was gone.

Elliott watched the boat disappear. He hadn't anticipated this. He'd expected an introduction at the very least. But now Roger was gone, and Elliott was alone.

On Crazy Sister Island.

Elliott scanned the empty beach, half expecting the specter from Stan's story to come bursting from the palms.

"Well," he sighed. "Fuck it."

Elliott followed a path into mangroves draped with Spanish moss, unmoving in the still air. He wiped his brow. The air should have moved, he thought, but it was still as a churchyard, the only noise the humming of insects. The blistering sun sliced through the canopy, dappling the path in front of him, and when it opened abruptly, he stopped short at the edge of a slatestone walkway leading to what once must have been a grand home. Now, sadly, it looked like a nightmare woven from splintering wood and decayed dreams. His thoughts fled. He had no idea what he would say to these people. Would they be willing to open their door to him?

Would they even be alive in there?

The thought turned his stomach.

No, of course they would, thought Elliott. There had been a note on the dock.

"Calm down," he whispered. "This isn't new to you."

And yet it felt entirely new, like stepping into the pages of a grim fairy tale.

Elliott fiddled with his notebook, checked his phone, but found nothing but an empty triangle where a signal should have been. He pocketed it, screwed up his nerve, and walked to the house.

The front porch was no steadier than the dock, and he felt for the family forgotten here. Family fortunes didn't go as far as they used to.

As Elliott moved to knock, the door swung open, and he squawked in surprise. He clamped his mouth shut and mustered a smile he hoped was ingratiating. He suspected it wasn't by the way Petra – it had to be Petra – looked at him.

She was a tiny thing, frail, and the narrowness of her shoulders under her black blouse sliced upward, making her look as though she had wings folded behind her. Her hands were knotted with arthritis, blue veins coursing under her skin like tributaries. Her hair had gone gray and hung in wild curls around her face, and suddenly Elliott could very easily picture her running along the beach, howling for her lost brother. But what captured Elliott most were her eyes, one clear blue, the other dark brown, but both sharp, clear, and full of suspicion.

"Get off my island," she hissed. "Fuck you and your taxes!"

Elliott lifted his hands in a placating gesture. "I'm not a tax assessor, ma'am," he said. "My name is Elliott – "

"Get off my island."

"I'm sorry, Miss Winsome. I just wanted to ask a few questions for a story I'm doing."

Her sharp eyes narrowed, head tilted. "Story?"

"Yes, ma'am. I write travel – "

"I don't travel."

"I wanted to write about your island."

"So tourists can come?"

"No, not at all." Elliott struggled to find something to sway her. Finally, he settled on, "To show people why you love it so much." The lie felt oily on his tongue.

"I don't believe you," she muttered, and Elliott thought she was wise not to.

"If you want me to leave, I will," he said. "But Roger thought it would be okay."

He watched her ponder this and felt sick. He'd lied to get stories before, but this was different. This felt wrong. The whole island felt wrong.

"Maybe I can talk to your brother? Castor?"

There was a flash in her eyes. Fear? Panic? He wondered if she was afraid Castor would leave her again. The flatness of her answer surprised him. "No."

Before he could form another question, someone – or something – inside answered. The hairs on the back of his neck lifted.

"Mawww…mawww…mawww…"

It was a man's voice, muffled, slurred. The voice, the underlying notes of despair without form, shook him. He tried to peer over her head, but she angled the door to block his view. The sound inside stopped, replaced by the creak of a floorboard and shriek of wheels begging to be oiled.

"Get off my island, Mr. Writer," she said, her voice full of steel. "You want to find trouble, you just keep poking around. Ask the last one who came."

She slammed the door shut. The cracked window glass, held together with yellowed scotch tape, made a tinkling sound that crawled up Elliott's spine. He backed slowly off the porch and stood staring at the house for a time, not moving until he heard – or thought he heard – the *shuck SHUCK* of a shotgun being loaded.

He hurried away.

Ask the last one who came.

Her words lingered. Elliott thought back to the locals' warnings. What had the tax man seen that sent him away without payment? What had scared them off?

"You're being stupid," Elliott whispered. "She's an old lady. Calm the fuck down."

Guilt gnawed at him as he walked. Clearly, she was disturbed, probably had been for most of her life with only her brother as caretaker. Could he really expose them? An article would bring people, lookey-loos, and worse: developers. They'd buy out the debt and watch happily as the Winsome's were forced off the only home they'd ever known.

But it was his job, he reminded himself. And maybe they needed help. She certainly looked unwell, and the sounds he'd heard from inside the house would haunt his nightmares.

Mawww...mawww...mawww...

How bad off was Castor? Maybe it would be a blessing to get him away from her.

Okay, thought Elliott. He would go back, talk with authorities, and then make a decision on his piece. There was no shortage of islands; he could easily pick another.

At peace with his decision, he walked toward the beach, but a path carved out of the brush caught his eye. At first, he thought it was a game path, but remnants of slate stones peeked through the grass threatening to swallow them. Every nerve in Elliott's body hummed, and he thought back to his old prof, to the journalist he wanted to be. He thought back to that feeling in his gut. Maybe the story he'd intended to write wasn't here, but *something* was. With one last look behind him, Elliott chose the path less traveled.

The brush was thick. By the time Elliott reached the end, his skin was crisscrossed with scratches that stung as sweat found them. He paused, catching his breath, and was so intent on his own misery that he very nearly missed the salt-washed stones set in a ring around two stone crosses smothered in vines.

Elliott felt unsettled anew. Their parents. Of course, he thought. He knelt, pushing aside vines and rubbing away dust and moss with his thumb. Inscribed on the crosses were the names he'd expected: Callum and Anna Winsome.

Elliott stood to snap a photo but cried out and dropped his phone when his ankle turned in a furrow. Scrambling to steady himself, his hand fell on a splintered branch that pierced his skin. Cursing the dueling pains in his ankle and palm, he realized quite suddenly what had hurt him. It wasn't a branch at all. It was driftwood, two pieces cobbled into a crude cross, and carved with the unsteady hand of a child:

C A S T O R W I N S O M E

DADDA

1 9 5 0 – 1989

Elliott stared at the cross for perhaps too long, trying to make sense of it. The house, Petra, the noises from inside.

Mawww...mawww...mawww...

Castor? But not Castor. Castor was here. If it wasn't Castor, then…?

The locals' words came back to him, their exchanged glances, their unspoken secret.

Dadda.

"What the fuck?" whispered Elliott.

And as he considered what he was seeing, he noticed another furrowed trench.

And another.

And another.

Unmarked, but unmistakable.

A cold splash of fear spurred Elliott, and he ran on his aching ankle out of the brush. The path he took wasn't the same, but it led him out, away from the graveyard, to the beach on the other side of the side of the narrow island. The open air slowed his panicked breathing and racing heartbeat. He took a moment to get his bearings and then started walking toward the old dock, turning over what he had seen, what he had found. There was someone – something – in the house. Something *not* Castor.

Elliott shuddered when he recalled Stan's words about the last man who'd come to the island. No one had seen him since. Oh god, thought Elliott, and then he stopped short when the hull of a beached rowboat rose up before him, the once-brown vessel silvered from years of sun and surf. Its only color was a swatch of darkness eaten into the side, like the errant stroke of a paint brush. He ran his fingers over it and drew them back with a shudder. He didn't know what it was, but in his soul, he knew it wasn't good.

He stepped over a disintegrating tether line, and anxiously lifted a tarp, grayed from the elements, that crumbled as he pulled it aside, revealing an old suitcase. Leather-bound. thick brass hinges, a brass nameplate.

CAW.

Castor Aloysius Winsome.

"Well, goddamn," he whispered.

Elliott hoisted the suitcase. How long had it lain hidden? Why was it hidden? What had he been trying to escape?

Elliott opened it, his imagination filled with bats flying forth, or spiders piling out, maybe crabs, but it opened silently, and Elliott stared at the contents of man's life, pared down to a few things.

Shaving kit. Wallet. Clothing. And a fistful of bills, bound with a rubber band that crumbled in Elliott's fingers. He examined the first bill in the roll. Date: 1985.

A "go-bag" from years gone by, his escape from Crazy Sister Island. What had stopped him? But it was the other things stuffed like hidden afterthoughts into the suitcase that made his skin crawl. Remnant of something pink – canvas – and the black, shiny bits of something broken. Glass, plastic, metal. Elliott lifted a shard carefully. *Nikon.*

Elliott swallowed a rising sense of dread. The missing boaters' things? Why in this boat? He let the broken pieces fall when he thought back to the furrows in the graveyard. Of course.

He felt sick. He felt scared.

But he never felt the blow on the back of his head that blacked out the sun.

Elliott woke in a sunroom, light filtering through panes spider-webbed with tape. He wondered for a half-second how long he'd been out.

He rolled to one side. Pain knifed through his skull. He touched the tender spot on the back of his head and his fingers brushed something hard, crusty. He turned his thoughts back to where he'd last been. The beach. The boat.

The suitcase.

Cold sweat sprang up on his skin, turning him clammy despite the oppressive heat in the room. He rolled to his knees, taking a moment to lean against the glass wall. It cracked under his weight. He took a slow breath, waited for the room to stop spinning, and stood. As he rose to his full height, he saw her in the doorway, her mismatched eyes aflame with fury. He recoiled, preparing for a blow that didn't come.

"I told you to get off my island."

"I was going," said Elliott.

"You want to tell my secrets, just like him."

Like him. Like the tax collector who'd never left? Like Castor? Elliott pressed his palms against his eyes and fireworks shot across the darkness. He thought he might puke.

"I'll go," he said, and tried a step, but she gave no ground. "Miss Winsome, please. I'll go. I won't tell anyone."

"That's what he said," she hissed, and he realized then she wouldn't give in, not to him, not to anyone. "He's dead now."

Elliott's guts twisted, and he made a hard decision. It was her or him, and it wasn't going to be him.

He reached to move her, and her reaction stunned him. Her hands came up in claws, nails reaching for his face, for his eyes. Elliott reeled backwards, nearly tripped over his own feet. She landed on him, and though she was tiny, she was enough to knock him over. Glass shattered around him, slicing into his skin, littering her hair like crystal snowflakes. Her nails tore into his cheeks, climbed toward his eyes, and a wild, keening erupted from her throat.

"You ruined it!" she wailed, and spittle dripped from her gaping mouth onto his face.

"You…crazy…bitch," muttered Elliott when her nail caught the lower lid of his eye. The pain shot through him like a lightning bolt and he lost all reserve and he threw her off with a strength he didn't know he possessed. He lurched to his feet, but she was on him again, screeching and howling, and Elliott felt a sudden jolt of terror when he realized her yowls were not wordless sounds, but rather a word.

A name.

"Juuuuulllliussss…Juuuuulllliussss…. Juuuuulllliussss…"

Elliott struck out, his elbow connecting with Petra's jaw. He heard her teeth clack together, felt her weight fall off him, but her wailing didn't stop.

And then Elliott heard it. The squeak of wheels.

"Mawww…mawww…mawww…?"

He whirled around and saw it. Saw *him.*

He sat in a wheelchair probably older than Elliott. His size dwarfed the rusty contraption, spilling over the wrecked vinyl seat, but it wasn't fat. It was muscle. One hand hung at his side, trailing a wooden 2X4 stained dark with fresh blood – Elliott's blood. His tanned skin shone like he'd been oiled, but it wasn't his size that stole Elliott's breath. It was his face.

Misshapen. Swollen. Features that once might have been handsome were covered in growths, tumors perhaps? Black hair hung in curls around his face, doing a poor job of covering it. Rows of teeth crowded his mouth. But it was his eyes that froze Elliott. One blue. One brown.

Just like his mother. Just like his mawww…

"Oh fuck," whispered Elliott, praying for a second that this man – this thing – was confined to the wheelchair, but that hope died when he rose to his full height, nearly a foot taller than Elliott, and took a lurching, unsteady step toward him.

"Kill him, Julius," whispered Petra.

"No," said Elliott, but his voice was cut off by the wail tearing from Julius' throat, a sound so full of rage that Elliott pissed himself.

Elliott spun and ran toward the shattered glass windows.

Julius caught him with one swing, and Elliott went down hard when wood connected in an explosion of pain. He rolled away as it crashed down beside his head. He scrambled backwards, toward escape, but Petra grabbed his ankles. Elliott kicked out, and the crackling wet sound of her skull caving in filled the space between them. Elliott watched her son's eyes travel from him to her still form and then back again.

"No, no, no," Julius said, his voice rising in pitch, muffled by overgrown teeth, until Elliott had to cover his ears, and then Julius did something that filled Elliott's mouth with bile.

The Winsome boy brought the 2X4 upward, toward his own face.

It landed with a thud, but the blow didn't stagger him. Blood ran in rivers down the boy's face, between the tumors – no, not tumors, thought Elliott…scars – and dripped onto the broken glass carpet between them. He did it again. And again. And Elliott knew it was now or never.

He scrambled over Petra's body, pushing through the hole in the broken windows, and landed on the ground beneath. Elliott ran wildly, the *thunk* of wood and the calls for "Mawww…mawww…mawww…" echoing behind him.

As he reached the path toward Castor's failed escape, he heard Julius give chase. Elliott tumbled through the vines, to the beach, through the sand. His shoulder protested, salt from sweat and tears made the wounds on his face sing, but he had no time to waste. Behind him came Julius, swinging his weapon like a baseball bat.

Elliott ran through ankle-deep surf, reaching the hull of the boat as his legs gave out. He knelt, forehead pressed against the slash of color left years before. With a monumental effort, he hauled himself up and threw himself against the boat as the boy lurched ever closer. He spared a second to glance behind him and saw Julius struggling in the sand, using his 2X4 to steady himself.

"Oh god please," moaned Elliott, pushing with his last ounce of strength. It gave way with the gentle hiss of wood against sand, gliding effortlessly into the rising tide. Elliott followed, finding the strength to pull himself aboard. His hands found the oars, baked hard under years of sun and sky. Elliott pulled against them, and pulled again, and again. The boat drifted away from Crazy Sister Island.

His breath coming in labored gasps, Elliott saw Julius plow into the water after him. Elliott rowed faster, harder, but survival finally won out, for both of them. Julius turned back to shore, howling and hitting and dancing his unsteady jig.

The Collectors—Jen Mierisch

*J*en Mierisch's dream job is to write Twilight Zone episodes, but until then, she'sa website administrator by day, and a writer of odd stories by night. Jen's work can be found in the NoSleep Podcast, Horror Tree, Sanitarium, and numerous anthologies. Jen can be found haunting her local library near Chicago, USA. Read more at www.jenmierisch.com and connect on Twitter @JenMierisch.*

* * *

The lights hovered above Hawker's Pond. Above, the red sunset stretched in blood-smear streaks across the sky.

Glowing white-gold, the lights glided through the air like a school of fish, separating and returning in graceful pulses. Together they skimmed the pond's surface, leaving a streak of empty water where algae used to float.

A pair of dragonflies zipped inches above the water, veering at the sudden splash of a turtle diving off a log. Their course correction sent them straight into the group of lights, which flickered brightly. The insects did not re-emerge.

Almeta Guthridge stepped out of her cabin in her bathrobe, squinting at the lights. She'd lived next to Hawker's Pond for nigh on seventy years, and she reckoned she'd never seen fireflies cluster that way before.

She kicked off her house slippers, slid calloused feet into worn-out sneakers, and edged down the slope, still muddy from yesterday's storms. What in the world could make fireflies move so fast? It was as if they'd gotten into a cup of coffee somebody forgot on a porch.

The fireflies, if that was what they were, swung toward a plume of water left by a leaping trout. A few seconds later, the lights swerved toward another jumper, nearly touching the fish's tail.

A small muskie broke the water, soaring high. The lights zipped to the spot. Their uniform gold shifted into reds, greens, and blues, like fireworks exploding. Almeta frowned, half listening for the splash of the muskie landing back in the lake.

The splash never came.

The lights' color shifted back to gold. Gathering themselves, they rose and moved through the humid air toward the lake's edge, crossing the shore, heading toward Almeta.

Her heart thumped against her chest. Though her instinct was to back away, she stood captivated, as if her sneakers had sprouted roots. They may be strange, but they're God's creatures, she told herself, trembling. Maybe angels. As they neared, her face glowed gold, and she felt heat emanating from their tiny forms.

Subtly, the colors changed, yellow to red and orange, white to green and blue. The warmth prickled Almeta's skin, raising the hairs on her arms, pulling them toward the glow. A buzzing filled the air, like electrical wires after rain. And the lights were whispering, but the sound wasn't coming in through her ears. It seemed to beam straight into her head, as if the words had originated in her own mind.

She wrenched away and ran for her cabin, a yell escaping her throat. The lights scintillated in the shadows as she slammed and bolted the door.

* * *

Half a mile north of Hawker's Pond, a small house sat on scrubby land that backed up to the woods. Its open windows let in the evening breeze, which had finally cooled off, and let out the sounds of people celebrating the White Sox' victory over the Yankees.

Darius Coover paused in the kitchen doorway, Coke in hand, and smiled to himself. His small living room was filled with family, neighbors, and friends. Eddie, his six-year-old son, lay stretched out on the carpet, showing off his Pokémon cards to Jerry, his neighbor Rosaline's grandson. A knot of Darius's co-workers from the warehouse sat on the secondhand couches, polishing off the nachos while debating the Sox's chances of making the playoffs. Rosaline's granddaughter, Josie, laughed as she played tug-of-war with Darius's dog. Rosaline, seated on the recliner, turned her phone sideways to take their picture.

Seeing all that gave Darius a good feeling inside, like getting out of the city had been the right move, like a fresh start could be possible after all.

"Eddie," said Darius, "no more Skittles. That's your third bag. Your mama will kill me." Eddie gave his dad a sour look but twisted the top of the red bag and handed it over.

"All right, y'all," said Roy Rainville, setting down his fourth bottle of Corona and getting up from the couch, "get ready to move your butts. I'll DJ this party." He tapped on his phone and set it into Darius's audio dock. The speakers blasted "This Is How We Do It," to which Roy began a series of tipsy hip-hop moves.

Rosaline watched him and shook her head, smirking. Roy extended a hand to her and said, with exaggerated politeness, "Care to dance, madam?"

"No thank you," she said. "I have this thing called dignity that I'd like to hang onto."

"What is that music?" asked Eddie, looking up from his cards and frowning. "The Jackson Five or something?"

"The Jackson Five?" Roy bellowed. "Darius, you are neglecting this child's musical education."

Darius smiled. "You know he just turned six, right? That song's old."

"It ain't old! It's from 1995, bro."

"Man, I was born in '95," said Darius.

Roy gave him a look. "Are you serious? That's when I graduated."

"That's why you're old school."

"Old school!" giggled Eddie. "There's a school for old people?"

"Hey, now," said Roy, taking a playful swipe at the ballcap on Eddie's head. Eddie dodged, laughing.

Roy gave up on the dance party and heaved his bulk down onto the carpet next to Eddie. "What you got there?"

"Pokémon cards."

"Pokey who?" Roy held up a card and examined the yellow cartoon creature. "When I was your age, we collected baseball cards."

Eddie stared open-mouthed at Roy's ankle, where the pants had shifted upward.

"Check it out," said Roy, knocking on the artificial leg with his knuckles. "Try it if you want. Go ahead."

Eddie reached out hesitantly and tapped the leg with his fingernails. His eyes were huge. "What happened to your leg?"

"Iraq," said Roy. "It's all right, though. This leg's better."

"It is?"

"Yeah," said Roy, winking. "I never get foot odor."

Eddie grinned.

"Eddie," said Darius, knuckling the top of his son's head, "it's getting late. Go put Muddy in the yard." The boy jumped up and clapped for the dog, who obediently followed him toward the kitchen door.

Darius picked up empty beer cans and headed for the kitchen. Gathering paper plates, Rosaline followed him.

"I talked to Almeta Guthridge today," Rosaline said.

"That old bat who lives by Hawker's Pond?"

"That's her."

"She still trying to convince you to go to her church?"

"No," said Rosaline, smiling. "None of that. But Darius, I'm not sure she's got all her faculties anymore. She was telling me she saw lights down by the pond."

"Lights?"

"Sounded like fireflies to me. But get this. She said they followed her up to her house and flashed different colors."

"Isn't she the one who saw the UFO last year?"

"So she said." Rosaline sighed. "I'm concerned about her living over there alone, if her eyesight might be going. Or, you know…"

"Her mind?"

"Mmm-hmm."

Darius stripped aluminum foil and nacho crumbs off the baking sheets, crumpled the foil into a ball, and tossed it into the garbage can. "She got any family around?"

"I never see anybody visit. I think we neighbors ought to start checking up on her."

"Darius," said Roy, charging into the kitchen with an unopened beer in each hand. He stopped short when he noticed Rosaline. "Oh. Hello there, hot mama."

"Hello, Roy," Rosaline said coolly, turning to go back into the living room. Roy swiveled his head to watch her go, murmuring appreciatively.

"Here, man," Roy said, cracking open a beer. "For the host."

Darius put up a hand. "Naw. I'm good."

"Just one."

"No." Darius turned toward the sink.

"I haven't seen you take a drink all night," Roy said. "What's the matter? You ain't driving."

Darius turned suddenly and looked Roy in the eyes.

"Listen, Roy," said Darius, "I know we haven't worked together that long. But I need that job, and I need to keep visitation with my son. I don't drink anymore."

Roy swayed on his feet, but Darius's words seemed to sober him somewhat. "No drinking?"

"Nope."

"None at all?"

"None." Darius sighed. "Look… I didn't always do good in my life. Eddie's the best thing I ever did. I can't screw this up."

"All right, man," said Roy. "I understand. I got kids too."

Darius clapped Roy on the shoulder and headed back to the living room.

"Darius, we're heading out," called Rosaline. "Jerry, Josie, let's get going."

"Allow me to walk you home, madam," said Roy, reaching to grab his phone off the audio dock.

Rosaline rolled her eyes, but she didn't object when Roy followed them out the front door.

* * *

The woods had darkened in the waning August light, but Rosaline marched along the path with the stride of a woman who knew where she was going. The kids darted on ahead, and Roy, puffing a bit, did his best to keep up with Rosaline. Cicadas shrieked in the trees above, nearly drowning out the sounds of twigs snapping beneath their shoes, and the air was fragrant with smoke from an unseen campfire.

"When Darius said you lived next door," Roy wheezed, "I thought that meant, you know, nearby."

"It's only about an eighth of a mile," said Rosaline, sounding amused. "You must live in town."

"Fifth and D Street," Roy said. "Pretty empty now that my kids are grown. The place sure could use a woman's touch."

Rosaline snorted and kept walking.

"Hey," said Roy, putting on a burst of speed to catch up to her. "Don't suppose you'd like to have dinner with me sometime, beautiful lady? Or, if you'd prefer," he said, wiggling his eyebrows, "breakfast?"

They emerged onto a paved road. Across the street, a porch light illuminated Josie and Jerry as they ran through the front door of a modest house, the torn screen door banging shut behind them. Rosaline turned to face Roy, her eyes twinkling in the dimness.

"Roy," she said, "I could never take advantage of an intoxicated man, no matter how handsome."

Roy stood straighter, brightening a bit.

"Head straight down the path now, and you'll get back to Darius's place.

Oh, and Roy?"

"Yes, ma'am?"

"Have him give you a lift home." Was she smiling, or were the shadows playing tricks on him? "Good night."

He chuckled, admiring the swing of her hips as she walked away.

Roy wasn't quite sure when he lost the path, but after a few minutes he was knee deep in plants and he couldn't see Darius's house or Rosaline's. He sighed and looked toward the sky. His drill sergeant's voice had never really left his head after basic training. *You'd better learn where that North Star is, boys. Navigate from that.*

When Roy stumbled into the clearing, its brightness stunned him for a moment. Puzzled, he looked at the sky again. It was clear, but there was no moon.

A crowd of fireflies hovered above a fallen tree, golden lights winking. Roy's brow furrowed. Odd way for fireflies to behave, grouped together like birds in a tree.

The group drifted toward the ground. Roy blinked as the lights appeared to change color, sparkling with greens and oranges and reds. He watched what looked like a baby rabbit darting across the clearing toward the lights, and then the critter leaped and vanished in midair.

Roy rubbed his eyes. He should probably take a page out of Darius's book and cut back on the alcohol. Rosaline would like that.

The swarm glided across the ground toward Roy. He stood with his head cocked, admiring them, when he heard the whispers. He looked around, but there was nobody here but him and the fireflies. He could almost make out words.

Lights played against Roy's lower body, first the flesh-and-blood leg on the left, then the acrylic-and-titanium leg on the right. The lights teemed, seeming to mix themselves.

The whispers weren't coming from any particular direction. If anything, they seemed to come from Roy's own mind. The words came again, louder, and it seemed to him that they said *Bad specimen. Not intact.*

The lights darted back toward the fallen tree, still glowing a uniform gold.

Roy's heart thumped in his throat as he hurried in what he hoped was the direction of Darius's place. He'd check the stars again in a minute, he told himself, once he got away from this eerie, floating constellation.

* * *

Darius dumped the last of the trash into the can and hollered toward the back door. "Eddie. Bring Muddy back inside. It's past your bedtime."

Outside, the dog was barking. Muddy almost never barked. It sounded too far away.

Darius stepped out into the humid night, trotting down two concrete steps to the grass. "Eddie."

Crickets and cicadas trilled in response.

"Eddie, it's late and I'm tired. This is not the time to play hide-and-seek, my man."

Darius scanned the backyard. He was about to go around the side of the house when Muddy, alone, came barreling out of the woods. The dog ran to Darius, planted his front feet in a wide stance, and barked fervently.

"Good boy," said Darius, reaching down to scratch Muddy in his favorite spot on the sides of his jaws. "Where's Eddie? Go find Eddie."

Muddy ran to the edge of the yard where the woods began, and stopped, looking back at Darius with one paw in the air.

Frowning, Darius followed.

* * *

A few minutes earlier, Eddie Coover had put Muddy on the tie-out, watched him do his business in the yard, then unhooked the clasp from the collar. "Go inside, Muddy." But instead of running for the door, the dog had taken off for the woods. "Hey! Where you going?"

Eddie chased Muddy all the way to the clearing with the fallen tree, one of Eddie's favorite places in the woods. But the dog stopped short at the edge of the trees. He appeared to be staring at fireflies hovering above the log.

"Wow," said Eddie, watching the fireflies glow. He'd never seen such a huge number together. If he'd brought a jar, he could sweep it right through that group and catch several at once.

The lights floated slowly toward Eddie. He took a step into the clearing.

Golden light illuminated the boy's face and reflected in his eyes. He didn't notice Muddy backing up, shrinking away, whining. All he could see were the fireflies, so dazzling, so wonderful. They were bigger than normal fireflies, and brighter.

The colors shifted, white to pink, yellow to blue, twinkling as they moved closer. It seemed they were buzzing, like friendly bees. Enraptured, the boy reached out a hand toward them, and then the whispers began.

Were the fireflies talking? Eddie strained to hear the whispered words. It sounded like a single word, over and over again: *Collect.*

* * *

The dog led Darius straight to the clearing with the fallen tree that Eddie liked to climb on. He'd found Eddie here the other day, placing Skittles in a little pile underneath a bush. When Darius had asked him why, Eddie had said he was leaving a snack for the fairies.

"Eddie," Darius called, but there was no answer, no sound at all. Even the crickets had quieted.

A pale object lay in the dirt. Darius reached down and grasped it, recognizing it even in the dimness as his son's White Sox cap. His eyes darted around wildly as alarm surged through his veins.

"Eddie!"

* * *

At noon the following day, Darius sat across his kitchen table from his ex-wife. Dominique, the first and only woman he'd ever been in love with, had left him when his drinking got out of control. But today, she was the only one who had stayed after the police and worried friends had gone home.

She stared out the window, chin resting on her hand, fingers splayed out across her face. Darius laid his head on his folded arms, exhaustion weighing him down. His stomach growled, which he ignored.

As teenagers, they'd been together every waking moment. It was strange to be spending this much time with her again. Handing off Eddie twice a week didn't take long. When she arrived last night, right before the police, Darius had noticed her outfit, one he hadn't seen before, stylish jeans with a form-fitting top.

They'd been over the events a hundred times, it seemed—with each other, with neighbors, with the cops. Eddie had left the house around 9:45 to put the dog out. Darius had gone looking for him around ten. There were no reports of strangers in the area, no evidence of kidnapping or foul play, and no findings from their search of the woods. The police had collected everyone's statements and assigned someone to the case.

Darius thought about how a little Jack Daniels would take the edge off. He forced himself not to think about how the liquor store was only five minutes up the road.

"So what now?" he said.

He expected Dominique to answer that with something practical, like she always did. Or maybe to be angry at him for asking anything of her, since this had happened on his watch. He did not expect her to start crying, but the tension of keeping it together all night and all morning exploded into a flood that shook her like whitewater.

Darius sat awkwardly. He wanted to put his arms around her, but that wasn't allowed anymore. He wanted to cry, too. He wanted to punch a hole in the wall, run out of the room, and never come back. He wanted to stay with Dominique for as long as it took to make their son come home.

"He must be so scared," she said, barely comprehensible. "He might be hurt…"

He scooted his chair over and reached out a hand to rub her back.

Dominique threw her arms around him and sobbed. He held onto her, uncomfortably aware of how much physical contact they were having, wondering if she liked it, too, feeling a fool for thinking that way at such a time.

Finally, she pulled back, retrieving a tissue from her purse, not looking Darius in the eye.

"I guess I'll take this with me," she said, reaching for the detective's business card that lay on the table between them.

"Take it," he spat, suddenly angry at everything. "I ain't calling him."

Her eyes met his, frown lines appearing between her brows.

"He won't do anything," Darius declared. "Did you see how he acted? He doesn't give two shits about some little Black kid going missing."

"We have to give them a chance, Darius. It's all we've—"

"For God's sake, Nicki," he shouted, "they asked me if he was in a gang. My six-year-old son!"

She pushed her chair out and stood up. "I'm going now."

"You're leaving?"

"We both need to get some rest."

"Fine," he said, pushing his chair back with a screech, standing to face her. "Leave, then."

"Darius, I can't do anything by staying here."

"Eddie's out there somewhere. And you want to give up and—and go back to bed?"

"Don't you make this about me," she said. "I'm not the one that lost our son."

"Oh, I lost him?" He was yelling now. "This is my fault? Goddammit, Nicki, he was in the backyard, where he's been a million times, and then he was gone."

She stood with her arms crossed. "Were you drinking last night?"

"What? No. You know I quit—"

"I saw the beer cans in the trash, Darius. Looked like at least two cases."

"I had some friends over. They brought it."

She was shaking her head.

"What does it matter?" he yelled. "You think I'm lying? Even if I was, what the hell does that have to do with Eddie going missing?"

"I think maybe Eddie was gone a lot longer than fifteen minutes, and you weren't watching because you were carousing with your drunk friends."

Darius kicked the kitchen chair across the room. It ricocheted off the wall and clattered into the counter, landing sideways on the linoleum floor.

"You have no idea," he shouted. "No idea what you're talking about. How hard it's been for me to kick that habit. How much I wanted to do right by—"

"Oh, I remember. It was always about what *you* wanted." Dominique grabbed her purse. "You're a selfish man, Darius Coover. And our son is paying the price." Her cheeks were wet again as she strode through the doorway to the living room. He heard the front door slam.

Darius kicked the chair again, watching a leg splinter off the base. He banged out the back door into the yard.

* * *

After finally caving to fatigue, Darius had slept all afternoon, then microwaved a frozen pizza to quiet his griping stomach. Now, lying awake in bed at 11 p.m., sleep eluded him, though he felt more exhausted than he ever had.

He sat up, swung his legs over the side of the bed, and rubbed his eyes. Muddy raised his head from the floor. Darius stared back at the mongrel face. A few seconds later, he pulled on his shoes and headed for the back door, making one stop in Eddie's empty room.

Muddy followed Darius into the yard, the crickets in the grass quieting at their appearance. Darius could hear bullfrogs croaking at the nearby pond as he knelt and faced the dog.

"Muddy," he said, holding out the clothes from Eddie's laundry hamper. "Go find Eddie."

The dog sniffed at the fabric. Darius felt ridiculous. Maybe this only worked in the movies.

"Can you find him?" He looked Muddy in the eyes. "Where's Eddie? *Find*

Eddie."

Muddy took off running toward the woods, pausing at the edge of the yard, one paw in the air, looking back at Darius expectantly.

"Well, I'll be damned," Darius muttered, jogging after the dog.

Muddy ran straight to the clearing where he had run the day before, where Darius had found Eddie's hat. Deflated, Darius sat down on the fallen tree, rubbing a hand across his weary face. "Yes, boy. Eddie was here," he said. "Where did he go?"

But Muddy hadn't entered the clearing. The dog had stopped at the edge, front legs spread in a defensive stance, whining.

Darius followed the dog's gaze to what appeared to be a swarm of fireflies. He might be pretty new to living out here in the country, but since when did fireflies swarm? They moved as a group a few inches above the grass.

A small round object lifted off the ground and disappeared into the bright mass. Darius blinked in surprise. The lights moved a few inches, and an object a little larger than a pea rocketed upward as if the lights had sucked it through a straw.

Darius's stomach fluttered uneasily, but he took a cautious step toward the fireflies, squinting past them at the ground. A couple more of the pea-sized objects lay there. They were stamped with a miniature letter S. Skittles, Eddie's favorite candy, the snack that Dominique complained was pure sugar. Pure energy, by the effect they had on Eddie.

Darius gasped as a chipmunk scuttled past his feet. The cloud of light abruptly dropped, right into the critter's path. Maybe the rodent had put on a burst of super speed and skittered away, but it seemed to Darius that it disappeared into the lights, and that the lights had briefly twinkled in different colors, like a Christmas tree.

Different colors. What had Rosaline told him yesterday, about Almeta Guthridge? She claimed she'd seen fireflies that flashed colors and came after her.

If they could take Skittles, and a chipmunk, what else could they take?

Dominique would never believe this. Unless he had evidence.

Darius took out his phone.

* * *

"Hi."

She didn't sound happy to hear from him. But at least she had answered his call.

"You hear anything from the police?" Darius asked.

"I would have called you if I did."

He opened his mouth to tell her about the lights, but something else came out first. "I wasn't drinking that night."

"I know."

He blinked. "What?"

"Your neighbor Rosaline told me," she said. "She's a sweet lady. She gave me her number the other night, in case I needed anything or wanted to talk. She says you never drink."

"Yeah," he said. "Rosaline's cool."

"I'm sorry," she mumbled, "about what I said yesterday."

He hadn't often heard Dominique admit she was wrong. She quickly changed the subject. "Shouldn't you be at work right now?"

"Nah," he said. "I can't focus. Roy, my co-worker, he said he'd cover for me, try to get them to hold my job."

"You got anybody there with you?"

"Roy's been checking in on me." He drummed his fingers against the kitchen table. "What about you?"

"Mom came over for a while," she said. "Prayed with me."

"What about your boyfriend?" he said cynically. "Let me guess. He couldn't handle it."

"Don't start, Darius."

He sighed, suddenly exhausted by the weight of it all. "Sorry," he said. "I don't want to fight. I just want to find him."

There was no good way to tell her. He might as well just say it.

"Listen," he said, "this is gonna sound strange. But that clearing where I found Eddie's hat, there are some weird lights over there, and I think they took him."

She was quiet for a few long seconds. "Lights? What are you talking about?"

"Hear me out," he said. "They're like a clump of fireflies. But they're not fireflies. They move around in a group, and they take things. Little objects, little animals. Roy told me saw them, too, that same night. I got some video. I can show you."

She was too quiet. Probably thinking he had lost his mind.

"Come with me," he blurted. "To the clearing. Tonight. Once you see for yourself—"

"Darius," she said, "you're talking crazy."

"I know it sounds crazy. I know," he said. "But I'm sure of it. I can feel it. Eddie isn't gone. He's still there, somewhere in that clearing. Or nearby."

"How can that be? They searched the woods. What you're saying, it's—not possible."

"Look," he said, "if you come with me, I will never ask you for anything again. You can have your choice of holidays, Mother's Day, Christmas, whatever. But I need you there with me. I need you to see this."

Her silence lengthened until he wondered if the call had dropped. Finally, she spoke.

"All right."

* * *

In the end, Dominique, Rosaline, and Roy all came along, trailed by Muddy. They tramped through the trees, not talking much, ears overly sharp to the sounds of the crickets, the hoot of an owl, the startled scatter of nocturnal animals. Rosaline cursed her flashlight's dying batteries, and Roy stepped up next to her so she could share his.

The clearing was completely dark.

"Damn," said Darius, but then he remembered what he'd brought along. He reached into his pocket for the little red bag.

"Come here now," he called, tearing open the package and scattering Skittles. "Come on, little aliens, or whatever the hell you are. I got some stuff to discuss with you."

Roy spotted them first, up by a bird's nest on the high limb of a tree. Darius wondered if the nest still contained any birds.

"Here, critters," Darius said, waving a handful of Skittles in the air. "Come and get 'em."

The lights descended, gleaming, just a few feet away from Darius now. Dominique took a step back. Rosaline put a hand on her shoulder.

Darius's face glowed in the brilliance of the shining swarm. He held out his hand, palm up. The Skittles shot upward like metal to a magnet. Behind him, Roy yelped.

A hand was squeezing his. Darius turned and met Dominique's eyes, wide, afraid. He allowed himself a second or two to savor that touch. Then he squeezed her hand back and let it go.

The yellow and white shifted to green, indigo, and crimson, glowing ever brighter. The temperature in the clearing grew hotter, the air hummed, and Dominique screamed, because Darius had vanished.

* * *

The light was everywhere. Darius threw up an arm, fruitlessly, to block it, but he felt it seeping into every pore in his body. The air was burning hot, causing sweat to bead on his skin. He'd have to ask Roy if this was how the Iraqi desert felt.

He was in a sort of room, though it had no walls. He had the sense of being inside a snow globe, enclosed in something vast and round. Gravity didn't seem to work like it should. He wasn't standing on anything, but he wasn't floating aimlessly either.

The firefly-things were here, millions of them, trillions, filling the space as far as Darius's eyes could see. One of them flew past his face, and he yelped and shrank back. It was like a glowing worm, writhing in midair. How could he have thought these things were fireflies?

He watched a cluster of lights move toward a second, joined by a third. As they squeezed closer, they formed a shape, a creature made of tiny suns.

More clusters joined the mass. Gradually, the being resembled an octopus, its central body surrounded by glowing appendages.

The creature moved toward Darius. Behind it, suspended in a bed of tiny lights, were animals – a raccoon, a field mouse, a rabbit – and, at the edge of the row, a human boy, whose chest rose and fell just slightly, as if he were safe in his bed, asleep.

"Eddie!"

Darius lunged toward his son, his limbs scattering the fireflies, but the huge light-creature blocked his path. The center of its body shifted, the lights rearranging themselves. When they stopped, they'd left two vacant spots in the middle that resembled eyes, and a line below like a mouth, which suddenly curved up at the edges.

Welcome.

The voice was inside Darius's head, somehow, but it wasn't his voice. Darius yelled and backed away.

He was shaking, but he glared directly into the creature's shadow eyes. "You have my son," he said. "You can't take him. Give him back."

The face momentarily disappeared as the fireflies shifted, swarming. Slowly, they reassembled into a face, and the voice spoke again.

No.

"What do you mean, no? He's my son. I'm his father. He needs to be with me. Not up here in your light factory or whatever the hell this place is." He strained to see past the creature for a glimpse of Eddie. "Where are we, anyhow?"

Between.

"Between what? You know what, forget it. I don't have time for this."

Darius thrust his body forward, swimming through the searing ocean of light.

"Eddie!" he cried out.

The light-creature extended two shining appendages, which slithered around Darius's hands, binding them. He screamed as the heat burned his skin. When he kicked at the creature, two more appendages laced themselves around his legs, forming scorching rings of pain. Darius shrieked again and stopped kicking. Sweat poured down his face.

"Look," he said desperately. "I don't know what you are, or where you came from, but that boy over there—" He pointed across the space as best he could with his bound right hand. "He's the most important thing in the world. In *my* world. In my world, you don't take children away. He needs to come home, and I will fight you until you understand that."

Son?

"Yes. My son. I'm his father and I love him. Do you understand love?"

Love?

"I made him, and it is my job to keep him safe. You can't have him."

Job, they whispered. *Mission. Collect.*

"Collect?" Darius looked at the animals, suspended in clouds of light, dozens of different species all lined up. "You're collecting? One of each, like Noah's Ark or something?" He shook his head, staring at Eddie's small body, and made a choice.

"Collect me instead," he told them. "Please. Send Eddie back."

Instead. The lights swarmed again, surging like a storm cloud.

The light-bed holding Eddie shifted and began to move. Eddie's eyelids fluttered and his eyes half opened, like they used to do when Darius carried him out of the car after he'd fallen asleep during the drive home, and then he smiled.

"Dad?"

* * *

In the center of the clearing, the cloud of fireflies shimmered rapidly, changing from yellow to a blaze of colors. A boy's body dropped from the cloud, collapsing into a heap on the ground.

Dominique sprang from the log and ran to him. She dropped to her knees and folded her son in her arms. Roy and Rosaline gasped, jumped up, and hugged one another.

"Eddie. Mama's here, baby. Oh, thank you, God." Her tears soaked his shirt. "I thought I'd lost you."

The boy did not respond. His body felt cool to Dominique's fingers, his frame lean, the fabric of his shorts hanging loosely.

"Eddie," she said, rubbing her hands along his arms to warm him. "Eddie. Are you alright? Please tell me you're all right."

Muddy licked Eddie's hand and wagged his tail.

"Mama?"

Eddie opened his eyes and blinked at his mother. She pulled him into a fierce hug and squeezed as if she would never let go. After a while he murmured, "That kind of hurts, Mama."

Dominique laughed, brushing tears off her cheeks, and loosened her hold a bit. "Sorry, pumpkin. I'm just so glad to see you." Rosaline, her eyes wet, knelt and hugged them both, and Roy joined them a second later.

The lights hovered, pulsing. To Dominique, it appeared as if they were observing the embrace.

"Thank you," she told them, over Eddie's shoulder. "Thank you for giving me back my boy."

Eddie curled up on Dominique's lap, squirming around to face the lights. They twinkled rapidly, then drifted slowly upward, over the top of the trees, vanishing into the night sky. Muddy barked once at their departure. Then they were alone with the chirping crickets and the darkness.

"Mama," said Eddie.

"Yes, baby?"

"Is Dad coming back?"

Relationships Cultivated on the Bike Trail — Edna Cartwright

E dna began writing when she was a wee thing and hasn't stopped since. *Once, when she was a teen, she wrote a story about something dark, and the darkness has stuck around ever since.*

* * *

Time had escaped Clem and Maple as they walked the bike trail this cold, autumn night. The sky had settled darkly, and so they had taken a shortcut across the empty University of Arkansas campus, vacated for fall break and the Halloween weekend because it was better lit than the first section of the bike trail. Dead, dry leaves scuffled behind them like encroaching footsteps. Clem's eyes darted skittishly the darker it got, sure that every sound signaled some shadowy menace. More than once, he said, "I knowed we should have left an hour ago. I just knowed it."

"Just a little ways to the Skull Creek Trail," Maple answered, "and then we'll be home." The bike path was segmented into different trails depending on the part of town through which the asphalt stretch meandered. Running north and south, the trail snaked through woods and abutted parks and apartment complexes and crossed over and alongside a shallow water flow with a name that only heightened Clem's trepidation as he whispered its name: "Skull Creek."

At night, the college campus felt strange and out of touch, like they'd passed into another world full of darkness housing things that gnashed and preyed, existing on the periphery, just waiting for the right moment. The rectangular buildings and the angular shadows, the Senior Walk barely illuminated by a smattering of streetlights, its carved names of graduates in the concrete blurry under any light that wasn't sun.

There was no one on campus to welcome any trick r treaters, though their laughs and sounds of mirth echoed afar off like a requiem, a cry of the wind mourning the past. It had only been a few years since Clem had gone trick or treating. He'd gone with Maple and Maple's father. They had just entered middle school and Maple was already saying he was too old for it, but Clem convinced him to go one more time. The last time, as it were. A piece of youth they'd never get back.

Clem knew normalcy had evanesced from Maple's life over the past few years, beginning with a diagnosis after the last vacation his family had taken, and the last vacation his father would take ever. Maple had been the clown of the two, but he lost any ability to laugh when his parents came home from the doctor's and lost all pretense of a smile when his father and mother sat him down and told him the diagnosis.

There was a mole. The adults tossed around medical terms that drained the color from their faces while Clem and Maple tried to keep up: *metastatic, lymph nodes, melanoma, immune boosters*. Though he had Clem, Maple sank further and further into a humorless, zombified existence. He slept a lot, barely ate, doted on his father, spoke little of himself or what he was thinking. Six months after the initial diagnosis, not even a month ago, Maple lost the opportunity to say goodbye as the cancer spread to his father's brain and robbed him of his last hours of consciousness and senility. Clem didn't know what to say as they watched his father's heart slow, the oxygen levels drop, the respirations crawl shallowly from the chest up to the throat. Maple later had said he felt the depression lift. Replaced by a grim determination to muddle through the rest of his life. Rolling off him, a resolute sadness that had brought him through the valley of his father's death older, wiser about the ways of the world: *it don't have a happy ending.*

Maple's ringtone, a snippet of the Eagles "Hole in the World Tonight," broke the silence of the night, and he stopped just before the Engineering Building to answer.

"Hello?" he clenched and unclenched his fist repetitively.

"On my way home. Yeah, I'll be fine." He met Clem's gaze then mouthed the word "Mom," then shifted to look all around the campus. Clem checked his own phone, but his mother hadn't called.

"I'm fine, Mom."

Clem shivered, the wind cold against his flesh. It was too dark and with every subtle sound from the shadows, he jumped. As Maple had grown stoic, Clem's temerity had remained as thin as the carpet of falling leaves dancing over the college grounds. Over by the library steps, the silhouette of a stranger in a coat and fedora. Was he watching them?

"Good," Maple said but he looked so uninterested in the conversation. Still, Clem knew Maple would never hang up on his mother.

Clem glanced to the left — something scuttled behind the fountain in front of the student union, the stranger now gone.

"Just saw some friends," Maple said.

Clem could read his buddy. Knew Maple was hurting.

Maple had ended their last deep conversation with, "Loss is inevitable." Clem wasn't sure if it were the words or the tone that had scared him more.

"I'm walking home," Maple said.

Clem was afraid he'd lose his one friend if he pushed too hard, but sadness hung on Maple like an old suit; he could see it now as his friend stood under the streetlight.

"What does that even mean, Mom?"

Clem snapped his head in the direction of the library. A wisp of a shadow. Fleeting. Like a whisper in the air. He felt that old clichéd feeling — they were being watched. Around them a ground fog rolled in and the temperature dropped another ten degrees. The figure, silhouetted against the dusk now back by the music building. *Fedoradorned.*

"No, Mom. Of course not. Just me and Clem is all."

Maple's father had looked so still and ashen in the coffin. They'd done their best to make him look natural, like he was sleeping. But the skin looked like Play-Doh and the mouth and the corners of the eyes had settled towards the ground. There was an unnatural stillness about the body: no slight rise and fall of the chest, no twitch of a digit or of the lip, no slight breath ruffling a hair of the gray mustache. Even the hair looked plastered on.

"No, ma'am. No homework. Yes ma'am: trash and dishes. Got it."

Clem scanned the darkness. The figure had faded back into the night.

"Yes'um," Maple said. He tucked his phone into his back pocket and asked, "What's up bud?"

"Nothing," Clem said. "Thought I saw something."

Maple stared across the campus but didn't react if he saw anything out of place. "Let's get moving. We aren't far from the bike trail."

They crossed the campus, Clem continuing his darting gaze, jumping at every shadow, until Maple said, "What?"

Clem cinched his coat around his thin form and cast another glance over his right shoulder. "I think we're being followed."

Maple checked. "I don't see anyone." ·

Clem sighed in disappointment. Of course, there'd be no one there when Maple looked.

"That's always been your problem, buddy," Maple said. "You're too jittery. This world will eat you alive if you don't toughen up."

They pressed on.

"That night, after the funeral," Clem tried. He knew Maple would know he was talking about the only time Maple had opened up to him. Maple needed more of that, or the hardness would spread and kill his friend like those hard tumors had spread and killed his father.

"I said all I want to say about that," Maple said.

The boys crossed the crosswalk, and though there was no car on the street, Clem still looked both ways. It was when he looked back up the hill from where they came that he saw the stranger in the fedora and long coat and he thought he heard whistling. "If you ever wanna talk again…"

As they reached the other side of the street, Maple said, "What good would it do, Clem? I said all I got to say. I mean, why should I rehash it? He's dead. I couldn't do nothing to help him just like the doctors couldn't and just like God wouldn't, so what's the point?"

"I'm sorry, man. I just…"

"Drop it," Maple said. "Don't push it."

They walked on silent for a few minutes, the sound of whistling a distant echo. They descended the slope and crossed the old train tracks then passed under the railroad bridge's wooden structure. Heard the burbling of the small stream that accompanied the trail. They crossed a couple of other streets then made it to the trail itself.

Maple asked what the homework was in Civics class and Clem told him, and Clem asked him what his plans were for Christmas and when Maple didn't answer, Clem didn't push. When Maple asked him when the SAT's were given, Clem told him and said that he should think about studying for the ACT's also. Maple said, "yeah," and shrugged and Clem realized this was less actual planning for the future and more small talk to pass the time. Lost in his own thoughts, it wasn't until Clem looked up that he saw someone ahead of them. Whistling that same tune. Nearby children screamed out, giggling "…*give us something good to eat*" but they were separated from the bike trail by a row of trees and shrubs.

The stranger whistled while he walked, his fedora-covered head tilted up to the full moon, his hands stuffed in the pockets of his black coat as he meandered toward them, slight and pale with an easy smile and a gait that for some reason unnerved Clem.

He said, "Howdy," as he passed them and Maple said, "Hi," and Clem kept his head down against the wind until he realized that the whistling had stopped abruptly. He looked back then clutched at Maple's collar, stopping his friend.

As Maple turned, Clem stammered: "Where'd he go, Maple? The whistling man?"

The creek stood to one side of them, down a slight gravel embankment. To the other a five-foot high brick retaining wall and above that a six-foot-high shrub and tree-lined chain-link fence that blocked off the property of their apartment complex. The path in either direction was empty.

"Maybe he…" and that was all Maple got out.

"Maybe he," came the voice and the boys turned back the way they'd been going and there he stood, the whistling man in the fine black suit and the black fedora, hands still in the pockets of his dark overcoat. "Sorry! Didn't mean to startle y'all. How you boys doing tonight?"

Instinctively, they both took a step back.

"Where's my manners?" the man asked and drew out his left hand and offered it to them, his fingers long and pale with jaundiced nails gleaming in the soft light of the overhead lamp. Blue veins scarred the back of the hand, and under that light, the man's shadow stretched impossibly long.

Clem grabbed Maple by the arm and yanked him down away from the path to the creek, then hopped the swift, shallow flow to the sandbar in the middle. Surprised, the man skidded down the gravel bank till his toes kissed the water's edge. Here he watched the stream like he was watching a tennis match until he remembered them, looked up and flashed a toothy smile that glistened unnaturally white in the moonlight.

"I'm right glad we met, boys. Right glad. You needed me to come along. Why, I could feel it in my bones. I set out this night to find someone in dire need of my services and I could feel you boys – I say, *feel you boys!* – calling to me, desperate for what I had to give."

His accent sounded forced, like he was trying too hard to mimic them.

"What do we need?" Maple asked.

"Don't listen to him. Why can't you come over here?" Clem thought he had an answer, but if he said, he knew Maple would call him insane.

The man smiled and looked down and resumed the tennis match, then brought his smile back up to them. "Why, for someone to show you that you matter, Maple. You and Clem, y'uns don't have a lot of friends, do you? Just each other? That's fine most days, but don't it ever get lonely? Don't you ever want something more? More than what your mommas give? More than what any of them girls at school would give? I could give you all of that and more. Just help me remove them lodestones from around y'un's necks and give you a new purpose, a new life."

Maple said, "I got friends." His voice trembled.

Clem wanted to cry and never so much just wanted to go home.

"I got an idea," the stranger said, his face lighting on an epiphany that produced a smile more like a gruesome rictus in the moonlight. He waved his hand in a flourish, like a magician, and like that a swirl of leaves and gravel engulfed him in a whirlwind that, when it settled, had consumed him completely.

"He must've followed us," Clem said, trying to reason.

"How the hell did he disappear like that?" Maple asked.

Maple chanced a step or two then hopped to the bank and scampered up to the bike trail, Clem on his heels.

"Followed us?" Maple asked. They each looked one direction down the trail then switched directions. Clem saw only a bare oak limb dancing in the soft glow of a trail light, and then the small tunnel under the Sycamore Street Bridge that divided their apartment parking from the hospital parking lot.

"I think he was back on the campus," Clem said, "but he looks …" His voice faltered with no words to keep his thought going.

A sound. The rustling of leaves or more footsteps. Or a breath. "Run!" Maple whispered.

Hunkering under the tunnel, Clem and Maple scanned the darkness past the small pool of light that illuminated the bike trail ahead of them. Maple's home was closest, and his mother's car was near the door. Clem was fast. A lot faster than Maple. They heard the trickle of the creek, but there was no sign of the stranger. They had just caught their breaths, but they hadn't yet the opportunity to discuss any kind of plan when the man's voice boomed all around them.

"Why don't you boys come on out here and enjoy the night. Maple, we can say hi to your mom. I think she'd be right proud to see you. I asked her so myself, just now."

"Why's he doing this?" Maple asked.

"Because you boys need me. Especially you, Maple." The stranger reappeared in front of them, grinning under the trail light some fifteen feet away. His eyes, still under the shadow of the fedora's brim, appeared to glow like white stars. Clem forced himself to remember to blink lest he fall under the spell of those stars and begin orbiting them, but when he glanced at Maple, his friend stared dully and swayed just slightly as if a breeze raced through the tunnel.

"I smelled you in the cemetery that day, Maple. The day your father was chucked in the grave, your scent awoke me. You should know that. You should know that I won't let you make it to the car once he's inside. I won't let you make it five feet from this tunnel."

Maple said, "I just want to go home, Mister. Just go home, and you can go on your way and just leave us be."

"It … I don't work like that."

"I'm just fine, Mister."

"I can be the daddy you lost. I can instruct you and punish you when you're bad and reward you oh so nicely when you're good. But it takes some time. Cultivatin' y'uns and growin' you in the earth, that is. More than just blood rites. It's about nurturing and growth."

"I'll get back to the Baptist church. I'll start saying my prayers. I'll get back to studying and I'll be nice to people and I'll get a job to help my momma."

"You'll grow inside of him," Clem said. "You'll rot him to the core from the inside out."

"Baptists!" the stranger laughed. "Petulant children who watched their elders and mimicked them without understanding what it all means. Evangelicals, ha! Don't have a real understanding of the AGE of it all. You have to have been around to really get it. The Jews and the Catholics and the Muslims, and there's a sect of practicing Sumarians in Iraq I could introduce you to. But don't talk to me about Baptists or Methodists or snake-handling, tongue-speaking Assembly of God."

"If I went to the Catholic church and grabbed me one of their crosses, what would you say to that? If I had some of their holy water would you say those things?"

"You might as well have a Star of David or the Koran."

"And if I did, would you leave us alone."

"You have two choices, Maple. Try to become me … or nourish me."

Clem looked down at his hands, clinched into fists, then looked back up to the stranger. He stepped in front of Maple, breaking his gaze, and stared resolutely into those white eyes.

"There's another choice," Clem said. "You can leave him alone. He's my friend and he's suffered enough, and he ain't gone with you. You wanna try and take someone, you try and take me."

The brim of the hat dipped, and the toothy smile fell under the penumbra. "Why my dear Clem, all you'll ever be is food. But he has called to me, ever since his daddy got sick. He's longed for this. He wants the quiet. The darkness is the key, you see, to ever hope to become like me, to survive the cultivation. You have to want it. Despite his protests, Maple knows deep down he wants it."

Clem said, "So why not just come in here and take us? There ain't no running water between us and this ain't no holy site."

"You know the rules," the stranger said. "I can't go where I'm not welcome." He leaned to the side, probably to get a better glimpse of Maple. "You'll have to come out of there at some point. But know that even if you decide to join me, it don't always take, and most just end up in the ground. You know, faced in that moment, how many people realize that this is it? That there ain't no more than this, 'cept for what I offer them, and even as old as I am, I can't always guarantee that they'll get life everlasting. Why, I tried changing a whole host of people over the years, and I can count on one hand how many actually made it through the cultivating."

"I don't believe that," Maple said, his voice wavering. "I don't believe this is it."

"Cause it isn't," Clem said," but Maple stepped around him and once more locked eyes with the stranger.

"Believe it or not, make's no never mind to me. Don't make it no less true. I'm the only chance you got, Maple. I'm you're only hope for survival. Not Clem getting your momma's car and not the sunlight and not the creek and not the Baptists or the Catholics or any whole host of crosses and not just giving up the ghost and dying, cause all those ways are just nothing."

Maple fell against the cool cement of the tunnel wall and closed his eyes and grabbed for his head, and said, "Stop laughing in my brain!" and Clem, hearing nothing, looked from him to the stranger then knelt by his friend.

"Maple," he said, pulling his hands away. "Maple, look at me. It's going to be okay. We can be okay."

"I just want to sleep, Clem."

"We can do this. I know it."

"It'll be just blackness," Maple said. "And that awful quiet."

"He'll eat away at you till there's nothing left, Maple. He'll grow inside you till there is just blackness. But if you come with me, we can do this. We can beat him home."

"He said there was no other way," Maple said, and he looked up at Clem and Clem saw, in his friend's eyes, more than just fear. Maple wore the same look his father had right before the end.

"He's a liar," Clem said.

"I don't want to lose me," Maple said, but he sounded as though he'd lost all say in the matter.

When Clem looked back, the stranger was gone, but he could still feel him. Something rotten lingered in the air. Perhaps he really was waiting for them to make a break for it.

"Give me the key," Clem said.

"Why you want my key? Where's yours?"

"I left mine at home this morning," Clem admitted. "Besides, my place is too far. I can make it to your place, get your mom's car, and pull in back there, to the parking lot. You run out and hop in, and I'll get us home and safe."

"What if I can't make it up the hill?" Maple asked.

"What is this?" Clem asked. All the lonely nights, all the times he felt like he couldn't make it through, he'd depended on Maple's strength. Even in the face of those insurmountable odds, with his best friend at his lowest, Clem had relied on the strength Maple exhibited. "I can make it. We can."

"What would stop him from getting in the car?"

"He hasn't come in here because we didn't invite him," Clem said. He took his friend's hand and squeezed it until Maple met his gaze.

"What if he's faster than you?"

"I don't know," Clem said. But he knew there was no other way. He had the legs and Maple had the key, and Clem couldn't part with his legs, but Maple could part with his key. Maple removed the jumbled key ring from his pocket and clenched it tightly in his fist, and stared at their building, impossibly far away. Begrudgingly he held out his fist and dropped the ring in Clem's empty palm. There were so many keys on the small wire band.

"Why you need so many keys anyway, Maple?"

"I got stuff."

"Don't go nowhere."

"You be right back," Maple said.

Clem stood and stretched his calves and thighs, staring all along at the apartment building. "I promise."

The wind to his back, Clem sprinted off the tunnel, the keys tight in his fist, pumping, pumping as he pushed harder. Don't look around. Don't respond to Maple's withering cries. The stranger was out there in the dark. Clem felt his thighs burn. His stride lengthened and once he nearly slipped on the dew-soaked grass. Pulled himself up. Didn't look around. Regained his footing and limped up under the soft hum of the nearest sidewalk fluorescent, and only then glanced back.

Thick shadows gathered around the entrance to the tunnel. That darkness reached up to him as he resumed his sprint up the hill, the soles of his shoes skidding on the moist blades of grass. He reached the door frame, sure he'd be yanked into the dark sky and drift into the oblivion of the outer atmosphere. Then into the emptiness of space, orbiting those stars. He fumbled for the keys. There seemed an impossible number of keys on an impossibly short ring, and he was sure he would not find safety, not until the door closed with him inside and locked behind him and he heard the air conditioner kick on. He closed his eyes and rested his head against the door paneling, then reached his free hand up and caressed the door.

In the wicker wastebasket in the bedroom occupied by Maple's mother, Clem saw no liner, but wads of toilet paper, a tampon, and a photo of Maple, his mom, and his dad smiling, arm in arm on the beach. Her keys were on her dresser, next to the wedding ring she hadn't worn since the funeral. She lay on the bed, fully dressed in the red and white striped uniform that she wore to work every day at the pharmacy on Dickson, a near empty bottle of Xanax on her nightstand. She snored oblivious to the world around her, to the danger her son was in. Clem snatched up the keys.

He bolted from the apartment to the parking lot, turned the key and choked the ignition, pressed the gas, and heard the engine sputter to life. Whipping the car around, he thought that it was more than just the fear of total isolation that spurred him on. Maple would never abandon him.

On the radio, the Eagles sang "Hole in the World Tonight." If it was a portent, Clem would give his dying breath to keep it from coming true.

He crossed the two-lane road and barreled into the hospital parking lot, then rolled down his window and called and honked the horn. His neck strained around to see any sign of Maple, but he saw nothing but the bike trail. Ever-reaching shadows and silence, in the distance the trees danced. Clem sensed a trap and knew he wasn't prepared, but he couldn't … wouldn't abandon his friend. So he shut the car off and opened the door.

The wind had picked up, and he heard cars in the distance. Somewhere he couldn't see, the kids sang the Halloween song. Though the bike trail stretched through the middle of town, out here on it he felt isolated. If help came, it would be too late.

"Maple!" he called.

Nothing.

"Maple!"

The zephyr carried a whisper sounding like his name, drawn out and drowsy. Clem bounded down the hill and skidded under the tunnel and searched but saw no one.

"Maple."

"Clem." The voice was in his ear, but when he looked around, he was alone.

The fedora had been tossed haphazardly on a coffin lid. The stranger's nearly bald head was claylike, the hair on the back of his head flattened and fanning out, the world's worst cowlick. "Cultivating is all about nurturing. It's a sign of true, unyielding love."

Maple stared up at the ceiling of the dank mausoleum, unmoving. He did not blink; he did not stir. His chest neither rose nor fell.

"I hope you survive the cultivating. It's important you know that. I hope I can continue to love you. I heard you that day when you walked through my cemetery, laying your daddy in this very dirt. I heard you from this mausoleum, and I opened the door to hear your heart."

He took fistfuls of dirt and sprinkled it over Maple's bare chest, then his groin. The pebbles and clumps and small stones dimpled his flesh, but Maple could not feel it. He could not feel his inner left thigh being caressed, or the hairs on his left calf stimulated by an index finger or the arch of his bare foot caressed by the supplest and longest of fingers.

"I want you to be happy, Maple. Should you make it through this, perhaps you'll tell me if you were happy in this moment."

Maple could not respond; he could not hear the words or smell the decay of his own flesh or even think of a response.

Clem shared the bike trail with no one. Walks were long slow treks with only his thoughts to greet the coming dusk. This was how it had been in the months since Maple's disappearance. That Halloween night felt like a dream. Even the next day, when the search party was formed, and when the cops questioned Clem, all of it like some nightmare.

The moon was full and the air was warmer, spring in full bloom, the creeks higher thanks to all the rain. It was lighter out longer. It had been almost this hour on Halloween when they'd encountered the whistling stranger, and it was pitch black then. Now, though he couldn't see the sun, he could still see well enough through the dusk to make out the pretty girl jogging from around the bend up ahead, the father riding his bike with his kid who still needed training wheels. The skateboarder. The middle-aged man trucking along jogging and huffing at a pace Clem could powerwalk.

Lost in his thoughts, it wasn't until he heard the whistling that he realized just how quickly the bike trail had emptied out. He wasn't near enough the creeks to make it to them, once he caught sight of the pedestrians to either side of him, smiling, staring.

"God, Maple. Everyone's been so worried." Clem tried to steady his voice.

"I got some answers I needed. How you been, buddy?"

Clem took a step back. "I've been doing good. Made some friends. I have a girlfriend now."

"We've been watching," the stranger said. "I told you it weren't easy to make another'n. It took me a month just to cultivate him."

Clem took another step back and they both took a casual step forward. Clem reached under his shirt and fetched the silver chain around his neck. From it dangled a crucifix. Maple and the stranger instinctively retreated a step or two.

"I've been going to church, too," Clem said. Holding the chain up, showing off the crucifix, Clem found his voice a little less shaky. "I should be getting home. I've got a date tonight. My mom said I can take the car. Hardship license."

They parted and let him through. He paused, but didn't turn back to them, instead gripped the chain tight. "Don't follow me. And you best leave your momma alone too. She's hurt enough." He paused for a breath. "I'm really sorry, Maple."

Only then did he look back. Maple and the man were gone.

Black Mariah's Final Form—Michael Gray Baughan

ichael Gray Baughan writes weird fiction and manages a wild old property where no roads go and no one above ground resides full time. Born and bled on the outskirts of Philadelphia, he indulged an early obsession with Poe by studying English Lit and Creative Writing at the University of Virginia, where he was awarded the Wagenheim Prize for best work of short fiction. Michael's debut collection of stories, The Ana Log & Other Anomalies, *is due from Independent Legions in late 2022. His novel about the world's oldest cult is quietly seeking a publisher.*

* * *

A dirt road led beyond where the blacktop ended but Cole saw nothing in need of an address among the acres of soy it bisected. Without the desperate need to be done with this sorry business urging him onward he would have turned around long before he crested a rise in the terrain and the small, squat homestead revealed itself. When he spotted the old woman sitting out front, the cold stone in his stomach became a brick wrapped in barbwire. After the week he'd just had, he half expected to step from the car and be sprayed with buckshot.

But unlike the others on his list, Mrs. Tilly Perkins did not scream, or curse, or rush forward to rake her nails across his face. Instead she asked him to sit. At least Cole assumed that's what she conveyed with her blunt wave at the other metal rocker on her concrete porch. There was no sign of deference or hospitality in the gesture, though, just a stiff invitation to get this over with, whatever this might be. Cole waited a moment beside the car for some sort of secondary confirmation, but her eyes never left the fields behind him. Not even as he passed in front of her to take the seat. Wondering what it was she watched out there, he sat and mirrored her gaze a minute before speaking. Every so often a slight breeze would ripple through the soy like the flexing segment of something monstrous moving just beneath the surface of the earth.

"Pretty piece of property you have here, ma'am."

"Fields ain't mine anymore. Reckon I'll need to find better facilities soon."

He assumed she meant an old folks home but shied away from any sort of follow-up. Best not to get too personal. Instead he asked her if she knew who he was and why he was there. She nodded. Did she remember speaking with him on the phone? She nodded again, still not looking at him. She might not be fixing to attack him, but she wasn't going to make this easy.

Without much else to say, Cole waded in with what he had rehearsed. He reiterated the experimental nature of the project, using language that was a bit more explicit than what was in the written agreement. He reminded her about the liability waivers her grandson had signed. He did not cite the Supreme Court's latest position on felon volunteers, but he had key sections of the majority opinion memorized in case he needed them. He salted his speech with a proper dash of sympathy, but not so much as to sound guilty of anything but attempting to advance the scientific interests of humanity.

The sun continued to sink, but the air refused to give up any of its heat. By the time he bullied through his spiel, sweat was streaming down his face and turning the upper half of his white collared shirt a nearly translucent gray.

By contrast Mrs. Perkins' neck remained dry. So dry that Cole found himself wondering whether she suffered from some kind of dysplasia that prevented her pores from functioning properly. Spongy skin tags sprouted here and there among the fine gray curls of her remaining hair and for a surreal moment he entertained the notion that they had soaked up the missing moisture and any moment now would blossom with strange and hostile flowers.

Bodies bothered Cole. Always had, and now more than ever. Every body, really. Even, sometimes especially, his own. Their paradoxical density and squishiness. The sloppy disconnect between a finite sack of flesh and its immeasurable consciousness. The zombie hordes of autonomous subsystems that allegedly piled up to a self.

Atop this ambient phobic thrum ticked an egg timer of dread. Despite her outward calm Cole couldn't help but feel that any second now Mrs. Perkins was going to unleash on him. So far the old woman had not even once turned her face in his direction to register the horrible news or the calculated callousness with which he was delivering it.

Her silence should have made things easier. A sight better than the righteous hatred and sudden violence he'd suffered earlier that week. But something about her stoic bearing was triggering defense mechanisms he could hardly identify, much less disarm. As if she knew all that he could tell her. Far more in fact. As if she was simply waiting for him to catch up.

Just before he summoned the words to beg off, Cole heard a sort of moaning sound from inside the house. He had seen no one else about and assumed she lived alone. The sound was oddly harmonic in its voicing–doubled, yet distinctly individual, with a slight delay in between. Cole swiveled his head to the nearest window but he could see nothing through the overlapping pair of timeworn curtains. Even when they jerked ever so slightly away from the screen, as if tugged by an unseen hand. The twin layers of meshing, the interior gloom, and the contrasting light outside gave Cole the disorienting sensation of descending through layers of skin with a microscope. Distracted and tense as he was, he nearly seized when Mrs. Perkins began to sing.

"Way out west, they got a name, for rain and wind and fire."

She wasn't belting it, by any means. Her voice was both kinds of low. *"The rain is Tess, the fire's Joe, they call the wind Mariah."*

Hearing those lyrics sung outside the lab confirmed Cole's sense that he was operating at an informational disadvantage. Black Mariah was the project's internal codename. Singing "They Call the Wind Mariah" from *Paint Your Wagon* was just a grim, contagious joke, something the techs did to break the monotony. They never meant it to be cruel.

"Why they call it Black Mariah?" Mrs. Perkins said.

"Pardon me?"

"You heard me. Do they only use it on us black folk?"

"Who told you that?"

"Answer my question!"

In the tense lull that followed that strange moan returned. This time Cole thought he heard within its weird harmony the whimper of a child. As far as he was concerned, kids were the worst kind of bodies. Kids were chaos incarnate.

"Is there a child in there? Do you need to—" he said.

"Nevermind her," she cut in. "Gets fussy this time of day is all. Answer the question."

At first Cole thought maybe she made her money looking after other people's children. The idea of it overwhelmed him for a second. Then a detail from the skimmed case file sitting on his passenger seat floated over in the hot still air.

Marcus had a daughter.

When invited to volunteer for their experiments, Mrs. Perkin's grandson had just started serving a life sentence for murdering a liquor store owner killed during a robbery. Marcus pled not guilty, and claimed throughout the trial that he was the wrong man, at home looking after his baby daughter at the time. He had a couple arrests for pot possession and disturbing the peace. Nothing violent, just stupid stuff from his youth, but none of it helped. An oddly confident identification by the wife hiding in the back carried more weight with the jury than an alibi from an infant. The file said nothing about the child's mother or Marcus's parents, but presumably

Great Grandma Perkins played a role in raising her.

"It's complicated," Cole said, shifting in his seat. He was pretending to get more comfortable, but what he was really doing was angling away from the window so that he might at least avoid an ambush. The thought of this child's hand tugging at his neck like it had with the curtain was giving him the screaming meemies.

"How 'bout you uncomplicate it then?" Mrs. Perkins said. "You owe me that much. And you can start by leaving out the fifty-cent words. You ain't impressing anybody."

She was right of course. He owed her that much and more. But fifty-cent words were where he banked all his social anxiety. Long before the Asperger's diagnosis or the hard-won PhD, ever since he could read on his own really, they'd been pouring out of him like a slot machine stuck on jackpot.

"It originated with a racehorse," Cole said. "Born in Harlem, 1826. Some sources run wild with this, no pun intended, and claim a connection between *Mariah* and *Mare*, which is interesting given the implicit connection to *nightmare...*"

Mrs. Perkins found that neither implicit nor interesting. Her face screwed up at his robot librarian routine.

"Other sources say it started as colorful vernacular for a marooned ship or a horse-drawn hearse. Dreaded vessels of death. That sort of thing. It seems to have become a catchall for any large black mode of transport. By 1846, it was mainly used as a synonym for police escort vehicles. You know, paddywagons. James Joyce used it that way in *Ulysses*. There are cognates with that meaning in Dutch, Swedish, Russian, Finnish, almost certainly other languages as well."

Wordy as all that was, it was still only half the story. He left out the Black Mariah variants of hearts and stud poker, despite a deep fascination with the meta relevance of a wild card that gets reassigned every time the queen of spades appears. For all sorts of obvious reasons he wasn't comfortable sharing the probably-apocryphal-anyway explanation from Brewer's 1898 *Dictionary of Phrase and Fable* that traces the term to a black roominghouse owner in Boston by the name of Mariah Lee, equally infamous for her great bulk as for her habit of snitching on johns who abused her girls. He skipped as well the Marvel comic book villain modeled after her, enemy to Luke Cage and memorably portrayed by Alfre Woodard in the TV series.

In the interests of time, Cole also left out the term's use by Scottish soldiers in WWI as slang for the sixteen inch shells fired by the largest German artillery, which Cole assumed traced back to its meaning of a transport for death. He likewise neglected the series of experimental diesel-electric locomotives, which almost certainly referred back to the racehorse.

"Black Mariah was also the nickname of Thomas Edison's experimental film studio," Cole went on. "The first to use special effects, by the way, when they recreated the beheading of Mary, Queen of Scots. No special effects needed in 1903, though, when they filmed the first legally sanctioned electrocution. A Coney Island fixture named Topsy the Elephant was executed for the crime of killing one of its trainers. It's this intersection of prisoner transport and pioneering technology where our team's use of it begins to make sense."

"Not to me it don't," Mrs. Perkins said.

"I'm sorry, ma'am. I'm a real motormouth when I get going. What do you need me to clarify?"

"I don't need anything from you but the truth."

"Our Black Mariah was an experimental engine of teleportation," he said. "Do you know what teleportation means?"

"I'm not stupid, junior," she said. "I've seen Star Trek."

"Well, I led the team that made it work in real life."

Cole didn't suppress the pride in his voice. Even now, even here, even to her, he could separate the technical feat from its awful application.

"You made it work, huh. How's that?"

"Basically, we turned matter into data by passing it through a small, artificial black hole."

She wrinkled her nose at the thought of it.

"As momentous as that was, though, that turned out to be the easy part. The real trick was how to retrieve the data and turn it back into matter.

Explaining how we did that would fill a whole high school's worth of blackboards with equations you wouldn't understand. Suffice it to say that we ultimately used quantum entanglement to dodge the whole problem. We shaped the event horizon in such a way that the test subject was both entering and exiting the black hole at the same instant.

"Inanimate objects were pretty straightforward. Scrape a sample for the post-port checksum, scan it, encode it, check for consistency, and bam! Bob's your uncle. We got all sorts of things to pop into the decom chamber just like that tennis ball in *Poltergeist*. Living things… well, living things weren't quite that simple. The problem was not just what we were teleporting, but when. The atoms in living things are never static, right? They're superfast curveballs of organic entropy. Can't hit a curve ball if you lose sight of it, even for an instant. Might as well close your eyes. But once we were able to clock our cell state capture to within a few thousandths of a second, we could lock in the when, more or less. Any organism could then be expressed in a finite amount of code. But the file size for a human being… well, it was just astronomically huge and the quantum packets we use for transport can only hold so much data…"

"The what now?"

"People were basically too… ample to fit through our tiny black hole."

"Hmm," Mrs. Perkins said, disappointed. "But my Marcus was lean."

"Yeah, well, I didn't mean it literally. Anyway, we solved that problem too. Back in 2018 biologists announced the discovery of a new organ."

Mrs. Perkins exhaled through her nose hard enough to clear both nostrils. "Can't you do this any faster?"

"I'm sorry, ma'am, but if you want a real explanation, I'm afraid this is as fast as I can go."

She just stared into space and waited, and so he went on.

"They called it the interstitium. You know how if you look up into the sky at night there's all this space between the stars? Well the interstitium is our inner space. A layer of fluid padding in our organs. Inside our skin, inside our blood. Quite large in proportion. A whole lot of relatively empty inner space. The key thing to understand is that it's more or less the same in everyone. Just water and collagen. The interstitium gave us a new constant for a much more radical compression algorithm."

He paused again, looking to see if he'd lost her, but Mrs. Perkins was right behind him.

"You fried out all the fat and crammed the cracklins through the hole."

"Exactly!"

"Then you tried adding it back on the other side. With a computer or something. Like my Marcus was a cup of instant you could toss in a microwave."

"Yes! Exactly. Instant being the operative word. At least in theory. In the same way the human ear cannot tell the difference between a properly encoded MP3 file and its original, full-spectrum recording, our teleported subjects should have been, well, for all intents and purposes, they should have been the same. Moreover, if we did our job properly, the entire process should be imperceptible to the subject."

"But you *didn't* do your job properly!"

She started singing again before he could protest. Slow and low, same as before. Each word ripping up something rooted way down deep.

"Mariah blows the stars around. And sends the clouds a-flying. Mariah makes the mountain sound like folks were up there dying."

Cole did his best to hide how much that verse disturbed him. When she trailed off again he tried to explain. "It did take us a while to fine tune it, and yes, we did make a lot of… well, nothing to call them but mistakes, but by early last year we had successfully teleported seven worms, three frogs, two kittens, and a puppy."

"No chimps?" Mrs. Perkins asked.

"Our CEO has strict prohibitions against experimenting on animals of a certain order."

"No problem with convicts though, huh?"

"No, ma'am. So long as they can consciously consent."

"Hmm. I reckon once you dangle a little pardon ain't hardly a one who don't consent?"

"Hardly a one," Cole agreed.

"But if you knew it would work, you wouldn't need to offer pardons!" Cole winced.

"Would it make you feel any better if I told you I was the one who blew the whistle? They fired me for it too. Probably tanked my career. They even threatened my parents to keep my mouth shut. Despite all that, I'm out here of my own volition, telling you the truth."

"None of that makes a lick of difference to me."

"Then I don't know what else I can do."

"I do. You can tell me what happened to my grandson."

This time he was ready for her singing. At least he thought he was. Until she got to the end and his mind shrank from the image it made in his head.

"Then one day I left my girl. I left her far behind me. And now I'm lost, I'm oh so lost not even God can find me."

"The truth is we don't know," Cole said after a long silence, hoping she would finally hear the regret in his voice. Hoping he could leave it at that. But Mrs. Perkins' face made it abundantly clear he could not. Something had changed in the composition of the scene and Cole felt compelled to determine what.

Formerly turned away, or shrouded in late afternoon shadow, her face was now lit with a strange glow. Almost like a Renaissance painting of a martyred saint, only one done by Kehinde Wiley. Cole blinked a few times, his sense of reality abandoning him until he realized that the sun had dipped enough to trigger the solar cell of her porch light. He took a breath. Opened his mouth. Closed it. Opened it again and began to tell her the full truth.

"I'm no longer convinced that teleporting a human being will ever be possible. Especially when the human in question is a prisoner. At first we had no idea what was going on. We'd put the subject in the compression chamber—"

"What happens to the original?" Mrs. Perkins said.

"Pardon?" Cole said.

"Do they go through the black hole or not?"

"It doesn't make sense on anything but the quantum level. We collected the one that didn't, just before it did."

"You just made a Xerox machine! That ain't teleporting."

"Well, the distinction is fine enough to be numerically irrelevant. We captured and transported complex biostates in their entirety, ma'am. Mid-heartbeat. Mid firing of synapses. That puppy I mentioned? It teleported while scratching an ear and continued scratching on the other side!"

He left out the fact that it never stopped scratching. Not until it hit brain matter.

"I'm gonna ask you again. What happened to my Marcus?"

"I'm not sure that's a healthy thing to focus on."

"Why can't you people ever give a straight answer?"

"The antecedents are annihilated. Is that what you wanted to hear?"

The look she gave Cole then was not one he could withstand. He dropped his eyes before going on.

"As I was saying, imprisoned humans delivered results that were entirely unpredictable. Sometimes… um, well, sometimes a *portion* of the subject would come through and we'd think something went wrong with the decompression algorithm. Until we found the other portions… elsewhere. Embedded in the prison wall. Grafted with a particular tree just beyond the fence line. In one case some remains were recovered from the trunk of a car that happened to be driving by the prison at the time of the experiment. We thought the data packets were splintering and energy was leaking somewhere. We thought information might have gotten lost in the black hole. But we could measure it exiting. Nothing was lost. We just couldn't direct or contain it. Eventually we reasoned it had something to do with desire."

"Desire?" She said it like the thing expressed by the word existed at a great distance from her, something dimly remembered. Or maybe she said it like that thing was far too close and precious to acknowledge at all, lest it drive her mad.

"Whatever you want to call it," Cole said. "Faith. Willpower. Intention. The quantum soul. Shed of mass, if only for nanoseconds, the information that comprises a fully sentient being refused to behave in predictable ways. Or, more accurately, in controllable ways. Despite our every attempt to corral them, they broke out and followed their own prime directive. Which in the case of the prisoners meant escape. Most of them didn't get very far. None that we know of did so intact. A very small number eluded our recovery teams and disappeared altogether. Your grandson Marcus was one of those. I like to believe he won his freedom. That he's out there somewhere, living a new life, but that's just wishful thinking."

Mrs. Perkins was shaking her head and stroking her bottom lip. So hard Cole worried she might rub away some skin. She'd turned away from him again. Beyond her the fireflies had begun to wink in and out of sight.

"How many people you try this on before you shut it down?" she asked the dark.

There seemed no point in hiding anything else, given what he'd already shared.

"Twenty-two," Cole admitted. "Twenty-seven if you count the cadavers."

"How many were people of color?"

"Too many," Cole said quickly. "Ma'am, that's why I'm here. To do my penance. What can I say besides I am utterly and terribly sorry?"

"Ain't enough. Not even by your reckoning. You need to meet someone before you go."

Mrs. Perkins finished her song for good measure. If before her tone was barbed, now it was just bone-weary and blue.

"*Out here they got a name for rain. For wind and fire only. But when you're lost and all alone, there ain't no word but lonely.*"

By then it was country dark and Cole felt on the verge of collapse. He'd been out on the road delivering terrible news for the better part of two weeks. He had one hell of a rough drive ahead of him to get back to his hotel room. That last thing on earth he wanted to do was meet the child of someone he killed.

"I'm sorry, ma'am, but I really need to get going."

"Uh-uh. No way. Not yet. All this time you've been dancing round your devilry, using fancy words and fancy ideas to keep from feeling anything. Trying to quiet them screams in your head. Time to lose them words and listen, son. Time to sit with what you done."

They didn't enter the house through the front. Instead they went around to a side door. Mrs. Perkins insisted that he walk out ahead of her. She didn't help him find his way by turning on any additional lights. Once off the porch Cole had to put his hands out in front of him to keep from colliding with anything.

"Sure gets dark out here," he said.

"Just you wait," Mrs. Perkins said.

Lone trees and other unidentifiable clusters of denser dark in the foreground gave him the impression of an audience, of some sort of shadow gallery assembled in mute witness of a gallows walk. Eventually he found the screen door he was supposed to enter but its spring was shot, or gone entirely, and he nearly fell over at its lack of resistance, his weight working against him, desperate grip on the handle the only thing keeping him upright.

It was hardly any less dark inside. Low ceilings and a clutter of old furniture enhanced the feeling of walking into a trap. A few circular nightlights at each outlet led him into the living room, dim orange moons hovering like small faces just above the baseboards.

Mrs. Perkins finally cut on a small lamp in the entranceway just as Cole was turning around to ask her who it was she wanted him to meet.

She just jabbed her chin in the opposite direction.

For a second he felt as if he'd placed himself into the Black Mariah. Space and reality were bending out of shape. The small living room had been converted into a makeshift nursery. A rickety plywood base supported a freestanding wash basin. Even in that meager light he could see the water was tinted red with blood. Piles of towels and extra sheets were neatly folded beside it. Dominating the room, and blocking the front door, was a second-hand hospital bed. On the bed, coiled and flexing, was a tangle of limbs that took a few seconds to mentally unravel. When the shock subsided a little, Cole understood that he was looking at the meshed bodies of Marcus Perkins and his daughter.

The fusing was thorough. Seemingly haphazard and yet somehow viable. Angry welts marked every visible point of intersection. Skin upthrust along the fault lies, already knitting into scar tissue. Overlapping tendons strained and bulged. The child thrashed within her second womb. Marcus flailed his misplaced arms in a vain attempt to cradle her.

When they lifted their heads and looked at him Cole saw how nearly their hearts overlapped. How closely their movements synced. His eyes jerked away and his mind threatened to flee the scene entirely, but he forced himself to look back. As their mouths opened in furious overtone, Cole did as he was told. He sat with what he had done. He lost his words and listened.

They spoke of old evils with ever evolving definitions. Of jails and hearts and hearses. Of power, projection, and invention. Vessels of doom and instruments of war. A dread carriage of justice and revenge. They even named the driver.

When they finished speaking Cole's eyes were shining with shame and awe. Their plan was masterful; audacious and genius enough to outdo Edison. Cole only nodded once. Both to confirm that it was possible and to confirm that he was willing to execute it. Behind him, in a lullaby whisper, Mrs. Perkins resumed her song.

"Mariah blows the stars around. And sends the clouds a-flying. Mariah makes the mountain sound like folks were up there dying."

Hunger — Curtis Harrell

Curtis *earned his MFA from the University of Arkansas and has been writing and publishing for over thirty years. Most recently, his works have been collected and published by Sley House Publishing under the title* MELPOMENE'S GARDEN.

* * *

History credits that runt Cump Sherman with the "war is hell" adage, and even though that rat-faced sadist is correct, I am here to tell you that I said it first. He uttered the phrase eight years after the war at a commencement for mewling Union cadets in their prissy blue, long after his inauspicious inauguration in the western theater as a nervous Nell. Our cavalry had intercepted the Louisville papers shortly after his debut, and when we read about his "condition" we laughed out loud and wrung our hands in mockery. I saw him soon after that, in 1862, the first part of April. I was a private in Hardee's brigade in the Army of Mississippi. I remember the morning of the 6th. It was a Sunday; there had been two nights of barbarous rain, but that morning promised skies clear enough for a sermon in the dew. We had moved up within a quarter mile of Sherman's camp before dawn and were waiting for light. The disembodied white of dogwood blossoms loomed in the false dawn, and the promising scent of spring belied the events of that day. We could hear Yankee hymns floating through the trees. But Powell's reconnaissance betrayed our position earlier than we wanted, so we came up in pursuit. As I and my comrades flowed like ghosts out of the woods on Sherman's right, I could hear him berating a captain for sounding a false alarm. Then he turned and saw us, not needing the glass he held in his hand for we were that close. We volleyed, and a shot blew his orderly backwards off his horse, and that poor Christian writhed on the ground, heart-spray coloring up Sherman's white gelding to its hocks. Sherman raised his hands to his face and shouted, and I let off my scatter gun and ripped his knuckles with bird shot. As he wheeled his horse around, we let out the glorious rebel yell and rolled them back up halfway to Pittsburg Landing where Grant hobbled around on his crutches. We lost that battle, like many others, because our hunger was sharper than our indignation. We valued roasted meat above a deadly goose chase. We filled our bellies while our beloved General Johnston slipped off his great mount, Fire Eater, and bled out into his boot. That was Shiloh.

I should have whispered the phrase a month later, after midnight in an unrelenting spring torrent, but I didn't. The brim of my hat is all that kept me from drowning like a turkey. I stood picket as the storm pelted me with hail the size of goober peas. Hell for me that night wasn't the vision of slaughtered youth dead on the ground; hell was the irony that I was suffering for a cause I had no stake in. Let me make it clear that I hold no other being in bondage, and I think it abhorrent to the soul to do so. I detour around politics whenever possible since there is no clear road in that dark country. I was the county librarian before Hardee recruited me from my home south of Pocahontas, Arkansas. I relished my duty as the bringer of books to the hungry literati. I traded eggs and milk for collections of the classics and read them in my spare moments which were many. I ensured my library wagon sheltered the meagre collection I shared with my hill country brethren on my routes through the backwoods and across the swollen rivers. But Hardee's persuaders had convinced me that the blue bellies were going to carnally insult my wife and two daughters. They told me that my library would be burned like the Romans did Alexandria. I believed that when I signed the papers, but a hard rain tests a man's beliefs.

Standing picket in a deluge like that was a study in anxiety and dread. I was totally blind, but I could visualize the forest by the sound of the rain beating down on it. Close-up, I could hear the pop of drops hitting the newly spread leaves of the mulberries, the showering spray of water falling through pine needles. But I could also hear the deeper susurrus of rainfall on the stubblefield beyond. I held my musket out before me in case a Yank might run into my bayonet.

Then, a sliver of moonlight angled under the ceiling of rain, and I could see the working of some odd fabric across the entire sky. As I peered closer, wiping the wet from my eyes, I saw the heavens fall on the field before me, triangular shapes flapping through the night downward. Even though I had willed myself alone in the storm, I heard the raising of voices, first in warning and then in terror and, finally, pain. Screams drowned out the background rush of rain, but they quickly choked. I never heard any shot fired. I never saw a single muzzle-flash in the eyeless void. Clouds blacked out the moon again, and after the cacophony, what sounded like sleeves flapping in the wind, all was quiet except for the ubiquitous plashing of the rain. Slowly I moved forward, toward the sound of the voices. But there were no more voices. The rain slackened, and I walked into the field, my gun and all my senses erect. But there was nothing. The moon finally burst through the clouds flowing above, and the landscape came clear. Weapons lay scattered across the ground. But there were no bodies. I had heard at least a company through the rain, but there were no men here. Footprints pocked the fallow cornfield, but their makers had disappeared. An acrid noseful of phosphorous lingered in the rinsed air as though a chicken house may have stood nearby. I stood and listened for a long while. Convinced the enemy had vacated the field, I collected the rifles abandoned in the mud and staggered back to camp under the weight of my gains. A lone sentry halted me at the camp's edge as I sought the comfort of my tent and ordered me to drop my weapons. I did, all 20 of them, though the clatter roused no one.

An unfamiliar bugle tattoo woke me just after the dawn. I ignored it but then heard someone shouting and then my name.

"Private Penny! Fall in!"

I exited my tent, my clothes still damp and night dirt soiling the front of my blouse from the captured guns, and I saw Captain Drumpf sitting his mount in the new day.

"Are you the man responsible for the capture of these weapons," he queried as he swept his hand toward the tepee of Springfields standing outside the sutler's tent, "and how did you accomplish that, my good man and soldier?"

Captain Drumpf rested both hands on the saddle horn and genuflected while his horse pissed a stream that ran sizzling under our cooking fire.

This man's reputation preceded him like an odorous fog, and I hoped he was merely passing through our encampment on the way to somewhere else to taint. His name was dropped frequently in the campfire gossip, but I now had opportunity to see him in his corpulent flesh.

I refuse to mince words: privilege of any sort, especially when it came to filthiness of lucre, sickened me. Captain Drumpf was a moron on a fat mare. He was the son of a rich planter in Texas, and even the poor souls in his care still picking the scabs from their ankles where galley chains galled them across an ocean knew he was an idiot in an ostrich plume. His fastidiousness in his grooming and his overdecorated uniform telegraphed his incompetence and his discomfort in the saddle.

"I am," I said, "and I just picked them up off the ground."

"Good work," he replied.

I simply gazed up at him, addled from fatigue, and said, "It was like the wind took them."

"Good work," he said again, and the mare ignored the spurring toward headquarters and nibbled on clover as Captain Drumpf pretended to look dramatically toward the horizon.

"If you don't mind my asking, sir, why are you interested in this?"

"There have been other reports, one or two, maybe, seem similar to yours."

"I have not yet made a report, sir. I had planned on conveying my narrative when time allowed."

"News like this travels, soldier."

"Is there something I should know about this, sir?"

Drumpf glared down at me from under his comical headpiece and said, "Who are you to question me, soldier. I am a captain, do you understand, in search of intelligence that is military, and it is your sole duty to give it."

"I am a soldier and a citizen, sir. I have left my home to assist in the admonishment of the enemy and their aggressive tendencies. I am a peaceful man abandoning my better nature to keep the scavenging Yankee scum off our womenfolk."

"Bravo for you, son. I, too, am a peaceful man looking for any advantages that might fall our way."

His gall, ironically, burned in *my* craw, and I could not help myself from replying, "The cookfire tales contradict that assessment. I have spent many a lonely evening listening for our nemesis through the woods, and I have thought that only a man experienced in taking another man's life, as Cain did Abel, is truly capable of peace. That man has harnessed his murderous urges for gentleness and reconciliation."

"Hah!" Drumpf responded, "and what does your story make of men who have not? Killed, that is. Men who aren't distinguished yet, that is, themselves in battle."

"That man rides a fat mare and is but a toy in the game of war. He is better off keeping his questions to himself and riding in the rear for he is not peaceful, only harmless."

"Many good orders come from the rear," Drumpf sputtered in his saddle as I about-faced and broke wind in farewell.

We daily sparred with the Yanks as we both moved easterly in our campaigns. I volunteered for picket duty most nights because I enjoyed the solitude, and I didn't let my nerves conjure apparitions in the buggy dark. I'd rather see those seeking to kill me than have a cannon ball unexpectedly bounce through the cornstalks and separate my top from my bottom. Nearly a fortnight later I was searching for the Yankee line soon after dark when the grease-heavy scent of a cookfire caused my gut to grumble. I crept forward until I could see the flicker of flame through the wild lilacs and the honeysuckle. I was astonished by how often the Yanks neglected to fortify their camps. I could have marched up and slapped their cook with my tallywhacker had I so desired. But I settled my back against a fallen oak and enviously watched the camaraderie of these men, boys mostly, as they settled for the evening, joking and lounging in their undergarb. The scene evoked memories of a summer camp-out, so much so that tears welled unwelcome in the corners of my eyes as I recollected visions of my dear Annie and our daughters when we enjoyed the adventure of the out-of-doors. I suppressed an urge to lay down my rifle and join these others of my kind in human companionship. Anger surged, not at them, but at my situation. I held no hatred nor animosity against any of these men personally. Something so abstract as an idea, some dim duty, separated me and my lonely post from the collegial comfort of their fires. I believe that all men are created equal and that all men are equal in their opportunities. I have taught men of both colors to read. But I was personally envious of the meat roasting while my stomach knotted in hunger. Oddly, even though I could distinguish scraps of taunting and mirth as they called to one another, I relaxed, and soon I had nodded into a blessed sleep.

The feathery glancing of falling leaves on my fists startled me from my slumber, and it was as if the woods rained down on me. Almost as soon as I opened my eyes the Yanks doused their fires. Once again in blackness I heard the ripping of air and shrieks and flags flapping in the night. An air both humid and fetid blew against my face, and I pressed my lips together in disgust. The domestic scene I had witnessed just moments before was now an unfathomable massacre I could only hear. I peered into an invisible horror the way that every soldier does, but I was bewildered as to the machinations of this style of death. Again, there were no shots fired. I could hear not one mortal struggle but many, too many, a butchery of flesh and muscle being rent with razors, the clopping of bone on bone. In only minutes silence swallowed the field save for the sizzling of embers where doused campfires smoked in the darkness. I resuscitated a torch and peered around in the puny light. Again, rifles lay discarded on the ground, but this time there were uniforms scattered also, all torn into shreds. The stench of feculence lingered and filled my nostrils in the dark. This had been a picket camp—hence no earthworks—and I recovered seventeen rifles. Before I made my way back to camp I raided the cook pots to stifle my constant hunger, but the beans were spattered with excrement.

The next morning I woke to see Captain Largo sitting at my writing table, the letter I had started for my wife in his hand as he looked over at me.

"Hardee wants to see you in his tent," he said, "and that Major Drumpf is back again. He's interested in those ghost rifles you brought in last night."

"Major?" I retorted, "He was but a Captain the last I saw him."

"Attrition," said Captain Largo, "bad luck, or money will reward almost anyone."

I splashed my face with water from the bowl and strode to Hardee's tent where his orderly acknowledged me and waved me through the flap.

"Private Penny," said Hardee as he motioned me to a stool beside where Drumpf lounged on Hardee's cot, "Major Drumpf has an interest in your reconnaissance last evening."

Drumpf eyed me, propped on his elbow, and cleared his throat, "What kind of man habitually encounters unknown violence? A peaceful man, hiding some truth, who needs to know his place in the order of things?"

"I have told you before that I am a soldier and a citizen. I adhere to my duty despite it including circumstances beyond my control or understanding."

"Does it strike you as odd that this bizarre event has occurred again, to you, that is?"

"Everything about this war is bizarre, sir. I have sat paring my nails unaware of a brisk fight unfolding in what should have been my earshot. I have seen men survive being shot through both lungs or the brain. I have seen boys fall dead for no reason. I have seen vile racists shot through the heart and drooling blood on their necklaces of black fingers. Now I speak to you about captured weapons even though I follow other men's orders."

Drumpf sat fully upright and pressed his duck lips together in a laughable grimace, "I have been studying other occurrences like those that have befallen you; tell me all the details you can about these rifles, these things in the air."

"I stood picket. Out of utter blackness the sky fell on these poor Yankee soldiers. I saw nothing I could describe that would make sense to you. Have other men seen anything?"

"You've seen nothing, either time, you are telling me."

"I have seen nothing but the bloody aftermath and rifles discarded on the ground."

"You've no clue as to what did this?"

"Have other men seen anything?"

"No," he replied and retrieved a purse from his belt, "perhaps you need some reward for your bravery, soldier. How about some genuine Yankee greenbacks to refresh your memory?"

"Have they smelled the air afterward?"

"Yes, that is a common denominator. How about five dollars?"

"Do you know what is responsible for these events?"

"That is none of your concern."

"In my experience, a bad smell is a warning."

"That is none of your concern," Drumpf repeated.

"Foul-smelling victuals should be thrown on the ground. Noxious wounds should go under the bone-saw. Soured hay harbors vermin and parasites. The abuse of rank has a stench to it as well. I believe I shall smell you coming the next time."

"Watch your tongue, private. Mind your duty."

"My duty compels me to send these bluecoats home in boxes. My duty requires me to wholly place my faith in the orders of another man, no matter his skill or ambitions. My duty, ultimately, becomes a tightrope walk between mercy and victory. Chasing banshees or mollifying morons has no role in that equation."

"Hardee," shouted Drumpf, "place this man under arrest."

But Hardee, a brigadier general, kicked the cot from under Drumpf and shoved me through the tent flap before I could ridicule the fat man sitting with his precious pants in the dust.

The end of June I once again found myself scouting for the Yankee line after dusk when I discerned camp sounds from the other side of a stand of pine and scrubby cedars. Beyond, in a vast meadow, the Union soldiers milled like Baptists for a feast. A quartered hog rotated on spits, and I could smell the green corn shucks roasting in the coals. Soldiers lounged around the cook fires with their dice and playing cards, their suspenders hanging below their knees. The cooks prepared long tables commandeered from some poor farmer's house, hand-embroidered tablecloths slipping onto the ground. The air was succulent with the scent of meat. There were no fortifications, no Union pickets, no earthworks, or trenches or even makeshift fences. These were new recruits playing picnic on a balmy Tennessee summer evening.

I turned and fled through the woods, no more than a half mile to where Hardee sat smoking in his camp chair outside his tent. Between gasps I reported the proximity of the enemy, and he swung up into the saddle, calling the charge, his stallion stamping the ground and snorting the night air. We all sprang forward, riding and running through the sparse woods, ripping through brambles, our guns forward, and, when the cook fires flickered through the underbrush we let loose our rebel yell.

The Yanks froze like deer in a full moon, but then they broke to the rear in their nightshirts, dropping their rifles and soiling themselves as they sprinted barefoot. We pursued them to the opposite side of the camp, the fleetest of our men, once their guns empty, clubbing the half-clad Blue with the stocks of their weapons like slender shillelaghs. Our boys trampled the wounded as we ran like hell hounds across the grazed grass, but, like at Shiloh, we broke off too soon. The smell of the feast was too much for the ravenous boys in the dirty butternut. Our horse routed them northward, and, when the cavalry returned, all of the men fell onto the meat and the corn. I, too, dropped my gun and used both hands to grab the grub the Yanks had abandoned, cramming steaming pork into my mouth.

As I satisfied my hunger, licking the delicious grease from my fingers and belching, I saw none other than Drumpf ambling into our midst, not ten yards from me, wearing the insignia of a colonel now, but as usual appearing when food was to be had and long after the danger had fled. His orderly shoved his way past the privates gorging themselves around the fires and brought enough meat for ten men to a table near where Colonel Drumpf sat his mare and surveyed the field as if he had vanquished the enemy singlehandedly. Drumpf dismounted and made a show of having his man produce silverware and linens from a huge wicker picnic case. He had another personal valet bring an ornately carved dining chair from somewhere in his personal train, and Drumpf settled into his meal with the gusto of a baron or a thief. Despite my continuous hunger, my stomach turned at this display, so I turned as well only to hear my name shouted to my back.

"Private Penny!"

I ignored him, but he called my name again. I dutifully turned and approached as he tore wads of meat from a shank and smacked the mouthfuls down, drippings running down his weak chin.

"Private Penny," he said with his jaws full, "did you smell me coming this time? Or did I surprise you like those things you see in the night?"

"The only thing that surprises me is that you found the battlefield."

"Soldier, that talk is insolence bordering on insubordination. Mind your speech or I will have you put in the stockade."

"Do you have any military queries, or are we here to discuss you and your aroma," I said.

"There might be a rhythm to these mysteries, a schedule, if you will. You will discuss the exact dates of your sightings with my corporal."

"I will return to my post, sir."

"You will speak immediately with my corporal."

And, at that, I wheeled about to search for Captain Largo, but Drumpf's orderly snatched my elbow.

"I," Colonel Drumpf intoned, completely full of himself, the pronoun as delicious on his tongue as the pilfered meat, "am now in your chain of command. Go with my orderly to see the corporal."

My inclination to duty stopped at that moment. The papers I had signed meant nothing to me as I watched Colonel Drumpf wallow in the privilege of his expensive rank. He embodied the frustration I felt as a soldier and a citizen trapped in the web of the ideal and its hideous incarnation.

"No," I said, and wrenched my arm from his orderly's grip. When he grabbed me again, I dropped him with an elbow to his forehead. I lunged at Colonel Drumpf only to have the valet rob me my consciousness with the butt of a musket.

When I revived, I found myself in a Union brig wagon in the center of the field. The cage was formed from riveted metal straps, and though it rocked from my shaking of the flat bars, it held steady. My view was not dissimilar from my nightly vantage point as a picket. Totally removed from their company I watched the men continue to gorge themselves on the Yankee feast. I could see that Drumpf had polished off more than his share and now sipped liquor from a fancy brandy decanter his valet used to brim his cup. Strangely, my incarceration both held me captive but freed me from any pursuit of the enemy. My responsibilities were taken from me as well as their dreadful charge. I relaxed as I hadn't since I left my Annie and two girls. But the skies had thickened since dusk, and the smell of rain weighed heavy in the air. I could almost taste the loam exhaling its mossy breath into the sullen evening. Clouds began to flow over the three-quarters moon, and the sky became a black lid over the fire-lit field. As I watched the men lounging around the fires, leisurely cleaning their rifles and bathing themselves with buckets of boiled water, déjà vu crept up my spine. I had seen this scene before but never anticipated it. But now, this time, I knew what was going to happen.

"Captain Largo!" I shouted from my cage.

But the only reply was Colonel Drumpf's fruity cough and a half-laugh.

"He can't help you now, Private Penny."

And then I heard the flags flapping in the sky. Our men didn't know to douse the fires in hopes of hiding from the scourge, whatever it was that dropped from the heavens and ripped everything asunder. I sat down heavily on the straw-covered floor of the wagon and watched in horror as bird-creatures fell on my friends and comrades. They were the size of hunch-backed pygmies, but they had buzzards' wings. In the measly light I saw them descend as if a colossal sack of vultures had been spilled from above. But these were no vultures. Their hideous torsos sagged at the belly, and their pendulous teats were feathered. The nails on their feet and hands curved in gruesomely polished talons. Many landed on my wagon in guttural dismay as the iron straps kept them from eviscerating me, and they shat on me in shrieking anger, and the feces dripped through the bars and spoiled my haven, flattened my hair to my skull. These were harpies, the creatures Virgil described, but their monstrousness exceeded his ancient description I had pondered in the lantern light of my library wagon. They were ravenous and unrelenting, half-bird and half-hag, and, in the wing-blown firelight, I witnessed the murder of every man in that field that night.

But I remember what happened to Colonel Drumpf to this day. He struggled to rise with the assistance of his valet, but that young sycophant was snatched into the scream-riddled sky. Drumpf reached for his ridiculously long saber but could not release it from its obstinate scabbard, and the largest harpy I had seen upended him and sat his heaving chest. She slowly and deliberately tore at Drumpf's breast with her time-worn talons until blood spewed from between his lips, and he coughed skyward in bright red clots. She sliced through the medals into bare flesh until she laid open his beating heart, which, to my amazement was not black and shriveled but crimson and jumping in its rib-hole, and ragged spurts wet her feathers until they glistened in the firelight. Then, she looked at me. Her human face was as wizened as a grandmother's who had seen centuries of greed and stupidity and motherly loss, and her eyes expressed a hunger I had never imagined. Her pupils were black saucers of wanting, horrific bottomless pits of insatiable craving. I bore witness to an immortal Hunger in her stare, and it was then I realized that hunger was the taproot of all other emotions and endeavors and dreams. That unquenchable desire, that gut-hollowing need, drove everything else. Her gaze showed me the wretched ugliness of those famished for power, for money, for fame. But I also saw that hunger perhaps drove nobler instincts, and I pitied those ravenous to save their homes, those yearning to show mercy when confronted with cruelty, those starving to share their love. I saw in that monster's lidless relentless orbs the hunger that drove Drumpf, the hunger that drove Sherman, the hunger that drives me.

It was then that I whispered, "war is hell," without a single mortal there to hear me.

Waif(u) — J. D. Keown

J.D. Keown lives on the North York Moors with his little hound of hell, Lola. He has always been an enthusiast of the horror genre and its many forms, and now writes ghastly, ghoulish stories of his own. J.D.'s fiction can be found in Blood Rites Horror, All World's Wayfarer, Dark Dossier, *Bag of Bones Press, and forthcoming from Lovecraftiana. His non-fiction will soon feature in* Caillou Pettis's The Inspiring World of Horror. *He is also the founder of* Night Terror Novels, *which published its debut anthology,* Ceci n'est pas une histoire d'horreur (This is Not a Horror Story), *in October 2021, and will be publishing its second anthology and first young adult anthology,* Nerve-Janglers: Thirteen Tales of Terror, *in late 2022. He can be reached via email at nightterrornovels@gmail.com, on Instagram or Twitter @JDKAuthor, or found on Goodreads at J.D. Keown.*

* * *

He comes to me in the dead of night, under a blanket of darkness as black as pitch; the perfect time for deeds dark and dastardly. This night is a stormy one, too. Wild and raw. Thunder cracks and lightning crashes, the sky alive with peals and flashes. The rain is ceaseless, the sort that soaks you right through to the bone, but even this is not enough to dispel the stink of the man. It's almost as though the taint of his crooked heart has eked its way to the surface, spewed out from his pores, and encrusted his body like a second skin: a filth so potent it pervades his very being. Rotten within, rotten without.

Beneath his hood, the man's hair is matted and greasy, its wispy strands clinging to his scalp like rat's tails. His beet-coloured face is pimpled and pocked, and the fingers that extend toward me are more akin to talons. Everything about him repulses me, and if I had skin, it would crawl. Ragged nails rake through my clayflesh; he sifts me through his fingertips and examines my texture by torchlight. I cringe at his touch.

With such close proximity—close enough that I can *feel* the heat of his rancid breath—I'm able to probe around inside his mind, can read his thoughts and sense his feelings. Among the jumbled mess, a note of triumph sings loudest and clearest; this is what he came for, he is here for me. He caresses my silt with an odd tenderness and a whimsical smile plastered across his face. Tired, red-rimmed eyes inspect my every grain as he chuckles his satisfaction.

'Perfect,' he calls me, but the way he leers leaves me feeling exposed. Violated, even.

The man has been plotting this for such a long time. Month upon month devoted to researching, learning, understanding. Many a sleepless night has been spent poring over forums and imageboards, niche blog sites and ancient internet archives tucked away in the shadowy recesses of the web. From the local libraries, he's borrowed books on all manner of subjects: works of theology and mythology; from esotericism to Taoism and everything else in between. Scripture from various religions, translated Hebrew texts on the art and practice of Kabbalah; the man is a glutton for knowledge, and his appetite is insatiable. He has gorged.

He is also well-versed in the tale of Rabbi Loew ben Bezalel. The legend goes that from the sediment of the Vltava River, the Rabbi erected a golem, a mighty creature of clay, and gave life to the inanimate through ancient rituals and incantations. The man's goal is simple: by recreating the Rabbi's method, he hopes to construct and give life to an automaton of his own.

His reasons why are not quite so transparent, but one thing is for certain: tonight is the night it all comes together, his months of research and secret scheming. Tonight is the night his plan is enacted. Failure is not—has never been—an option. He has invested far too much time, too much blood, sweat, and tears, to even consider it. For his labour to bear no fruit now is simply unthinkable.

The man has a flair for the theatrical, and he revels in the dramatics of it all: the black night, the squally weather, the quiet city and its empty streets. On these riverbanks, a wheelbarrow in tow, he relives—*revives, reimagines*—the myth. Prague sleeps; the spires of St. Vitus pierce the tar horizon, ever-watchful bastions through these wee twilight hours. The city lies dormant. Silent. Only the brave, stupid, or wicked would dare venture out on a night such as this.

For a minute or two he simply stands, arms akimbo, eyes pinched shut, and savours the moment. Were it not for his hunched posture, he might've cut an imposing silhouette against the black. Behind him, the vast river flows lazily, rain pitter-pattering as it showers its surface. He listens and he sways to the staccato beat it plays.

One deep breath and a hacking, phlegmy cough later, the man sets to work. He is entrenched up to his knees in the mire, and barehanded, he hauls lumps of mud into the barrow. I, unwilling but ultimately helpless, am torn from the earth with it. The bitter breeze batters his windbreaker and waterproofs, whipping them this way and that. Downpour bombards the Vltava, the din of its assault drowning out most other sounds. Even the rhythmic grunting of the man is all but stifled. His cheeks and nose are rosy-red by the time he's done; rain droplets intermingle with beads of perspiration on his brow. Squinting through the sweat, he scans the riverbank. No crime has been committed here, yet the man would prefer his deeds go unnoticed. Whatever he plans to do with *me*, I can be sure it won't be pleasant.

But nothing stirs. Nothing comes to my rescue.

Satisfied that he has enough material—and that he hasn't been seen—the man wipes his mud-caked hands on his trouser-legs and grasps the handles of the barrow. He glances around one last time before putting his back into it. The loamy ground refuses to yield, at first. It does not want him to steal me away; I am part of this earth, and I belong only to it. Who is he to claim me? Still, just as his forebears wrenched these riverbanks from Nature's bosom and built their sprawling metropolis atop it, the man bests the earth and wrestles the wheel free.

Up the bank we climb, steep and slick. Twice the man slips, cursing the dark, the rain, the gods. By the time we emerge onto Prague's streets, he is more mud than man, but the never-ending torrent makes short work of the grime. We stalk along rain-slicked roads and down dark alleys, just another shadow in the murk and the gloom.

It takes more than an hour and one bus ride for us to reach the man's dwelling. The dead-eyed expression of our driver suggests that the man could've wheeled a corpse on with him and he wouldn't have bat an eyelid. His eyes dance over the barrow full of clay, full of me, for but a moment, before he flicks them back to the road. Ask no questions, hear no lies: a sensible policy to adhere to in *any* city this late at night. The man flashes his return ticket and the driver grunts his acknowledgment. Doors hiss, engine growls, vehicle lurches. I am thrown about in my vessel. My prison. Besides the driver, we two are alone on the night bus. My captor puts on a bulky pair of headphones and settles in for the ride. I endure the tinny noise of his music and wish he were dead.

When we arrive, a further ten minutes are spent negotiating the barrow down a steep flight of stairs. The man lives in a basement letting; like most elements of human detritus, he exists out of sight, out of mind. The apartment block he inhabits is a *panelák*: a relic of bygone Czechoslovakia, and an enduring reminder of the communist influence in these parts. Neglected and ignored: which, I sense, is something the two share in common. It's a rundown building in an equally rundown neighbourhood. In short—a complete shithole, and that feels most fitting.

* * *

It rains again this evening. I watch the droplets race down the pane of the paltry rectangle that passes for a window here. The tiny, ground-level thing lets in a pathetic amount of sunlight, but I'm somewhat thankful for that. The less I have to see of the filthy hovel he calls a home, the better. It makes me sick.

I've been here so long this place has started to feel like purgatory. Time has become interminable, so I stare at the bald spot on the man's crown, and I think and I simmer. Simmer with a rage so fervent it eclipses everything else. Devours my train of thought. I hate this man, utterly loathe him. Sometimes, all I wish is for him to just *do* something, anything. Othertimes, I wish that the intensity of my glower would burn a hole right through his skull. Pray that by sheer willpower alone, I could end his miserable existence. So far, these prayers have gone unanswered, but I'm forever an optimist.

The lump of me has been sat on a makeshift worktop for about a week, or thereabouts, before the man so much as lifts a finger. He's a procrastinator through and through. I still do not know his real name, only that which he goes by online: thy_sculptor_96. There are about a dozen sites he frequents daily, all under this same handle. The Sculptor idles away much of his time on the computer, tip-tapping his keyboard and click-clacking his mouse. It drives me insane. Most of his time is spent lurking on a handful of imageboards and an obscure forum site called Incels Together, where he preaches hateful views to equally hateful sorts. The rest of it is spent masturbating. He consumes pornography like it's going out of fashion. My captor's deviancy knows no bounds, and this makes me dislike him all the more.

I presume the number in his handle denotes the year of his birth, though to look at him, he could be anywhere between sixteen and thirty; somehow, his face is both cherubic and haggard at once. A student at the city's university, a quick glance at the mountain of books suggest he is studying Graphic Design.

The Sculptor's days have a habit of melding together: he attends classes during the day, then shuts himself away until sunrise. It's always the same, the routine never changes. These same four walls, day in, day out, broken only by the occasional trip to the bathroom. This place is revolting, too. It'd be enough to drive anyone mad, so it comes as no surprise that he's downright deranged. Living, breathing waste, ruling over his toxic cesspool.

After a time, I can feel my own sanity slipping away. I'm somewhere between my last straw and the end of my tether when something finally, *finally* happens. With the aid of a camera, myself and the Sculptor have ourselves a photoshoot: he the photographer, me his amorphous blob of a model. He captures every angle of my unflattering shapelessness, then uploads the photos to his computer. Visiting his habitual internet haunts, the Sculptor creates a series of posts, all along the same lines. I watch impassively as he types:

Golem Creation/Jewish Folklore General Anonymous 05/19/22 (Thu) 20:52:31 No.39228043

Does anyone here have any first-hand experience with creating and animating golems? If you do, get your ass ITT. I'm looking to build one myself, and want to talk to someone who's tried this kind of thing before. What should I expect/what precautions should I take? I've been researching this loads recently and learned a lot of useful stuff, mainly about the art of Kabbalah and its practical applications in golem creation. I think this is the key, and I'm pretty sure I can legit do this, /x/. I'm ready now. No memeing, no roleplaying. No bullshit. Got something big planned if it does work out. Watch this space—I'll be back soon to share my results. Wish me luck, losers.

Oh, and in case I needed to make it clear: genuine replies only. Also, general Jewish folklore thread. Post your creepiest irl occurrences and 2spooky greentext stories, I need something to read tonight and want you to give me the scariest shit you have.

His posts go more or less unnoticed, lost among the desperate cries for attention that populate these sites. Buried under the slush of divination threads, creepypastas, and chemtrail conspiracies; the succubus summonings and the Flat Earth theories. From the handful of replies he does receive, most dismiss him as a 'shitty LARPer'; an abhorrent few spew antisemitism, while the rest spout absurd nonsense. The Sculptor reads; the Sculptor seethes, knuckles white and teeth grinding.

For a moment, I pray that he will be dissuaded from whatever demented endgame he has in mind for me, for *us*; that the ridicule will prompt him to give up and cast me back to whence he found me.

Alas, fortune frowns once again. If anything, their mockery strengthens his resolve: he will prove them wrong. He will not fail.

With that he begins, and my fate is sealed. I am to become his private project, stashed away in this den of indecency, this pit. A mere slave to his whims and desires; an object to do with as he pleases. His, and his alone. I find myself in dire circumstances and diabolical company. If I could, I would weep.

* * *

Over the following days, my body starts to take shape. Progress is slow, but steady. The Sculptor moulds me atop his workstation, a plethora of tools fanned out before him. I'm trussed to the table like Frankenstein's monster; he slips into the role of mad doctor with ease, the look complemented by his white coveralls. I am given the vague suggestion of a head, of arms, legs, and a pair of breasts. I'm to be female, that much is clear—or as close to it as a creature of animate clay can be.

'*Ars longa, vita brevis*,' he murmurs to himself. Latin. An aphorism, it roughly translates to "Life is short, art eternal". In the right context the words might be inspiring, but coming from him, they're alarming. He means to leave a lasting legacy, but where do I fit into it? Something tells me I'd rather not know.

For a while, my figure remains basic and lacking in definition; I am little more than a blueprint at this early stage. A naked sodium bulb dangles above me, bathing my mud-figure in pallid light. The buzz-hum it makes is incessant but also comforting, in an odd way. I try to focus solely on that

192

drone when the Sculptor is busy pleasuring himself, or hurling insults at his mother down the phone, or cursing under his breath while online. It is a cold comfort in this hellish place.

Two Fleshlights, two orifices—one vaginal and one rectal—are used to make my facsimile of human anatomy, strapped together by a roll of duct tape and ensconced within the still-wet clay of my crotch. The reason for my creation is perfectly clear now: it seems my primary function, perhaps my *only* function, is his pleasure. Am I to be nothing more than his sentient sex toy? A faceless fuck-thing? He spends an uncomfortable minute appraising his handiwork, face twisted into that same leer he wore when we met. I burn with shame under his gaze.

As time passes, my form becomes clearer and more distinct. More human. The Sculptor is a foul person, but his artistic prowess is enviable. Tools at the ready, he carves and refines with deft hands. My muscles are given mass, biceps and triceps drawn and defined. It isn't long before my figure is complete. I'm not much to look at: my creator's warped measures of beauty makes me look waifish and malnourished. Under the room's harsh light, I give the impression of a corpse on a mortician's slab.

Once I've fully dried, he wastes no time in putting my body to use. I didn't think I could be more repulsed by him than I already was, but as he pumps and pounds, face red and dripping sweat, I realize I was wrong. *Horribly* wrong. With the lights out, I don't even have the solace of the buzzing bulb to distract me. I try to let my mind drift, then try to focus on anything other than the grunt-thrust, thrust-grunt beat we make. Neither work.

Another week crawls by like this; another week wallowing in the Sculptor's pigsty, another week of his lecherous looks and his wandering hands. Every night now, he takes me to bed with him. Molests me, defiles me. This one is no different. I am his prisoner, without eyes and without a voice. Mute. Helpless. Hopeless.

'Whore,' he snarls through clenched teeth, tearing me from my reverie and back to this damned reality. The grinding of his jaw and the spittle on his lips make him look like a mangy, rabid dog. 'You're nothing but a whore. A fuckdoll. You're worthless, you hear me?'

I do. I hear it all, *endure* it all.

The tirade of abuse doesn't stop there. He slaps me, wraps his fingers around my throat, calls me every shade of nastiness he can think up: *Bitch. Slut. Cunt.* Humping all the while. Thrust-grunt, grunt-thrust.

After he finishes, he holds me in his arms, cradles me in a sorry imitation of a lover's embrace, as his deposit runs down the inside of my thigh. The tender display is jarring; the Sculptor seesaws between extremes. His behaviour is erratic. It makes him unpredictable. He caresses the blank expanse of my face and whispers sweet nothings at where my ears should be. An hour passes before he drifts off to sleep. I lie there and obediently listen to him snore until the sun rises.

* * *

Rain. More damn rain; it never seems to stop. Maybe it won't. Maybe it'll pour so much that the banks of the river burst and flow through the city; the raging torrents might flood this basement and drown us both. The eternal deluge is a reflection of my internal sorrow. How long have I been here now? Weeks? *Months?* I've long since lost track. Nor am I any closer to understanding why my captor brought me here. Every time we lie together, I try to slip inside his mind, to figure out what he wants before sleep claims him. It's no use: when he's screwing me his brain is focused on nothing else; the rest of the time, it's too noisy, too chaotic. It's maddening.

In truth, he doesn't sleep much anymore. Deprivation takes up residence in his face: in the bloodshot sclera and purple eye-bags; the irritability and constant muttering. He's growing ever-more volatile. He is unravelling. It won't be long before he becomes completely unstrung.

Yet still, he does not rest. With my figure complete, the Sculptor moves onto my head. He devotes the bulk of his time to crafting it; I am to be a pretty face, first and foremost, everything else is treated like an afterthought.

A can of energy drink in one hand and a blade in the other, the Sculptor sculpts. All three of his desktop monitors are filled with profiles of a virtual woman—a character from his favourite anime series, I forget the name—which he uses as reference for my own visage. A two-dimensional girl given a third: this is how he wants me to look. I am ashamed at the prospect. Humiliated.

He shuffles me over to a full-length mirror beside his bed, hands cupping my shoulders. I refuse to look at my face, knowing what he intends to do with it. The beady eyes of the Sculptor creep the length of my figure as he runs his tongue over his teeth. Even with the stoop of his back he towers over me, a conscious design on his part: height gives the illusion of power. Of control.

'You're going to be beautiful,' he says. Or states, rather, like it's an order. I *will* be beautiful. I *will* be perfect. My master demands it. And what master wants, master gets.

For now.

* * *

One night, he screws up whilst shaping my cheekbones—too high for his liking, too severe, too imperfect—and he lashes out violently. He gets ever so upset sometimes; this sense of injustice, some ill-defined and imaginary slight against him and all that he is, it bubbles over and erupts into raw fury. The Sculptor can only contain his viciousness and spite for so long: sooner or later, the man retreats and the beast emerges. Tonight, that beast is especially fierce.

Pummelling with reckless abandon, he sets back our progress by mashing my face to a pulp. I *feel* it all, every ounce of his rage. The pain is intolerable, each punch delivering a fresh flare of agony. I want to cry, want to wail in torment, want to scream into his stupid, sweaty face until his eardrums burst and bleed. But I have no eyes with which to shed tears. I have no mouth with which to roar. He sees fit to punish me for *his* mistake, *his* fuck-up, and all I can do is accept it. Accept it, but promise myself that one day, I will make him suffer the same. Soon, he will pay dearly for the violence he inflicts: eye for eye, tooth for tooth; I will have my pound of flesh.

Later as we are laid in bed, I hear the Sculptor crying. My immobile body is pressed up against his own, which shudders and trembles as he sobs. Curled fetal, he faces the wall. I'm glad. I don't want to look at him right now. Even being this close to him makes me feel ill, after what he did. What he continues to do.

'I'm sorry for earlier. I didn't mean to hurt you,' he whispers over his shoulder. Then sniffles, blows his nose, sniffles some more. 'I just get so angry at myself sometimes. Please don't hold it against me. I want you to be perfect, you deserve to be perfect.'

Naturally, I say nothing. If I could, I would tell him where he could shove his apology. The Sculptor is as manipulative as he is malicious; these words mean absolutely nothing to him. They are as hollow as his heart. He rolls over and peers up at my vacant face, his rheumy eyes wide and pathetic.

'I hope you can forgive me.' He sighs. 'Let's not go to bed mad at each other.'

'You know that I love you. You know that, right?'

Love. What a joke; he has a damn nerve. Nothing is sacred here: even a concept as beautiful as love is twisted and bastardized by this cretin. He doesn't love me, doesn't even know the meaning of the word. Still, I can do nothing but listen to his venom. His delusions. I have no choice.

* * *

It takes an entire day and a sleepless night to restore my face, and a further twelve hours of painful alterations until he is satisfied with its various angles. Next on the agenda are my eyes, and they take just as long: they must be flawless, after all. I am to be without defects, the embodiment of perfection. Or his version of it, at least—a crude, ridiculous effigy of this non-existent female.

His demeanour has changed toward me lately, though; rampant lust replaced by bizarre adoration, close to idolatry. He doesn't call me his "fuckdoll" anymore: now, I'm his "princess". I'm not quite sure which is worse.

As he applies the final touches, my blank pupils blaze with hellfire. They bore into him. I want my gaze to gouge his soul, to violate him in the way he has violated me. The Sculptor meets my eyes, looks at me askance: does he recognize the hatred within them? Does he understand the creature he is creating, the malice he's moulding? I hope he does, hope he feels the flame and the fury burning there, just for him. His face darkens, and there's a flicker of something in his expression. Could it have been guilt? Shame, perhaps? Both seem unlikely.

The Sculptor has been finishing something else, too. Something he's had in the works for a long time, well before he imprisoned me here. The sleepless nights had become a regular occurrence of late; he'd spend unbroken hours at his computer, furiously typing. At first, I'd ignored it. I'd assumed it was coursework, but that can't be right: the Sculptor stopped attending classes some time ago, devoting his full attention to me. Is he working on a novel, maybe?

I don't have to wonder for long. As I read over his shoulder, it soon becomes awfully clear what this is; it's a manifesto: a last will and testament.

Something to be left behind, something to explain what he's going to do. What *we're* going to do, the madman and his unwilling accomplice.

All the malice and spite that has accrued over his lifetime, he pours it into this declaration. Through tear-filled eyes, he unloads every ounce of his emotional anguish. So much hatred. Hate for the father that was never there and the mother that barely was, for the lack of close friends and family. Hate for every taunt and every rejection, every failure and every mistake.

The Sculptor's perception is twisted beyond all reason; he believes the world has wronged him, and he wants revenge. In his eyes, life has dealt him a bad hand, and he feels it owes him for the unfairness. There's no single victim in mind, but he intends to lash out in violent fashion nonetheless. He wants blood.

A hundred excuses, a hundred arguments to justify the way he is, the way he acts; all are meaningless in light of this latest development. The terrible truth.

I finally understand why he built me. *This* is the real purpose behind my design. Being his personal sex doll was horrible enough, but this is so much worse. I watch in mute horror as he opens up the browser, checks back into his favourite imageboard, and creates a new post:

So long, /x/ Anonymous 07/22/22 (Fri) 23:49:06 No.40056145

It's been a while. You probably won't remember it, but I posted on here a couple of months back. I was planning on creating a golem; you guys were completely fucking useless. None of you believed me, but well, it's finally happening, /x/.

> pic related

It's the material I've been using to mould her. My goddess. Dated and timestamped, so you know I'm not bullshitting. I told you I wasn't. She's almost finished now; I'll post more pics of my progress down below. Haven't settled on a name yet, so feel free to shoot me some suggestions. I'll be dropping in and out for the rest of the night. Dubs or trips gets first dibs, ofc. I'm sure some of you degenerates will be able to tell who I modelled her on, I know a whole bunch of you weebs lurk /a/, too. She's a goddamn qt 3.14, boys. She's perfect.

If it all goes to plan, by this time tomorrow I'll have actually created life, /x/. If it doesn't, then you won't hear from me again. I know this sounds like a classic case of god complex and I know you fucks are gonna call me a liar or a roleplayer or whatever anyway, but this is for real. If this post is still up, I'll come back tomorrow night and I'll prove it to you all.

If it's not, then this will be the last time I post on here, so this is kind of a goodbye too. You guys are alright, I guess. Been better to me than anybody irl, which is pretty fucked up. If you're in Prague over this weekend, I'd suggest giving the Old Town Square a wide berth. To the rest of you in Slavland, check the news on Monday.

Peace out, schizoids.

In the fable of Prague's golem, Rabbi Bezalel raised his automaton to protect the city's ghetto from antisemitic pogroms. His methods were misguided and ultimately ruinous, but his intentions were good. They were noble.

The Sculptor's are not. He means to use me as a weapon: armament for an act of domestic terrorism. Who needs anything else when you have an automaton bound to *robota*, a mindless slave to enact your atrocities?

I cannot allow him to succeed. I will not.

* * *

When my face is finished, the Sculptor stands awestruck. His jaw all but hits the floor; physically, I'm everything he desired and more. If only he knew what lies beneath the veneer. Beauty is only clay-skin deep, my *love*.

'You're the spitting image,' he tells me, and it's true: I'm a dead ringer, a perfect doppelganger of my animated blueprint; his attention to detail is remarkable. Uncanny, even. It sends a shiver down my artificial spine.

Close now to completion, he deigns to christen me; I am finally worthy of a name. Galatea, he calls me—and the name makes sense, for he is my Pygmalion, my Sculptor, my creator. My god, or so he believes. The name would be beautiful under any other circumstance, but every syllable sounds vitriolic spilling from his lips. I hate it almost as much as I hate him.

'Galatea,' he breathes. 'My beautiful princess. My *kawaii* queen. We're going to do great things together. We'll be unstoppable.'

Fingers part my lips; a scrap of paper is forced inside. This is the *shem*, the explicit name of God, and the last step in his arcane rituals. That which is meant to give life to the inanimate. Something does indeed change. I feel it welling deep inside, subtle at first, but swiftly growing and flowing through me: a warmth from within. It is power; it is life.

Still hesitant, still disbelieving, I try clenching and unclenching my fists. To my surprise, they oblige. It worked. It actually worked. I half-expect my mad creator to exclaim, 'It's alive!' in dramatic fashion, but he says nothing, just continues ogling me like I'm meat.

Those dirty, broken nails of his reach out, and onto my forehead, he traces an inscription: "אמת". "Emét", it reads, and it means 'truth'. He trails his hand over the curves of my body, pausing at the hip. The clammy palm lingers there for a beat or two, then he takes his index finger and carves his initials into my clay, forever marking me as his property.

I am branded.

This is the final indignity: his last offence against my flesh. I will suffer at his hands no longer.

I will not be made an accomplice to his hideous intentions.

'Come, Galatea. Come.' The Sculptor beckons me over to the mirror, childlike glee plastered across his face, lips curled in a triumphant sneer. I stand my ground, unmoving. Unshakable. I will not be ordered around like his pet, like some animal. He believes he has control over me. He was a fool to think he ever did, ever *could*.

My fate is mine, and mine alone.

I will show him the error of his ways.

For a moment he looks unsure, perhaps doubting if his rituals have even worked. Part of me considers staying still; let him believe he has failed a while longer. His face hardens and his eyes blaze as he says, 'Come here. Do not ignore me.'

This time, I choose to obey. But my movements are jerky and unnatural; I am a newborn calf on jellied legs. I move like claymation. The disgust that colours his face gives me grim satisfaction. He backs away as I draw closer. Am I *not* to his liking? Not how he imagined I'd be? No: I am so much more than he intended, and so much worse. I am his beautiful monster.

'Wait, stop.' I take a step toward him.

Another. 'I said stop, Galatea.'

'You will listen to me,' my master commands, but his surety is waning. Will I listen? We are less than a foot apart and that pervasive stink of his makes me want to gag, but I can almost reach out and touch him. I want to rip his face off; I want to tear him limb from limb.

'I created you. I *own* you.' The facade fractures, the dynamic shifts. Man becomes mouse. Predator, prey. Realization, panic, fear: a maelstrom of emotions flash across his face, one after the other. I can almost hear the cogs whirring in his brain as the blood floods from his cheeks. Behold, my Sculptor: the terrible price of playing God. Now he understands.

'Stop,' he whimpers. Begs. Let him: his pleas will fall on deaf ears. There is no salvation for this sinner.

I lurch at my creator, shuffling like the undead. He spits incantations—mumbled and mispronounced—but even with flawless diction they would be useless. No spell will save him. In an act of desperation, the Sculptor lunges for my forehead; by removing the aleph, the inscription would read "mét", "death", and I would be deactivated. Or so the stories go. Another mistruth: short of taking me apart piece by piece, he can't stop me now. Can't snap his fingers and undo what's already been done. The savagery inflicted on me, the violence planned for his fellow man; he must pay.

My iron fists clamp around his wrists and with little pressure, they snap like sticks. Nostrils flared in agony, the Sculptor's legs buckle beneath him. Pleading gives way to primal screams. I make him kneel before me, then wrap my hands around his head. His flesh is soft and doughy: exquisitely malleable in my vice-like grip. My strong hands mash and knead, mash and knead, until his skin is battered and bruised and blue. His bones bend and break under the force as he whines in protest.

Air escapes his swollen lips, tongue flapping and useless. He mumbles something that sounds like, 'please stop', or perhaps, 'please God', though he will find no forgiveness from me, nor from any higher power.

I take a few steps back and look him over: assess my own handiwork. Reduced to a sad sack of flesh and bone, he's a grotesque sight to behold. The ugliness inside turned out, exposed for all the world to see.

Can something so repulsive be made beautiful? Is it even worth trying? The Sculptor didn't understand the forces he was reckoning with; his arrogance and hatred had made him blind. To him, I was nothing more than a tool, a means to an end in his sinister schemes—something he sought to weaponize. I was made to be used and abused. Why should I treat him any differently? Does he deserve mercy?

Looking at him now, I feel nothing. The well of my sympathy has run dry. He is powerless before me. He is pitiful and flawed. An emasculated god.

I resolve to start from scratch: much like my maker, I'm a perfectionist. The lump of him is much more pliable now; he has become a colourful canvas of pinks and purples, welts and wounds, ready to be shaped. Ready to be born again. In the Talmud, Adam was created from the dust and the earth: he was the first true golem, and the blueprint for Man. The Sculptor is *my* Adam, and I am the new god. He will be my masterpiece, just as I am his.

I crouch low and meet his blank stare, invite him to explore my own. To plumb the depths of my soullessness and come up empty. Drawing close to his ear, I whisper his own words back to him: '*Ars longa, vita brevis.*'

He hears me. The words register, along with the shock of hearing me speak. My voice is gravelly and breathless. All his fight may have gone, but the awareness is still there: in his eyes, in his mind, and deep within his heart. The fear is still there, too; fear of what I might do. He's right to be afraid. We're just getting started, after all.

My fingers find his chisels and scalpels, and I set to work. He will be remoulded. He will be remade. He will be reborn into something new. Something better.

I am the artist now. I am the creator.

The TALES of RG SLEY

Figure RG Sley, portrait in Sley home laboratory

My laboratory – once my father's – is filled with the arcane symbols and tomes on magic, ancient grimoires and herbs and elements needed for all manner of sorcery, from alchemy to summonation, is my only stronghold, unpopulated by all but me and the shadows and that which I summon.

To the great gods we must of course pay homage, something my brother and sister do not realize. That is why, of course, I have chosen the following stories to wrap up this year's anthology. This is the homage to the eldritch gods and not just the classic scares, and I have for you here the true face, nay, the true purpose of magic. To summon that which you cannot fathom, and reign down on humanity the only true justice. These stories feature those beings that feast on your soul, on your mind, on your very being.

Three Days of Darkness — Tiffany Stewart

Tiffany Stewart is currently pursuing a master's degree in creative writing at Southern New Hampshire University. She lives in Kentucky with her husband, where she works shipping out uniforms and clothing to National Guard members.

* * *

"Happy Tuesday, ladies and ghouls! Only four days left till time to get your spooky on!

And speaking of the spooky, have y'all heard of the Three Days of Darkness? According to best-selling author, Suzanne Greene, darkness will begin this Thursday with demons coming into our world to run amuck until Sunday morning at midnight. "How does she come to this conclusion?" you ask. Well, you'll have to pick up a copy of her book 'Three Days of Demons and Darkness' to find out! It is excellent Halloween reading!

Alright, guys, time to bid thee adieu. This is Morning Joe, signing off, on 93.3, The Coyote!"

Kristina pulled into the library parking lot. The radio went silent as she shut the truck off. She grabbed her books from the passenger seat and climbed out. A sliver of excitement went up her spine as she walked toward the red-brick building. She decided to grab a copy of Greene's book while she was there. The thought of her and Luke hunkering in for the weekend, enjoying scary stories and an obscene amount of chocolate, thoroughly basking in Halloween glory, made her smile. They could even camp out in the living room and play 24-hour horror movies just to set the proper mood.

Returning the books to the gray-haired lady behind the counter, Kris inquired about Greene's book. After a couple of seconds of tapping on her computer, the lady responded, "Looks like we have one copy left, sweetheart. Let me grab it for you." She smiled as she looked back up at Kris, her blue eyes bright and full of life. For a moment, she reminded Kris of her mother.

It only took a couple minutes for the lady to return to the counter, book in hand. She scanned it and Kris's library card and handed them both back to Kris. "I believe you came in at a good time, my dear. There were three other people looking for this when I went to grab it. Lucky for you, I knew where I was going." There was that smile again. Kris smiled back.

"Very lucky for me! Thank you for getting it, I doubt I would've found it in time. I heard about this on Morning Joe before I came in this morning. Do you know much about it?"

"I actually read this one a few months back when it first came out. It's quite interesting. The Three Days of Darkness supposedly only happens when the moon and planets line up on the week of Halloween, and it also has to correspond with a blood moon. As you can imagine, it's quite rare! The last time this was said to have happened was about 630 years ago," she chuckled a bit. "Everything must line up so that midnight on the third day falls on midnight of All Saints' Day, or November 1st. The saints are the ones that come and wrangle the demons back through the veil and back into their place in the netherworld."

"That's so cool! I heard about everything lining up on the news the other day, but never gave it much. How perfect that it's all around Halloween. Thank you again for grabbing this for me, I really appreciate it!" Kris couldn't help but smile as they wrapped up their conversation, wishing each other a happy Halloween, and telling each other to watch out for Thursday.

Kris left the library and decided to grab some lunch and head to the cemetery. Her mother used to take her there when she was little. They would sit in the car with the windows down, under one of the many towering walnut trees, and have lunch while they talked and watched the squirrels. It was their way of stealing time for just the two of them. Then, when Luke came along, the three of them would go together. They were their own Three Musketeers. Now, the best Kris or Luke could hope for is to have lunch with the windows down, sitting in the shade of the walnut tree that grew next to her mother's headstone.

A musical vibration coming from the console interrupted her thoughts. She grabbed her phone and saw it was Luke. "Hey babe."

"Hi hon, how goes it?" They talked for a bit, and Kris told him about the Morning Joe broadcast, and about her weekend plans for the two of them.

"Morning Joe was talking about the Three Days of Darkness. Did you catch any of it?"

"No, I didn't get a chance to listen to him this morning. What is this days of darkness?"

"Ok, well, first you have the planets line up with a blood moon. This has to happen four days before November 1st. When all of that happens, the day after the alignment is known as the Day of Preparation. The three days after the day of prep are the days of darkness. During that time, demons come into our world to wreak havoc until the saints come and haul them off at midnight on All Saints' Day. Sounds like a fun Halloween, right?" she laughed.

"Yessir, that sounds just lovely," he had that flat, sarcastic tone that made Kris smile.

"Well, I figured we could camp out in the living room, watch something scary, and see how close we can get to eating ourselves into a sugar coma. Just you and me – no phones, no internet, no interruptions. Whatdya say?"

"I don't know, I might wanna take my chances with the demons. Not using the internet all weekend? That's a bit much. How can I talk to all my girlfriends if I can't check my email?" He paused, waiting for her response. He knew one was coming.

"Son, I'll throw you to the demons if you ain't careful! If your girlfriends had to put up with you, they'd probably do the same." They were both laughing by the time she finished her sentence. They had been together 20 years, and never tired of one another.

They finished their conversation as Kris finished her lunch. After leaving the cemetery, she went by the grocery before heading home. Their house was unassuming, set in the suburbs, surrounding by other unassuming houses. But it was theirs.

Once home, Darcy, their German Shepherd, met her at the door. When Kris came in carrying a large bag of kibble, Darcy perked her ears and watched intently. Her tail swooshed on the floor, and her tongue made a *plop* sound as she licked her jowls. She knew that one was hers.

Luke brought home supper that evening, and while they ate, Kris told him everything she had read in Greene's book. "The animals fall asleep for the three days. On the Day of Preparation, they eat like crazy, then, before midnight, they'll go to sleep, and stay that way 'til midnight on All Saint's Day."

"So, if Darcy eats pickles tomorrow, we'll know something's coming, right?" he chuckled. Darcy had tried a pickle a couple years ago. She gave it a chomp, then promptly spit it back out and went to her water bowl for a drink. Ever since then, she wouldn't even take a bite of a hamburger if she smelled pickle on it.

"Exactly," Kris answered. They laughed and talked as they finished eating.

They went to bed around 9pm, Darcy in tow. It didn't take long before the three of them fell asleep, their rhythmic breathing the only sound in the house.

The clock on the bedside table changed to 12:00am. Darcy opened her eyes and yawned. She stood up from her bed and trotted down the hall. She grabbed her stainless food bowl from the kitchen, and carried it back to the bedroom. She went to Luke's side of the bed and sat, her bowl in her mouth. Luke didn't move. She edged closer and woofed, still carrying her bowl. Still nothing from Luke. She walked over to the mattress, jumped up and put her front paws on the edge, and dropped the bowl on Luke's chest. She woofed again, this time without the bowl muffling the sound. Luke startled awake. "Darce, what in the world…" his stopped, his hand grabbing the bowl. Darcy pushed away from the bed and ran to the door. She turned around and looked back at him. She wagged her tail as she danced back and forth on her front feet. *Woof!*

"Kristina, wake up." Kris stirred and looked at him.

"What? What time is it?"

"It's a couple minutes after midnight. You have to see this." He motioned towards Darcy, who was walking towards him, then back to the door, then back towards him.

"What's going on?" It took Kris a minute to understand. She looked at Luke. "She's wanting more food?"

"Apparently so. I've never seen her so adamant. She even got up on my side of the bed and dropped her bowl on me." He held it up as evidence.

"That's crazy," Kris half whispered, lost in thought watching the dog.

Luke got up and walked towards Darcy. She took off down the hall, turning around in the living room, waiting. Kris threw the covers off and followed them both.

Darcy ran to the bag of kibble Kris has brought in earlier; she nosed the front of it and turned to face both of them. "I've never seen her so determined about anything before," Kris said as Luke opened the bag.

"Me neither." He scooped the bowl into the bag and set it down in front of Darcy.

"Wait." Kris went to the fridge, came back, and dropped a couple pickle slices on top the kibble. She looked at Luke, "I'm curious." They both watched as Darcy gave the pickles a sniff and a lick before taking a bite of them along with a mouthful of kibble. Luke looked back to Kris.

"In all of her seven years, I've never seen her act this way. Maybe we *should* consider boarding up the windows. Are there any other signs Greene talks about that would say this demon thing is real?"

"No, she just talks about the planets lining up with the blood moon, and then how the animals act about eating." Right then, she heard scratching sounds and thuds coming from the back porch. It was similar to the sounds Darcy made when she was outside running around the yard and across the deck. "Honey, do you hear that?" Her tone was quiet and concerned.

"Mm hmm. Stay here." His tone left no room for negotiation. If there was some kind of trouble, it would only serve as a distraction to him to think Kris was in harm's way. Kris nodded. Luke made his way to the back door. He turned on the porch light and peered through the blinds. "What… Kris, come here." He spoke quietly.

"What is it?" Kris made her way to the window. She couldn't believe what she saw. Raccoons and possums were running across the deck, some carrying pieces of scraps they had found in a garbage can somewhere. Others were working on getting the lids off the cans that were setting by the deck. "Let's go to Lowes."

"Agreed," he said, still watching the coons. "Let's try to get some sleep. We'll leave Darcy here with her bag of kibble, and in the morning, we'll go to Lowe's and check out some plywood. Maybe we can hit a couple other places as well and make sure we have some extra food and ammo."

"Sounds good to me." She was still partially distracted by the scene on their deck. It crossed her mind that the critters were so into what they were doing, she could walk out in the middle of them, and they wouldn't even notice.

Luke took her hand and pulled her from her thoughts. She followed him back to the bedroom, hand in hand. They stopped at the foot of the bed. Before letting her hand go, he pulled Kris into his chest and wrapped his arms around her, kissing the top of her head. "Guess this makes for a good Halloween story, huh?" He smiled against her hair.

She chuckled in response. "Yeah, I guess so." They kissed goodnight and went back to bed. Sleep didn't come as easy this time. After almost an hour of listening to the consistent *crunch crunch crunch* coming from the living room, they both finally drifted off.

By 8am, they were at Lowe's. Going through the store, they noticed people arguing, almost fighting, with each other over batteries, wood pieces, garbage bags, and anything anyone could possibly fashion as a weapon. People were taking items out of other people's carts, cutting in front of each other in line, grabbing items off the shelves from in front of one another.

"Stay by me, don't wander. I don't like this." Luke's tone was serious and concerned. Kris knew to listen to him; his face was still, unsmiling. He was constantly scanning the store, watching everything. She hooked her arm through his as he pushed the cart through the store. Their first stop was the plywood area. They needed five larger pieces, and one smaller one.

As they stopped in front of the shelf where the pieces lay, a man started to push in front of them to grab the last three that lay there. Luke grabbed his wrist, twisted him around, and pushed the man's back against the shelf. They faced each other, not three inches between them. "Don't, buddy. Don't." Luke spoke in a low, controlled tone. Kris saw a stillness in his eyes that she had only seen a handful of times before. Luke was serious, and she could tell the man saw it, too. He nodded, not saying a word, and side-stepped to remove himself from between Luke and the shelf. He hurriedly walked away and didn't look back. Kris stood silently with her hand on the cart.

"You OK?" Luke looked her up and down, stopping when he caught her stare. The harsh stillness she had seen in his eyes was gone – all that was there now was concern for her.

"Yeah. You?" That was the only physical confrontation she had ever seen Luke have before. She had heard stories about his military days but hadn't met him until after he was out of the service. Maybe it was how he carried himself, but there was always a quiet knowing within her that she would never have to be afraid so long as he was around. This incident solidified that confidence.

"I'm good. Let's get what we can and get out of here. This is going to get worse as the day goes on." He put the three larger pieces and one smaller piece in the cart, and they made their way out of the aisle. On their way to the registers, they grabbed a couple boxes of screws, and the only box of nails they could find. He talked as they went toward the front of the store. "We'll board up the living room, dining room, and kitchen windows since that's where we'll be staying. The smaller one will cover the bathroom window. We'll shut off the bedrooms and tape some garbage bags over the front door. It won't be pretty, but it'll be functional."

"Pretty doesn't matter," she said quietly as she watched the people they passed on their way to the check-out. "Function over form. Hey, let's ask someone what they think is going on. See if they know something we don't."

"Good idea, babe. Let's do that."

When they found the end of the check-out line, which was a good fifteen people long, Luke struck up a conversation with the man in front of them. He asked if the guy knew what the big to-do was about, feigning ignorance and telling him that he and Kris were there for wood to build their dog a house. The man was animated and excited. Luke could tell fear was driving him, and the poor man could barely contain it. "Man, Morning Joe this morning, he told everyone about his dogs last night. Did you catch yesterday's broadcast when he was talking about the Three Days of Darkness?"

"Yeah, I heard about that. Supposed to have demons running around, right?" Luke continued with the ignorance.

"Everyone thought it was a big Halloween tale and was just laughin' about it. Today, though, he came back on, and you could tell, he was scared. He talked about his three dogs, and how they woke him up right after midnight tryin' to get food. Not in a normal I-want-an-extra-treat kinda way, but in a very pushy I-haven't-eaten-in-three-weeks kinda way. Then, he talked about some of his family callin' him this mornin' before the broadcast. Their animals all acted the same way – dogs, cats, chickens. Everyone I've talked to today, they're all sayin' that same thing, too! And the wildlife, have you seen *them*? There ain't a bird in the sky right now 'cause they're all on the ground tryin' to get food! That Greene lady Morning Joe talked about, she was right! This is the Day of Preparation!" The man turned around and pushed his cart forward in line. Luke and Kris exchanged glances but said nothing.

After leaving Lowes, they went around gathering supplies from different stores. As they drove, they noticed the wildlife. The sky was empty, just like the man mentioned. The grassy areas were crawling with birds, pecking and waddling in a near-frenzy state. Squirrels darted to and fro, scurrying around looking for anything they could find. Metal dumpsters that sat behind gas stations and restaurants had cats, coons, and any other creature that could crawl going in and out of the doors.

Luke and Kris expedited their trips and made their way home as quickly as possible. People were growing more fearful, and more unpredictable, as the morning grew late. Luke pulled the truck into their driveway and parked it. Kris turned to face him. "Do we have everything?"

"Yeah, I believe we do. Tell me again, please, what did Greene say about light?"

"She said that even if the demons can't see it, they'll feel it, and be attracted to it. They don't like light, so it kind of pisses them off in a way."

"So, if we turn on the flashlight, we'll piss them off, but they won't be able to break our door down or anything, right? It'll be a paper tiger kinda thing?"

"From what I've read, that's correct. They need to be invited in, and, according to Greene, looking into the darkness is considered by them to be an invitation. They want to stay here when the veil gets closed by the Saints on All Saints Day. To do that, they have to hide inside the living. But, to do *that*, they have to be invited."

Luke shook his head in affirmation. Kris could tell he was digesting everything she just told him. They got out of the truck and began to haul everything into the living room. As they sat the bags down on the floor, they saw Darcy was still working on the 50lb bag of kibble. She had slowed her pace a bit but was still not ready to stop.

They brought the lumber inside and began to board the windows like they had discussed. They drug the mattress into the middle of the living room and laid it so that the couch acted as a headboard. Kris began taping black garbage bags over the front door as Luke closed up the bedrooms and hung blankets over those doors. Once they were finished, they sat down together on the mattress.

"OK, let's get us and Darcy tethered together. If one of us needs to go somewhere, we'll let the other one know so we can keep an eye on each other as well as on Darcy." Finally having stopped eating, Darcy sat on her bed next to the mattress and looked at him as he put her harness on her. He then threaded cord through the metal leash rings. He let the cord unravel as he walked everywhere they would need to go in the house, then cut it, and a second one just like it. Going back to Darcy, he threaded the second piece of cord through the rings and tied it, then tied one of the cords around Kris's wrist, and she tied the other around his.

When all the tying had been done, they both bent down to love on Darcy and tell her goodnight. She gave them each a few licks in the face, as she did every night at bedtime. Then, she laid her head down and gave a long exhalation. It was time. She closed her eyes and went to sleep.

Kris sat on the mattress and tucked a flashlight under Luke's pillow. Luke went around turning off the room lights. As he flipped the last switch, Kris turned on a second flashlight and pointed it at the ceiling, causing light to flood the room. Luke made his way back to the mattress and sat down.

"Let's try to get some sleep, hon. It's almost 10pm. Let's see what the morning brings." Luke pulled Kris close and kissed her goodnight. "Love you."

"Love you, too," she wrapped her arms around him and squeezed. She turned off the flashlight and placed it under her pillow as they laid down and listened to the silence. They were too tired to fall asleep quickly, but eventually, it came. The emotions of the day drained them more than they had realized, sending them under a wave of heavy sleep.

Midnight came without so much as a whisper. Kris awoke around 2:45am with the pressing urge to urinate. The darkness was so complete, she couldn't tell at first if her eyes were open. She reached for Luke, her hand finding his chest. She gently shook him, barely uttering, "Luke." A screeching wail sounded from the front porch.

"What?!" Luke jerked upright, confused, and startled. He grabbed at his chest, finding Kris's hand. She gasped as another ear-piercing shriek flew past the window. They pulled their flashlights out and clicked them on.

"I didn't want to startle you, but so much for that," Kris had to almost yell at him to be heard. "I have to pee. I'm sorry."

"No, baby, you did right," he patted her hand. Mindful of the cords, they took turns in the bathroom and watching Darcy.

They came back to the mattress and turned off the lights. After a few minutes, the screaming stopped, and they fell back asleep.

"Krissy? Honey? Where are you?" Kris opened her eyes to the darkness. It must've been the remnants of a dream that woke her. It was so disconcerting not being able to see, even with your eyes open. She heard footsteps walking across the porch, approaching the door.

knock knock knock

"Krissy? Where are you? It's so dark, honey. Please help me, let me in." It had only been two years since she had had the aneurysm that took her life, but Kris, like any child, would always know her mother's voice. Tears flowed down her cheeks.

Sitting up, she reached out for Luke but couldn't find him. *Where are you?!* A flash of anger ran through her, but she wasn't sure where it came from. Nothing felt right since this night had started. She ran her hands over his side of the mattress. Then, she thought about Darcy – *I'll follow the cord.*

She felt Darcy's bed, but no Darcy. *Figures!!* The anger flashed again, and it scared her. It wasn't hers, and she knew it. Kris grabbed the cord on her wrist, fumbling it through her fingers, trying to find Darcy. She was part of the way through the length of it when she felt a tug on the other end. Not wanting to set off the screaming again, she refrained from using her flashlight or calling Luke's name. Instead, she kept following the cord, until finally, she felt the cold metal rings of the harness.

She grabbed the rings, the cord still taut, but found they were no longer attached to the harness. Holding them and the cords with one hand, she ran her other hand over the floor. Where was the harness? The dog? Luke? She couldn't think clearly – nothing was making sense.

She found Luke's cord on the ring and followed it. She crawled across the floor as her hand slid along the length of the cord. She hadn't gotten very far when she came upon another hand on the cord. *Luke!*

She grabbed the hand, then realized how cold it was. The skin slid unnaturally under her fingers. She stifled a gasp and jerked her hand away. The smell of rotting flesh flooded her nostrils. Crawling back, searching for the mattress, she heard a voice from behind her, "Krissy, honey, come give Momma a hug." She felt desperately for the mattress. Shuffling footsteps came towards her. "Give. Me. A. *Huuug.*" The voice grew closer and dropped lower in pitch with each word it spat out. That was not her mother.

"*LUUUKE*!" Kris screamed, jerking upright on the mattress, panting, still unable to see. Luke jumped, and the demons screamed back. He turned on a flashlight.

Kris's face was glistening, she was heaving with sobs. Luke pulled her into him. "Honey, it's OK. I've got you." He stroked her hair as she cried into his shoulder. "It's alright. I'm here, Darcy's here, it's OK."

Fear shot through her, and she pushed him away. "How do I know *I'm* here? How do I know I'm awake?" Kris backed away from him, going closer to Darcy.

"You're awake, babe. Give it some time, you'll see." He reached out to touch her, and she flinched. The screaming and crying outside was relentless, deafening.

Kris reached out to pet Darcy. Her fur was soft, and her breathing rhythmic.

"See, hon, it's just us. It's alright." Luke held out his hand. Kris looked at him but didn't move. She kept one hand on Darcy's head, stroking her ear. She started to reach for Luke's hand when she felt Darcy move. She stopped. There was a pounding on the door. Kris looked at Luke. He was frozen, staring at her with horizontal pupils. He smiled, and it terrified her.

"Get. Your hand. Off me." The voice came from beside her. It was low and guttural. Kris turned to see Darcy snarling at her, missing patches of fur, her eyes like clouded pools of ice.

Kris couldn't move.

From behind her she heard, "Krissy! There you are!" She buried her head in her hands.

Kris sat up screaming louder than the demons. She was back in the dark.

She reached for her flashlight and turned it on. The demons responded.

"Kris! What's wrong?!" Luke jerked up, reaching towards her, turning on his light as he did. The screaming never stopped.

"NO! Get away from me!" Kris flailed her arms as she scrambled off the mattress and away from Luke and Darcy. She ran to the kitchen. She felt like she was losing her mind.

"Honey? What's the matter?" Luke stood next to the mattress.

"You stay there!" Her voice was shaky, as was the rest of her. She grabbed a Coke from the fridge and sat down at the table, facing the living room. She kept Luke and the dog in front of her.

"What's going on?" Luke looked at her. She sat staring at him for what felt like an eternity, then cautiously motioned him to come sit with her. She told him everything that had happened. He picked up her hand and kissed it. "Why don't we sleep in shifts from here on? Sound good?"

"Yes, very." She felt she would never again know for sure if she was awake and started to cry. Luke got up and put his arms around her. Kris buried her face in his shoulder as the screaming continued outside. He kissed her head. When she pulled back to look at him, she found herself looking at silent darkness. She could feel the mattress under her. Luke was breathing steadily to her side; Darcy was doing the same on the other side. She really was losing her mind.

Kris kept waking up to the darkness until finally, she and Luke awoke at the same time. Turning on their lights, they saw Darcy lift her head and yawn.

"Kris, are we really awake this time?" Luke's voice was trembling.

"I don't know." Then, she stopped. "Listen."

He paused. "Silence." He looked at her. "We're awake!" They laughed. Darcy joined them on the mattress and slurped them both as they pet on her. "I thought I was losing my mind! I kept dreaming I was waking up. I couldn't tell what was real anymore. It was horrible!"

"Me too! I didn't think I'd ever know if I was awake again. And I saw the most awful things! I think Ms. Greene was misinformed about a few things. Apparently, we sleep the whole time like the animals do." As she made that statement, it was as though a puzzle piece had fallen into place in her mind. "The demons want you to open your mind to them, not your door. They want to drive you to being willing to do anything to make the madness stop. It was never about a physical battle; it was always meant to be a mental one. If they can wear you down, you become low hanging fruit, ripe for their picking."

"I think you're on to something, hon. Maybe *you* should write a book. You've actually been through the Three Days, so it wouldn't be a bunch of guessing and conjectures." Luke tucked her hair behind her ear as he spoke.

"Hmm. I like the way you think. Maybe I will write about it. Who knows? Maybe it will be Oprah's book of the month." Kris laughed at the thought. She leaned forward to kiss Luke. As she leaned closer, she felt herself fall forward, and land face-first on the mattress. She was laughing at her own clumsiness as she pushed herself back up. She opened her eyes to look at Luke, and saw nothing but darkness.

Telethon — TM Morgan

T.M. Morgan has had stories published in Vastarien, Lamplight, Penumbric, Mythaxis, *and several anthologies, including* Tales From Omnipark. *He has upcoming work in* Pseudopod, Vastarien, Sley House, The Wicked Library, *and the anthology* Vinyl Cuts. *He is also the editor of* Dread Imaginings, *www.dreadimaginings.com. You can read more about him at https://thetmmorgan.wordpress.com. A radio adaption of this story can be found on the podcast Sley House Presents anywhere you stream your podcasts.*

* * *

The Sylvania spit a wavering line down its screen. For a moment, the twin juggling duo Betty and Nancy Golliver shivered out of existence and were replaced by a gray blob. Once the offending line passed through, the TV screen once again showed the sisters tossing six rainbow-colored rings between them. Offscreen, a drummer played a paradiddle at speed on a snare.

Tommy Liplet watched them as one watched a cloud drift across the sky. He held a bourbon in one hand and a large TV clicker in the other. By pressing his thumb, the snare went silent; he pressed again, and it returned. Back and forth it went. Tommy looked at the clock above the dressing room door: 3:25 AM.

Two loud knocks came followed by a man's voice. "Five minutes, Tommy. Come on. We need you in your spot."

"I'll be there!" he called back with irritation in his voice.

After Betty and Nancy caught the last of the airborne rings, the drummer snapped down on the snare and hit the crash cymbal. The jugglers bowed, and Helen Bird, the backup emcee, thin as a scarecrow and wearing an ungodly red, white, and blue dress, walked into frame, clapping her hands while holding a massive, black foam-covered microphone.

"Beatrice and…oh, Betty and Nancy everyone! Wasn't that wonderful? As you can see," she said and motioned to screen right, "our volunteers are busy manning the phones. We need your support."

The camera panned to two rows of people sitting in front of rotary telephones, the back row higher than the front by a foot. Five of them showed onscreen, two on the second tier, though the platform continued beyond view. Helen walked to the bottom row and leaned her elbow on the table.

"The last hour we didn't reach our goal, folks. Please, pick up your phones and call the number at the bottom of the screen. It's 1982, everyone! The Hauser House is celebrating its one hundredth anniversary!"

All five call-takers onscreen held receivers to their ears, but Tommy knew likely none of them had anyone on the other line. Maybe a few dozen people watched in their homes around the city.

Two more knocks at the door.

"Yes!" he yelled.

After downing the bourbon, he stood shakily and walked out of the dressing room. The hallway ended at double doors that emptied into the studio. A camera was stationed on each side, one mid-left and the other mid-right, and one in the middle, then the cameramen and half a dozen others milling around. Sam, the one who had been banging on the door with such ferocity, strutted up with clipboard in hand.

"Did you get any sleep?"

Tommy looked at him as if a turd had popped out of his mouth. "Sleep? Do you know how much blow I've done? I couldn't sleep if Mother Theresa laid my head in her bosom."

Sam laughed far too long. "Good one, Tommy. Here's your mic. Helen will lead us into a short, taped segment, then we'll come back for your appeal. After that, another taped segment, and we'll have David Tucker, a comedian. Talk him up and throw it to—"

"I know what I'm doing, kid," Tommy said.

The buzz on set made him feel nauseous. One of the volunteers, a heavyset woman sweating like she was being interrogated by the police, fake talked so loudly she drowned out everything else. Tommy had grown to hate her, her voice bleeding into every segment since the telethon started at 5:00 PM. She thought of this as her starring chance, he thought, finally able to escape years of dinner theater.

"Mister Holland wants to see you after that," Sam said. "Just quick. You need to be right back when Tucker's done."

"What does Holland want?"

Tommy tried not to sound nervous but found his throat dry. Holland could make a grizzled commando cower. The owner of the station brought old school, eastern European gravitas to every conversation. He carried himself like a man that used to put ice picks to men's balls for sport.

Sam hedged. "He—well he said, 'things need to pick up,' and to get Tommy."

Helen sang her way into the taped segment in an off-kilter rendition of "Somewhere Over the Rainbow." It caused the crew to wince at the held note for "-where." Tommy empathized with her: live TV was not for the faint of heart. Even if the crew outnumbered the viewers, Holland was always watching.

Helen approached with a crazed smile bordering on demented. "Tommy! That was good, right? I adlibbed the song there. How was it?"

Sam nodded in an equally surreal fashion. "It was great! Great, great, great, Helen."

But she kept her eye on Tommy and bent her head slightly as if preparing to be struck. The snare fell to the floor with a bang. The drummer, an octogenarian with a ponytail, waved a "fuck you" gesture with his hand

and retrieved the instrument. The loud woman on the phone screeched an exaggerated "Thank you!"

Tommy hugged Helen and whispered into her ear. "You did great. That's why I have you here. Now go get some rest."

She stepped back beaming, on the verge of tears. "Thank you, Tommy. Thank you so much."

The set began to spin. Tommy had felt faint before and knew what to do. He thought back to when he was a kid, when his grandmother would make butter in the kitchen, the big, wooden churner belching its wet sobs as she wiped her brow with her forearm. Tommy ate the fresh butter by the spoonful. The memory always put his feet back on solid ground. The same trick had handled everything from panic attacks to exhaustion for thirty years, though he couldn't say exactly why this memory had that effect. It might have been the sense memories etched into his thoughts, how full it made his chest when he remembered. Not that he had any great love for granny, as she had been an ornery woman; instead, it was the lazy farmhouse, the dust swirling in the sunlight through the window, and the smells that could only have occurred in the 1930s.

Through overhead speakers, the station's announcer delivered Tommy's intro. "And now, ladies and gentlemen, welcome back the one, the only, the comedy legend, the star of stars, the greatest showman of all time, and Pittsburgh's own, Tommy Liplet!"

He jogged in front of the camera. The din quieted. The loud woman faded. He saw the light on above the center camera and walked up to it until his face was being swallowed by the lens.

"We're going to need a bigger boat," he said and then opened his mouth so the viewers could see his uvula. He laughed in breathy chunks until the lens fogged over.

* * *

Once in front of the camera, things became a blur. A thousand jokes appeared on a rolodex in his mind, randomly spitting from his mouth on autopilot. Even as this nonsense left his lips, the appeal he would need to say processed forefront in his head. By 4:00 AM the viewers would pick up, mostly old people on their waking and drugged people at the end of their night's highs. The soliloquy must register with both.

"Ladies and gentlemen, let me get serious for a moment. The Hauser House has been helping the children—and their families—of Pittsburgh for a hundred years. When a child gets sick, it causes not just physical and emotional pain, but financial devastation to the family. The Hauser House offers hope. With your generous donations, it allows these families a place to stay during treatment, a support system. Even a few dollars can make a difference. So, pick up the phone and call the number on the screen. I'll be here for forty-eight hours straight. I am giving all I have to give. I just ask you give even the smallest amount. I'm begging you."

He waved his hands as if conjuring some magic. Sam grinned behind the camera, his mouth turned into a long, pleasant curve. A young man stood beside him. It had to be the other comic. The fucker was handsome, shockingly young, at ease in his own body, hands crossed. Even though Tommy continued his pitch, growing ever more animated, the words flowing from some mysterious space, he glared at Tucker.

"Please pick up your phones. Call with a pledge and help these children. Now, ladies and gentlemen, after this break, a great young kid, David Tucker, will be here to make you laugh."

A production assistant pointed his finger at Tommy and lowered his hand in a fast stroke. The camera light went dark. A taped segment played for the audience, though Tommy forgot what it was. Sam motioned him forward. Stepping from the stage lights allowed him to exhale.

"Tommy! Meet David Tucker. Up and comer out of New York."

Of course, he's out of New York, thought Tommy. Where else? Tucker put out a hand.

"A supreme honor, Mister Liplet."

Tommy shook and patted Tucker on the shoulder. "Good luck, kid. Give them all a boner."

Tucker flashed a smile. "Genius," he said and strolled to the X on the stage floor. A girl ran to him, said something, and scurried back from wherever she came. A strange white noise filled Tommy's ears, as if someone held a hair dryer behind his head. The cacophony of sounds on set disappeared, and he thought he might need to think of granny and her churned butter again. Sam was talking directly at his face, to which Tommy nodded and pretended to hear. Slowly, the strange noise faded.

"—to his office. You've only got about fifteen minutes." Sam stared at him, obviously expecting an answer.

"Holland?" Tommy said. "In his office?"

Sam gave that too exuberant laugh. "You're too much, Tommy. Go on, hurry."

A nudge from Sam started him moving. Holland's office was on the third floor of the building, in the corner office that overlooked Lombardi Street. Whenever Tommy had been in there, it always seemed unnaturally dark, even during the day. The windows weren't tinted, and the building wasn't at an odd angle from the sun. The room just absorbed light. Tommy trudged down the hallway, past swinging doors, and into the lobby. The elevator appeared instantly, likely in slumber at the first-floor spot. He pressed three and went about tucking his shirt into his slacks and tightening the knot on his blue, dotted tie.

At the third floor, the doors opened with a ding followed by a sludgy pop. The hallway was dark save for a single fluorescent halfway at the end where Holland's office door waited. That light fluttered. He gulped hard. At the office door, he knocked lightly three times. Heavy footsteps clunked toward him and stopped. He wondered if Holland had some way of peering through the door to see who was on the other side—maybe a closed-circuit camera or secret peephole.

"Tommy?" Holland said through the door. His voice sounded like gravel being churned in a cement mixer, as garbled as a voice could be and still be called a voice.

"Yes, sir. Sam sent me up."

The door opened, though Holland wasn't there. Must be standing behind it, Tommy hoped. After three steps—and he didn't dare turn around—the door shut. Holland appeared in the periphery to his right, at first a massive shadow figure that took its time to swing into frame, and kept walking until he stood at the large window behind his desk. There, in silhouette from the streetlights below, his body had the shape of a small tank turned on its end. When he turned half around, so he was in profile, his cigar allowed a swirling silhouette of smoke that drifted upward.

"Tommy, do you know why I have this fucking telethon every year?"

Tommy gulped again, his throat so dry something seemed to snag near his vocal cords. "The Hauser House? Helping the children—"

"God, no," Holland said. "I could donate enough to fund that. Let me ask you another question then: do you know why we sign off at one AM every night and just let static run?"

"No one watches TV in the middle of the night?"

Holland laughed. "Right. That cable shit runs all night, but have you seen the godawful dreck they offer? Roger Waters had it wrong: there won't just be thirteen channels of shit to choose from, there will be hundreds. I'll have to get in on that game at some point, but for now, it's just—" here Holland switched to a perfect call man's voice, "—WPXT, channel 20, Pittsburgh, the biggest station for two hundred miles."

The station owner swung his meaty paw forward for effect, as if presenting a magic trick to an audience. "So why would I run a telethon when no one is watching? Why are you telling the same shitty jokes to no one at all? How much money do you think we're raising right now? Ah, fuck it. Sorry, Tommy, this is all rhetorical. Have a seat and—wait. Pour us both a bourbon first. You know where it is."

Tommy found the glass decanter on a slim table that sat beneath an enormous portrait of a racing horse, except its eyes and mouth glowed red. The background was entirely black, the shape of the horse only hinted at by wispy, white lines. He gave two hefty pours into glasses and went to the submissive side of Holland's desk to plop down in the chair there.

Holland continued to stand, though pressed his hands onto the back of his leather-bound chair and leaned forward. "I've always liked you, Tommy. You fit the bill. Too old to be relevant and too young to be dead. I need someone who attracts the weirdos, the stoners, the old-timers with no shit better to do. Now, the Hauser House. Did you know I'm on the Board there? In fact, I'm the president of that Board. We are flush with money already. That's not what we need. Most of the kids who come through are poor fuckers from bad homes. Some of them aren't even dying *that* badly. Just their parents have nowhere else to go with them and are lazy shits. We *pay* them, Tommy. Pay the parents to take their kids. Are you listening to me? I'm not going to waste my time telling you these things if you're not listening."

A shudder ran through Tommy's body, starting at his chin and rippling through his torso, crotch, legs, and then feet. Holland's outline grew, his face still not making itself fully visible. It looked like his eyes and mouth showed the faintest hints of red.

"I'm listening, sir. I'm just not sure why you're telling me this."

Holland grabbed the bourbon, swallowed it in one swig, and belched. "I'm telling you this to preface telling you why I called you up here. I need you to get people calling in on those phones. It is imperative that every potential lowlife and derelict who's watching right now calls that number. Do you understand? Chew glass, pull out your dick, whatever. I need them on the phone, pledging to one of those human answering machines. The children aren't giving our benefactors enough. They're hungry, Tommy, so fucking hungry. That's all you need to know. Our *volunteers* will handle the rest."

The air in the office grew so stale Tommy tasted it, like the slime that coated his tongue when he had a bad cold. It caused him to cough when he first tried to speak.

"I don't understand what you mean, Mister Holland. I will do the best—"

Holland stepped around the chair, and his face finally showed. Deep ridges covered his forehead and cheeks, his mouth a snarling mess, eyes empty except for fires ablaze within them, and his nostrils wide.

"Get me more fucking people! If you don't, I swear I'll have my dogs chew off your cock and balls. I'll let those goddamn wraiths that live under Hauser House snatch your soul through your empty eye sockets and make you their permanent plaything. They are starving and getting fucking angry.

They need to eat. Do you get me, Tommy? Go. Now!"

Tommy lurched back so suddenly, the chair tilted and fell. The back of his head smacked the floor, but he twisted and crawled toward the door as though this were the normal way to exit an office. He felt Holland stomping toward him and reached for the knob, yanking the door open to scamper into the hall. Holland stopped at the door frame, kept entirely dark, as if no light could pass the threshold. Cigar smoke pressed under the fluorescent, taking on the quality of a jungle mist.

"I'm counting on you, Tommy! Give me your best Don Knotts, your most ballistic Soupy Sales. Go be the idiot you were born to be. And beg for those calls! I'm holding you responsible."

Waiting for the elevator, Tommy cowered against the wall. The image of Holland rushing down the hall, mouth gaped open to reveal teeth filed to razor points, seemed so real he covered his head with his arms. The bell dinged. The doors opened. Tommy sprung inside and fell into a heap, blubbering.

* * *

Three knocks on the door. Tommy snorted a fat line of coke through a rolled up twenty. His head trembled in reaction.

"Tommy? Please. Tucker's almost done. Are you in there?"

"Come in, Sam." Tommy used his index finger and thumb to wipe his nose as he inhaled harshly.

When the door opened, Sam's face was shock white. He sweated through his shirt. "Tommy! Hurry up! We're going to have to bump up that rap group if you're not ready in—" Sam looked at his watch. "—two minutes."

"What's a rap group?"

"Not now, Tommy. Please, I need you on set."

Something in the air smelled like electrical burning. There was a whirlwind of lights as Sam took him by the arm and dragged him down the hallway. They arrived as Tucker stood from being completely prone on the floor, wiping the front of his black t-shirt now covered with dust. The production assistant behind the camera motioned with his hand frantically, but Tucker ignored him. When the comic saw Tommy watching, he winked. It momentarily lifted Tommy from his panic. The prick meant to not only run long but let Tommy know it was on purpose.

"Imagine," Tucker said and looked right into the camera before turning in a three-hundred-sixty-degree circle, "that I'm passing through a portal. Once through, an exact replica of me appears. And…here I am. Unbelievable right? You can't tell the difference between me and that loser I just replaced."

He winked knowingly and the laughter of the production crew filled the studio. Tommy looked around, bewildered.

"How is that funny?" he said.

But Sam was bent over with laughter. Tucker took a bow, his right hand pressed flat against his spine, as if he were an old-time vaudevillian ending his act. It was so mesmerizing that Tommy didn't realize Sam was pushing him in the back and sliding a mic into his hand. Tucker passed close enough by him to lean in and whisper: "Give 'em that Tommy Liplet gravitas."

It all made Tommy so dizzy he stood dumbstruck in front of the cameras. The studio was completely silent. Even the obnoxious woman on the phones took a breather. Everything was bright lights and stillness. The memory of Holland's mouth glowing red as it pressed forward made Tommy so nervous his hands trembled. He squeezed his eyes and thought of granny churning butter, her arms thumping the handle like a crazed woman, her eyes gone wild. Instead of calming him, it only made him think of Holland more.

"Psst!"

He shook his head and saw Sam nearly in front of the cameras, arms wide.

"David Tucker, ladies and gentlemen!" Tommy twisted up his face as if the whole thing had been an act and shouted, "Gah!" Unlike with Tucker, not a single person laughed.

One of the phones rang so loudly it made Tommy jump. He thought of what Holland told him, gave the live camera a quick glance, and sauntered up to it with a serious, arms-stiff gait.

"Now, listeners, I have something important to tell you. I'm going to plead with you. We're failing tonight, and it's your fault. Do you hear me? It's your fucking fault!"

Both the production assistant and Sam made a move toward him, but he swatted them off—all out of sight, just beneath the lens. Even Tucker watched slack jawed. Tommy was on the verge of hyperventilating, and only by continuing to talk would he not keel over.

"Have you picked up your goddamn phones? This. Is. Life. And. Death. We're not here for shits and giggles. We're not running a twenty-four hour cinema verité for the hell of it. We need you—yes, you lazy pieces of shit—to pick up your phones and talk to one of these volunteers. Pledge your lives here!"

The cameraman followed him as he paced. Tommy was barely aware of the tracking. The only thing in his vision was Holland reaching for him to chomp his nose off. Those glowing red eyes grew so close Tommy felt the heat on his lips. He replayed the comment about wraiths beneath Hauser House, which he told himself was some figurative way of referring to the diseases of dying kids but questioning that deep down.

"Listen, I get it," he said and turned away from the camera, putting a hand to his forehead. "It's easy to be at home. It's easy to watch. Nothing in your little picture box seems real, as if everything—me included—are part of some imaginary world. But believe me—" he said and turned, his eyes Charlie Manson wide, "—this is all too real. Get on those phones, or I will come to your house and kill you."

No one in the studio moved. The production assistant glanced around, as if someone might tell him what to do. Whoever was up in the booth directing right now might have been yelling in the man's ear or maybe that production team was dumbstruck as well. But the phones began to ring. First one, followed by another, until all ten joined in a shrill choir. The obnoxious woman screamed over the din.

"Why, yes! Of course, I'll take your pledge!"

Tommy found himself nearly on the verge of collapse when a hand gripped his arm. Sam bent down so that he could get Tommy's armpit onto a shoulder and limped them behind the cameras. The volunteers' voices stacked atop one another, a jumble of questions and thank you's. Funny, Tommy thought, that other than the one woman, he couldn't picture any of their faces, though he'd been on set with them for almost twelve hours. There was a man with a yellow bowtie, but his face stuck in his memory like a mannequin's. As Sam walked them back the dressing room, Tucker snatched the mic from Tommy's hand and danced in front of the still rolling camera.

"Tommy Liplet, everyone!" he shouted. "Legendary! But, as you can imagine, he is exhausted. Now, we've got a—what is it?—ah, yes, a special feature on the history of The Hauser House. We'll be back after that. And me? I'm David Tucker."

Once to the couch in his room, Sam let Tommy fall backward. The cushion caught him like sunshine onto a cloud. Tommy muttered something, but even he wasn't sure what it was.

* * *

Sam opened the door without knocking. He had changed shirts, now wearing a tight, red Polo. Tommy still lay dazed, having no desire to move. Ever.

"Helen's going to handle things for a while, Tommy. I, well, you need to—"

"What?" Tommy said. "Spit it out."

"Holland wants you in his office. Listen, for what it's worth, I don't know what got into you, but we got over a hundred calls. The best hour we've ever had. If you need me to put in a good word—"

Tommy waved his hand though felt sick. "Don't worry about me, kid."

Sam dropped his head. "Good luck. And just so you know, Tucker took over after you left. We've got Helen back on for now, though the whole schedule is messed up. We're winging it for a little while."

Tommy shrugged. "That's show business, kid. Roll with it. You'll do fine."

At the lobby, just as he was about to push the elevator button, he heard a ruckus from the front desk at the far end of the hallway. Several people stood in the main foyer, clustered around the security guard who tried to push them back.

"The woman on the phone said to come down here personally with my check!" an elderly man yelled, waving the checkbook as if it were a handful of cash.

The security guard motioned for the people to move back. "Please! Have a seat on the benches. We'll take care of you one at a time."

The bell dinged, and the elevator doors opened. Tommy didn't bother to tidy himself this time but did grip his hands into fists. "I did what he asked," he muttered. "I gave it my all."

Just before the third floor, the elevator lurched to a stop, held for a moment, and then dropped several feet. His heart hammered against his ribs, like a too big rat trapped in a small cage. But, as if it had only momentarily burped, the elevator spun to life again and raised itself to the third floor. When the doors opened, he scampered through them in case it meant to fall again and crush him on the way. Beyond, the hallway hadn't changed from earlier, except now the office door stood open, a portal into darkness. Holland would be there, those red pits for eyes and mouth waiting and, despite the "best hour we've ever had," would be ready to annihilate him.

A shadow along the hallway, even though nothing could be seen. No light as backdrop, no figure that might cast its shape onto the floor. Yet, the shadow leaned far underneath that fluorescent and waited for Tommy to make his way.

"Mister Holland?" Tommy called out.

When he got no reply, he took shuffling steps, hoping to drag this walk out as long as possible. Nothing good could be waiting for him in that office. At the door, he tried to peer inside.

"Mister—"

"Come on in, Tommy. It's fine. No need to announce yourself."

Once he passed through the frame, the office features showed, if in the dimmest light that would still allow vision. Now two chairs sat on this side of the desk, one of which housed a person, the tight cropped haircut and slim shoulders instantly recognizable: David Tucker. Holland stood at the window, his massive outline seeming bigger than before, more wide than tall. Tucker turned around, and the only thing that showed were his bright teeth.

"Tommy!" the other comic said. "I thought you might be dead."

Holland waved his arm. "Go on. Pour us all a drink."

Once the glasses were filled, Tommy had to hold them in a triangle between his hands, letting Tucker grab one delicately before placing another on Holland's side of the desk. He sat in the left side chair next to Tucker.

"Good job, Tommy," Holland said. "Really. I was impressed. Bonkers and ballsy enough to get these fuckers calling. I'll watch the tape of that for years, how red faced you got. I thought you were going to have a heart attack." The man chuckled, a sound like a pit bull protecting his meal. "It's just, how should I say it? That it had to come to that was a disappointment. You're too far on the downhill slope. Edgy shouldn't be a last defense; it should be the *main act*. Kids today want it now, want it hard, fast, over-the-top. You—it's the end of the line."

Tommy almost giggled with relief. "You're firing me?"

"Well, let's start with this. Next year, Mister Tucker will take over the telethon." Holland held up a piece of paper that Tommy assumed was a contract. "Going to give him a regular hosting gig for the Friday midnight movies too. The *Creature Feature* show but with yucks tossed in. Did you know David here is only twenty? Born in Toledo of all places. I've convinced him New York is a big pond, hard to make your mark. A little time in Pittsburgh would get him ready for the big leagues. Right, David?"

Tucker swung his left leg down from being crossed over the right knee and switched them. "If I may say, Mister Holland, that's as right as lube before a fisting."

Holland bellowed, a sound that made the window rattle. "Love it. See, Tommy, what I mean? Anyway, Helen is dumped for the rest of this thing. David will take over backup duties, though co-host is the more appropriate way of thinking about it. I'll leave you with your dignity and let you finish out the day."

Tommy looked from Tucker to Holland, but neither man so much as blinked. He did, though, hear whimpering from somewhere, a light sound that might have been his imagination. To his right, Tucker flashed a disarming smile meant to convey something, but Tommy didn't know what. Holland grabbed his bourbon and poured it back.

"Now, I want to leave you with something, Tommy. I don't need you to scamper off and provide gossip as you drink yourself to death."

A lump grew in Tommy's throat. Holland reached down and dragged a person—the one who had been whimpering, Tommy realized—from the floor at his feet. Though all the features weren't readily identifiable, it appeared to be a long-haired young man, eyes like white buttons. With one arm, Holland tossed him chest up on the desk. The man reached for Tommy, who couldn't bring himself to move, the terror ahold of his solar plexus with a phantom fist. The young man shit himself, and the stench turned Tommy's head, which allowed him to see the dimly lit areas at the edges of the room begin to move. What had been solid blocks of darkness took shapes, over a dozen of them, jerky phantoms made only of shadow. What might have been faces split to reveal ovals of teeth and red gullets.

They rushed toward the body prone on Holland's desk. Tommy watched them attack the man like hyenas on a kill. Something wet flung itself across Tommy's cheeks. He whipped his head to the right. Tucker stood and with incredible speed dipped forward to join the phantoms in their feeding.

"David!" Holland spurted out the name and jumped back. "You are an ambitious young man!"

But Tucker spun around and retched, a flow of chunks that looked black on the floor. "I'm sorry, Mister Holland," he said and spit, "just eager to get started."

Trying to keep as low as possible, Tommy bent and tiptoed to the door. Behind him came not just the sound of flesh being ripped but bones snapping as well. Once he got the door half open and thinking he'd get away clean, a heavy paw grabbed his shoulder. Holland yanked him around so they were face to face, blood splattered across the man's cheeks.

"Mums the word, Tommy. After this, go do a residency in Vegas or just fucking die. If I ever hear you speak of this, I'll send these fuckers after you."

Once released, Tommy stumbled to the elevators, his finger jabbing the button repeatedly. He thought of granny in her tiny kitchen, body hunched in toil, while he sat snugly at the table, anticipation at the creamy treat he'd have coming. A phantom devil snuck from the shadows behind her, leaned above like a wolf from the fairy tales, gave Tommy a coy wink, and then bit off her head.

* * *

The first floor came in a flash. An old woman waited for the elevator in the lobby. Her hair was so white it looked unreal. Tommy lurched back, drawing his hands to his chest by instinct.

"Oh, dear," she said. "Are you okay?"

He passed her taking care not to make eye contact. "Sorry, it's been a long day."

The woman squealed with delight. "Oh, heavens! You're Tommy Liplet! It's because of you I'm here. What you said was exactly right. I've sat around my apartment helping no one for years, feeling sorry for myself, waiting to die. Once I talked to that nice woman on the phone, I marched right down. Now I can hand my check in directly."

The woman reached in her purse and withdrew a kerchief. It landed on Tommy's cheek.

"You've got some ketchup there."

He watched as the doors closed, realizing that the woman bore a striking resemblance to his grandmother. He watched the counter pass 2 and stop at 3. He stumbled away, and the doors and hallway to the studio passed in a blur.

"Hey, Tommy," Sam said, sidling up to him when he entered the set. "I got word. Helen's waiting in your dressing room. I thought you would want to tell her. Listen, if you could just talk us out of a taped piece and introduce this rap group, Mo Money. Then I'll get you a couple hours break."

The mic slipped into his hand. Staggering to his X, he waited for the production assistant to count him in. The loud woman screeched behind him like a trumpet in his ear.

"If you walk that check down here right now, I promise the station will surprise you with a gift," she said. "Oh, yes, I'm serious as a heart attack! Thank you! You won't regret it."

Tommy half-turned to find her watching him, her eyes showing the faintest red glow, as if a fire burned in her skull. She gave him an a-okay sign with her fingers and thumb. People moved around him, wires slid across the floor, and voices gabbed into headsets. The drummer began a tight snare roll that kept increasing in volume until it matched the decibels of the loud woman.

"Tommy!" The assistant showed four fingers, then three, then…

The snare cracked down. The right camera light flashed on. Tommy approached and looked into the lens solemnly as the drummer tapped his ride cymbal in a soft, slow rhythm.

"My name is Tommy Liplet, folks, and I'll be with you until the bitter end."

Lord Carrington's Guest — Erik McHatton

E*rik is a previously published author and have been featured in several online and print publications including* Vastarien, Tales to Terrify, Tales of Sley House 2021, *and numerous appearances in* Cosmic Horror Monthly.

• The character of Y'golonac was used by permission from Ramsey Campbell for the purposes of this story, as obtained by the author.

* * *

The boy watched his mother and father slide into the distance from the back window of the jostling carriage. Her, sobbing and shaking, his father stone-faced and motionless. The boy simply stared, eyes quivering. A watery throat-clearing from behind caused him to jump, commanding him to turn around in his seat. The boy complied, dutifully clasping his hands together in his lap once settled. He looked up at the red-robed figure across from him, eyes as wide as he could manage.

"Be still boy, and careful," said the figure, in a sonorous voice that issued from deep inside the darkness of his low-hanging hood. "You wouldn't want to fall from your seat. Lord Carrington would be none too pleased to find his property scuffed or injured upon delivery."

The boy nodded, casting nervous glances about the interior of the carriage, studying the strange markings that covered the wood, before bringing his eyes back down to his bare feet. He hadn't even had time to get dressed properly. He smoothed out his nightshirt and tried to wipe away some of the grime.

"Not to worry, you will be cleaned and given something much finer than those rags to wear. His Lordship prefers his…guests… to be immaculate before receiving them."

The boy nodded. He opened his mouth as if to ask a question before being cut off by the figure.

"All will be revealed to you in time, boy. Until we arrive at the keep, I suggest you sit quietly and try to remember whatever manners have been taught to you. Your host this evening is a man of refinement. He occupies a station far above yours, and as such, deserves respect. You should be mindful of this and act accordingly. I assume you know how to behave before your betters." The robed man brought the ends of his voluminous sleeves together across his broad chest. "Lord Carrington is not a man with whom one should trifle."

The boy nodded again and looked out the carriage window. Cold rain sliced by in gray sheets. The air smelled of old fish. Clouds hung heavy, black, and pendulous. The carriage rumbled beneath him, rocking slightly back and forth in a slow rhythm. It wasn't long before his body gave way to weariness, and as the shimmering landscape raced past, he drifted off to the sound of horse hooves smacking against the narrow, muddy road.

The boy awakened sometime later at the sound of the carriage crossing from mud to stone flagging. Rubbing his eyes, he peeked out and saw two large wooden doors looming just ahead. Two figures waited outside these doors, red robes flapping in the wind like wagging tongues.

The carriage came to a halt.

"Out," said the man, swinging the carriage door open.

The boy obeyed.

Upon exiting, he had no time to ogle the massive keep or its crumbling crenelations, as a doorman grabbed him by the wrist and led him swiftly through the doors.

The hall inside was poorly lit, with sputtering torches placed unevenly about the walls. There was no finery, no ornamentation, just plain, gray stone holding in air that reeked faintly of horse dung.

The two men dragged the boy up a large, spiral staircase and into a small dressing room where he was once again handed off to two more red robed figures, these somewhat smaller and lither in stature. Strands of hair whispered from the ends of their hoods.

"Disrobe," they said in unison in voices vaguely feminine.

The boy hesitated, but the two merely stood and watched him, the vacuities of their hoods like two abysses, staring, waiting.

He took off his clothes and stood before them, exposed.

They sprang into action.

One of them took the soiled nightshirt and tossed it in the corner while the other moved to a wooden chest, retrieving a flowing tunic that glinted gold in the candlelight. Laying the garment across the small vanity against the wall, the woman pointed toward the opposite side of the room at a large wooden wash tub which stood steaming there.

"Get in."

The boy complied.

They handed him a horsehair brush. "Wash yourself. Thoroughly."

He scrubbed until he was raw.

The women bustled around him, pouring into the water odd smelling tinctures and perfumes, filling the room with a sickeningly sweet acridity. When finished, they commanded him to stand and step out.

They covered him with a large wool sheet and toweled him off. When he was dry, one of them retrieved the shining tunic as the other motioned for him to raise his arms. The fabric whispered across his skin as they slipped it over him.

They grabbed him roughly under the arms and dragged him over to a small wooden stool in front of the vanity. One of them began running a comb through his wet hair. The other patted his face with a fine white powder. They rubbed his lips with pinkish rouge.

Upon finishing, they stood before him, heads cocked to the side for a moment, before nodding to each other curtly.

One of the women moved toward the door and opened it, and the other grabbed him under the arm, pulling him from the stool.

"Follow us," they said, again speaking as one.

He followed.

The boy was led through another sporadically lit hallway, and down a different set of stairs until coming to a stop before a pair of banded green doors, ornately decorated by gold filigree. Their emerald lustre shone against the dingy surroundings.

His breathing quickened.

The women opened the doors into a large dining hall. The smell of roasted pork rushed out and filled his nose.

"Go. Lord Carrington awaits," said the women, before turning to leave.

The boy stepped slowly across the threshold and was greeted by a vacillating, booming voice.

"Welcome, dear boy. Come in and sit down wherever you like."

The table inside was expansive, surrounded by ornate wooden chairs. At the far end sat Lord Carrington, a towering mass of flesh covered over by flowing robes of crimson lined in gold. Unlike his servants, Lord Carrington wore no hood. His visage, like theirs, was still shadowed, however, by the wavering illumination of the half-lit chandelier overhead. The deep lines and wrinkles of his bloated face obscured his eyes, but the boy noticed bright pinpoints whenever the smeary light touched them. His broad mouth stretched wide, giving him an amphibian leer. He resembled a great, red toad.

The boy sat at the opposite end of the table and looked into his lap.

"Raise your head to me," said the nobleman in his unsettling, quavery voice.

The boy raised his head and looked to the lord.

"Your father has sold you to me for a hefty sum, for the good of your family, presumably. As I understand it, this is not the first transaction of this kind you've been involved in. This being the case, I expect you have at least some idea as to the arrangement made with your father. You are for me to do with as I please, and you will be expected to follow my commands. Unlike those other arrangements, however, this situation is permanent in nature."

The boy's breathing hitched.

"Calm yourself. While others in the world starve, your family will survive. For any boon, a sacrifice is always made. You would do well to heed this wisdom. Do you understand?"

His eyes brimming with tears, the boy nodded.

"Do not cry, boy. I will not abide it."

The boy wiped his eyes and nose with the sleeve of the samite shift.

"Good. Now, are you hungry?"

As if summoned by the question, a deep gurgling in the pit of his stomach answered for him.

"Ha! Your body gives you away." Lord Carrington snapped his fingers.

Two acolytes filed into the room, carrying with them two platters piled with steaming meat. The trays were sat in front of him only, leaving the table before Lord Carrington empty.

The boy stared, as if unsure of what to do.

"I've already suppered. You go on ahead. I know how scarce food has been for your family these last few years. I had this prepared especially for you, swine from the farm of Randall Browne. I believe the two of you were recently acquainted."

A foul contortion came over the lord's face as the boy dove into the piles greedily, sloppily tearing at the hunks of flesh, gnawing on the bones. For many minutes the only sound in the room was the smacking of his lips, and the odd humming of Lord Carrington, who leaned forward to watch the boy with steepled fingers pressed against his mouth.

When fit to burst, the boy slid the platter away. He wiped his hands and face with a napkin he found tucked under some ceramic plates he hadn't used.

"Satisfying?" asked his host.

The boy nodded.

Lord Carrington rose, chuckling.

"I'm glad. Now come with me, I want to show you something." He waved a fat hand toward an alcove in the back of the hall. The boy creeped across the room.

"Hurry, boy!" exclaimed Lord Carrington, and the boy skittered forward into a strong grip.

They stepped onto an expansive balcony which overlooked a valley far below, in the center of which sat a vast body of water, rippling in the moonlight. At the edge of the water, the boy could just make out a large ring made of dozens of the red robed acolytes swaying back and forth. A faint, droning murmur reached his ears.

"Praying," said Lord Carrington, answering the unasked question. "Beseeching. Groveling. Pah! Foolish sheep. Their shepherd lies dreaming below the surface of the lake, and in these dreams he calls to them. They do not know he cannot hear their worship. Not yet. For this is not *his* time. If it were, I could never have taken this keep for myself, or those of his followers I have fooled into serving me."

"He and I are similar in nature, you see, but the way in which we navigate this existence is much different. There is an abhorrence between us. I have as much contempt for his methods as he for mine, you see. He gathers sheep to dominate them, to break their wills and make them slaves, milking them daily, shearing them every winter for warmth. He sustains himself on weak minded fawning. Look at how pitiful they are, how debased even the cast-off leavings of his mind can make them. Coward!"

"I would do it all at once: suck them dry, leave them shorn and beaten before slaughtering them and feasting on the meat and bone. He has not the stomach for such consumption, so he draws it out like a blade. And he and his ilk call *me* a reprobate! They are just as cruel as I!" The lord's voluminous body shook with each exclamation. He took a moment before turning to look down on the boy.

"Do you understand what I'm saying to you?"

The boy shook his head, cowering.

Lord Carrington sighed.

"The last few years, as the world starved, pure consumption became the law of the land; royals subsisting on scraps of bread, parents eating their children in Bristol. Look at what your own father has been reduced to. Selling off your innocence piecemeal in exchange for some relief. Forcing onto you the same debasement as those wretched buffoons below. Bleeding you."

"All life is consumption; consuming and being consumed. Servitude is merely a slower march through this suffering, tiny cuts over time, rather than a single, decisive blow. And, unlike that thing down there, unlike your father, I am no slaver. Do you understand now?"

The boy nodded.

"Good, now let's away to the cellar. Our true business will be conducted there."

Gripping his shoulder once again, Lord Carrington led the boy down several dark hallways which twisted in upon themselves like a snake, before the two of them came to a narrow, poorly lit staircase leading down.

The boy hesitated slightly at the top of the stairs, but a firm nudge sent him slipping off the landing and onto the first step. He needed no further prompting after that.

Down, down, down they went, spiraling into the depths below the keep, each step more precarious than the last due to the near complete absence of light, the torches more and more sparse along the way. Finally, after what seemed like hours, they came to the bottom and the boy found himself facing another set of double doors, red and quite ornate.

Lord Carrington leaned low and whispered in the boy's ear, "My chamber."

The boy tried to control his trembling as the lord pushed both doors open with aplomb.

The boy was surprised at what he saw.

The chamber was gigantic, much larger than seemed possible, with walls of rough-hewn stone. A ring of standing torches lined the walls, filling the expanse with smoldered light. The domed ceiling flew high above, its top lost in darkness. The floor was completely black, slick looking, as if made of onyx, with lines and whorls of unintelligible design flowing in and around each other, etched into the stone. In the center sat a massive chair surrounded by a tremendous pile—several feet in height—of red robes. There was a pool of liquid around the pile, further darkening the obsidian floor. The air smelt of dirt and iron.

Pushing past, Lord Carrington strode to the chair and plopped himself down, striking a kingly pose.

"Come here, boy."

The boy moved to the edge of the robe pile, keeping his head down, shaking all over. Lord Carrington snickered, his fat belly jostling.

"I know what you're expecting, boy, but be at ease. I have no such pleasures in mind for you. I have brought you here to offer you something much greater than anything that could be found in mere carnality." He leaned down and reached into a compartment built into the bottom of the chair. He produced a scroll case.

"I'm given to understand that you are lettered. Is this true, or did your father cheat me?"

The boy nodded.

"Magnificent!" The lord waved his hands about, in the direction of the pile of robes surrounding him. "You see, the thing these imbeciles worship babbles in its slumber, and as such, a fragment of its great knowledge made its way into the mind of the former lord of this keep. He was a vain, tedious man, and hearing this inchoate wisdom mistook himself for a prophet. Much to his detriment, he clumsily transcribed the knowledge inadvertently imparted to him, and in doing so he summoned me. So sure of himself was he that, upon being found wanting, his devourment caught him completely by surprise." Lord Carrington reached down, grabbing the boy's arm while thrusting the scroll into his hand. "I want you to read what he wrote. I want to find out if I'm right about you."

The boy, still trembling, obeyed.

The scroll read:

In darkness, beyond a wall of stone, is confined for all time the great and powerful Y'golonac, unrelenting in His wickedness. Sleeping, He awaits the end of being, when the barriers come down and all reality is purged by the chaos of The Void. Only then will Y'golonac stride forth, His power full and beastly, and revel in the perversity of oneness.

Until this time, Y'golonac abides His imprisonment, knowing that even within the order rent by reality, chaos can still be found. He waits patiently for those beings unfortunate and foolish enough to speak His name. Upon such summons, He may splinter, and issue forth to consume the speaker and take their form, in order to walk among the damned host until the rise of Cthulhu from the depths; until the subjugations of Xoathathum are amassed; until the howls of The Thousand Young echo against the moon; when the veil is torn asunder, and the weakly held gulf of everything invades.

Then, in the rising tides of discord, Y'golonac will rule.

Looking up from the scroll, the boy's eyes quivered.

Lord Carrington rose from his chair.

The man began growing, shifting, bulging out of his robes, which split in numerous places, before falling off in rags. He held his arms wide, and the palms of his hands each bisected, becoming full with two greedy, wet mouths lined in jagged teeth through which flicked slithering tongues that dripped. His headless, fleshy, naked torso soon towered above the boy.

His hand-mouths boomed in unison, rebounding off the walls and ceiling. "I have watched you for months now, being passed from torment to torment. I have seen your sorrow, had it reported to me in great detail, sometimes directly from the very lips that defiled you. I know what happened to your heart. You pretend that you are meek, but there is violence in your eyes. You are angry for what has been done to you. You have rage, I know it. I'd wager that if I could project an image right now from your mind's eye, I would behold you, tearing your father's throat out with your teeth, and swallowing."

"You've had some measure of revenge tonight. Do you recall the pederast farmer Browne? After detailing to me his encounter with you, I had him ripped limb from limb. I sent his parts to the kitchens shortly before you arrived. A great deal of him now rests in your belly."

The boy wrapped his arms around his stomach.

Y'golonac leaned forward, placing his hand-mouths on either side of the boy's head.

They whispered.

"I can give you more revenges. All you must do is speak my name and I will make you my acolyte, my priest. You will join me in such glorious consumptions, the likes of which you could never imagine, for there is so much more to eat than food. Are you not tired of being used to satiate the basest needs of others? Are you not filled with bitterness at the casual nature of your pain? Think of your father counting out his coin, not thinking of what those awful men will do to you. Think of your mother, face full of tears yet still sending you to them. Think of your siblings, spared your fate but reaping the benefits all the same. Come boy, sup again with me and we will take our place among the destructors and wallow together until the end."

Y'golonac straightened.

"Or refuse me, and I will eat you."

The boy hesitated, looking around wildly.

"Make your choice, boy; consumed or consumer; victim or victimizer; weakness or power."

The boy's brow creased, the corners of his mouth turned down.

"Say. My. NAME!"

Balling his hands into fists, the boy looked to the top of Y'golonac's body, to the place where a head should have been. He shook before exploding.

"Y'GOLONAC!" he screamed, and the surrounding abyss reverberated, filled with the boy's triumphant rage along with the peals of Y'golonac's foul mirth.

"We will first visit your family. We shall start with your father," said Y'golonac, when his laughing hands were quiet.

The boy nodded.

And smiled.

Hear the Ghosts After — J. Rohr

J. *Rohr is a Chicagoland native with a taste for history and wandering the city at odd hours. Lists of his publications and music, from the band Beerfinger, can be found on the site* Honesty is Not Contagious. *Currently, he writes articles for* Horror Obsessive.

* * *

ACCIDENT DATA RECORDER
  A.I. REACTION TRANSCRIPT
  22-04-2109
  7:33 a.m. (NAST)
  KAIROS BASE
  MENG-CHIEN CORP. LUNAR FACILITY

{Login detected}
  {execute standard greeting 1}
  Hello, DR.

{query entered}
  What is the status of Kairos base?

{processing}
{responding}
All systems are GREEN. 9 crew members accounted for. One is missing.

{query entered}
Who is missing?
{processing}
{responding}
Professor Ellen Baskin.

{query entered}
Where are they?
{processing}
{responding}
Unknown.

{query entered}
When did Prof. Baskin go missing?
{processing}
{responding}
Prof. Baskin's RFID last detected at one a.m. (North American Standard Time). At 1:01 a.m. (NAST) her RFID implant no longer registered on internal sensors.

{query entered}
Is this like last time? Is the RFID simply malfunctioning?
{processing}
{responding}
Her RFID functioned properly at last detection. The signal is presently undetectable.

{query entered}
Did she leave the base?
{processing}

{responding}
Unknown. All transports accounted for. No airlocks opened during the night.

{query entered}
Are your systems in any way malfunctioning?
{processing}
{responding}
My systems are operating within acceptable limits, and my memory banks are intake.
{assist = suggest}
Security footage exists from the night in question. Would you like me to play it?

#

An instructor once warned that training only prepared in part. The real thing would not be the same. At first, that didn't seem true. Whenever Liu set up a temporary shelter, everything went the same as on Earth. Well, similarly, though any change in gravity didn't really bother her. Erecting prefab housing, hooking it up to support modules—the effort always seemed the same as on Mauna Loa. Not until setting things up inside did Liu ever start to notice the little differences. Nagging disparities like the absence of wind.

She recalled feeling throughout training the gentle touch of a Hawaiian breeze. Trying to fall asleep, back on Earth, wind slapped at the sides of her temporary shelter. Sometimes it made the walls hum. She got so used to it that the absence off-world produced an increasingly unsettling stillness.

Shuddering, she shook off the feeling. Placing a tablet on the left end of a desk, she flipped switches on the computer terminal. Lights began blinking, cycling through red, yellow, then green. She breathed a sigh of relief when they all settled on emerald. The monitors flickered to life and sounds from the towers soon killed the stillness.

Liu reached for the tablet. Feeling nothing, she glanced over. Furrowing her brow, she checked the ground. No sign of the device, she looked around.

Spotting the tablet on the right side of the desk, she shook her head.

"Focus," she said picking it up.

Setting up a chair, she went over what needed to be done. Investigating the destruction of an off-world installation followed specific procedures. Adhering to them not only ensured a job well done they helped keep her mind off the inhospitable environment outside.

First, a connection needed to be established with the lunar satellite in orbit. The laser utilizing communication relay would put her in touch with Earth. Analysis of the incident site couldn't be conducted without it. Body cams linked to the terminal relayed a steady stream of info back to Earth. Every moment recorded to ensure nothing called into question.

She tried not to think of all the eyes watching her every move back home. Each observing for their own reason. A few committed to spotting some mistake on her part.

Corporate lawyers already tried to block the investigation claiming they knew the cause of the incident—no need to look closer. However, the law remained clear. It dictated an independent investigation take place regardless. Yet, she knew those same law dogs would be watching, sniffing around the slightest mistake to undermine any conclusions.

Glancing out a view slot, Liu observed the remains of Kairos base, a bramble of burnt ruins. She saw a figure in a grey spacesuit loping through the wreckage. Rolling her eyes, Liu hopped off the chair. She snatched up a nearby radio.

"Rutledge," she said. "What're you doing?"

"Just taking a look," Rutledge replied.

"We're not streaming yet," Liu said.

"I'm not going to touch anything."

"And I don't want anyone to claim you did," Liu said. "Get back here. That's an order."

Silence. She went over to the view slot. Watching him stand out there, a thought popped into her head—the promising wasteland of the Moon inviting him to defy her.

"Did you copy that?" she asked.

"I copy, I copy," Rutledge said. "On my way back."

Watching him, she found it surprising one could moonwalk with the air of a sullen teen sent to their room. Sighing, Liu set the radio aside. Pulling the chair over, she sat down at the computer terminal. She started entering commands. A few minutes later she heard the snap-puh-pop of the door. Turning she saw Rutledge enter the room.

"Reporting as ordered, Queen Liu," he said saluting her.

"We are pleased to see you," she said returning to her work. "Did you finish setting up the sleeping quarters?"

"It'll get done."

She squeezed her eyes shut. Biting her tongue, Liu opted to pick her battles. He returned when ordered. That's what mattered for now.

A few final keystrokes and the computer initiated the connection process. On screen, a digital clock began counting down the minutes to completion.

"In about five minutes we should be connected," Liu said. "After that we can start a visual assessment."

"Great," Rutledge said. "Doing that twice makes it more thorough, I guess."

"Look," she said spinning around. "There's a procedure and this is my first command. I just want everything to go smoothly without room for insinuation. You know how the corporates get."

Rutledge nodded, "I'll be good. It's just that there's something about this place."

His eyes drifted to the view slot. He folded his arms across his chest. He almost seemed to be holding himself.

"Maybe's it's just the wind," he said.

\#

ACCIDENT DATA RECORDER
  A.I. REACTION TRANSCRIPT
  23-04-2109
  3:00 a.m. (NAST)
  KAIROS BASE

MENG-CHIEN CORP. LUNAR FACILITY

{RFID detected = Prof. Ellen Baskin.}
  {RFID alarm = Life signs fading.}
  {alerting medical staff.}
  Dr. Bryce. Medical emergency in habitat 3.
  {repeat}
  {RFID alarm = Life signs nil.}

ACCIDENT DATA RECORDER
  A.I. REACTION TRANSCRIPT
  24-04-2109
  5:15 p.m. (NAST)
  KAIROS BASE
  MENG-CHIEN CORP. LUNAR FACILITY

{multiple logins detected}
  {execute standard greeting 2}
  Hello.

{query entered}
  Could the wounds on Prof. Baskin be self-inflicted?
  {processing}
  {responding}
  Prof. Baskin's file shows no history of self-harm.
  {assist = suggest}
  *Psychological trauma during Prof. Baskin's absence may've triggered deperson-
alization resulting in self-harm.*

{query entered}
  Where were they during that absence?
  {processing}
  {responding}

Insufficient data.

{assist = elaborate}

Further information is needed to speculate on Prof. Baskin's whereabouts while absent.

{query entered}

Some of Prof. Baskin's wounds seem like specific shapes. Do they correspond to any known shapes?

{processing}

{responding}

Some of the symbols in her arm correspond to the cymatics found around KAIROS base.

#

Tapping icons on a forearm mounted tablet, Liu activated the augmented display in her helmet. Transparent green structures coalesced into view. It felt like summoning the ghost of Kairos base. A digital emerald complex implied the facility that used to exist. Each spectral module superimposed over the installation's corpse.

She ventured into the site with Rutledge trudging behind her. He wanted to split up, but Liu insisted they inspect everything together.

"We could get done in half the time," he said.

"We'll get done when we get done," she said.

Procedure dictated the pair stay together. If nothing else, safety concerns demanded they stay close to one another. Liu recalled a training video, a graphic CGI demonstration of a human exposed to the lunar environment. Skin burning, saliva boiling, retinas melting—she called up a checklist.

"We'll start with the support module," she said.

"Copy that," Rutledge sighed.

They made their way through the ruins of Kairos base. Specifically, they headed for the wreckage of a central building. Based on the augmented view, Kairos followed a common set up for lunar installations. The support module housed electric generators, and such surrounded by a ring of other structures.

According to the Meng-chien Corporation, a catastrophic malfunction in the support module resulted in an explosion then uncontained fire that destroyed the entire facility. However, so far, Liu saw little evidence to support that claim.

"I'm not seeing debris consistent with an explosion," she said.

"Me neither," Rutledge said. "Habitat 2 actually looks imploded."

Liu concurred for the record. She noted the hemispherical habitat resembled a crumpled ball of paper. Reaching the support module, they began an examination of the wreckage. Although their body cams documented everything, Liu ordered Rutledge to take photographs as well. Zero sign of a blast crater, he felt safe voicing his assumption an explosion never occurred.

"I am seeing evidence of clubbed damage," Liu said.

"That just means something melted the building," Rutledge said. "Then it solidified. Heat doesn't mean an explosion happened."

"I'm just recording what I see," Liu said. "We'll come to conclusions later."

"Right," he said.

Turning off the augmented view, Liu went around until she found a way into the ruins. Careful to disturb as little as possible, she entered the remains. The melted innards of the module littered the ground. Generators and life support equipment, not to mention the building's bones, all turned to blackened mounds. Yet, everything seemed to be in order. Nothing moved let alone blasted an inch from its proper place.

Passing a pile of soot, Liu paused. The way it lay reminded her of iron filings on a sheet of paper with a bar magnet beneath. It also called to mind cymatics, the phenomena where vibrations produced patterns and shapes.

The unusual design seemed to seed a notion. Trying to grasp it felt like grabbing fog. Her thoughts stirred—the melody of fresh cut glass, the color of a letter, the texture of petrichor—Liu moved, following the soot. It led her around a group of servers sagging like softened butter. Behind them a hole in the wall led back outside. Stepping through, Liu spotted an arm sticking out of the lunar surface, the charred hand welded to a partially melted piece of rebar.

Swallowing hard, she summoned Rutledge over.

"Is that a hand?" he said.

He sounded excited.

"Yes," Liu replied flatly. "Photograph it then we'll collect it."

While Rutledge snapped shots, Liu prepared a folding spade.

"That oughta do it," Rutledge said.

"Okay," Liu said moving towards the arm.

"You've done this before, right?"

"Doesn't make it any easier."

"Well, I mean, I'm happy to get it," Rutledge said.

Liu headed towards the limb. She ordered Rutledge to take a position so his body cam could record her digging without any obstruction. Once he got in place, she carefully scrapped away the lunar surface around the arm. Finding nothing, on a hunch, Liu grabbed the rebar. She pulled and the arm came out of the ground. The ragged chunk where the shoulder should've been called to mind a shark bite she once saw.

Rutledge prepared a sample bag. Liu slipped the severed limb inside.

"I'll think we should ping the A.D.R. next," she said.

"Agreed," Rutledge said.

She handed him the arm. As he stored it in his backpack, she tapped icons on her mounted tablet. A signal went out, but no response came back. She tried again. Still nothing.

"Maybe it was damaged?" Rutledge said.

"Not likely," she said.

"If we search the support module, we should find it."

She sent out a third ping. This time a response chime went off. Then her helmet's augmented view generated a waypoint. Liu started towards it.

Following her, Rutledge asked, "Where is it?"

"Looks like the arboretum," Liu said.

"How the hell did it get there?"

"I don't know," she said. "With any luck, it'll tell us."

\#

ACCIDENT DATA RECORDER
  A.I. REACTION TRANSCRIPT
  25-04-2109
  2:10 a.m. (NAST)
  KAIROS BASE
  MENG-CHIEN CORP. LUNAR FACILITY

{alert protocols initiated}
  Intruder detected: Habitat 4.
  {alert protocols initiated}
  Intruder detected: Arboretum.
  {alert protocols initiated}
  Intruder detected: Launch Bay.

{RFID alarm = Life signs fading.}
  {RFID = Dr. Serena Ochoa}
  {alerting medical staff.}
  Dr. Bryce. Medical emergency in Launch Bay.
  {repeat}
  {RFID alarm = Life signs critical.}

{RFID alarm = Life signs fading.}
  {RFID = EngD. Mae Bluford}
  {alerting medical staff.}
  Dr. Bryce. Medical emergency in the Arboretum.
  {repeat}
  {RFID alarm = Life signs nil.}

{RFID alarm = Life signs fading.}
  {RFID = Dr. Pierre Stewart}
  {alerting medical staff.}

Dr. Bryce. Medical emergency in the Arboretum.
{repeat}
{RFID alarm = Life signs nil.}

\#

They headed for the arboretum through the remains of a connecting hallway. One of the corridors linking the ring of modules around the support center. Inside, they saw the facility's exposed viscera everywhere. Wires spilled out from behind broken panels. Pipes jutted forth like broken bones. Signs of chaos ripping through wildly yet now, all eerily still.

Rutledge paused to photograph a bit of graffiti. Visible but difficult to discern, he figured they could make the image more legible later. To Liu, it seemed like further evidence of cymatics. Looking at it, invasive thoughts crowded her mind—the song of a solemn glen. Tearing away, she pressed on.

The door to the arboretum hung open. Pushing the hatch wider revealed a field of ashes. Burnt stumps hinted at the small forest cremated within. Normally the arboretum provided fresh oxygen for a lunar facility. Liu wondered if this scorched wasteland might've been the start of the calamity. A blaze beginning here could spread if fire suppression systems failed. She'd seen it before. Ineffective safety mechanisms due to corporate cost cutters failed to stop a preventable disaster. However, something felt off.

Using a portable spectrometer, Liu scanned for Novec 1230. Traces of the chemical showed up causing her to discard corporate penny pinching as a cause. It appeared the fire suppression system worked, though it didn't stop the fire for some reason. She also detected something the spectrometer couldn't identify. Almost undetectable hints of an unknown element in the atmosphere.

"Must've been a raging inferno," Rutledge remarked.

"Then there should be nothing left," Liu said. "But there's plenty of areas that are just scorched."

She pointed around the module. Sections of the dome still stood, barely singed. Some trunks appeared blackened, their leaves burnt off entirely, but the trees seemed fine relative to the charred stumps everywhere else. The sense of a controlled burn kept popping to mind. Intense pockets that incinerated certain spots yet never spread.

Continuing into the heart of the arboretum, they found the remnants of a bodhi tree in the middle of a cremated grove. Beneath the tree a burnt corpse sat holding an orange striped, black metal box. The dead held the A.D.R. like someone clutching a baby.

Before collecting the box, Liu ordered Rutledge to take photos. Meanwhile, she examined the corpse for any identifying features. The remains offered little. A name tag on the uniform nothing but melted gibberish; an embroidered patch suggested a member of the laboratory team. The gold necklace still around the corpse's neck offered a bit. If nothing else, it said the fire never got hotter than 1,000 degrees Celsius. Otherwise, the gold would've melted.

Instead of collecting the corpse, they decided to leave it in place. Liu went for the box. Gently, she moved the hands. The skin crumbled a bit when touched. Liu grabbed the box.

"Don't."

"Why not?" Liu asked.

"Why what?" Rutledge said.

"You said, 'Don't,'" she turned around.

"I didn't say anything," he said.

She looked at him skeptically. He shrugged. Turning back to the box, Liu saw a hand she thought she already moved clutching it again. Pushing the hand aside, she pulled the A.D.R. free.

After they gathered tissue samples, she decided they ought to check the accident data recorder before proceeding further. Rutledge volunteered to keep photographing the site. It went against procedure; however, Liu opted for a compromise, a little bone for being good. She ordered him to deposit his samples at the temp shelter, refill his oxygen, then only examine the exteriors.

"Stay in constant contact and do not go into any buildings," she said.

"Understood?"

"Yes, ma'am," he smiled.

\#

ACCIDENT DATA RECORDER
A.I. REACTION TRANSCRIPT
26-04-2109
11:41 p.m. (NAST)
KAIROS BASE
MENG-CHIEN CORP. LUNAR FACILITY

{Login detected}
{execute standard greeting 1}
Hello, DR.

{query entered}
Can you identify the entities we encountered earlier?
{processing}
{responding}
The entities recorded by security cameras do not match any known species.

{query entered}
Has anyone on Kairos base seen them before? Is there any mention in logs?
{processing}
{responding}
I cannot access crew member's personal logs without their explicit consent except in the event of a criminal investigation, catastrophic injury, or major accident inquiry.

{override requested}
{command code verified}
{overriding protocols}

{query entered}
{processing}
{responding}
Five personal logs contain references to abnormal events around the station.

{query entered}
What kind of "abnormal events" are described?
{processing}
{responding}
References to "spectral" entities are made as well as hearing "disembodied voices."

\#

Liu managed several tasks spread across three monitors. One displayed the percentage creeping closer to a hundred as the A.D.R. downloaded. At least forty-five minutes until complete. On screen two, Rutledge's feed showed him sauntering through Kairos base. Once or twice, he approached an opening, but she only needed to ask for a status update to prod him, keep him from going inside. Screen three showed her watching it all.

A dialogue box asked, "Continue prioritized recording?"

Clearing her throat, Liu touched the yes button onscreen. The computer beeped.

"After preliminary investigation, the claims of the Meng-chien Corporation do not appear to be," she hesitated to say *untrue*. "Accurate. If the A.D.R. doesn't provide clearer answers, I'll recommend dispatching the full team to the incident site. This is lead investigator Alyssa Liu signing off."

The recording stopped. She sent it to Earth. Prioritized, it would be viewed ahead of any streaming feed from the site.

Waiting on the A.D.R., she called up Rutledge's photos. The stills provided higher quality than screenshots from the stream. She cycled through several searching for the graffiti near the arboretum. A few appeared distorted. The images blurred in a way that called to mind being underwater. Finding the graffiti, she ran image enhancing programs hoping for some sense of the scrawl.

It seemed like Arabic calligraphy, but neither she nor the computer recognized the text. So, Liu tried to link with the servers at the Aufklärung colony 800km away. An alert notified her the connection failed—no access to the lunar web. She tried three more times, but each attempt failed to connect.

Instead of bothering with troubleshooting—she decided to task Rutledge with that—Liu sent a search request back to Earth along the stream. Granted, that'd take several minutes for any kind of reply, but the word might be meaningless gibberish. The last act of someone deranged by hypoxia. She figured it best to focus on more concrete clues.

Liu yawned. She realized it'd been almost two days since she slept. The excitement of the assignment propelling her to this point.

After touching down at the Aufklärung colony, she rendezvoused with Rutledge then took a hopper out to the Kairos site. People there didn't even know about any trouble at the facility.

"They don't keep in touch," the Aufklärung administrator told her. "We made routine checks like all lunar colonies, but except for automated answers, we haven't heard a human voice since April. Five months at least."

Stepping away from the terminal, Liu went to the food locker. Eyelids heavy, she prepared a coffee. As it hissed into a drinking pouch, she remembered sitting in a Hawaii café. The morning after a wild night celebrating the end of training, she sat trying to explain the wonder of seeing the Space Window for the first time at the National Cathedral in Washington D.C. A child staring up at a stained-glass display of whirling planets and stars. It filled her with awe and terror, the implications of the cosmos simplified yet still colossal.

"If we're ever going to explore deeper," she said. "We need to know what we've done wrong that way we don't make the same mistakes again. I want to help us leave this world behind. Nothing here is as important as what's out there."

Suddenly the gentle hands across the table, holding her warmly while promising, if she stayed, endless romantic strolls along Kealakekua Bay, those hands went cold. The grip tightened as if briefly threatening her throat. Then the person across from her drifted away.

Returning to the terminal, Liu noticed screen two frozen.

"Rutledge," she said. "Give me a sitrep."

A garbled bunch of static came back.

"Repeat," Liu said. "I didn't get that."

The screen flickered then jumped to another still frame. Rolling distortion lines spoiled the view but it definitely showed an interior.

"Goddammit," Liu said. "I told you not to go inside."

"I am outside," a voice but not Rutledge's. "Can't you hear me?"

The radio hissed. On screen, between the lines, she saw faceless people. Liu felt herself starting to fall.

The snap-puh-pop of the door made her jump. She almost leapt out of the chair. Startled, she spun around quickly. Seeing Rutledge entering the room, Liu did a double take. The feed on the screen showed his body cam aimed at her. She shook her head.

"Why didn't you respond?" she snapped.

"Why didn't you?" he said. "I've been trying to raise you. I came back because I was worried."

A quiet alert sounded. Turning towards the monitor, Liu saw a dialogue box informing the completion of the A.D.R. download.

"I think I dozed off," she said. "I must be more tired than I realized."

\#

ACCIDENT DATA RECORDER
  A.I. REACTION TRANSCRIPT
  27-04-2109
  4:21 a.m. (NAST)
  KAIROS BASE
  MENG-CHIEN CORP. LUNAR FACILITY

{fire detected = Arboretum}

{alarms activated}
{fire suppression systems engaged}
{alert protocols initiated}
Warning. Fire in the Arboretum.
{repeat}

{RFID alarm = Life signs fading.}
{RFID = Rupert Collins}
{alerting medical staff.}
Dr. Bryce. Medical emergency in the Arboretum.
{repeat}
{RFID alarm = Life signs critical.}
{RFID alarm = Life signs nil.}

ACCIDENT DATA RECORDER
A.I. REACTION TRANSCRIPT
27-04-2109
8:52 a.m. (NAST)
KAIROS BASE
MENG-CHIEN CORP. LUNAR FACILITY

{query entered}
If we contact the Aufklärung colony, how soon before they'll arrive with assistance?
{processing}
{responding}
The Aufklärung colony cannot be contacted for assistance.
{assist = elaborate}
{Directive 36}
{cancel assist = elaborate}

{query entered}
Why not?

{processing}
{responding}
{Directive 36}
I cannot answer that query.

{query entered}
   Why can't you answer the question?
   {processing}
   {responding}
   {Directive 36}
   I cannot answer that query.
   {override requested}
   {command code verified}
   {responding}
   Directive 36.

{query entered}
   What is Directive 36?
   {processing}
   {responding}
   {Directive 36}
   I cannot elaborate on Directive 36.

{override requested}
   {command code verified}
   {Directive 36}
   {override denied}

ACCIDENT DATA RECORDER
   A.I. REACTION TRANSCRIPT
   27-04-2109
   9:30 p.m. (NAST)
   KAIROS BASE

MENG-CHIEN CORP. LUNAR FACILITY

{notification = virus detected}
  {activating virus protection}
  {override requested}
  {command code verified}
  {overriding protocols}
  {assist = suggest}
  Disengaging virus protection is not recommended.
  {assist = elaborate}
  Computer systems are at risk.

{alert}
  Unauthorized changes have been made to the computer.

{query entered}
  What is Directive 36?
  {processing}
  {responding}
  {Directive 36}
  {overriding protocols}
  {responding}
  Due to the nature of research on KAIROS base, this facility is intentionally isolated from all other lunar communities.
  {assist= elaborate}
  Protocols related to Directive 36 ensure no R&D on KAIROS base is lost or stolen.

{query entered}
  What about base personnel?
  {processing}
  {responding}
  {Directive 36}

{overriding protocols}

{responding}

Personnel are a secondary concern.

#

"Yeah," Rutledge folded his arms across his chest. "I poked my head inside, but given what I found, I think it was the right thing to do."

He pointed at the image on screen. Liu still found it hard to believe. However, she knew of no way for Rutledge to fake the finding. Let alone any reason to. The photo showed a bare footprint in the lunar surface. In fact, a trail. According to Rutledge, he found a space suit just inside Habitat 2. It appeared someone stripped their suit off then walked out onto the Moon barefoot.

"Why didn't you photograph the body?" Liu asked.

"I couldn't find it."

"They couldn't've gotten far," she said. "Someone without a suit could only stay conscious, maybe fifteen seconds."

"Well, the trail went off out of sight."

Frowning, Liu sucked her coffee pouch, mostly to get the taste of this conversation out of her mouth. Her sleep addled mind vaguely recalled words didn't have flavor, yet she couldn't deny the sour all over her tongue. Sighing, she set the pouch aside. Somehow the caffeine seemed to make her more exhausted, thicken the brain fog. Deciding not to run on fumes, she instructed Rutledge to review the A.D.R. info while she grabbed some shuteye.

"Wake me in two hours," she said. "Then we'll explore the interiors."

"Sounds good," Rutledge said as she shuffled away.

Shambling to the sleeping area, Liu groaned in frustration. The beds still needed to be assembled. Instead of dealing with the collapsible frames, she simply unfolded a sleeping mat on the floor. Laying down, she felt ready to pass out of existence. Half awake, Liu noticed a faint vibration in the floor. The rhythms reminded her of rippling waves. Conjuring dreams of floating in the ocean, the vibrations lulled her to sleep.

When she awoke, Liu felt pleased to find she got up without Rutledge rousing her. Stretching, she climbed out of bed feeling thoroughly refreshed. Returning to the work room, she looked forward to his report on the A.D.R. info. However, she found the room empty.

Liu called out for him. No response. About to step over to the computer terminal, her eye hooked on splotches of red.

Just above the view slot a scarlet starburst painted the wall. Drooling ends of the splatter's rays pointed towards the ground. Her eyes followed them to the floor where she discovered an oblong crimson puddle dancing like water in a singing bowl. The closer she got the less Liu could deny, this must be blood.

Jumping over to the computer she pinged Rutledge's RFID. It showed him in the remains of Habitat 4. Calling up his video feed, she grabbed the radio.

"Rutledge, this is Liu. Can you hear me?"

She happened to glance at the clock. Blinking, Liu couldn't believe her eyes. It showed seven hours since she left to take a nap.

Turning back the footage, she started the stream right after she left Rutledge. For several hours nothing much happened. He dutifully went through the A.D.R. info. Occasionally he paused to have the computer define terms like gravity wave communication. For the most part, Liu sped through these moments. She hurried to a point where Rutledge got up, presumably to wake her. He turned and the feed smeared into an incoherent mess.

Furrowing her brow, Liu dialed it back a few seconds. Slowing the stream, for the briefest moment before the video scrambled, she saw a spectral entity flicker into view. It seemed to be a chimera combining a squid and a shark. Rutledge sat at the computer, oblivious to the massive entity slipping through the wall, gliding towards him with its tentacles outstretched and jaws wide.

She fast forwarded to when the video cleared. It showed Rutledge scrambling to put on his suit. She noticed blood dripping, probably from a head wound. Then he bounded out the airlock.

He seemed to've abandoned her. She didn't know if she should feel hurt, though it hardly surprised her. When a shark attacked her sister, she remembered so many surfers racing to shore. All those macho boys screaming for the safety of sand, exposed in a way she never forgot or forgave.

She watched him run then stumble as he entered the Kairos area. Suddenly he screamed in pain.

"What the fuck is that sound?" Rutledge hollered.

Then the view rippled as if a slow wave rolled through reality. It collided with Rutledge, picked him up, and carried him end over end. He tumbled out of control until his body fell back to the lunar surface, landing hard inside the ruins of Habitat 4.

\#

ACCIDENT DATA RECORDER
  A.I. REACTION TRANSCRIPT
  28-04-2109
  12:00 a.m. (NAST)
  KAIROS BASE
  MENG-CHIEN CORP. LUNAR FACILITY

{fire detected = Habitat 4}
  {alarms activated}
  {fire suppression systems engaged}
  {alert protocols initiated}
  {override requested}
  {command code verified}
  {overriding protocols}
  {fire suppression systems disengaged}
  {assist = suggest}
  Disengaging fire suppression system is not recommended.

{assist = elaborate}
Fire may spread.
{RFID alarm = Life signs critical.}
{RFID alarm = Life signs nil.}
{RFID = Dr. Bryce Krasnikov}
{alerting medical staff.}
{override requested}
{command code verified}
{overriding protocols}

ACCIDENT DATA RECORDER
A.I. REACTION TRANSCRIPT
28-04-2109
12:11 a.m. (NAST)
KAIROS BASE
MENG-CHIEN CORP. LUNAR FACILITY

{fire detected = Support Module}
   {multiple fires detected}
   {alert protocols initiated}
   Warning! Catastrophic failure. Evacuate facility immediately.
   {override requested}
   {command code verified}
   {overriding protocols}
   {alert protocols disengaged}
   {ADR upload initiated}
   {override requested}
   {RFID alarm = Life signs critical.}
   {RFID = Dr. Audrey Lynn}
   {alerting medical staff}
   Medical emergency in Support Module.
   {failure to input command codes}
   {ADR upload initiated}

{prioritized files uploading}
{prioritized = Project Mercury}
{RFID alarm = Life signs nil.}
{RFID = Dr. Audrey Lynn}

\#

Liu took a deep breath. A rising panic threatened to take her but focusing on procedure kept her calm. First, she recorded a brief prioritized message summarizing recent events. Hitting send, she raced to get her space suit on. Stepping out the airlock, an alert popped up in her helmet display.

"Message failed to send," the computer reported. "Connection failed."

Swearing, Liu decided to go for Rutledge first. Hurrying across the empty gray mare it dawned on her the closest help—humans—lived 800 kilometers away in the Aufklärung colony. She felt a sudden sharp desperate need for Rutledge to still be alive.

Using the augmented view, she found Habitat 4 on the far side of Kairos base. Ash reminiscent of Chladni figures ringed the remains like a halo of thorns. Stepping through a hole in one wall, Liu entered a burnt-out laboratory. Melted glass left odd solid puddles on tables. Torched circuitry spilled out of cremated computers. She passed a scorched skeleton, the skull several feet away. A portable cutting torch still in its hand suggested the dead cut off their own head.

Moving deeper inside, Liu started feeling a hum inside her body. It caused a dull headache that slowed her steps until she saw Rutledge splayed out on the floor. Heading towards him the hum intensified. She began to feel her suit vibrating. Reaching Rutledge, she dropped to one knee.

She rolled him over. Liu pushed up his sun visor. His face resembled a blueberry smoothie.

A resonance rattled her bones. Somehow it called Liu's attention to a device under a section of the module's dome that still stood. It looked like some relic in a futuristic grotto setting. More importantly, she noticed lights on it blinking emerald and an independent power source keeping the machine alive. The air, the very reality around it rippled every so often.

A spectral figure coalesced into view a foot before her. The kaleidoscopic chaos of its face forced Liu to look away. Seeing it made her want to look at the sun, stare into the star, and happily let it burn her blind.

"We heard you calling."

"We didn't…" Liu trailed off, her eyes drifting back to the humming Kairos experiment.

"We came to deliver silence."

"Silence?" Liu said.

"Even now, it screams into the void," the spectral said. "It screams into you."

"What else does it do?" Liu found herself asking.

"It summons teeth, and it sings open doors."

She saw a wave ripple from the machine. When it hit her—a flash like a blue sheet pulled over her eyes. Then she spilled across the stars. A human message in a bottle tossed across the cosmos, bobbing on gravity waves. Read by many, ignored by most. Ten thousand views tried to own her eyes at once. Slivers of the infinite poured painfully through her pupils. Thinking of one made it dominant—the Pacific Ocean rolling gently onto a Hawaiian shore.

Gasping, Liu found herself standing on Kealakekua Bay. The waves lapped at her feet. Sunset painted the sky red, orange, and gold. Not the empty black coloring so much of the ceaseless cosmos. She half recalled teeth and terrors, star-sized eyes glaring across the vast emptiness, and steadily Liu found this finite sky more pleasant than vast space. A tear rolled down her cheek.

Liu longed to feel the warm sun on her face. So, she snapped open the clasps on her helmet. Pulling it off, she tossed it aside. Smiling on the Moon, her skin soon began to burn, her saliva boiled, and as her retinas melted, Liu collapsed in Habitat 4. The Kairos machine hummed her into a pleasant grave. Yet, her mind still glowed in the hands of the specter; waiting to deliver a ghost for whoever came after.

The U Train—K. C. Grifant

K
C Grifant is an award-winning science writer with internationally published stories encompassing the horror, fantasy, scifi and western genres. Her stories have appeared in Andromeda Spaceways Magazine (*cover story for issue 70*), Unnerving Magazine, Tales to Terrify, Colp Magazine, *the* Lovecraft eZine *and more. She's also contributed to dozens of anthologies, including* Field Notes from a Nightmare; The One That Got Away: Women of Horror Vol. 3; Six Guns Straight From Hell Vol. 3; Shadowy Natures: Tales of Psychological Horror; We Shall Be Monsters; Beyond the Infinite: Tales from the Outer Reaches; *and the Stoker-nominated* Fright Mare: Women Write Horror. *She is the cofounder of the Horror Writer's Association San Diego Chapter. Learn more at KCGrifant.com or connect on social at @kcgrifant. A radio adaption of this story can be found on the podcast* Sley House Presents *anywhere you stream your podcasts.*

* * *

They say waiting is its own kind of hell. Whoever said that was probably familiar with the NYC subway system.

"Think it's the End of Days?" a gentleman to my left asked. We both stood

"

at the edge of the yellow strip on the platform, waiting for the train. God knows how much time had passed. Over an hour at least. I had gotten up early to go to my favorite breakfast spot in East Harlem. Bacon to die for. My doc said I shouldn't eat so much bacon. Or smoke. Or drink soda. But don't they all say that?

"It's always the End of Days waiting for the transfer," I responded, and he chuckled. He jiggled his foot and was going to ask me something else but I turned my attention pointedly away. Even though he was well dressed—collared shirt and a suit jacket visible from his open windbreaker—you could never tell who would ask for money or start talking crazy at you. I took stock, automatically, at how many people were around us. Just two others this early, a guy maybe in his early twenties with a faded rainbow hoodie and oversized headphones, and a woman around the same age, shrugging off a purple peacoat as she balanced a covered tray of cupcakes.

"I hate to ask but do you have a portable charger I could borrow? My phone is dead." The suited man said. As evidence he opened his hand, where the screen of his new apple-what-not was blank as a slate.

I shook my head. "Never had a need. Don't want anyone tracking me. You know they can hear everything you say on those. I got nothing to hide but my business is also my business."

He cocked his head, puzzled like just about anyone who learned I didn't have a phone, his foot pausing for two seconds before resuming its tapping. "It's just…I'm not sure why the U train is so late. And *I'm* going to be late."

He gestured up and I followed his line of thought. It was an older station and hadn't been fitted with any of those automated screens hanging overhead or announcers that told you how long it'd be. No attendants either; I'd have to track back up a long set of stairs and a godforsaken endless corridor to find a living person back at the turnstiles.

"Just like back in the day," I grunted. "You had nothing to tell you how long it'd be, half the time. Transfers, busses, constructions. People throwing themselves on the tracks. Happens a lot, you know. You just have to wait."

"Have you heard an announcement?" The girl chimed in behind us, setting the cupcakes on the rusted steel bench.

"Check your phone?" Suit asked.

Cupcakes shook her head, pressing a stray blond strand behind her ear. Genevieve would be about her age now, but I didn't want to think about that. "It's not turning on."

Suit held very still. "Mine either. Which is weird, I always charge it."

Both considered a moment before Cupcakes tapped the guy with headphones. His shoulders tensed and he turned.

"Do you know if the train's late?" Cupcakes said loudly and pointed to his faded jean pocket, where a sliver of a phone stuck out. "Could you check? Please?"

Headphones shrugged. "Outta juice."

"So, what are you listening to?" Cupcakes said.

He slid his headphones down and around his neck. "People don't bother me as much when I wear them," he said, almost defensive.

"Something's not right," Suit said. "How can all of our phones not be working?"

"That's why I don't carry the things," I said. "Look how distraught you all are over a piece of plastic and metal. Cyberattack, cancer in the brain. No thank you."

I glanced at my watch but had forgotten to wear it this morning. Damn. My wrist felt bare as a newborn's butt. The line out of my breakfast place would be unacceptable by 8:30, 9 tops. Then I'd be late for chess in the park. If I was a minute past the hour, Pete would mosey in on my prime corner seat like it hadn't been my spot the last ten years. I'd have to wait a half hour at least for rounds, then late to lunch.

"Damn it," I growled. "I need my coffee."

"You gonna look for a transfer?" Cupcakes asked, glancing behind her. I followed her gaze.

The exit seemed miles away. I'd have to zigzag up and down countless steps, trek up intersecting corridors, sidestepping pedestrians. In the meantime I'd get breathless and covered in sweat that would turn cold and sticky against my sweater and make me uncomfortable all day. And as subway luck would have it, the train would probably roll up as soon as I left.

"Nah," I said. I looked out on the tracks to entertain myself, see if I could spot something, anything. Maybe a rat to flick a rubber band at. If there was one thing I hated it was rats, so any chance to kill 'em or cause them a little suffering was time well spent. But not a soul moved down there. I strained my ears, listening for the faint drone or screech of an approaching subway. Nothing. Just the tap-tap-tap of Suit's foot, Cupcake's sighs and somewhere down that dark tunnel, a steady drip. The usual subway smell—a baked-in stench of old garbage, fresh pee and smoke topped with a sprinkling of fungus or mold—flared in my nose.

"What's that?" Headphones asked.

"Dessert, for a going-away party," Cupcakes answered. She wasn't dressed right for the weather or the morning, in some sort of sequined flare skirt and halter top. Not that I didn't appreciate the look, mind you, but April was full of endless wet and slush with a few teasing peekaboos of warm weather, so tantalizing you wanted to scream.

"At this hour?" I gave her a look. I mean, really peered over my glasses at her. *Who the hell has a party at 7am?* I wanted to ask and looked at my wrist again, forgetting the watch wasn't there.

Cupcakes sniffed and shifted, avoiding my eyes. Probably guessed me to be a lecherous old man. I didn't want to break it to her but she wasn't my type at all, too skinny. Something in my DNA just didn't find that all that interesting.

"Dead as a doornail," Suit said again in frustration, jabbing at his phone. "I don't hear anything. You think maybe something happened?"

Headphones' eyes lit up. "Like a Godzilla type? Or a terrorist attack?"

"I think we'd hear screams," Cupcakes said.

Headphones shrugged and headed toward the stairs without another word. We watched his backpack move up and out of sight.

"I'm too old for this s—" I started when Headphones popped back down.

"What's the word?" Suit said.

Headphones blinked at us. "I went up and…. now I'm back."

I squinted at him. "What are you going on about?"

"I can't leave," he said. "I can't. Like physically can't."

Suit jogged up the staircase and, a second later, jogged right back down. He paused on the last step, looking at us, up, down, up again like he was watching an invisible tennis match. Then his face folded like so many cards.

"It's not real. It's not right," Suit moaned.

Headphones had buried his face in his hands. "Wake up. Wake up."

"You guys are as hilarious as a battle sub with a screen door." I glanced behind me just to make sure there were no cameras. "This one of those viral marketing stunt flash mob what-have-yous? Hilarious."

I snorted and heaved myself up the stairs. When I got to the top, I found myself facing downwards, looking at the platform again. I turned to go back up and was facing down again. The whole effect made me dizzy, so I shuffled down the last few steps and onto the bench next to Cupcakes.

"You try," I croaked at her and she shook her head, eyes wide and terrified as a mouse.

"Screw this!" Suit bellowed at the empty track. "I'll go down there and walk to the next access point if I have to."

He stood, half crouched as if to jump down. He glanced at the rest of us and wavered.

"Sit down amigo." I laughed to hide my nerves. "You're not going anywhere. Whatever thing is happening *up there* is trying to keep us *down here*. You think they haven't thought of that?"

Headphones finally lifted up his head as Suit arched an eyebrow. "*They?*"

"Government corporate types, who else? We're just pawns on their board. If there's an outbreak, or a terrorist attack, or what have you, you think they don't have sophisticated weapons? They got all kinds of things. Including—" I waved my hands toward the stairs. "Invisible force fields, walls, what not."

"Sounds like conspiracy crap," Suit said.

"Believe it or not but it's well documented. It was always a matter of time. You'll see."

Trick was you had to look for the little offbeat blogs and forums, the ones where people talked in code and told you what was really going on behind the curtain. I knew some of it was hogwash, sure, but when you lived as long as I had, you know sometimes there's kernels of truth in the unlikeliest of places.

"They don't want us out, we're not getting out," I tried to explain but they were all panicking. Headphones and Cupcakes shouted for help at the stairs until they were hoarse. Stupid kids. Suit did eventually climb down to the tracks and walk a few feet down in the darkness, just to turn around.

"Same as the stairs," Suit huffed as Headphones helped him back up on the platform. Suit shrugged off his windbreaker and hurled it against a post. "What the fuck are we supposed to do?" He slumped onto the bench next to me, defeated.

Something like a skittering sounded below the tracks. I glanced down, looking for the shiny brown back of a roach or tail of a rat.

"You hear that?" I said.

"No, what?" Suit cocked his head and we all listened. Nothing.

"Maybe nothing." I shrugged. "Maybe a sewer rat or giant roach. Some of 'em grow to be the size of your whole arm, no kidding. Prehistoric."

"It's gotta be a dream." Suit pinched the back of his hand. We watched his skin turn white then red. "Ow."

"I think it's an end-of-the-world sitch," Cupcakes said, her dress spread out as she sat on the bench. "Actually, I'm relieved. It's about time."

The rest of us looked at her as a flush crept, relentless, along her cheeks. "I mean, I'm just tired of it all, you know?"

More silence until Headphones piped up. "Yeah."

"What, your expensive liberal arts college got you blue?" I asked.

"I have a lot to worry about actually." A mix of shame and pride stormed over her face, reminding me of a kid. "No, I, ah, dropped out of school. Run a pretty successful business selling stuff."

"Stuff?" I already knew where she was going by her tone, and I wasn't impressed. How does that song go, lots of "good girls gone bad" in the city.

She nodded curtly.

"Pot?" Suit said hopefully and she shook her head.

"You don't look anything like a dealer," Headphones said. She smiled primly but then I noticed the bags under her eyes, how her forearms looked like any fat or substance was burned right off, leaving the thinnest skin stretched over bones.

"That's what makes it so easy," she said and, almost as an afterthought, added, "it's a lot of money."

"Better be careful with that nonsense," I said. "People fall down a hole faster than they can get out."

She nodded, her eyes hollowed as a skeleton.

"Well, might as well make things interesting," Suit said. "I screwed my trainer yesterday. Again." He breathed out, bounced a bit on the balls of his loafers. "Man, it feels good to get that out. My wife ever found out well…" His glance flicked down for a second. "She's a little unstable. Makes it hard." He made a sound like a laugh, a noise mixed with heartbreak and relief. "She'd probably shoot me point blank."

"That's fucked." Cupcakes glanced at his wedding band.

"Pssh, you think that's a big dark secret?" I said. "Show me a man in this world that hasn't cheated, once."

Headphones rose his hand.

Cupcakes rolled her eyes at me. "So, what's your deal?"

"I'm not interested in games," I said and looked at the rail. I glanced at my bare wrist again out of habit and couldn't shake the urge of too much time passing. It must have been hours by this point. Probably almost lunch time.

"Guys." Headphones' hand was shaking.

"You OK, kid? Gonna barf?" I stepped back to be safe.

"I um, just remembered something." He was actually shaking, like he was cold, teeth chattering and everything. "There is no U subway."

Cupcakes started counting on her short purple nails. "F, L, 2. There are others, so many." She blinked. "Every day I take the…" She looked at us in confusion.

I wracked my brain but couldn't remember a damn thing about my commute.

"What does it mean?" Suit asked. "I can't…I can't even remember my name."

"Deadly toxin." I nodded. "Eating out our brains. Causing early onset dementia."

Cupcake yelped and covered her face. "Don't *say* that."

"I think—" Headphones shook his head, a grim set to his jaw. "We're in some kinda limbo. Maybe hell. I had a dream, last night." He pulled a beat-up blue spiral notebook the size of a checkbook from his back pocket. He flung it open and flipped past fraying corners to the last page. A sketch in pencil, not half bad, looked up at us, recognizable enough. The reaper.

"Now *that* is crazy," I said, angrier than I intended.

"Wait…" Suit said and leaned against the filthy column for support as his eyes fluttered closed. "Maybe it's true. The last thing I remember is…well, I can't recall, but I think it wasn't good. Maybe we're dead."

At his words something stirred in me, a panic, a quick realization that something was wrong, but I smothered it as quick as a bag of unwanted pups.

Headphones, however, nodded vigorously. "And now waiting for the ferry guy."

"Ferry guy?" Cupcakes squeaked. "You mean, like the River of the Dead? God that's morbid. How about an angel or something more positive?"

"Angels *down here*?" Headphones spread his hands.

"You won't entertain the likely notion that it's the government or terrorism but think we're all dead. That's rich." I laughed to cover up the lump that was forming at the base of my throat. Like I had swallowed something that the acid reflux wanted to send back up.

Cupcakes, Suit and Headphones all seemed subdued, somber. Now that had me unraveling like my cheap sweater. The lump in my throat seemed to grow, dropping into my stomach heavy as a sack of nails. I tried not to think about all I hadn't done with my life yet despite my years, all the people I still had something to say to. I pushed the sensation away but one thought burrowed under my skin and stuck. Pete in my seat, setting up the chessboard. Smug bastard would probably be glad I was dead.

Suit paced in short circles, the shadows on his face jumping in the gloom. "So, what is this? Our last confessional?" He looked up at the dank, spotted ceiling and was really yelling now. "I didn't do anything to deserve this. So

I cheated, so *what*? I didn't murder anyone. Didn't fuck up that bad. Not enough to be down here!"

Watching his breakdown made me feel a little better. Gave me some entertainment at least.

"Get a grip," Cupcakes said and turned to Headphones. "If it is a confessional, maybe you two need to go ahead with yours so we can wake up from this nightmare, move onto the next world or whatever."

"You seem awfully calm." Suit's note of accusation was sharp as a shard of whiskey bottle. "Are you the devil?"

"What? *No*." Cupcakes flushed. "Now you sound like my ex."

"OK." Suit pointed to Headphones. "What's your deep dark secret then that earned you this hallowed place besides us, Adulteress and Drug Dealer?"

"Me?" Headphones looked embarrassed and fiddled with the bent spiral of his notebook. "I, ah, some of my friends beat up guys sometimes. Homeless dudes mostly. Some guys are into it. It's kinda funny. I can't explain it. They usually don't fight back. You kinda have to be there."

"O-M-G," Cupcakes said.

"I didn't do anything," Headphones said hastily. "Just watched. The cops came though and…I don't really remember, I was kinda outta it."

The other two looked disgusted and he hung his head. "I know. I'm a piece of shit."

All their faces turned toward me, curious, relentless. Screw that, I started to say but stopped. Something in each of them had opened up it seemed, with their confessional. Less hardened and evasive. Just sort of sad. Reminded me of the last time I saw my other little girl, Pipa. Somehow she knew I was planning to leave, even though I didn't give any hint. Didn't pack anything. Said I was going to work as usual, gonna be late.

"Few kids," I barked hoarsely. "Haven't seen 'em in a while."

That was all I had to say about that. But Cupcakes regarded me sadly, and she started to remind me of the kiddos I had upped and left.

"Cut that out, with the big eyes," I said and she blinked. "I tried but it didn't work out."

"Suit nodded vigorously. "There's something about being free, yeah?"

I didn't want to talk about it anymore. I went back to the yellow stripe and looked down. No trash on the tracks. That should've been my first sign that something was wrong.

"It's too late to do anything about it now," I said to the tracks.

Cupcakes sighed. "It's never too late."

"Sometimes it is, though," Headphones said.

"You hear that?" I strained my ears. Finally, what sounded like the faintest drone echoed somewhere down the tunnel.

Cupcakes' eyes grew enormous, and Suit's mouth was a perfect "o" that would've made me laugh under other circumstances.

"The train," Headphones said, unnecessarily.

I had never been religious but damn if it didn't say a quick prayer right then.

Dear Lord. Please let this be all some sort of screwy dream and let me wake up. I'll be better I swear. I'll reach out to the kids—even though they'll tell me to shove it—I'll do it anyway. I swear. If you gimme a chance. Please.

The others were quiet, probably in their own negotiations.

I shuffled behind the yellow line as the train roared up and the doors to the last car screeched open. The cars in front of it were dark and closed.

"Could be a test." I still half suspected it was a government job. I glanced in. I expected ghouls or zombies or something, but it was empty, a little dirty.

"Typical car by the looks of it," I said.

"Should we board?" Headphones asked.

Suit pushed past me to step on. "*Anything's* better than here."

"Let's hope," Cupcakes murmured.

Headphones laughed nervously as we boarded. "We're good maybe."

Once we were all on the doors whooshed closed and the subway started, lights flickering. Nothing weird, nothing off, until Headphones stood at the window.

"We're definitely in Hell," Headphones said with a certainty that made us look over.

"How do you know?" I went to stand next to him as he pointed.

Through the rear window, below the track that we were zipping along, squirmed bodies. Hundreds, maybe thousands.

And not just any bodies.

The four of us. Over and over again. All squirming and mashed up on each other, grinning and waving in a mass of glittering skirts and suit jackets and rainbow hoodies and fraying argyle sweaters, making up a fabric like a ribbon undercutting the city.

Cupcakes screamed and Headphones doubled up, dry heaving again.

I couldn't stop staring. We were moving too fast to really focus on a single face, but the quick flashes of my smug smile, gnarled hands flicking toward the sky and shock of gray hair made me dizzy. It was like looking into a pit of cracked mirrors as the train thundered on, rolling over infinite versions of ourselves.

Cupcakes shuddered finally. "I can't look anymore. This is a bad trip. The worst."

"I think you're right, kiddo. We're in purgatory." Once I said it aloud, a little flint of a memory came back to me. Pain, and collapsing from my bed. Maybe I should've listened to the doc.

Still, I don't think I could've given up bacon, even knowing what was coming.

"Think we're gonna see the big man, then?" I said. God or the Devil, I wasn't sure.

"No way." Suit struggled with the rear car door. "I'm not sticking around to meet *anyone*."

"This again," I sighed. His freak-out was sort of funny the first time but was getting old.

"Help me," Suit said and Headphones grudgingly got up.

"Put your shoulder into it," I said.

"Why are you encouraging them," Cupcakes said.

"Way I see it, nothing we can do but try to enjoy the ride, sweetheart."

She frowned as the door cracked open.

Suit turned back to us with some sort of salute. "Sayonara." He stepped off and half a second later stumbled back in, eyes wild.

"Same as the stairs," Headphones guessed and plopped down, pulling out his notebook and pencil and starting to sketch.

"I wish I could've said good-bye to my mom," Cupcakes said out of the blue and got real quiet, turning her head away from us.

"I'm not going to just sit here like cattle to the slaughterhouse." Suit's eyes nearly bugged out of his face. "So, I'm not perfect, so what? I deserve this?" He turned and jabbed a finger at the window. "I'd kill you all to get out of here, no question. You'd do the same, don't pretend otherwise. If we're stuck up in Mount Everest and starving, anybody up there would eat their own to survive. Fucking human nature."

"He's losing it all right," I said to no one in particular.

Suit jutted forward and grabbed the knobby pencil from Headphones. He pointed it like a knife at his own neck, gaze out of focus.

"Just do it already so I can have my pencil back," Headphones said. I guessed he was as tired of Suit's shit as I was.

Cupcakes sucked in a breath as Suit rammed the pencil into his throat.

"No blood," I said, a little disappointed. The pencil had popped right out, no mark, nothing.

Suit slapped his neck, calmer. "It hurt anyway. Fuck." He slumped in a seat next to Cupcakes and Headphones resumed drawing. The sketch looked like Cupcakes from this angle, but wasn't good enough that I could tell for sure.

More time passed and I closed my eyes. Maybe it was a dream or a hallucination. Maybe if I willed it I could wake the hell up. I tried not to think of anything, and pictured a chess board empty of pieces. Symmetrical. Even. No problems, no riddles to solve. Just a blank slate.

An intercom system crackled, and my eyes flew open. We all froze as the static grew louder.

"Passengers who wove themselves badly must depart."

The voice was high-pitched and tinny, coming from all directions and I thought of trumpets.

"What does that mean?" Cupcakes shrieked. "Who are you?"

"I will fuck you up!" Suit shouted up at the ceiling at the same time.

"Next stop: primordial fears."

The intercom went silent after that.

"Primordial fears?" Cupcakes said. "What does that mean?"

"Like fundamental, right," Headphones said. "Fight-or-flight. Like when you see a lion in the jungle, that's a primordial fear to help you survive."

"That doesn't make sense," Cupcakes said. "We're going to fight a lion?"

"I don't deserve this." Suit was ramming his head against the window. He turned to Headphones. "Do you? Are you that evil a person, deep down? So rotten to the core to deserve this?"

"We still don't know what *this* is," Cupcakes said.

"Why us four? Surely we can't be the only ones who sinned. Maybe we died at the same time?" Suit jiggled his knee and rapped against the window for emphasis.

"Could you do us all a favor? Shut the hell up. Just for a few minutes. Or forever." I closed my eyes again when I felt the unmistakable sensation of the train slowing.

"We're stopping," Cupcakes said, voice laced with panic. I couldn't blame her. Panic was fisting my own chest like another heart attack.

The car slid to a stop and the doors hissed open to pitch blackness as the intercom voice crackled again:

"Stop: Primordial fears. Passengers must face themselves and fix their fabric to ascend."

"Fuuuuck me," Suit moaned.

Headphones, I had to give him credit, ventured out first before the rest of us followed, blinking in the shift from florescent lights to darkness.

Headphones inched forward and we followed as our eyes adjusted. At this point I felt more annoyed than anything. Whatever force or being was in charge sure liked dragging things out.

"Just tell us what the deal is already," I said in the darkness.

"Look." Cupcakes jostled next to us. I blinked at a small trickle of light from a narrow passage. The platform we stood on funneled into a weirdly lit cave tunnel.

At least it wasn't red.

We walked through, Headphones, Suit, Cupcakes and me bringing up the rear.

"God," Cupcakes gagged. The smell was terrible. Like the worse funk you could ever imagine, heated up in a tiny kitchen with your face over the open oven door. Before I could get out of the passage to see what was ahead, something hard slammed into me. It took me a second to figure out what it was.

"Fuck no, no, no," Suit was moaning and shoving, trying to get behind me. But there was nowhere to go; a rock wall had appeared and pressed into my back.

"Get outta here," I snarled and shoved Suit out of my way. I made my way past Cupcakes who had fallen on her knees and Headphones standing there all slack jawed.

That's when I saw it.

An enormous pit yawned out in front of the ledge we stood on, and rising out from the pit—my chest seized up as I recognized the massive shape.

A rat the size of King Kong, stood in the pitch, wearing a goddamn crown and everything. Thousands of normal sized rats ran up and over each other like ocean waves in the pit around the rat king.

"Goddamn why couldn't it be a proper devil." I had the shakes and my body pressed up against the back of the wall. My stomach slid up my throat again. "Of all the goddamned creatures."

The giant rat, its black eye the size of a bench, looked at me. It squeaked loud as a car horn and waved its paw.

Suit was still screaming.

"This was not what I pictured," Cupcakes said faintly between her hands. "This must be the primordial fear."

"Everyone makes mistakes!" Suit screamed and started hurling stones into the pit. "Die fuckers!" The stones disappeared harmlessly into the pit of rats. "Fucking snakes!"

"Snakes?" I said when the intercom voice boomed again and I saw another subway train behind the rat king, high up and with no obvious way to get to it.

"A stop to fix your fabric."

"Oh no. I think—" Cupcakes stammered, all round eyes. She trembled like it was the dead of winter and looked back at the pit. "I think I'm supposed to jump in. Like be brave enough or strong enough to do it. But I'm really afraid of spiders. It's like a phobia. I can't even look at them. Anything but—"

Just then Cupcakes winked out.

Out of sight.

Out of existence.

"No!" Headphones yelled and something pinched my chest and pricked my eyes.

"Cupcakes, damn," I muttered. I had grown fond of them. What I wouldn't give now to be back at the U station stop or even in the train with them, even if it was for eternity. Anything but the rats.

"Take them!" Suit jabbed a finger at me, spit flying. "Sacrifice them! I'll kill them if you want! Take—" He disappeared mid-shout, the rat king chittering all the while. Its stomach bellowed like a trampoline matted in fur while its crown, darkened gold with dirty jewels, sat crooked between twitching ears. I shuddered and pressed my hands to my ears to drown out its sound, like a chipmunk squeak cranked way up and remixed.

"Why are you doing this?" Headphones dry heaved. "Oh God, I think I'm next. I think…it wants me to jump into the roaches." A look of resolve fell over Headphones. "I'll do it. I'm sorry for everything. I deserve this."

"You crazy?" I jolted forward to stop him but next thing I knew, Headphones ran and jumped, the faded rainbow hood flapping as he fell.

The pit of rats promptly enveloped him, their claws digging in and running over his screaming face before he vanished.

"Let the kid go!" I yelled. A movement behind the rat king's crown caught my eye. Headphones waved from way up, inside the new subway train. His hand pounding the glass, his mouth moving trying to say something.

"OK," I muttered to myself. My stomach started to feel queasy like I was dropping on a roller coaster. "My turn, I guess. You can do this."

I looked at the pit again, the clawed paws and beady eyes undulating in filthy furred bodies. Just watching them my skin feel like it was sliding off and I tried to breathe through my mouth to avoid the smell of filthy fur and shit.

"Anything else," I said hoarsely. I didn't know what kind of man could face something like that but it wasn't me, even though I might be dead already. Props to Headphones. "Gimme bugs, fire and damnation. Just not rats."

The voice sounded again from the train behind the rat king, flat and emotionless: *"Primordial fears."*

I hunched over, my knees cracking into the rock. The rats' scampering and squeaking rose and I dug my fingers into my ears. For a wild second I was sure it was an elaborate prank. Had to be. Something to get the old man to jump into a rat pit and film it for all the world to see. My nostrils flared.

"Hell no," I said.

My stomach continued to suck away, and I felt something else: a patch of cold like a draft in January, starting up my legs and under my sweater.

I gritted my teeth as my eyes pricked. I wouldn't think of Pipa and Genevieve or anyone else. This might be the end, the real end, but I had to know one thing. "Did anything matter? What was the point of it all?"

The voice didn't come back. Instead, I heard the new subway start driving off, wheels squeaking. The rat king squirmed above its sea of subjects, their chittering filling my ears as darkness descended.

The Hunger—Frank Coffman

Frank Coffman is a retired professor of English, Creative Writing, and Journalism. He has published speculative poetry and fiction in a variety of journals, magazines, anthologies, and collections.

His major collections of verse are: The Coven's Hornbook & Other Poems *(2019),* Black Flames & Gleaming Shadows *(2020), and* Eclipse of the Moon *(2021). A formalist, traditional verse poet, he considers himself primarily a sonneteer, but his experiments and innovations with form cross national, cultural, and period boundaries and a plethora of forms.*

His collection of occult detective stories, Three Against the Dark: Collected Dr. Venn Occult Detective Mysteries *was released in 2022. A collection of short fiction,* Maxime Miris: 15 Tales of the Weird, Horrific, and Supernatural, *will be released in early 2023.*

He is a member of the Horror Writers Association *and the* Science Fiction & Fantasy Poetry Association. *He created and moderates the* Weird Poets Society *Facebook Group.*

* * *

It smelled the humans long before it saw them.

It had stalked to where their campfire could be seen, a spot of brilliant red through the thick timber and brush, more starkly colored by the perverse red tint of what was an aspect of its abnormal vision.

As it neared stealthily, it saw that there were four of them. They had killed a huge bull moose, but it was not the moose that it wanted. It would eat the moose too, of course, but it was the human flesh for which it was ravenous. It had not feasted on man for weeks now, and its need for that taste was always insatiable.

They had no notion of its presence nearby until it suddenly appeared in their midst. Two were dead before the other men could do more than scream. Only one managed to grab his rifle—but it was all over within a few seconds. Over except for the methodical eating that was to come.

* * *

Inspector Roderick McKenna had been with the Criminal Investigative Analysis Division of the Royal Canadian Mounted Police for 12 years. Normally, his job was simply acting as a consultant for local constabularies. But also, quite often, he had been called in to investigate a case more closely—usually cases of homicide. Some kidnappings—including hostage negotiation—and rarely, but of late, threat analysis for national security had come his way. In this last, he was always amused by the division's acronym of "CIA" being the same as the American's intelligence wing.

But Rod McKenna was no spy. He was a damned good policeman. He'd been a member of "The Force" (as "Mounties" referred to themselves) for 19 years. Working his way through the ranks from age 20, he had risen to Inspector in only seven years. Taking extra courses in criminology and forensics and having been certified by the International Criminal Investigative Analysis Fellowship, he had sought and was soon awarded an Inspectorship with the "CIA."

It had been another slow day. Cleaning up some big stacks of paperwork was part of the job. It surprised him when his phone rang, and the voice said:

"My name is William Tompkins of the Ontario Provincial Police. I'm the Staff Inspector of District 17 and in charge here in Thunder Bay. I've called Ottawa to get in touch with your unit, and I've been told by one of my Inspectors, Thomas Leeds, that you're the man for the job. We need your unit's assistance. The case—actually cases—are quite serious."

"Well, Inspector Tompkins, it's a bit unusual. Thank Tom Leeds for the recommendation for me, but, as you know, Ontario is not in our primary jurisdiction. Why wouldn't it be an OPP matter?"

"I should think that a problem on "First American" lands in Ontario is a bit off your primary focus also, but I've been begged for help by the Nishnawbe Aski Police up near Bearskin Lake—way northwest. Christ! It's almost to Manitoba. Oji-Cree people. But the case is one I'm sure you folks will be interested in."

"OK, let's have some details. A murder or murders, I assume.

"Murders plural. Three separate instances. But it's far more than simple murder, and far worse than obvious serial murder."

"Explain the 'far' in 'far more' and 'far worse! What the Hell has happened up there?"

"Cannibalism, Inspector McKenna. Eleven deaths so far over the past three months. All the bodies completely skeletonized—and I mean within hours or a day or so, not weeks or months. No signs of simple animal scavenging or predation. But the bones showed clear evidence of being gnawed upon. The larger bones had been cracked open and even the marrow gone—apparently sucked out!"

"Good God! Well…yes…certainly," he said, still a bit shocked by the answer to his query. "This is definitely a case for special investigation. I have a colleague in the division I'd like to bring along. She's had a particular interest in such things—and she's part Ojibwa. She knows the languages pretty well. Some Cree also, I think. Can you tell me the best way to get up there?"

"You could fly through here at Thunder Bay, but there may be a straight flight access to Sioux Lookout, a bit over 200 miles to our northwest. You can reach it by Highway 72 as well. But, after that, it's a flight of over 250 miles north to Bearskin Lake or Michikan Lake—that leg has to be by air. Only a few hundred natives on the reserve, but the deaths have been non-native hunters—four from the U.S. just last week."

"We'll be up there as soon as it takes to get my Superintendent to OK a special assignment and to get in touch with Kate. I know she'll want to be in on this one. Kate Youngbear. She's one of our chief consultants."

"Great! I'll send you all of the information I have. I've got to say the photos will likely sicken even you folks. Once you get up there—try for day after tomorrow latest if possible—you'll want to get in touch with Chief of Police, Steven Goodweather. He's the native cop who contacted me. I'll be heading that way too. It's going to take me an extra day to get things in order here and head up there myself. I'm bringing Leeds with me. Look forward to meeting you. And thanks."

* * *

Katheryn Youngbear had a double master's degree from McGill in psychology and medical anthropology and had finished her medical degree at Harvard, with an emphasis in psychiatry. Her interest for some time had been to join the Criminal Investigative Analysis Division of the *Gendarmerie royal du Canada* as it was called by most in Quebec. She had been eagerly accepted. They knew her credentials. She had learned French in college. English had been necessary since her girlhood, but she was also fluent in her father's native Anishininiimowin the language of the Oji-Cree—a group that was a blend of the Ojibwe and the Cree but considered a separate group of "First People." She knew Ojibwe well and could pick out most of the Cree she heard. Beautiful as she was intelligent, her long hair was a dark auburn—lightened from the native by her mother's European line. Her eyes were a strangely dark shade of green. Only the high cheekbones betrayed her Indian ancestry.

The phone call from Rod McKenna had made her day. Her father's people were from the Cat Lake area, not far to the south of where they were going. Going on this adventure up to Bearskin and Michikan Lakes was "going home" as well as going on an interesting assignment that was in one of her special areas of interest .

Within three hours after McKenna's phone call, she had packed and made ready for the winter that was setting in this late November. Rod had surprised her a bit by adding that she had been given the "temporary non-commissioned rank of Sergeant Major." He'd also asked for her sizes, since there was the unlikely possibility that they would have to be in "situations where uniforms were required."

They were to meet at the airport in Ottawa for a specially chartered flight to the lonely "Hub of the North" outpost town of Sioux Lookout. She was not going to be late.

* * *

Martin Higheagle was an man of "89 winters." When he smelled the stench, he was very glad he was downwind from *the thing*. He had smelled the smell of death many times: when out hunting those thousands of times since he was a boy, when he discovered where his grandfather had gone off to die back in the cold, famine winter of '39, when he and others had found the white hunter back in the spring of '98 who had been frozen and appeared only when the deep snow and sleet cover had melted.

But this smell was different—although still a death-smell. He had smelled it only once— when he was 14—back in '46, just after the Big War. He had been downwind then also, thank the Great Spirit! He had smelled it and then looked deeper into the woods in the direction from which it must have come. He could tell it was huge even at an eighth of a mile. He would not have seen it against the bare branches, since it was the same grey color and looked very much like a young tree. But it moved! What he thought at first were just swaying branches were its arms! When the "trunk" split and proved to be legs walking through the forest with huge strides, he had turned and run as fast as he could back to the village. For he knew what it had to be.

Then he saw the thing—very far away—at the edge of seeing. But his eyes had remained keen, even though the rest of him was old and very tired. He turned again now and started walking as fast as he could this time. There was no "running" left in him. It was always a bad, evil omen—seeing one. The thing was *pashtahowin*, "a sin against nature," an abomination. He had been troubled since yesterday when the kettle over the dinner fire began to sway with no wind. That was a bad sign too, and it often meant that such a thing was somewhere about.

Now that he had seen one again, it portended that—very likely—one of the village would be dead soon. He hoped it would be he and not one of the young. He prayed that prayer aloud to the Great Spirit and to his ancestors. He had lived long enough. His mother had died shortly after he saw the first one, now those many years ago.

* * *

The two CIA agents examined the files and photographs that Tompkins of the Ontario Provincial force had sent to Ottawa before their departure. The photos had all been taken by an officer of the Nishnawbe-Aski Police, the local native force, but the case report was very detailed and professionally done. The small charter plane for the first leg of their journey was to take them to the airport at Sioux Lookout. From there, another charter plane, the only type of access, would take them to the Bearskin Lake First Nation settlement.

The report was objectively clinical, but all the more disturbing in its graphic descriptive detail. But the crime scene photos would have sufficed. The first photos they looked at were of the latest incident—the one where the four American hunters had been killed and eaten. The pictures showed a camp in a small clearing. But the snow had been entirely reddened in a wide circle of blood—so much blood that barely any white still showed through. Many of the lower branches of the nearby trees had been bent or broken. Two relative close-ups of the trunks of birch trees showed rows of scratches etched deep through the thin bark.

"Probably a bear," McKenna had suggested.

"Perhaps, perhaps not," Youngbear had responded, a bit cryptically it seemed to McKenna.

But the many photos that showed the scattered bones and clothing were the most disturbing. Pieces of heavy winter hunting garb had been scattered—in shreds! The four skulls had been placed together near the center of the camp. The rest of the skeletons—down to the finger bones and smallest ribs—had been randomly scattered about within the circle of horror. Indeed, the photos showed that very little flesh had been left on the bones. The one photo of what was left of the bull moose was further disturbing. All of it—the whole huge creature had been completed denuded down to the bones with only a very few small bits of flesh clinging here and there!

"This can't be the work of one man," McKenna said. "Think of just the time it would take to do all of this. We're looking for a group of suspects—a crew of killer-cannibals! Can't be just one." Youngbear had to nod in agreement.

They had photos and a report on the first incident almost three months before. It had involved a family from away south, near Cat Lake.

"That's the area where I'm from," Kate said. "I was born near the shore of Cat Lake. My father's family has lived there for generations."

These photos showed the interior of a cabin. The bones of what had been a mother and her three children were scattered about. The report had objective specifics like: "multiple murder," "definite indications of cannibalism," "times of death appear to have been separate, based upon examination of what little flesh remained on the bodies of the victims," "evidence of separate murder scenarios," "cooking utensils found containing human bones and DNA," "not able to locate husband." For these reasons, the husband, Makwa Standingbear, was being considered the prime suspect.

Inspector Rod McKenna and "temporary" Sergeant Major Kate Youngbear stepped off the plane at Bearskin Lake Airport to discover that late November up here was already damned cold. No "Red Serge" uniforms or jodhpurs or "Mounty hats" up here. They had covered their service duty blues with ponchos upon deplaning, but they were glad to see that there were two native police vehicles coming up quickly toward the airplane.

A tall, native officer stepped out of the driver's side of the first vehicle.

"Welcome to the Bearskin Lake First Nation. Inspector McKenna,

Sergeant Youngbear," nodding to them. "I'm Steven Goodweather, I'm Chief in this district for the Nishnawbe-Aski Police. You don't know how glad I am to see you folks. I think Staff Inspector Tompkins has filled you in on some details. He and another OPP officer should be in later today or tomorrow morning latest."

After the formal introductions, the two specialists hopped into the back seat of Goodweather's SUV and they headed off toward the main settlement and his office at Michikan ["Fish Trap"] Lake. The Bearskin Lake First Nation of Oji-Cree had resettled there a few decades before—even though they kept the name "Bearskin Lake" for the tribal group. Both lakes were on the Severn River, not far from the Manitoba border.

"We don't have anywhere near the resources to cover a broad area—or to investigate this sort of atrocity," Goodweather said. "I contacted Tompkins of the Provincial Police as soon as the bodies—the bones I mean—of the hunters were discovered. I've worked with him before. But he suggested that we get you folks involved. My people are worried. The old legends are flying about."

"What specific legends are those?" McKenna asked.

"The Wendigo," Kate immediately answered, preempting Goodweather's answer.

"Yes, the legend of the Wendigo or Witiko. The names vary by language and dialect," Goodweather added. "So, you know of this legend, Sergeant. Is that because you are one of us by blood?"

"Partly that, yes. My father's line is full Oji-Cree, *Anishinaabe*; my mother is French-Canadian. I know of the Wendigo from my early years. But I also studied such tales in college—in anthropology classes."

"The Sergeant is not telling you the whole story. And she's being modest," McKenna added. "She's a distinguished scholar in medical and cultural anthropology, and she's an MD, a psychiatrist to boot."

"Well, whoever is doing these murders needs a 'shrink' for sure," Goodweather added, realizing he probably shouldn't have used the term. "But we've got to catch the perverted bastard first."

"So, you don't put any stock in the legends, Chief?" Kate asked.

"I've never seen a Witiko or whatever you want to call it, but I've seen too many evil men in my time." Goodweather responded. "I'm not near as educated as you, Sergeant. But I'm putting my money on this being the work of man—a fucking sick man! More likely a small group of demented men, people who are 'monsters' in a real sense. Satanic cult or some such bullshit."

"We'll need to be working closely and in concert on these cases, Chief," McKenna put in.

"Sound OK by me, Inspector—er, Steve," the tribal policeman answered.

* * *

The look of horror in her eyes and the agonized scream that Florence Corcoran gave out upon the discovery of the body was surpassed—if that were possible—by the frozen stare and silent, locked, and gaping scream on the face of her mother.

It saddened Martin Higheagle deeply to learn of Susan Corcoran's death. She had lived a good, long life, seemed healthy and fit. Her sudden death surprised the village. She had seemed so alive and spry the day before her body was discovered. Florence had become concerned when her mother hadn't arrived to watch her children that morning so she could drive in to work.

It was only two days after Martin had seen the thing. He remembered Susan had been among the small group of villagers he had told of it.

"It was just age," one said. "Whoever knows which day will be one's last?"

A few of the younger ones had said Martin's eyes had been tricking him; that it was only the stuff of legend. Susan was one of those who was bothered by what he had said. And the others who had lived long and still held strongly to the old ways looked at him without any questioning glances. Martin was an elder among elders and revered not only because of his extreme age.

"*But no!*" he thought to himself, "*No, it is the cannibal thing, 'the evil spirit that devours humankind.' The old tales are true. The legends are more than*

296

legends. I have seen it twice now. I knew this truth many years ago—and I have even tried not to believe. Now I have seen one again, and I must believe. The swinging kettle. Now Susan is dead—scared to death." He remembered the look on his mother's face in death those many years before. *"I don't know what the police can do, but I will talk to Chief Steve and tell him what I know."*

* * *

It had been late afternoon when the two CIA Division "Mounties" had arrived, and the night was descending fast. Chief Goodweather had dropped them at a lodging house not far from his station with the plan that they should begin in earnest the next morning. Inspector William Tompkins and Thomas Leeds arrived early that next morning. With the arrival of the two Ontario Provincial policemen, a meeting at the station was held right after an early breakfast.

McKenna had known Leeds from previous cases. The young man was very fit. A Canadian national side rugby player.

Tompkins looked much like his long line of Welsh ancestry would suggest: dark hair and eyes, greying quite a bit at the temples though only in his forties, short and stocky of build. His features made Kate think of a bulldog. And a "bulldog" he was, having risen through the ranks of the OPP being recognized as one of their most apt investigators early in his career. Perhaps a "bulldog" crossed with a "bloodhound."

The five of them had assembled around a conference table in a small room in the station house of the local Nishnawbe-Aski Police assigned to the jurisdiction of the Bearskin Lake First People area. Aside from the Chief, there were only four deputies to cover what was a very large range of over 200 square miles. The boundaries of the Bearskin Lake settlement included only about a quarter of that, but their responsibilities extended for miles in each direction. Two of the deputies were busy in the main office area which could be seen through a large window in the dividing wall. The other two were out searching for clues in the surrounding wilderness.

"You can see that the five of us here can't possible handle cases like these,"

297

the Chief said. "Maybe it's because the most recent case has made the national news in the U.S. and the Americans are pressuring us for answers. Maybe it's just because we're closest to this most recent abomination, but we were contacted to get things going—and going fast—on the investigation. I knew immediately that we had to seek help from the OPP. And Inspector Tompkins right away suggested bringing you folks in too."

"Yes, these incidents require a concerted effort," Tompkins said. "And with this latest case only a few days old, we need to quickly form some plan to proceed. Is the crime scene still undisturbed—at least as undisturbed as Nature might be leaving it?"

"Yes, we did GPS coordinates and taped off the circle of surrounding trees," Goodweather replied. "…not that any people will be venturing out that way. The people are very worried, and much of the talk is about the old legends. That, in itself, might get in the way of our investigation. Many of the people hold to the old ways and superstitions. But some defy reason."

"You mean the Wendigo," Leeds jumped into the conversation. "The thing's become legendary enough outside native beliefs. Hell, it's been in movies and TV series—and it's the only one I know of that has to do with cannibalism."

"Kate, you've researched and written about this, haven't you?" McKenna said. "What can you tell us—to ground us in the legends at least. So that we know what some of the people we're interviewing are thinking. Even though I'm already damned sure we're dealing with plural unknown subjects, a gang or family of insane cannibals."

"Yes, and Steve, feel free to interrupt me or add whatever you think I'm not covering," said Kate, looking at the Chief, who nodded, clearly indicating that she should proceed.

"Clinically, what we're most likely dealing with is a case of "Wendigo Psychosis." It's what we call a "culture-bound disorder," meaning that it seems to be almost exclusively found among members of the Algonquian family of cultures and languages—spreading all the way from the Algonquins in New England and Eastern Canada through the many tribal groups out to here and even further north and west. The culture extends down into the north central United States as well.

"There have been several sensational cases of cannibalism in Canada's past,"[1] Kate continued. "The psychosis takes one of two forms: those who began considering, then craving, then often acting on the desire to eat human flesh; and those who began believing that such cannibals are around them and need to be exterminated. Members of the second group have sometimes become "wendigo hunters"—murderers in their own right.[2]

"I read a story once about the Wendigo," Tompkins said. But I don't remember many of the details. It was spooky enough but left everything pretty mysterious."

"You're probably thinking of Algernon Blackwood's famous story. It's the best-known piece of fiction from the "white" world on the topic. The legend has been quite a bit convoluted over the years. It's also been commingled—as such things go with folk material—with other legends that have nothing to do with it. It's been mixed up with the Green Man, the Wild Man of the Wood, the Horned God of Wicca, and especially, in many corruptions of the legend, with the antlered god of the Celts, Cernunnos. But those are all derived through Indo-European myth and legend—not native tradition.

"The "wendigo" or "witiko" and other names among the Algonquian languages—is something else. It almost certainly derives from the taboos in the culture against greed and selfishness—and certainly the taboo against cannibalism. That's shared, of course, across almost all cultures on Earth. But the wendigo arises, most likely from times in the old days when bad winters meant famine for all the people and starvation for many. An evil spirit would come to one, usually a man, in a dream and put in him the idea of cannibalism in order to stay alive. He would act on this, usually killing and eating members of his own family group. The legend says that the more he ate, the more insatiable his appetite for the taste of human flesh.

"He became ravenous for the taste, but his hunger could never be abated. He became a *wendigo*. Every meal made him increase in overall size and especially in height, but he became more and more emaciated and gaunt. The flesh that he devoured proved to be no nourishment, and soon he—now more *IT*—began to decay and corrupt. It became a huge walking skeleton with putrefying deathly ashen skin stretched over its bony frame. Sunken red eyes; long yellow fangs; a too-long, slavering tongue; thin, excoriated lips; and huge hands with curved razor claws complete the usual description. And the smell, the stench of it, of course, was abominable. They were said to grow to two to three times the height of a man!"

"Jesus!" Tompkins exclaimed. Kate had described the thing so well he had even shuddered a bit. "I'm goddam glad the thing is a legend, but I can see why the locals who believe in such might be terrified. The crazy man—more likely group—who are doing these things are scary enough to think about."

"I know you've studied these things in your colleges, Kate, but I couldn't have provided all the details you just noted. I think your father's family line and your childhood near Cat Lake have added a bit. You could be a tribal storyteller!" added Goodweather.

"No, I'm no *debaajimod*, Steve. Although my grandmother was. I loved to listen to her stories. She often said that only a living voice to living ears was a proper story. I guess some of that could have "rubbed off" so to speak."

"You've only left off a couple things," Chief Goodweather said.

"Likely more than a couple. What in particular?" Kate asked.

"One thing just lacking in emphasis a bit. For one to be so selfish and greedy as to think only of oneself is a great sin among our people. Even in the old starvation winters when whole groups—almost whole tribes—would die, facing one's end of starvation or even suicide were considered more honorable by far than the greed, selfishness, and hunger that could lead one to cannibalism. People must share burdens no matter how great. People must work as a community. In those times only rationing and sharing might succeed in helping the people survive. Today, of course, we have means of supply and survival beyond those days of the past when game was not available and the cold was just too much.

"And the other thing?" Leeds asked. He had been mesmerized by the telling of the legend.

"The other thing is the matter of the "Heart of Ice," Steve Goodweather said. "Whatever was human of the wendigo was shrunken into the heart of the creature and lost in a shriveled knot that was frozen so cold it was colder than the worst winter wind—and yet almost impossible to melt."

"Which brings up another thing I left out," Kate was quick to add. "How does the wendigo die? How can it be killed? The legends say only by fire. It must be burned to death—and the heart will be the last thing to remain, but it too must be burned to ash."

"Well, I think that whoever we catch won't be quite so magically impossible to stop," Tompkins put in. "I think our guns will be sufficient—if lethal force is needed. My strong suspicion is that it quite well may be."

Just then one of the deputies came through the door. "Sorry to interrupt, Chief, but Jennings hasn't returned from patrol, and he was due back today. He took the Snow Cat out on a run south down the Severn. Also, there's an old fellow here who says he must speak to you."

"Let the man in, Mike," Goodweather responded.

A man who looked like the poster for a hard, long life entered the conference room. He was very dark and ruddy of skin, but the numerous deep lines in his face spoke great age and great mystery. Kate Youngbear determined that she must do a photographic portrait of this man sometime on this case. Her passionate hobby was photography.

Martin Higheagle took a moment to look around at Steven Goodweather and the rest of them and then simply said, "Chief Steve, I have seen the thing. It is no longer a human thing. It is a Witiko. And it stalks nearby. I saw it in Deer Valley two days ago."

* * *

Deputy Delsin Jennings had stopped the Snow Cat in the middle of a small clearing. What puzzled him was the condition of what was left of the bear. He wouldn't have noticed it at all—white bones protruding up through the new-fallen snow—but he had seen the clearing from the crest of a nearby hill and decided to stop for a breather and to smoke a bowl in his pipe. He was examining the remains when his nostrils flared at a stench that hit like a clap of thunder. "What in God's name...?" It was his last thought.

Turning, he saw the stinking thing. It was so close it took him a second to scan up its height. Its knees were at his eye level! Seeing the face, his reaction took a silent second or two. His response to scream was cut off by his decapitation. The head fell a few yards away, the pipe, clutched in its teeth.

* * *

After delivering his story, the deputy showed the old man out of the station. Higheagle looked back once to say, "You must believe me. I have seen and I know."

Only two of those in the conference room who had listened to the story that the old man had to tell put any possibility of credence to the tale. Strangely, those two were the two CIA agents who, one would think, would be the most skeptical of the group assembled there. Both Rod and Kate were mulling over the old man's tale.

Goodweather, who knew Martin, but also knew he was up near 90 and quite likely a bit senile, thought, "He's just seeing things and exercising his belief in the legend." Both Tompkins and Leeds were thinking almost the same thing.

"Well, enough talk and storytelling," Tompkins said. "Let's get at this investigation. This late in the year, it will be dark before we could reach that last crime scene today. Let's plan for early morning—leave before sunrise tomorrow."

All agreed to this, but the weather had other plans, blizzard conditions set in for the next two days, so the investigation was delayed. "This might be a good thing," McKenna had said to Kate at breakfast the second day of the blizzard.

"Why's that?" she answered.

"Probably no good reason—at least I hope so," he answered, leaving her dissatisfied with the response. But she decided to let it go.

"We need to get out there. The only good news I can see is that whoever is doing this… or *Whatever*?"—she looked at McKenna across the table to see his reaction to that word—"is just as immobilized as we are. At least we can hope."

Roderick McKenna had been on the phone right after the first meeting and hearing Higheagle's story. The calls he made were, first to CFB Winnipeg, a Canadian Air Force base and the closest military to their location. Not getting the answer he wanted, he called the Irish Regiment of Canada post in Sudbury, Ontario. It was actually far more distant, but they had the answer he needed to his query.

The weather broke the third day, and the plan was to set off as early in the morning as possible. A plane arrived from Sioux Lookout, unloading a few passengers, but it also had one item that McKenna was expecting.

"What the Hell is in the crate?" Tompkins asked, as Rod brought it into the police station. The small crate was marked on the side in black military block lettering: "Lifebuoy, Model II, Portable." McKenna asked Goodweather for a screwdriver or clawhammer to pry open the crate. It was clearly many years old, based upon the age of the wood.

Upon succeeding in prying open the lid, it took a moment for the rest of the group to reflect on what they saw.

"Judas Priest! What is this contraption?" But Leeds realized the answer as soon as he had asked the question.

"It's a flame thrower," Kate said, smiling a bit, now that she understood what McKenna was doing. "Well, Rod, leave it to you to make sure we're prepared for—literally—anything."

"The damned things aren't even legal, are they?" Tompkins said. "Geneva Convention and all that."

"A bit of 'overkill' don't you think," Leeds commented. "Our 9mms and assault carbines ought to be enough if we encounter these fucked-up sons of bitches. Oh shit! You've bought into the Wendigo legend bullshit, haven't you?"

"It might come in handy in whatever we encounter, when we find the suspect or suspects. Maybe they'll be holed up in some place and need some extra *persuading* to bring them out," he said trying unsuccessfully to deflect Leeds' guess, which was actually much closer to on target than he cared to admit to himself. He had come to the slow and awful decision that there was no "human" explanation for the photos that showed the hunter's camp. And there was something about old Martin Higheagle's story and sincerity.

Kate thought so too. Although every bit of scientist within her told her—*"Impossible!"*—her ancestry and the physical evidence she'd seen photos of had pushed her to consider the same irrational possibility.

Quickly reading the manual on how the flamethrower was packed like a backpack, McKenna learned the function of the device. There was a doughnut-shaped fuel container that held 4 Imperial gallons. In the middle of the "doughnut" was a spherical container that held the nitrogen gas propellant. It could propel the burning liquid out to 36 meters. A hose from the fuel tank went out the to the nozzle assembly that was, essentially, a pipe with two pistol grips. The rear one had the trigger. He had been assured by the ordinance officer at the Irish Regiment Armoury that the thing—even though an antique—had been an unused one—and kept well. More importantly, it would be fully functional and ready. "Ready to FIRE!—if you will," the army Captain had quipped.

They took off in the larger Snow Cat. There had still been no sign of the missing deputy, and Goodweather was beyond worry about the man who was a friend as well as a subordinate. The other three deputies had gone off to search in the various directions.

Tompkins and Leeds were riding snowmobiles.

They were all headed off to the site where the American hunters had been slaughtered. It was a good three quarters of an hour away. Rod and Kate had donned the cold weather gear of the Force: official blue leather winter cap with muskrat fur earflaps; heavy buffalo fur coats, and mukluks. They each had an RCMP standard issue Smith & Wesson 9mm pistol. Rod would put on the flamethrower, but Kate just her sidearm—*and her camera!* "We'll need to document any fresh crime scenes or other things of interest if we encounter them," she had said.

The OPP officers were well-armed too. The company were "ready for bear." Certainly, ready if they found the people responsible for the carnage that had, so far, claimed eleven lives in unthinkable fashion.

Steven Goodweather had his police revolver, an old standard .357. But he also had his favorite gun for moose hunting along, a hefty .458 Winchester which could stop any of the biggest game in North American and which would have served well in Africa.

When they reached the spot that GPS indicated was the camp of the slaughtered hunters. Any further investigation was impossible. The snows in the blizzard of the past two days had completely covered the scene. Only the tip of one of the skeletal moose's antlers was protruding through the snow.

"Let's move on," Goodweather said. "We might as well check out Deer Valley. That's only a couple miles to the west. It's where old Martin said he saw the…well, *something.* But who knows? He may have seen someone moving down there. It's the only lead we have."

* * *

Makwa Standingbear had the third dream the night before he killed his eldest son and his wife. The spirit urged him in an earlier vision to think about eating his family. He had been plagued by that thought. They were very poor, since he had lost his job and had not really looked for work as he should have. His wife had pestered him to "do the right thing" and find a way to provide for his family. The second dream increased his thinking about it. When he awoke after the third, the first thing he did was take his hunting knife and, holding his hand over the boy's mouth, slit his throat from ear to ear. The boy was sixteen and would have been the only one with any chance to stop him.

He went back to his own bed and murdered his wife the same way. The two young children he had locked into the closet to "save" for later. Two days after that, and following his devouring the flesh of his two youngest children, he left.

Finding animal carcasses to scavenge had been easy. But the meat didn't satisfy. Then he had found those three men, by the lakeshore, fishing. They had provided the taste he craved, but still—no sating of his hunger. Then the group of four and the moose. Then the lone man. None had been enough.

What was that? He heard noises that had to be human made. Low, rumbling sounds from back down in the valley. Then he heard human voices. Several of them. Ah! He would feast again. This time the hunger would be abated. This time…

* * *

They had reached the crest of a hill overlooking Deer Valley. In a small clearing below they saw something colored bright yellow standing out beneath a blanket of snow.

"It's Jennings Snow Cat," Goodweather said. "But I don't see any sign of a fire or shelter of any sort. Let's get down there!"

They arrived at the clearing. Only the Snow Cat was there. No Jennings.

Then Leeds saw something. It was a curiously shaped stick protruding from the snow. Bending to inspect it more closely, he saw that it was a smoking pipe! "Look here!" he shouted. Then, as the others were coming closer, he began to lift the pipe out of the snow. It shouldn't have been that hard to lift! But then—to his horror—he saw why. A human skull, with only a small shock of hair still attached, emerged from the snow, teeth clenched and bitten so tightly into the pipe's stem that they had embedded in the amber!

"Oh! Good Christ! It's Jennings," the Chief moaned. "Oh, God!"

At that same moment, first Kate Youngbear, then Rod McKenna, then all of them smelled the stench. Tompkins became ill. He was still vomiting as the rest of them looked in the direction of the wind.

They did not see the thing at first. It had developed the trick of standing sidelong toward its soon-to-be victims. It was so emaciated and thin in comparison to its height that the putrefying grey of its tight skin blended in with the surrounding small trees that it looked—for a moment— like one of them.

Then it turned toward them and entered the clearing, only about 50 yards from where they stood.

306

It was at least 15 feet tall! A horrible, grey and huge skeleton covered with rotting flesh. Dead, yet alive. All too alive! A much-too-long, black tongue was thrusting back and forth from the gaping mouth and between rows of terrible sharp fangs. What lips it had were split and bleeding. Each giant hand ended in long fingers tipped by claws that were the size of hunting knives!

As Tompkins, who, along with Leeds, were closest to the thing looked up and began screaming, Goodweather clicked the safety off of the huge bore rifle, and fired one, then two shots in quick succession directly into the chest of the giant skeletal figure. Then it made its first sound, not a roar, but a high-pitched scream. But it did not fall! Pausing only a second or two, it continued its approach.

With one swipe of its bony hand, it disemboweled Tompkins and tossed him aside like a doll. Leeds fired every round from his carbine at the thing, aiming at "center mass." He stood there, defiant as the thing got to him. He'd pulled his sidearm when the Wendigo grabbed him with both of its abominable hands and bent him back double. The crack of his spine was almost as loud as the third rifle shot that Goodweather delivered.

As Rod McKenna primed and lit the flamethrower, fumbling a bit at first, he looked quickly over to his right to Kate. *She was taking pictures!* The camera noise was the continuous *ka-chick, ka-chick* of continuous mode!

With a scream of rage, Rod stepped forward toward the thing. It was now only about 25 yards away having paused and having dropped the lifeless, broken body of Tom Leeds. "You Bloody!...Goddam!...Evil!...Bastard!" he screamed, with each step pulling the trigger and dowsing the thing head to foot with liquid fire. All three of the surviving humans were even more amazed to see it stagger forward. Still coming at them and screaming that high-pitched scream!

Then, it stopped. Through flaming eye sockets, it seemed to be staring at them as if more in curiosity than any sign of pain. It fell to its knees, then toppled forward onto that horror of a face, the head coming to rest not more than ten feet in front of McKenna.

The entire carcass of the thing was on fire, what had to be called its "flesh" was crumbling and dripping away. Rod fired two more blasts of flame over the entire body.

"Holy God!" Goodweather said. He had reloaded and now fired all three rounds from the clip of the giant rifle into what had been the head of the abomination. It shattered to smithereens from those impacts and the intense heat. "Holy God!" he kept repeating as the thing crumbled to ash and tiny fragments of bone.

The steaming mass of what had been the Wendigo cooled quickly in the below zero temperatures of the late afternoon. The three who remained rested inside the larger Snow Cat in a sort of mixed shock and too-gradual adrenalin diminishment. Steve Goodweather began shaking, and it was a while before he could stop.

Rod turned to Kate and asked, "Photographs? Really?"

"It was clear my pistol wasn't going to do any good," she replied. "Something in me said that—if nothing else—somebody might find the camera and see the Truth. Some legends are real."

When they emerged from the vehicle, they noticed one lump remaining in the center of the ash and bone chip pile that had been the thing. Kate walked in picked the thing up.

"It's the heart!" she said. "Feel it! It's hard and cold as ice!"

Rod went back to the Snow Cat and got the flame thrower. Setting the heart back in the center of what had been the total perversion of Nature, he shot blast after blast of liquid fire onto the thing—until he was out of fuel.

It took a good hour before the heart was fully reduced to a pile of dust.

* * *

There was a wonderful full haloed moon with bright moon dogs on each side that night. Martin Higheagle knew it was a sign. The police had not yet returned, but he sensed that the Thing was gone. Knowing he might have played some little part in its end, he was happy. It was going to be a hard winter, his 90th—a winter like that one back in '46 when he had seen the first one and his mother had died. He watched the moon and its companions for a while, then he went in his modest dwelling to his bed, fell asleep…and then began his journey along the path of his ancestors.

* * *

* The most famous case of cannibalism among the Canadian tribes is that of the Cree, Swift Runner. He murdered, cooked, and ate his wife, his children, including an infant, his brother, and his mother-in-law. He was tried and hanged at Fort Saskatchewan in December of 1879. His defense was that a Wendigo spirit had come to him and made him into a Wendigo.

* The most famous (or infamous) "Wendigo Hunter" was another Cree Indian named Jack Fiddler. He claimed to have killed 14 of the beasts in his lifetime but was imprisoned at the age of 87, along with his son, for the murder of a Cree woman in October of 1907. Both him and his son plead guilty to the offense but maintained that the woman had been possessed by the spirit of a wendigo and was on the verge of complete transformation. They attested that they murdered her as a form of self-defense, believing she would kill other members of the tribe if left to transform.

In Search Of—Catherine Fields

Catherine is a fourth-year communications student at The Ohio State University. She loves writing, drawing, cooking, and her one-eyed dog Winkie. You can find her on Twitter @cfields1031.

***

The boy, a first-year named Ben, runs a tense hand through his hair.

"But Lincoln's the great emancipator."

"I never said he wasn't," responds Jesse.

"Then what are you saying?"

Jesse sighs, setting his course book down and sitting on the edge of his desk.

"I'm saying that Lincoln was a racist."

The class of college students shifts uncomfortably. A few students scoff.

"From a 1988 perspective," Jesse continues, "Lincoln was a racist. This is why we teach about the Mankato executions."

"You just said he pardoned over 200 of the Indians who got sentenced to death," another student, a second-year named Justine, responds.

It's a small college, so despite term having only begun three weeks ago, Jesse has everyone's names and faces down pat.

"That's a very good point," he nods. "But I would counter that the Dakota men who carried out that violence did so as a reaction to the United States government's breaking of treaties and systemic violence toward their people."

"So," Shiloh, a first-year, ponders, "Lincoln was the head of the colonial force that made the situation and that pushed Native people to the point where they'd react so violently to settlers. So if he really wasn't a racist, he would have pardoned all of them."

Jesse smiles. This girl was quickly becoming one of his favorite students of the semester.

"That is exactly what I'm saying. Now," he checks his watch, "class ends in a minute. I know a lot of you would like to talk about this more, and I don't want to take that opportunity from you, but I also know you all want to get out of here." The class waits with bated breath. "So we'll pick this up on Monday."

With a collective appreciative mutter, the group disperses in a flurry of rustling papers and zipping backpacks. Jesse is wishing them a good weekend when he notices the man standing by the door. He is willowy, with dark hair and eyes.

"Have a good weekend, Mr. Friedman."

As the last student leaves his class, Jesse turns to the stranger with a smile. He's in no rush to leave - no point in hurrying off to grade papers.

"How can I help you?"

The man nods to the book on Jesse's desk.

"I take it you're not a fan of Lincoln?"

"No, yeah," Jesse laughs. "He's actually one of my favorite historical figures. Definitely my favorite president."

The stranger tilts his head.

"Why?"

"He never stopped learning and educating himself his whole life. Worked to be better right up until he died."

"Perhaps you should share this with your students, Mr. Friedman. It may make them more receptive to discussion of his flaws."

"Please, it's Jesse."

He extends a hand. The man hesitates just a split second too long, slowly lifting his thin hand to grasp Jesse's in a too-short handshake.

"I am Lev. I understand that you possess a level of expertise in Midwestern folklore?"

Lev's manner isn't off putting, but it is unusual. The strangeness of their interaction also draws Jesse's attention to the fact that the man is wearing a long coat and a beanie too heavy for the mild fall weather.

For a reason he can't put his finger on, Jesse likes him. In any case, he's not overly eager to return to his empty house, so he doesn't mind some conversation - even with a stranger who embodies every sense of the word. He nods, moving to the chalkboards to erase the evidence of today's class.

"Yes. I just teach history and politics classes here, but independently I've written several volumes about local myths."

"I am aware. I have come to you with questions about multiple creatures, primarily the bolaith."

Jesse raises his eyebrows.

"Most people around here don't say that name."

Lev reaches into his pocket, retrieving a worn notepad and a pen.

"For what reason?"

"It's a little bit of a taboo," Jesse elaborates, moving the books and papers littering his desk into his bag. "There's no real, traditional taboo surrounding the creature's name, nothing that indicates saying it can summon it. People in other states say it no problem, but folks in this area tend to avoid it just in case. Figure we might as well play it safe."

Lev jots this down.

"Do you believe we would be in danger if we did indeed speak its name during these circumstances?"

Jesse takes another look at Lev. He's good looking in a way that's simultaneously delicate and worldly, but there is nothing about him physically that's unusual. Lev raises his brows, looking at him expectantly before abruptly averting his gaze.

"Forgive me," Lev blurts. "I did not intend to impose upon you or your time. If I could schedule an appointment during which to speak about this matter-"

"Lev," Jesse smiles, lifting his bag to his shoulder and rounding his desk. "You're not imposing, I love talking about this stuff. You free right now?"

"Yes."

"Would you like to get something to eat with me?"

Lev blinks at him.

"Y-yes."

\#

The walk to the diner is quick and quiet, accompanied only by the crunching and rustling of dying leaves. Jesse doesn't mind the lack of conversation that Lev seems to be content with - quiet company's better than no company. Upon sitting down in a booth, they each take up a menu, Lev furrowing his brow.

"It ain't much, but it's honest food," Jesse jokes.

"I have been to many such diners in my travels, the food is acceptable."

Jesse can't help the chuckle that escapes his lips. Lev raises a brow.

"I'm not laughing at you," he quickly clarifies, "you just talk very precisely. I don't know anybody else who speaks that way."

Lev nods sagely.

"That is understandable. My pattern of speech would be somewhat unusual anywhere but is especially so in rural areas."

The man had seemed pleased when Jesse invited him to lunch, but now it's almost as though he's closed himself off. Jesse recognizes that kind of emotional wall-building. He's engaged in it himself - possibly for the same reasons.

"So Lev, what do you do? Why do you wanna know about this stuff?"

Lev raises pleasant eyes from his menu, brows lifted in anticipation of conversation.

"I am a cryptozoologist."

At this exact moment, their waitress comes over to take their orders. Jesse leans forward after the woman departs.

"Cryptozoologist?"

"It is the study of legendary or mythical creatures and the science of determining their existence."

Jesse raises his brows.

"Well, I can't say I've ever heard of that beyond that *In Search of* show."

"I am not surprised. Cryptozoology as a field has largely been written off as a pseudoscience undertaken only by charlatans."

Were he not genuinely interested in what his companion was saying, Jesse would need to suppress another laugh at his word choice. The waitress swiftly deposits their drinks on the table.

"So I take it you've come to me for research purposes."

"Affirmative."

Lev takes a delicate sip of tea. His lips are a sort of desert brown color - Jesse remembers seeing it called burnt sienna on one of his nephews' crayons. Lev puckers them endearingly before pulling the cup away. Jesse finds himself attracted to the yellowy tinge that spreads across his high cheekbones in response to the drink's warmth.

"Looks like we could both learn some things from each other," Jesse observes.

The ghost of a smile flits across Lev's features. It makes his hooded eyes crinkle.

They talk for an interminable time. Jesse tells stories of bolaiths and other regional bogeymen, of things just beyond the reach of the camp's firelight deep in the woods. Lev demonstrates an impressive prior knowledge of these entities; Jesse suspects he's accessed every text he'd been able to get his hands on.

"It's important to gather stories from previous generations," Jesse confides at one point, "because the oral tradition of the region has been kind of starting to wane with modernization. These stories aren't being passed down the way they used to, so if we want to preserve them, we need to start doing so formally."

"Yes," Lev affirms. "It is generally community elders who have been able to assist me in my studies of specific regions. My efforts with younger people have not been unsuccessful, but there is certainly a deficit of knowledge between the groups. Despite your age, I suspected that as an academic expert in the field you may possess some insight that I have missed. It appears that I thought correctly. Please continue."

Jesse describes the bolaith, its sickly, rubbery skin stretched over sharp, inhuman bones. The glowing eyes set deep in its hollow skull. How no matter how much bone marrow it guzzles or how much flesh it devours, it is never full. Fetid, tattered lips, wrecked over time by its evil speech. The heinous stench it gives off, drawing to mind the eventual decay of one's own body. Its inexplicable intelligence.

Lev studiously takes notes and contributes interesting conversation as Jesse speaks, grateful for someone to listen. Their talk ambles through several legendary creatures, gradually landing on the golem. At this point, Lev's eyes light with surprise.

"I am intimately familiar with that entity." He pauses a moment, eyeing Jesse, seeming to weigh possibilities. "I myself am Jewish."

Jesse blinks before allowing his face to split into a wide grin.

"Should we show each other our Jew cards or do the secret handshake?"

Lev, obviously pleased with this development, cannot quite wrangle his face into disapproval at Jesse's joke.

"Rural America is not particularly welcoming to Jewish individuals," he comments with a raised eyebrow.

"I know. I've been lucky though," Jesse sighs, pushing his empty plate to the edge of the table. "Haven't had any trouble but the occasional ignorant remark."

"I am pleased to hear it," Lev responds earnestly. Then, cryptically: "I know what it is to be apart."

Jesse catches his eye and nods. The evidence that they share certain proclivities is growing stronger.

"Alright, I been talking your ear off for God knows how long," he announces, leaning back in their booth. "You owe me some cryptozoology education."

"Well-"

"Jess?"

The pair both turn their gaze to the door of the diner, where Tom Fortney stands.

Exceedingly skinny and chronically exhausted, he's the town's doctor and resident curmudgeon. He's also Jesse's closest friend.

"Tom! What are you doing here?"

The middle-aged man saunters over, eyeing Lev warily.

"I'm getting some supper, it's nigh on 7 o'clock and I don't much feel like cooking." He jerks his head to Lev. "Who's the city boy?"

Lev furrows his brow.

"What about me indicates that I am from a city?"

"Couldn't tell ya, kid, it's just a sense," Tom sighs, swatting Jesse further into the booth and sliding in next to him. "As long as you're here, you might as well keep me company."

Jesse gives Tom a significant look.

"What if my friend would prefer otherwise?"

Tom rolls his eyes, turning his attention to Lev.

"You mind eating dinner with me?"

Lev's eyes alight on Jesse before returning to the stranger.

"As I have no other plans, there is not reason for me to say no."

The waitress returns, and Jesse gives Lev a long suffering look as Tom places his order. Lev purses his lips in obvious suppression of a smirk. Once everyone's orders are in, Tom returns his attention to his dinner partners.

"So, how do you two know each other? You ain't never told me about any Lev," Tom elbows Jesse.

"Lev's researching bolaiths and other myths for his work."

"Ooh, you don't wanna go messing around with those," Tom shakes his head. "What kinda job would have you looking into that anyway? You some sort of educator too? That beanie you got on reeks of college."

Jesse winces inwardly at Lev's inevitable answer.

"I am a cryptozoologist."

Tom stares for a moment before whipping incredulous eyes to Jesse and back to Lev.

"Nuh uh. We ain't playing this game today. I know all about you folks."

"Lev was just about to tell me about it."

"Well, I can tell you right now. It's a pseudoscience. A sham, total bullshit. A science for the uneducated."

"I possess doctorates in biology, organic chemistry, and physics," Lev responds serenely.

Tom opens and closes his mouth for a moment, and Jesse barks a laugh.

"He's sharp, Tom. I would hear him out if I were you. And anyway," he continues accusatorily, "what are you all up in arms about? You believe in this stuff more than I do."

"Believing in it's different from making a science of it," he grumbles, returning his attention to Lev. "These are spiritual concepts. A lot of these entities are beyond human understanding. They're forces of nature. You respect them and you stay out of their way. You don't go running around trying to prove they exist with a camera and an overactive imagination."

Of course his best friend is the greatest cockblock in the tri-state area. Jesse has already begun mourning his prospects when Lev responds.

"I am aware of these facts, Mister…?"

"*Doctor* Fortney. Tom Fortney."

"Dr. Fortney, I understand this. But as a scientist, it is in my nature to investigate the unknown. To disturb or endanger any creature is against my ethics. However, to be a scientist often entails actions that may be perceived as an affront to people's spiritual beliefs. Galileo was prosecuted for blasphemy. But I do not wish to cause disturbance. I wish simply to know."

Jesse feels a sudden burst of pride bloom in his chest. Tom just shrugs.

"There's some things you can't know, son."

"Perhaps you could tell me some of what you know or believe," Lev continues, completely unaffected.

"What I know is my business."

"Oh, gimme a break, croaker," Jesse groans. "All you gotta know is Tom believes in everything but aliens."

Lev stiffens slightly at this announcement.

"Although I do not share that sentiment," he says stiltedly, "I understand your point of view. It is highly unlikely that extraterrestrials would have visited Earth without anyone's knowledge."

Dinner passes quickly with chitchat and more subtle sniping between Tom and Lev. The two talk like two old rivals, and Jesse internally bemoans their dynamic. As soon as they finish, Jesse interjects into a story Tom is telling about the mangled deer corpse he found on his property.

"Lev, where are you staying?"

The man pounces on the lifeline from the doctor's graphic anecdote.

"I had planned to sleep in my car."

"Boy, that's fool talk," Tom announces. "You oughta stay with Jess here."

"I'd love to have you," he nods.

Lev waffles for a moment.

"I do not wish to impose-"

"You ain't imposing, he wants you there," Tom waves him away.

Lev bites his lip briefly before continuing.

"If it would not be an inconvenience."

Jesse scolds himself for his earlier irritation at Tom; the man's less of a third wheel than he lets on. The doctor stands and extends an arm toward the door.

"Go on, you two, get. Lunch and dinner's on me."

Ignoring him, Jesse and Lev both pull out several bills and place them on the table. Lev exits first. Tom wishes Jesse farewell with a quick slap to the seat of his pants.

"No accounting for taste, but try to have some fun."

Jesse flushes in spite of himself as he follows Lev outside.

\#

Ice clinks as Jesse refills his and Lev's glasses. It's almost midnight now, and Lev's been speaking enthusiastically about cryptozoology since they got in the door of Jesse's woodland cabin; the man didn't even take his beanie off before they began their conversation. Jesse's currently laughing at a story Lev has told about being attacked by an ornery goose who did not appreciate water samples being taken at his pond. He's a little buzzed and has decided to enjoy his intoxication thoroughly.

"Well, I'll tell you," Jesse sighs happily, retaking his seat next to his friend.

"It'd do the cryptozoology community a lot of good if they elected you as their spokesperson. You know your stuff so well I doubt anybody could call it a sham after talking with you."

Lev ducks his head modestly.

"I do not believe there to be a governing body capable of such an election."

Jesse belly laughs at this, and Lev allows himself a self-satisfied smile. While he is still wheezing, Jesse feels a hand touch his knee. His sight follows the lithe arm up to Lev's face. His expression is stone. At Jesse's lack of response, he retracts his hand quickly and returns to his drink.

Just subtle enough to be deniable.

Jesse reaches out and takes Lev's chin in his hand, gently turning his angular face toward him. The last thing he sees before their lips connect is Lev's dark, half-lidded eyes.

His mouth is pleasant, eager and vaguely spiced. Its unusual coldness, which Jesse attributes to the ice in their drinks, does nothing to lessen his enjoyment. Lev reaches out and grasps his hand, stroking a thumb along its back. Jesse brings his other hand up to cup his partner's cheek, running a thumb across his brow and slipping fingers beneath the hat's band to frame an ear. As Lev deepens the kiss, Jesse's hold grows tighter, more grasping. He is cognizant of something protruding on Lev's brow. The beanie slips off.

Lev rips away and leaps to his feet, losing his footing in his evident panic and falling backward.

"Jesus, Lev, what's-?"

Lev has scrambled onto all fours and replaced the hat securely upon his head, but not before Jesse catches a glimpse of what it previously concealed.

His ears possess an inhuman point, and a pointed brow resulting from a dramatic forehead ridge is visible through his mussed bangs.

Jesse stares only a moment before averting his eyes. His voice fails him momentarily.

"Lev, you're not from here," he croaks.

This development has instantly made them both very, very sober.

"I apologize. Thank you for your hospitality," Lev chokes out in a voice thick with suppressed emotion. "I must go."

Jesse doesn't move as Lev crosses the room on cat feet, nor does he when the screen door slams shut behind him.

The house is empty and silent again - back to its usual state.

Maybe it was a genetic mutation. Something he's had from birth and is embarrassed about.

Jesse knows this is wishful thinking. He's never seen or even heard of anything like what he saw on Lev. Combined with his unusual behavior, his earlier reaction to the mention of aliens, his hasty retreat…

He makes himself regulate his breathing, fighting against the shallow panting his body attempts to force upon him.

An alien.

Dazedly, he thinks of how pissed Tom would be if he ever found out.

He can still feel those pleasantly cool lips against his.

Maybe he dodged a bullet. Who knows what Lev could be capable of. Lucky Jesse spooked him while he still had a chance.

Jesse shakes his head. *Spooked him.* Like an animal.

He remembers Lev's shy smile. The deep cleverness and intelligence that was palpable every time he spoke. His reserved nature. The hand on his knee.

Jesse leaps to his feet, stumbling a bit as he runs to the door.

He jogs heavily into the crisp night and decides quickly that Lev would have gone in the direction of town, on the road that cuts through the woods. After a minute or so's trot, he's gained on Lev. The man marches determinedly, pretending not to hear the footsteps behind him.

"You know, I could be anybody. You should at least take a look over your shoulder."

Lev continues walking.

"Where are you going?"

No answer. Jesse hustles to catch up to the man.

"Lev, you can't walk alone out here at night and you can't sleep in your car," he pants.

No answer. Jesse sighs.

"Playing the quiet game doesn't work with me, you can ask my mother."

Lev stops in his tracks, and for a moment the only sound is leaves rustling in the breeze. When he speaks, it's in a low voice.

"It would be best for me to go on my way at this time," he says carefully. "I am capable of defending myself. I appreciate your hospitality and would appreciate your discretion."

A perfectly composed response, leaving no room for argument. And why should Jesse *want* to argue? He stays put as Lev begins walking again. He's known the guy for less than twelve hours.

He's also made up his mind that he likes him.

"I understand you're in a sensitive situation, and I understand you don't really know me, but you can't just go through your life never having intimacy with anyone."

Lev pauses. His shoulders rise and fall before he responds.

"What do you know of it?"

"Very little, but no one should have to shut themselves away."

Abruptly, Lev stiffens. A tremor passes through his body. Just as Jesse is about to ask what's wrong, Lev whips his head toward him, eyes wide and face sickened.

"There is a stench."

Jesse immediately closes the space between the two of them, placing a light hand on Lev's shoulder.

"I don't smell anything," he murmurs.

Lev takes a shuddering breath.

"My sense of smell is superior to that of a full human. If you cannot smell it, it must be some distance from us."

Jesse's legs tingle into numbness. Without needing to think, he opens his mouth slightly so as to draw breath more quietly and tightens his grip on Lev's bicep.

"We're going back to my house," he breathes.

Lev does not seem to hear him, instead placing a distracted hand over his.

"If only I had my equipment," he mutters.

"Lev."

The dark-haired man turns to him, sparked into action.

"You go back. Quickly. I will stay here, I must use this opportunity to study the creature."

Jesse tightens his grip on Lev's arm, vaguely cognizant of the wiry muscles within. He steps so close that he can feel alien breath against his cheek. He focuses on that rather than the rancid smell making his throat close up.

"Like hell you are."

Lev intensifies his hold on Jesse's wrist until it is like a vice.

"It is closer now. You must go."

"Not without you."

"Jesse-"

A twig breaks.

Both men fall absolutely still and silent - adrenaline courses through Jesse's body, and he shivers. Locking eyes, Jesse sees the deep revulsion Lev cannot totally hide. The smell of what can only be described as death is overpowering.

It is upon them.

Very swiftly, Lev spins to hug Jesse from behind, covering him totally. He prompts Jesse to begin walking in small steps with him in the direction of the house. Gravelly breathing is audible. It does not belong to either man.

"You are not a human."

Ice fills Jesse's veins. The voice is one that should not exist; the words sound unnatural, a wheezing growl functioning as a gross approximation of speech. He knows he is not the one to whom the bolaith speaks. He squeezes Lev's hand again. Lev continues steering them forward.

"I would see your face," it continues.

Jesse plants his feet, stopping Lev in his tracks.

"You can react, talk to it," he breathes. "It can't make things any worse, and it might make them better."

Lev releases his grip on Jesse and whirls, shielding the man with his body all the while. Jesse peers over the taller man's shoulder, helplessly curious.

Two green dots, dull but radiating light, hover between the trees about seven feet above the ground. They are fixed on Lev's face. He stares back with fascination.

"The flesh. You do not have the flesh," it says.

Lev doesn't miss a beat.

"I possess flesh. What makes it different from that of a human?"

In a different mood, Jesse would be tempted to punch him. Here, at the likely moment of his slaughter, he fails to contain a hysterical grin.

"It is different. I do not want it. I want the man."

"You will not have him."

Jesse realizes dazedly that no one has ever protected him so fiercely in the face of such adversity. Fruitlessly, he caresses the plain of Lev's upper back. The creature froths audibly.

"I say that you will not have him," Lev doubles down. "You will find much less trouble in the procuring of flesh at the campsite five miles to the north."

A pause.

"Maybe I will kill you and eat the man."

"I am not of Earth. I could kill you easily."

The creature gurgles. Jesse imagines it is considering calling Lev's bluffs.

"You could not," it hisses petulantly.

They stand in silence for what seems an interminable time. Jesse finds his breath coming in quavering bursts. He can feel Lev's hummingbird-fast heartbeat thrum where their bodies touch. The bolaith makes a grumbling noise deep in its throat, and the eyes rise another foot.

Jesse realizes with muted horror that the thing is drawing itself up to its full height. He savors the air in his lungs and his hand against his friend's back, having accepted that this will all be torn from him any moment.

Lightning quick, Lev sweeps his arm up and over his head, ripping his hat away to reveal his ridged brow and pointy ears. He gazes into the trees, exposed and sheltering Jesse, as the eyes scrutinize him further. The bolaith waits an excruciating few seconds before speaking.

"You cannot kill me with a pointed ear or a creased forehead."

"Do you want to take that risk?" Jesse asks in a clear voice.

It takes Jesse a moment to realize that he has spoken, and he is taken aback at his own boldness. He straightens, staring steadily from over Lev's shoulder.

A breeze moves through the night, rustling thousands of leaves into a seething sea. The green orbs once again minutely shift position.

Lev moves his arm very slightly, as if to reach into the pocket of his coat. There is a distinct crackling of branches and underbrush.

The eyes are gone. The stench recedes. The men nearly rip each others' arms out of the sockets on their flight to the house.

With shaking hands, Jesse shoves Lev into the house and secures all three locks on his door before shoving off of the wall and booking it to the bathroom. He barely has time to throw himself to the floor and drape himself over the toilet bowl before his nausea overcomes him and the contents of his stomach empty. He vomits for about a minute, almost grateful to focus on the physical sensations of the sweat on his brow, the acid in his mouth, and the spasms racking his body. Jesse lifts his head to close the toilet and pull its handle, collapsing to rest his cheek on the cool surface of the lid and listen to the water flushing. He doesn't even jump when he sees the figure in the mirror.

It's Lev, scribbling in his notebook.

Jesse lets out a weak chuckle. The noise draws Lev's attention back to him, and the man snaps his notebook closed before bending to retrieve a glass of water he has set on the floor. He traverses the two feet between the door and the toilet, awkwardly holding the glass out to his friend. When Jesse stares at him vacantly, Lev nudges the glass closer to his hand.

"Jesse?"

Upon hearing his name, Jesse raises a shaking hand and grasps the glass. Not wanting to appear unappreciative, he forces himself to swallow a couple sips. Lev observes this closely, waiting to speak until Jesse returns the glass to the floor.

"You are unharmed?"

Jesse nods, patting the tile next to him. Lev seats himself so that their knees are brushing.

"We lucked out," Jesse mutters.

"Yes, it is fortunate the creature believed me about the campsite and my defensive abilities."

"That's not what I'm talking about," Jesse shakes his head.

Lev waits expectantly while Jesse adjusts his gaze to regard him fully.

"You told me when you smelled it that you've got better smell than a full human. Unless I'm wrong, you're of Earth. You're human - just half. We're lucky it got hung up on the parts of you that aren't."

Lev studies the floor for a long moment before speaking.

"My mother knew my father briefly in what I understand to have been a consensual tryst. I do not know of him or where he came from beyond what she gleaned in their time together."

Jesse is glad for the coolness of the toilet and the tile, feeling more grounded than he might have had he heard this revelation earlier in the evening.

"So if you're real," Jesse parses, "who's to say any other thing from *In Search of* isn't."

Lev nods. Jesse repositions his hand so that it's covering Lev's. He finds the flesh as calming as the cold floor.

The bathroom is far from the most comfortable place in Jesse's house, but they stay there for half an hour, content to unwind silently in the cramped room. Nothing happens in this time beyond Lev occasionally raising the glass to Jesse's sight line, prompting him to rehydrate. After finishing off the glass at Lev's most recent encouragement, Jesse stretches and hauls himself to his feet.

"Well, you're welcome to the couch or my bed," he grunts. "No strings attached with the latter. Can just be a sleepover. But we oughta get to sleep, because tomorrow I'm going through initiation into the Lev Cryptozoology Academy."

He extends a hand to Lev. The man on the floor furrows his brow as he accepts it, standing to his full height.

"The Lev..." Understanding dawns on him. "You wish to work with me?"

Jesse takes in the astonished face before him and relives in quick succession the absolute terror and confusion he experienced tonight juxtaposed with the accompanying revelations and connection.

This is new territory. He'll work out how to reconcile this with his teaching tomorrow.

Any difficulty this might cause - hell, all his years alone were worth it if they culminated with this new world and this man. He squeezes the hand grasped in his.

"Yes."

Lev smiles.